KIND OF CURSED

STEPHANIE FOURNET

Kind of Cursed

Stephanie Fournet

www.stephaniefournet.com

This is a work of fiction. Names, places, characters, and events are either the products of the author's imagination or used fictitiously. Any similarities to actual events and persons, living or dead, are purely coincidental. Any trademarks, service marks, artistic works, product names, places, or named features are assumed to be the property of their respective owners, and are used only for reference or world building. There is no implied endorsement if any of these terms are used. Except for review purposes, the reproduction of this book whole or in part, electronically or mechanically, constitutes a copyright violation.

Cover design by Cayla Zeek

Dedication

For Tara, Shane, and Rebekah Grace

Author's Note

When I started writing *Kind of Cursed*, I was very conscious of the fact that this was the first time I had written a romance with a person of color as one of the principal characters. I was also conscious of the fact that, with this being my ninth novel, it was about damn time.

In 2016, my then seventeen-year-old daughter and I had the good fortune to sit in the audience of a panel discussion on diversity in romance at the RT Convention in Las Vegas. The overall message was that romance is for everyone and we shouldn't shy away from writing about everyone. I completely agreed, and yet I was still afraid to leave the relative safety of writing about my own race and culture for fear of making mistakes. After the session ended, my daughter, also a writer, and I approached author Alisha Rai, and my teenager bravely shared that she wanted to write characters of color but that, like me, she was afraid of accidentally writing inaccuracies or stereotypes. Ms. Rai very wisely said, "It's good that you're afraid. That's the first step in getting it right." And then she advised us to be curious. To widen our social circles. To get to know people. And to ask them about their experiences.

I hope I have done that well enough to have succeeded in writing Luc and the Valencias with respect, dignity, and an abundance of love.

On another note, in addition to being a multicultural romance, *Kind of Cursed* is a romantic comedy, but some serious themes emerge. Miscarriage is one of them. To any reader who lives with the pain of this unforgettable loss or who has struggled with infertility, know that this book is dedicated to dear friends who share that experience and have inspired me with their strength and outreach. You can read more about them in the acknowledgments.

Finally, I hope you love Millie, Luc, and their families even half as much as I do. Happy reading!

Prologue

MILLIE

Fertility. It's something of a curse in my family.

I'm sure a lot of people who've had to deal with the curse of infertility probably wouldn't appreciate me saying that, and to them—or anyone else—I mean no offense.

But anyone who's heard about my family, that is, the *maternal* line of my family, would agree that *curse* isn't too strong of a word. I come from a long line of remarkably fecund women. And I'm not about to offend a whole other subset of people by claiming that any of my maternal ancestors were the result of an *immaculate* conception, but something supernatural (and I'm just stating for the record here that my term for it is *curse)* has to be at work.

Either the women in my family have been graced with wombs that are teeming with eggs like a caviar sturgeon, ripe and ready for that magical moment three hundred sixty-five days a year, or we have all had the uncanny ability to attract the most virile of virile men who spread sperm—indestructible, everlasting, and navigationally superior sperm—like mean girls spread gossip.

I could probably go back ten generations to make my

point, but let's just take three. Starting with Great-Grandma Mildred, whom I happen to be named after, but that's a different family curse. Great-Grandma Mildred had two sets of twins—the first, boys, the second, girls—separated by three babies, all born in the span of seven years.

That's *seven* kids in seven years.

The poor woman wasn't even twenty-five by the time she had the last one. I'm not sure what put a stop to it, but either my great-granny's uterus fell out or she started sleeping with a hot poker to keep Great-Grandpa Hubert on his side of the bed.

Granny Matilda—whom my little sister Mattie is lucky enough to be named after—didn't have it much better, even with the invention of the Pill in the 1920s. She used to say Grandpa Ernie just had to look at her across the dining table, and she'd be with child.

That must have been some look. Two boys, then a set of twins—also boys—then my mom, and finally, my Aunt Pru. At least Granny Matilda spaced hers out a little better than Great-Grandma Mildred, but that just meant she was changing diapers for more than a decade.

Mom turned up pregnant with me when she and Dad were sophomores in college. They'd been dating for all of three months. Mom knew about The Curse, of course. It was part of family lore. She had even warned Dad. They figured the Pill and condoms would be enough.

They figured wrong. Medical advances are no match for the supernatural. And a week after seeing the plus sign on that pregnancy test, they tied the knot at the parish courthouse.

I've always thought that decision said everything about what they felt for each other. I mean, they'd barely known each other for a whole season. I can't imagine that kind of certainty, but they always had it.

And back then, they didn't have much else. No money,

that's for sure. I remember us eating Toasted O's for breakfast, lunch, and dinner for a whole week while Dad was in med school and Mom was between waitressing jobs.

Mom once told me that during those years, they'd relied on three different kinds of birth control. They weren't about to take any chances with the three of us in a tiny apartment. But as I've said, I don't think birth control actually matters. Maybe The Curse took a break. Or maybe my parents were just too tired to do it back then.

But midway through Dad's surgical residency, The Curse returned with a vengeance, and we got the twins, Harry and Mattie. By then, I was ten, and mom had gone back to school and finished in interior design.

Money was still tight, but I remember Mom and Dad being insanely happy when they found out our family was growing, so I was happy too. Mom told me they'd never wanted me to be an only child. The twins just showed up a little earlier than they'd planned since Dad was still just a medical resident and Mom was a student.

And three was supposed to be the magic number. I got this piece of information when I started dating in high school. The twins were about six at the time, and one Saturday, Dad took them to the skating rink, and Mom and I went shopping.

That's when she told me about The Curse.

Of course, she didn't use *that* word. That's mine. If I remember correctly, she called it an *uncanny potential for procreation*. At the time I thought she was just trying to scare me away from sex.

And I might still think that if it weren't for Emmett.

Emmett is my eight-year-old brother—who was born six years after the twins and five years after my dad's vasectomy.

I don't care what anyone else calls it. That's a curse.

I mean, don't get me wrong, I love my brother. And the twins. Harry, Mattie, and Emmett are the greatest. I'd literally do anything for them. And while all of my parents' pregnan-cies were unplanned, I never thought for a moment they were unwanted. It's the powerlessness I take issue with.

The life-altering powerlessness.

My parents never seemed to mind this haplessness, this state of being at the mercy of the fates. But they had each other, and they were so in love. I don't think it really mattered what happened to them as long as they were together.

And they were. Right up to the end.

Maybe that would make any curse bearable. I wouldn't know. For me, The Curse has just struck the once, and it was the most unbearable time of my life.

Chapter One

MILLIE

EMMETT IS COUGHING.

My alarm hasn't even gone off yet, but he's awake. Coughing. And I can tell just by the sound that he's faking.

School refusal, the guidance counselor called it. My eight-year-old brother doesn't want to go to school. So he pretends to be sick as often as he can.

I can't say I blame him.

He knows I'm off on Mondays. Someone would be free to watch him, so why not make it a three-day weekend? We go through this almost every week. Some days he rasps through a sore throat... or moans with stomach cramps.

It's the coughing that woke me today. Or it woke Clarence, and Clarence woke me. I'm not sure which, but I can feel the puffs of his canine breath through the blanket over my knee. His ears are perked toward the door, listening to Emmett's cough, but being the good boy he is, he's waiting for me to make the first move.

I glance at the glowing red numbers on my alarm: *5:26.* I have four minutes until the thing goes off. Five minutes until I have to wake up Mattie. Ten minutes until I have to wake up Harry. And fifteen minutes until it's Emmett's turn.

Except he's awake already. Plotting.

With a sigh, I roll onto my back and stare at the shadowed ceiling, asking the question I've asked every day for the last five months.

What would Mom do?

She'd be patient... cheerful... and absolutely uncompromising. And Emmett's ass would get to school.

I close my eyes, marshaling my will power and letting myself catch a few more seconds of peace and solitude—

And then the beeping starts.

I deliver the alarm clock a vengeful slap. Clarence lifts his head with a jingle of tags.

"Yep, buddy," I sigh again. "It's time."

When I toss back the covers, my roommate/bedmate/soulmate and four-year-old Great Pyrenees rises with lumbering ease, stretches his massive limbs, and jumps off the bed.

"Let's go wake Mattie," I say, wrapping up in my robe before opening the bedroom door. It's technically not *my* bedroom door. It's the guest room.

Or, rather, the guest suite.

My room—the room I lived in until I left for college—is now Mattie's. Before I moved out, she roomed with Harry. Like most twins, they were inseparable when they were little. When I went to Tulane, they were only eight years old, and I don't think either one of them had ever thought about rooming by themselves until Mom offered Mattie my room. I guess Mom figured the two of them bunking together any longer would be weird, and the offer of my room—with its private bathroom and its balcony overlooking St. Mary Street—might be just the thing to get her to take the plunge. Mom was right, and Mattie moved. All the way down the hall.

I pass both boys' rooms because Mattie needs to be woken

first. Not because she's a girl. Not because she primps or changes outfits five times before she leaves. But because she stresses when she's rushed, and I don't need her to be stressed.

Her door is closed almost all the way but not latched, so when Clarence pokes it with his nose, it opens soundlessly, and he slips in. I stand in the doorway and squint to see him boop her in the face.

The sight of it makes me smile.

Mattie, who sleeps on her side, makes a muffled sound, reaches out a hand, and scrubs Clarence behind one ear. "I'm up, Millie," she says softly, and I can tell she's smiling too.

Because if your mom's not there to wake you up in the morning, a one-hundred-and-ten pound Great Pyrenees is the next best thing.

And, yeah, I learned that the hard way, but at least I learned it.

The wake-up routine is almost the same for Harry, except Harry is a stomach sleeper. This means he somehow roots his way under the pillows during the night. He may be fourteen years old, but when he's asleep, he still looks like one of Peter Pan's Lost Boys. Boney. All elbows and knees. Hair sticking up like a turkey tail from his pillow diving.

So most mornings, Clarence has to do a little excavating. He snuffles and snorts and pokes his big head under the pillow pile. And since Harry isn't as easy to wake as Mattie, there's usually licking involved.

"Ugh!" Pillows scatter.

I grin. Yep, he's awake.

"Morning, Harry."

"Blech. His tongue got in my mouth," he whisper-shouts across the room. He's not really mad. Or even grossed out. He's trying to make me laugh, so I do.

"Clarence, mind your manners," I say, chuckling. "So, what'll it be? Waffles or eggs?"

After we lost Mom and Dad, I quickly learned that even if Mattie and Harry were technically old enough to make their own breakfasts, they didn't actually have the maturity to do it. They'd say they weren't hungry just to sleep later.

But then the calls started coming from school about them falling asleep or sneaking snacks in class.

So I make breakfast for everyone now.

"Eggs. Three scrambled, please. Got a game today."

My eyes bug, and I'm glad it's too dark for him to see. "Right!" I say as if I totally remembered his soccer game, and I so totally forgot. I cross my fingers for good luck. "A home game."

Please, God, let it be a home game. Away games are a logistical gamble, and I'd hate for him not to have anyone in the stands cheering him on.

"Yeah, like I told you last week." Harry sits up and scrubs his head, and in the dim light of the hallway, I can see he's frowning at me. "Did you forget?"

"No, no. I didn't forget… Just making sure," I sing-song, crawfishing out of the room.

I still have a few minutes before I have to get Emmett. Just enough time to negotiate. So.

I dash back to Mattie's room. The outline of light tells me she's in the bathroom, so I tiptoe through her room and press my lips to the door jamb. I can hear water running.

"Mattie," I hiss whisper. The water cuts off.

"What?" She sounds irritated. And I have to admit, if one of them came to the door while I was in the bathroom, I'd be irritated too. But I only have a few minutes, and I need to be strategic about this. As Mick Jagger says, *you can't always get what you want.*

Well, none of my siblings is going to get what they want today, but maybe they'll get what they need.

"Can you stay at school today for Harry's game? So I can pick up Emmett and get him there?"

I hear my sister's annoyed sigh, and I brace myself. Mattie likes routine. She wants to come home every day, straight after school, and start on her homework. At five-thirty on Mondays and Wednesdays, Mrs. Chen arrives for Mattie's piano lesson, but at five-thirty every day even when she doesn't have lessons, Mattie is still at the piano, practicing for an hour.

Except Saturdays and Sundays when she practices for two hours.

Harry's game starts at three. Emmett loves Harry's games. The chance to go to one—which means me picking him up from school instead of having him ride the bus home—might be just the bargaining chip I need to get him up and out without a fuss today. But instead of picking her up like I normally do, Mattie will have to stay after school until the game ends, which won't be until around four-thirty. Messing with her routine is going to carry a price.

"Fine," she drones, "but can we have Chick-fil-A for dinner?"

And here it is. Harry likes Cane's better. Emmett *says* Cane's is better, but I really don't think he cares. He just wants to be like his big brother. I don't like either, but at least Cane's is closer. And local. To get Mattie's precious Grilled Cool Wrap and waffle fries, I'll have to drop the kids off at home first so Mattie will be there in time for her lesson, get back in the car, and drive all the way to the Ambassador Caffery location.

Not to mention having to listen to the boys gripe about why we aren't getting Cane's.

Like I said, no one's going to get exactly what they want here. Emmett's not going to get to skip school. Mattie's not going to get to come home right after school. And Harry's not going to get the dinner he wants when he wants it. He'll have to wait another hour—after a full day of school and a soccer game—to get the dinner he doesn't want.

But they'll get what they need.

And, bottom line, that's what I need. Forget what you want. I know I have. Getting what you want is overrated.

Chapter Two

MILLIE

"CAN I GET A COKE AND A POPCORN?" EMMETT ASKS, slamming the car door before catching up with me. The soccer game is just minutes from starting and I want to be in the stands when it does. "I'll share it with you."

I glance down at my red-headed little brother and his manufactured look of wide-eyed innocence. "I'm not falling for that again." The last time I did, Emmett drank all but the last two swallows of Coke and zipped around the soccer field like a bumblebee on Vyvanse. "How about we get a popcorn and two waters?"

His whole body sags. "I hate water."

"You're made of mostly water."

Emmett screws up his face and looks at me through his long bangs. The kid needs a haircut. When was the last time he had one? How often should he get one? It's shit like this I haven't figured out yet.

"I'm mostly made of *water?*" His look of bewilderment is priceless, and I wish he'd hold it long enough for me to snap a picture with my phone. But he doesn't. And who would I show it to anyway?

"All humans are," I say, tucking my self-pitying thoughts away. We make our way to the concession stand.

"What about dogs?" he asks a moment later.

"Dogs too."

He giggles. "Even Clarence?"

I grin. "Even Clarence."

"I figured he was mostly gas."

I try not to laugh because laughing at Emmett's fart jokes only encourages him, but he sees me struggling and beams with pride.

"Get it?" he asks, digging in.

I roll my eyes. "Yeah, I get it. You're too much." We move to the front of the line and get our snacks. I lead him away from the concession crowd and scan the bleachers. "I wonder where Mattie is."

"Probably hiding with her homework somewhere," Emmett mutters.

"You say that like it's a bad thing." I find us a spot in the stands with enough room for Mattie to join us and dig out my phone.

"It *is* a bad thing," Emmett says with conviction. He takes the popcorn from me and plants the bag on his lap. "A *boring* thing."

If he's ready to talk about school, I'm ready to listen. I just have to find Mattie first. I tap out a message on my phone.

Me: At the soccer field. Where are you?

I grab a handful of popcorn and scan the field for Harry, making my question come out as casual as possible. "Is your homework boring?"

Emmett snorts like I've just said something ludicrous. "No. It's dumb."

My little brother gets his homework done—at least on the days he goes to school—because I make him. He sits at the kitchen table while I fix dinner, and it never takes him long. But if I didn't drag it out of his book sack, he'd ignore it and probably fail. He may fail anyway, his counselor has warned me, if he misses too many more days.

But if school is boring and dumb, maybe he needs more of a challenge. Maybe I should ask the counselor about having him tested for gifted. Mattie and Harry are in the gifted program here at Lafayette High. I did it too when I was in school. Maybe Emmett is ready for that now.

"Do you think school is boring?" I ask, still not looking at him, but I've said the *s* word. Classic misstep. Even out of the corner of my eye, I watch his shoulders slump.

"I don't want to talk about school."

"Well, we probably should." But even as I say it, the Lions kick off the game, and I know I've lost him.

"Let's watch," he says. "That's why we're here, isn't it?"

I sigh just as my phone chirps. I glance down.

Mattie: In the library. Can I stay here and finish? Be done in about 20.

I stifle another sigh. She'll miss most of the first half. I know I shouldn't complain. She's in the library finishing her homework.

But going to Harry's games has always been a family thing. Just like Mattie's recitals and Emmett's T-ball. Mom and Dad thought it was important for us to do stuff like that together. Living in a different city while I was in school meant I didn't share this the same way, but if I was home visiting, I was expected to go too. We all were.

Maybe it's silly to try to keep this part of their lives the same when so much else has changed. Still, when I text her, it feels like conceding failure.

Me: Okay, but be here by 3:30.

She replies with a thumbs up.

I put my phone away, ignoring the too-familiar sinking feeling in my gut, and lift my gaze to the field. Harry is the starting goalie, and even from this distance, I can see the coiled readiness of his limbs, the way his eyes track the ball as it zig-zags across the grass.

The season just started. The Lions are three home games in. Last season, back when everything was the way it was supposed to be, Harry and Mattie were still in middle school. He played, of course, but I was still in vet school, and I could only make it in town for one game. The same thing for the years before that. Before this year, I'd seen maybe three soccer games. This season I've figured out about half the flag signs, but I still don't understand most of the offside calls.

I'm trying to understand why one of the assistant refs has his flag in the air when four people—arguing in rapid-fire Spanish—approach and sit on the bleachers in front of us. I can't help but notice them because, besides the arguing, out of the four, two of them walk with canes, an older man and a woman who looks adorably ancient.

But it's the man between them, steadying each with a supportive arm on either side, my eyes find. I swallow. Dark. Chiseled. Flawless… Oh, except for that scar that scores his left brow. It would make him look kind of scary if he didn't have those long, curling eyelashes.

This is what I'm thinking when the eyes behind those dark, curling lashes flit to mine—and I suck in a breath and choke on a piece of popcorn.

The rogue kernel triggers an instant coughing fit, and I wrench open my Dasani bottle, trying to silence my struggle in a flood of water.

"You okay?" Emmett asks, frowning up at me.

Eyes streaming, bottle pressed to my lips, I nod. It's touch-and-go for moment, and for one terrifying instant, I'm afraid I'm about to spray Emmett and the entire Spanish-speaking family with a mouth shower. But then the beastly popcorn kernel washes away, and I can breathe again after a few wracking coughs.

Thankfully, most of this has happened while the family in front of me has been busy situating the two cane-bound members, still arguing in Spanish.

Dear God, for future reference, if I'm going to choke to death, please don't let it be in front of an audience, I pray, dabbing my eyes dry on the cuff of my sweater. *Definitely not in front of Emmett. And no cute guys. I know I shouldn't care about that part, but I really do—*

I halt my prayer as one of the strikers from the opposing team aims a powerful and arrow-straight kick right at the Lions' goal. Harry leaps, limbs splayed like a five-pointed star, and deflects it with his right hand.

The home side goes wild. Emmett and I spring to our feet, screaming for all we're worth.

"HARRY! YEAH!" I yell.

"WOOHOO!" Emmett whoops. "THAT'S MY BROTHER! WOO!"

I hear chuckles from the crowd around us, and I don't miss Mr. Dark, Scarred, & Chiseled glancing over his shoulder, the corner of his mouth tipped up in a grin. But I quickly drag my gaze away, cheering again for Harry before I sit down.

I grab the water bottle and guzzle. Cheering is thirsty work. And my face is hot. And I am definitely not here to make eyes at the dark, scarred, and chiseled of the world. Not today, and not anytime in the near future.

That is the last thing you need right now, I tell myself, a mental image of Carter Fox darting through my mind. And that image does the trick. A frosty rush replaces the heat in my cheeks, and I draw my thin cardigan more tightly around myself.

One thought, and I am prepared to live like a nun until Emmett finishes high school. That's me. Sister Mildred. I sniff a laugh at the ring of it. Sister Mildred sounds more chaste than Mary Poppins and absolutely, positively impregnable.

Impregnable. That's the critical point.

So with impregnable focus, I turn my attention firmly back to the soccer game and cheer as the Lions make a goal.

The blocked kick and the first score rev up the crowd, and the bleachers rattle as feet stamp in time to "We Will Rock You!" Emmett and I are stomping, clapping, and laughing when Mattie finds us.

With her backpack slung over one shoulder, she gives us a wry smile. "Having fun?"

Oblivious to her irony, Emmett practically vibrates with excitement. "Harry blocked a kick and then that guy scored!" He bounces in his seat, jabbing a finger toward the field. Mattie and I follow the trajectory of his pointing to see Number Seven, a tall, wiry boy with thick dark hair who is already in pursuit of the ball again, frowning in concentration, the moment of triumph clearly already a memory.

And then the guy on the row in front of us turns. "That's *my* brother," he says with a grin for Emmett, but his gaze flicks to mine, and I quickly look away.

"Really?" Emmett squeals. "He's good!"

I glance at Mattie to have something to focus on besides the gorgeous guy in front of me, but I find her blinking, looking almost startled, her eyes glued to the figure on the field. Number Seven.

"He *is* good," she says, sounding breathless.

Oh Jesus.

I yank the bag of popcorn out of Emmett's grasp and thrust it in front of my sister's face. "Want some popcorn?"

She turns to me with a confused frown.

"I-It might be a while before dinner," I stammer. "Are you hungry?"

She takes the bag from me, answering absently. "Sure." She looks back, searching, I know, for Number Seven, but in the frenzy of activity on the field, no one person is easy to spot.

Don't look for him. I'm not ready to have The Curse Talk with you just yet.

"Did you finish your homework?" I ask, my voice blaring.

Mattie's face when she looks at me is one of keen irritation. "God, why are you shouting? Are you okay, Millie?"

No, not really, I want to tell her. *Take your eyes of the cutie on the field, and I'll be fine.*

Instead, I nod. "Yeah...You just made a big deal about finishing your work, so I'm curious. Did you?"

She rolls her eyes at me and tosses her chestnut hair over her shoulders. "I finished math, but I still have to study Spanish."

I swear, every muscle in my body tenses when she says this, and from my peripheral vision I catch the guy in front of me react ever so slightly. He's heard her. He's listening. His eyes might be on the game, but his ear is angled just a little more in our direction, the line of his shoulders taut and alert.

Why did she have to take Spanish? Why couldn't Mattie have picked French like Harry and I did?

"I can help you study after piano," I say in a rush, ready to change the subject.

My sister's lip curls like she smells something off. "But you don't speak Spanish."

And I know I'm not imagining things. Mr. Dark, Scarred & Chiseled chuckles at this. He doesn't make any noise, but those shoulders—broad and impressively muscled though they are—bounce with silent amusement.

He's laughing. At me.

I ignore the rush of heat this delivers to my cheeks. It doesn't matter if this cute guy is laughing at my expense. Sister Mildred does not care such things. I clear my throat and try to sound as confident as ever. "I can still quiz you. Call out vocabulary words or something."

Mattie just shrugs, and her eyes drift back to the game. And no sooner does she do that then Number Seven breaks away from the cluster of players, the ball clearly under his command, and makes a bold kick toward the goal. It's blocked, but the crowd still roars, electric with the near miss.

"Good push, *hermano*," the guy in front of me yells. "Keep 'em on their toes!"

And before I can stop him, Emmett leans forward and shakes him by the shoulder. "Hey, your brother's name is *Hermano?*"

Three things happen at once. My stomach forms a cement ball. Mattie snorts a laugh. And the guy twists around, hitting me with a smile that is so beautiful I feel the absurd urge to cry. In a nanosecond, my brain catalogues every nuance of its radiance. The natural rose of his lips. The hint of dimples there on his cheeks. The white of his teeth, which are almost perfect except for the one lateral incisor. The left one on the bottom. It's just a little crooked, leaning against the central incisor like a tipsy friend after a night of clubbing.

Stop it. You're making up stories about his teeth. Look away! I scold myself and then scold Emmett.

"Buddy, let the man watch the game."

"It's all right," the guy says with a shake of his head, his eyes moving from me to Emmett. "His name is Alex. *Hermano* means brother."

It's faint, but his words hum with an accent. The hum tickles the back of my neck. I lift a hand to sweep away the sensation, then grab the popcorn from Mattie and thrust it back at Emmett. "Want more popcorn?"

But my brother just ignores me. "Alex? I think Harry's talked about him."

"He has," Mattie adds in a gauzy tone I've never heard from her. My gaze whips to her to find her staring onto the soccer field looking drugged, a slow smile lifting the corners of her mouth.

Oh shit.

I need Emmett to stop talking to this guy and Mattie to stop mooning over his brother, but I realize that's not going to happen when the woman beside him—not the ancient one, but the other one—swivels around too. One look at her eyes, and I'm sure she's his mother.

"Is your brother in ninth grade too?" she asks, smiling, her accent more pronounced than her son's. She's looking at Emmett, but I am acutely aware, as if every cell in my body is receiving a satellite signal, that her son is looking at me.

I force my gaze to my brother. Emmett nods. "Yes, ma'am." I should be proud of his good manners, but the weight of this guy's stare has my system on overload.

Turn around, dammit.

How can I ignore him and stick to my ten-year chastity plan if he's staring at me like that? I refuse to meet his stare, but it might as well be a hand reaching across the space that separates us, seizing me by the belt. I feel like I'm being tugged forward. And maybe it's not an invisible hand at my belt. Maybe it's grabbing my chin, insisting that I turn to face him.

Well, I won't do it, I silently tell him, keeping my gaze fixedly on Emmett.

"They're the only freshman starters on the team," the guy's mother says with obvious pride.

I swivel my focus to her, completely bypassing Dark, Scarred, and Chiseled. His mother is safe territory. I meet her smile with my own and nod. I don't mean to be rude to her. She has no way of knowing what I'm dealing with. Everything I'm dealing with. She can't possibly know the threat both her sons' very existences pose to my sanity. Still, I don't want the conversation to continue, and I need the temptation of her older son's eyes to ease up, so I don't actually speak to her.

Instead, she turns to her son. "Luca, didn't you start as a freshman too?"

The question is a Godsend. He finally turns away and faces his mother instead. "Only during the playoffs when one of the seniors tore his ACL." He pauses for a moment, and I allow myself a glimpse at his profile. The dimple in his right cheek winks at me. "But don't tell Alex. He'll never let me forget he's the better player."

His mother snickers, shaking her head. "Alejandro wouldn't rub it in. He has too big a heart."

Out of the corner of my eye, I see Mattie drop her elbow to her knee and lean forward, resting her chin on her raised knuckles. I'm not a hundred percent sure, but I think I hear her whisper with dreamy appreciation.

"Alejandro..."

Chapter Three

LUC

I OPEN MY EYES AND PICK UP MY PHONE: 4:57 A.M.

Across the apartment, coffee hits the bottom of the carafe, right on time. Tapping the clock icon on the screen, I swipe the green dot, killing the alarm before it kills the silence.

But I don't move. Instead, I lie still, eyes closed, and figure out my Daily Three. Today's top three priorities. According to Papi, anyone who says you can have more than three priorities a day is full of shit. To-do lists are long. Priorities are short.

Priorities determine to-do lists, not the other way around.

Yesterday's Daily Three were Resources, Quality Control, and Family. I review yesterday in my mind. Repair costs on the Series II Crawler. Lumber orders. My visits to each Valencia & Sons job site. Hector's fuck-up with the dirt delivery. Papi's leg. Alex's two soccer goals.

Eyes the blue of spring fever...

My lids snap open and I stare at the ceiling, but all I see is that redhead. I reach a hand behind my head and squeeze the back of my neck, surprised I don't have a crick in it from turning back to look at her so many times—instead of watching Alex's game.

"Pendejo," I mutter to my empty room.

I should have stopped that shit the first time she yanked those blue eyes away. She might as well have held up her hand. *Not interested in you.* Message received.

But I didn't stop.

I tried, but looking at her felt like striking a match. No. It felt like *I* was the match. I tried telling myself she was an ice princess. No warmth for some first-gen Chicano who works with his hands. But that wasn't it. Even a minute or two listening to her with her little brother and sister made that clear.

No ice princess would stamp her feet to Queen songs. Or yell, "C'MON HARRY! TURN ON THE SCARY!" at the top of her lungs. Or keep her cool when the little brother spilled soda in her lap.

And, yeah, each of those moments made me turn back for a look. Nothing icy about her. Just hot.

Only not for me.

"Not a priority," I say, flinging off the covers and pulling my mind back to the Daily Three. I make my bed and decide they're going to be Customer Satisfaction, Staffing, and Bros.

I text my brother to see if he wants a ride to school today, and then I text Cesar. Maybe he has time for a beer tonight. Alex won't answer for another hour, but my best friend is already up.

Cesar: Time and place?

I move to the kitchen and fill a mug with coffee, tallying up the tasks that fall under my first two priorities. Call the Sterling's and find out if they want to change anything else before we start framing the house. Check in with Mike and Ella Lambert to smooth over any hard feelings about yesterday's mess. And try for the twentieth time to reach that woman with the kitchen redesign. I might just have to go over there if she doesn't pick up this time.

And I can't iron out staffing until I know where that third job stands. But I won't make Cesar wait on me. If I have to work a couple of hours at my desk tonight after we have drinks, so be it.

Me: 6:30. And you're the restaurant expert. You pick.

"You bought lumber from Stine's? Why not Menard's? I always bought from Menard's?" Papi says, frowning up at me from the kitchen table.

"Stine's had a better price for three-quarter-inch moulding," I say, crossing to the counter to refill my travel mug. "Coffee smells good, Mami."

My mother flips the last pancake onto a short stack and turns toward the table. "Help yourself. You want some pancakes, Luca?"

"No time," I say, shaking my head, and then I realize she's setting the plate down in front of my father, and I frown. "You sure you should be having pancakes, Papi?"

He makes a dismissive grumble and reaches for the syrup.

"Don't worry, *mijo,*" Mami says. "His doctor increased his Metformin, so it's okay."

I look from Mami to Papi. "Um… I don't think that's how it works, guys." They both know that's not how Type 2 diabetes works. We've been over this for months.

Scowling, Papi slathers his short stack with ribbons of syrup. "So, I'm supposed to go without breakfast?"

I take a slug of coffee and swallow my response. No use in mentioning green smoothies or steel-cut oats. None at all.

I lean down and kiss my mother on the cheek. "Tell Alex I'll be in the truck."

"Without greeting Abuela?" Mami gasps, scandalized.

"What was I thinking," I mutter.

In the living room, Abuela sits in front of the *Today Show*, propelling herself in her glider like a champion sculler. Her eyes are trained on the TV screen and she's clutching her rosary when I bend to kiss her.

"Buenos dias, Abuela."

Abuela doesn't speak English. I would bet my life on the fact that she *understands* English perfectly. The woman watches the *Today Show* religiously and without subtitles. She just won't speak it. My cousins and I have a theory it's just to make sure we all learned Spanish despite being American born.

"¿Qué hay en las noticias?" I ask her.

My grandmother makes a face like she's tasted something rotten. *"Centros de detención,"* she hisses. She rubs her rosary beads between her thumbs and forefingers and mouths the *Hail Mary*.

In the time it takes me to send up my own *Hail Mary*, Alex tears down the stairs, and we head out to my truck.

"Good game last night," I tell my little brother when his butt lands on the passenger seat.

"Thanks." When his seatbelt clicks in place, I put the truck in reverse. "And thanks for the ride. I hate the bus. I can't wait 'til I can drive."

I eye him with a smirk. "What're you planning on driving?"

"A car." His sarcasm has me biting back a growl.

But I just nod and let his answer hang there as we snake through the neighborhood.

A minute later. "Did Mami and Papi buy you a car when you turned sixteen?"

"Nope."

"Mierda," he hisses under his breath, staring at his lap. "Did you buy your own? When you were sixteen?"

"Not sixteen." I shake my head. "I was seventeen."

He blinks. "Why not sixteen?"

Alejandro is twelve years younger than me. We may have

the same parents, but we didn't have the same childhood. He doesn't remember the years when Papi was in Mexico, waiting for his green card after he got deported as an illegal. He doesn't remember the days when it was just Mami, Abuela, and me, the two of them working to keep the rent paid, to save for the day Papi would be allowed to come back and start a business while sending him a little money every month.

But I do.

"I couldn't afford one until then." I take a sip from my travel mug. I know better than to lecture Alex. He listens more when he's asking the questions.

He turns to me with a frown. "You worked?"

I nod. "Mowed lawns and pressure washed houses for three summers." We're stopped at the intersection of Meaux and South College, so I don't miss his double blink.

"You started cutting grass when you were my *age?*" His voice cracks on *age*, and he clears it forcibly, embarrassed. I hold my mouth as firm as granite, even though I'd love to crack a smile.

"Yep."

"What kind of car did you get?"

Now I free my grin. "You don't remember the Geo?"

"The Easter egg?!" His voice climbs at least two octaves.

Breath leaves me in a laugh. "You *did* call it that," I say, chuckling at the memory. "Yeah, the blue egg."

He's quiet until we stop at the light in front of Rouse's Grocery. "You worked for three summers before you could buy that piece of shit?"

I aim my glare at him. *Yeah,* I curse, but Alex wouldn't know it. That might make me a hypocrite, but he's fourteen. I don't want him to sound like some *naco* punk. He can curse in front of me when he's older.

Alex rolls his eyes. "You look just like Abuela when you make that face."

"You'd better not be cursing like that in front of Abuela."

"You think I'm *loco?*"

I eye him like the jury is still out, but he knows I'm joking, so he just snorts. "So, if I promise not to curse, can I come work for you this summer?"

I keep my focus trained on the traffic in front of me. A construction site is the worst place to park him if I don't want him to curse. But it will be the best way for him to decide if this is the life he wants.

Papi named the business Valencia *& Sons* Construction when I was Alex's age and before my brother was even potty trained. To say Papi had hopes and dreams for us would be an understatement. And that worked for me.

But I want Alex to have choices. For him to know what to choose, he needs to know what he wants and what he doesn't. I don't want him to go into Construction Management at LSU just because I did.

"I think I could put you to work," I say simply.

From the corner of my eye, I see a smile break over his face. "That'd be awesome."

I shrug. "Don't thank me yet. You'll be low man on the totem pole. Hauling dirt, picking up trash, sweeping sawdust..."

This doesn't seem to faze him. "Yeah, but I'll be making bank," he says, rubbing his palms together.

I scoff. "You'll be making minimum wage."

"*What?!*"

His shriek makes me wince. "You heard me."

"*Minimum wage?*"

I join the line of cars waiting to pull into Lafayette High's horseshoe drive. "You think your knowledge and experience deserve more than that?" I don't have to look at him to know his mouth is hanging open, but I glance over in time to see it close. He narrows his glare at me, and now he's the one who looks just like Abuela.

"Does everyone you hire start at minimum wage?"

I shrug. "Everyone with zero experience and zero training."

"Hmmph." His lips press together and he mutters, "You'd think you'd give your own brother a break."

He's not really upset—at least, I don't think so. And if he is, he needs to get over it. "I *am* giving you a break, " I say, nudging the truck into the drive and braking as cars crawl through the drop-off line. "By paying you what you're worth, I'm making sure the business with your name on it stays profitable."

He doesn't have to like this, but I'm glad when I see the corner of his mouth turn up just a little. "So you're saying keeping me poor is making me rich?"

My chuckle is low but automatic. "Appreciate the paradox."

Alex sniffs a laugh. Then he looks at me and shakes his head. "You're not fooling me."

"I'm not trying to fool you."

Shooting me his best wise-ass face, my brother shakes his head. "You're trying to fool everyone, but you don't fool me."

He looks so smug, I have to reach across the seats and mess with his hair.

"Hey!" His skinny arms shoot out to defend against my attack.

Wait a minute. They used to be skinny. They look bigger, more solid. When did that happen?

"Serves you right," I say as he rakes his fingers through his hair, restoring the order of his dark waves.

"Yeah, that's what I get for speaking the truth. I see through you." His voice holds a teasing note, but something in the way he averts his eyes has me frowning.

"What's that supposed to mean?"

Alex shakes his head. "Nah. Forget I said anything." We're at the front of the line, and it's his turn to get out. His hand is already on the door, but I grab one of the straps of his backpack.

"Hermano, what do you mean?"

He opens the door and leans out, tugging against the backpack. "I gotta go, Luc."

I firm my grip. I'm wearing a grin, but I have no intention of letting go. "Tell me."

He climbs out of the truck and the backpack forms a link between us, neither one of us letting go. The car behind me honks.

"C'mon, Luc." His eyes widen with exasperation.

I hold his gaze with my own determined one. "I'll let go when you talk."

The car behind us honks again. An on-duty teacher motions for me to pull forward. I ignore her.

"Luuuuuc." He drags my name out until it's at least three syllables. "Forget I said anything."

"Can't. Won't."

He rolls his eyes. "Ugh. Fine." He throws up his free hand in defeat and then gestures at me with it. "This. Your big brother routine. All work and no play."

I frown. He tugs at the backpack, but I hold on. "Work is important." It has to be. I'm running the family business now.

"Yeah, but it's not everything," he says, all smugness. "And the way you were looking at that *bonita* at the game last night tells me you know it too." Alex jerks hard on the backpack, and the strap pops from my grip.

My brother tips me a two-finger salute, turns, and melts into the crowd before I can utter a single word.

By TEN A.M., I've ticked off almost half of the tasks on my list. I've logged a brief report about Hector's dirt dump into his employee file, realizing when I did that it's not the first time his failure to show up on time has cost the company.

Papi had a three strikes policy. As far as I'm concerned, three strikes seems excessive. Why should I let anyone fuck up a third time? What's wrong with getting it right the first time?

Don't get me wrong. Accidents are one thing. I'm not talking about accidents. I'm talking about dumbass moves. About being somewhere else when you're supposed to be waiting on a dirt delivery.

I'm not eager to fire anyone. I've done it once right before Papi went into the hospital. He'd asked me to do it, and even though the guy I fired needed to be fired, it still wasn't a fun time.

Hector probably needs to be fired, but I decide to give him one more strike.

Before I break for lunch, I reach out to my clients—or try to anyway. The family with the new construction is easy enough to contact, and the good news is they don't want to change a thing. We'll have some framing up by tonight. I leave a message on Ella Lambert's voicemail, asking her to call me if the clean-up didn't meet her satisfaction.

And then I try the lady with the house on St. Mary, but instead of the call going to voicemail this time, I hear the three-tone beep and then,

"We're sorry, but the number you are trying to reach has been disconnected or is no longer in service…"

I hang up. She must have changed her number. I look down on the papers from Papi's meetings with her and grimace. He took her deposit last spring. Her orders for cabinets, lighting, and appliances were filled weeks ago, and the tile and granite should come in soon. I know we fell behind schedule when Papi got sick, but this is bad. We should have started the job in September. She's probably ready to sue us by now. I roll up her plans and head for my truck.

A SILVER INFINITI QX80 sits in the driveway at 1021 West St. Mary Street. Somebody's home. I pull up and kill the engine.

As soon as I step out of my truck, the red front door opens and a baying, bounding white blur surges off the front porch.

I halt on the spot. *Jesucristo.*

"Clarence!" A woman's voice calls from the porch, but I can't spare her a look because this dog is *huge.* He's not even a dog. He's a polar bear.

The bear stops three feet in front of me, tips up his chin, and bays again, aiming his warning to the treetops. Hell, they can probably hear him in the Space Station. See him too.

"Don't worry. He's friendly. Can I help y—Hey, do I—Are you—"

I look up, and I blink. It's her. The redhead.

What the hell is she doing here? She's wearing dark green scrubs over a long-sleeved gray shirt. Is she a nurse? Does she work here?

Maybe I'm in the wrong place. I glance down at the roll of plans in my hand. *Delacroix, Eloise and Hudson.*

Delacroix? Is that the name of Alex's teammate?

"I—" I look up again and see she's frowning. Definitely confused, but those blue eyes are sharp with wariness. "I'm Luc Valencia. I think we met at the soccer game."

Her posture stiffens. She doesn't move an inch, but, I swear, every line in her body hardens. "We didn't *meet.*" Her voice is hard. Flinty.

She looks angry. Why the hell is she angry? We may not have been introduced, but I'm sure she remembers me. And by the look of it, it's ruined her day. I might have to rethink my Ice Princess conclusion.

I take a step forward and offer my hand. "We did. I—"

She steps back. "Stop right there." At her words, I hear what sounds like distant thunder, but the sky is clear. No rain in sight. And then it dawns on me.

It's the giant dog-bear.

He's growling. His lip curled in teeth-baring menace. At me.

"Whoa—" I step back, both hands—the one holding the plans and the one I extended—go up in surrender. "Whoa. Whoa. Whoa. Maybe I've got the wrong house."

She narrows her eyes as though trying to make sense of my words. The dog growls again. I take another step back, and that monster takes a step forward.

I jerk a thumb over my shoulder in the direction of my truck. "I'm with Valencia & Sons Construction. I'm looking for the Delacroix house. Maybe they're one of your neighbors," I say quickly, but fuck this shit. I don't need to get directions from her. "You know what? Never mind."

I'm already moving toward the truck, walking backward, not giving the dog my back.

"W-wait," she says, her eyes flicking from me to my truck with its Valencia & Sons decal. "Construction?"

It's the look on her face that makes me stop. It's not just confusion. It's more like…

Shock.

She bites her bottom lip, and just like that, everything in her posture changes again. She sort of just… wilts.

"Are you okay?" The question leaves my mouth, and without thinking, I move toward her. The dog growls again. I halt.

"Clarence." She says the dog's name again, but now the sound is so different—a plea instead of a command—both the animal and I look back at her. He trots to her side, sits on his haunches, and sniffs the air around her as if searching for something.

"Can you tell me wh-who…" I watch her swallow, her face now pinched, the wariness gone and a kind of devastation taking its place. "Who contacted you?"

I glance down, tilt the plans, and read the names aloud. "Eloise and Hudson Delacroix?" I say, hoping I'm pronouncing it right. "Do you know them?"

I flick my gaze back to her and my stomach drops. The woman has gone completely white.

Yeah, of course she's white. But a minute ago, she was a creamy white and high on her cheeks a rosy white. Like vanilla and strawberry swirl ice cream.

But now she's ash white. Bloodless white.

I move then because nobody can look that white and stay upright. And just when I do, her knees give. The plans and my keys fall to the ground, but she doesn't because my left hand catches an elbow while my right arm hooks her around the waist.

"*¡Ay!*"

She staggers back, but I've got her, and I lower her to the porch steps. Her eyes are open but unfocused. On instinct, I guide her head down until it's even with her splayed knees. Curious, but no longer threatening, the big, white Clarence hovers, sniffing, but his attention is all on her. Not me, *gracias Madre Maria.*

"Just breathe, okay?"

Slowly, she nods, but she's shaking. All over.

Under my hand that rests on her back, I feel the exaggerated filling and emptying of her lungs. Once. Twice. Once more.

Then she groans.

I shut my eyes and pray she isn't about toss her cookies on my shoes.

But she doesn't puke. Instead, she draws her elbows in and covers her face, her body still folded over her legs.

"Jesus Christ," I hear her whisper, but it's no prayer. She sounds kind of disgusted, and I fight the urge to smile.

She brackets her face with her hands and straightens up.

"*Ten cuidado...* Easy," I caution.

She sniffs and clears her throat. "I'm fine," she says.

"You sure?" I realize my hand is still on her back when she rolls her shoulder to shed it. I drop it and inch back.

Clarence steps in and noses her. Still shielding her face with one hand, she lowers the other and pats him absently.

"I'm okay, big guy," she tells him.

She sounds better, so I get to my feet and step back, giving her space.

Her shielding hand moves to her forehead, and she looks up at me from beneath it as though shading her eyes from the sun. And then I see. She's embarrassed.

I don't want her to be embarrassed. It surprises me how much I really don't want that. So I say the first thing I can think of.

"Most people don't usually faint until they get my bill."

Chapter Four

MILLIE

I STARE AT HIM. BLINK. AND THEN HIS WORDS PENETRATE. A joke. I want that to be irritating. I really do. Yet it takes away the sting of my embarrassment. Just a little.

But, yeah. I fainted. Again.

At least I'm definitely not pregnant this time.

My fingers tremble when I wipe my forehead, so I ball up my fist and lower it to my knee.

"I-I'm sorry about that," I say to my shoes. Meeting his dark-eyed gaze straight on isn't really an option right now. "That... uh... that took me by surprise."

My parents have been gone for five months, so there's no way they called a contractor. I'm not sure what's going on, but there's got to be some mistake. Still, I miss them so much, I want them back so badly, just hearing their names—hearing that this man is looking for them—gives me a moment of absurd hope.

Maybe it has all been just a big misunderstanding. Maybe the Coast Guard got it wrong. Maybe they're really fine. They've just been marooned on an island... like Tom Hanks in *Castaway*.

It can't be true. I know that. But even the temptation of such a possibility is enough to make anyone light-headed.

"Are you okay? Should I call someone?"

I risk a glance up at him. He's frowning down at me, and that scar through his left brow makes him look a little scary, but only until I notice concern in his dark, watchful eyes. It hits me again that he's the guy from the soccer game. Alejandro's brother. But I can't process that right now. One thing at a time. Answer his questions.

The first one's easy enough. "I'm... fine." It's true. I am fine. My little fainting spell has left me misted in sweat, a slight ringing in my ears, and my limbs feel like jelly, but that'll pass in a minute.

As for the second? There's really no one. Who would he call? Kath at the office? Aunt Pru on her Norwegian cruise ship? Harry, Mattie, and Emmett, my next of kin, are all minors.

"No, you don't need to call anyone." When his frown deepens, I quickly add, "I'm fine, really." To prove as much, I push myself—carefully—to my feet.

He steps closer, as though to offer me a hand, but stops before actually touching me. Good. I don't need to look any more helpless than I already do.

Standing, I brush my hands against my scrubs and offer one to him, pretending that nothing at all weird just happened. I didn't just faint in a heap in front of him, and I definitely didn't give him the stink-eye before that—when I recognized him from the soccer game and assumed he'd looked me up.

Who? Me?

Let me just say for the record that I feel like an ass for that one, but, really, who could blame me? Even after it was clear last night that Mattie had developed and insta-crush on his little brother... even after the chit-chat between his mom and

Emmett, the guy kept eyeing me. Stealing glances behind those curling lashes. Checking me out.

At least, that's what I thought.

So when I stepped outside and saw him, I was more than a little freaked out and, frankly, annoyed that he'd looked me up. If I go out of my way to avoid making eye contact with you, you'd better not show up on my doorstep the next day, looking like you just stepped out of a Calvin Klein underwear ad.

I mean, yes, of course he's dressed, but that T-shirt he's wearing doesn't look like it's up for the job of actually keeping him decent, clinging to his muscles the way it is. I guess it's not the T-shirt's fault. If I were hanging on that chest, I'd probably lose all my strength too.

So that's why I was rude to him before I even knew why he was here. Self-preservation.

And then he mentioned my parents, and I fainted. Yeah, nothing at all weird here.

But he shakes my hand anyway, still watching me closely. I willfully ignore the warmth of his hand. The way it surrounds mine.

"I'm Millie Delacroix," I manage. "Hudson and Eloise were my parents."

I don't know what it's like for anyone else, but using the past tense to talk about people we've lost should be its own stage of grief. Denial. Anger. Bargaining. Depression. Past Tense Usage. Acceptance.

Or maybe Past Tense Usage comes before Depression. God, I hope not.

But the past tense definitely gets Luc Valencia's attention.

"Were?" His eyes widen a fraction, but that scary frown sharpens so that he looks both confused and horrified as things fall into place. It's a look I've seen enough times over the last five months to know I've just made someone feel supremely

uncomfortable. He glances up at the house and back at me.
"That's why—" He stops and clamps his mouth shut before
visibly swallowing.

I'd feel sorry for the guy if I had the room. Or the time.
But these days, feeling sorry for my sibs and myself is pretty
much all I can manage.

"That's why," I echo because it's true. That's why... pretty
much everything. That's why I live in this five-bedroom house
instead of an apartment like a normal twenty-four-year old.
That's why I took a part-time position at a vet clinic in
Youngsville instead of looking for jobs in places I'd always
thought I'd try living. Austin. Charleston. Nashville.

Nowhere *too* far away, but someplace different. Someplace
buzzing. With people. Music. Cool stuff to do on the weekends.

That's why I don't even want to so much as look at a man
—especially one as stunning as he is.

"I tried calling," he says, and I hear regret in his voice. "I
didn't mean to disturb you, but..." His gaze shifts to the
ground, and he lowers to pick up his dropped keys and the roll
of papers he was holding.

I see it's drafting paper, and as soon as I do, a memory
smacks me across the face.

A phone call from Mom. A week or so before they left. She
was excited because they were finally—after living in this fixer-
upper for eight years—redoing the kitchen. Of course, I never
saw the plans, but I know what this contractor is about to
show me.

A breakfast nook with bench seating at the bay window.
Dark stone countertops. A cobalt blue statement oven with
brass knobs.

One more thing my parents were looking forward to that
they'll never get to see.

I point to the rolled up plans. "That's the kitchen, isn't it?"

Surprise glints in his eyes. "So you know your parents hired us?"

I shake my head. "No, but I heard about the remodel." It's my turn to frown. "But that was supposed to happen over the summer. Like late August, right? Why are you just showing up now?"

The look in his long-lashed eyes turns rueful. "I'm afraid we're a few months behind schedule." He makes a face like he'd rather be talking about anything else, but he goes on. "My father was the one to meet with your parents. He's... uh... he's been in poor health since the summer. It wasn't planned, but he's had to retire. I'm sorry that it has taken me this long to get to your parents' project."

I remember the older man with the cane at the soccer game. That must be his father. I shrug off his apology. "We lost them in May," I say, my voice fading out a little. I clear my throat and press on. "They had no idea you were behind schedule. No need to apologize."

This information doesn't ease his expression. Not that I'm really worried about making him feel better, but his frown is back, and it's etching deeper. I've never seen anyone with such dark brows. Almost black. His hair is the same. Like a raven's wing.

And he's staring at me like I've just ruined his day. "Your parents paid a deposit to secure our services and place orders," he says stiffly.

I shrug again. "Okay?"

"I'm... we're not in a position to pay that back."

Now I'm the one who's surprised. "I wouldn't expect you to pay it back. They put down a deposit. You prepared to do the work. That money is yours."

He tucks his chin, his gaze hardening. "That doesn't sit well with me."

I stare at him. "You mean when a job falls through, you don't keep the deposit?"

"Not one from a bunch of orphans."

On another day, I might have cried. That's how grief is. Maudlin one day, hysterical the next. I can't help it. I bust out laughing. It's the wrong reaction. I can tell he doesn't appreciate it. And no matter how many times he turned to look at me last night, I don't think Valencia likes me very much right now.

Good.

But I shake my head, fanning away my laughter. "I'm sorry, Mr. Valencia. That's very noble of you, but," I look back over my shoulder at the two-story Victorian that was my parents' pride and joy, "my parents made sure we were taken care of, and, frankly, I'm a little old to be considered an orphan."

His expression doesn't soften. He's not amused in the least. Nope, he doesn't like me very much.

"What about your brothers and sister?" The words and the hard edge to his voice do the trick on the last of my laughter. Harry, Mattie, and Emmett are orphans. No doubt about it.

I clear my throat. "Like I said, my parents left us in good shape."

The early days of my parents' marriage may have been tight financially, but after that my dad had been a successful heart surgeon for more than a decade. And maybe it was because he had the four of us, or maybe it was because he knew how fragile life is, or maybe he was a sucker for a good sales pitch, but Dad believed in life insurance and monetary trusts. Even before my parents died, the house was paid for and so was college and grad school for all of us. The rest will see my brothers and sisters safely into adulthood.

I worry over a lot of things these days, but money isn't one of them. Maybe I'll never forgive my parents for being out on the water when the weather forecasted storms, but I'm grateful every day for their careful planning. I don't know how we'd manage otherwise, and I don't want to know.

"May I ask what your plans are for the house?"

The question knocks me off balance. I realize this guy's dark eyes are still fixed on me with a brooding stare.

"What do you mean?"

He purses his lips together in a way that, to my annoyance, makes me notice again how full and perfect they are. "I mean do you plan to stay in the house or sell it?"

The thought of selling our house is like a splash of ice water. "We're *not* selling it." My tone is indignant. Offended. His brows twitch in response.

"Okay." His tone softens, and he lifts a hand in a placating gesture. I blush, embarrassed over the force in my response. It's not like he was threatening to take the house from us. I shift my weight on my feet, wanting to shake off this awkward moment.

"My brother Emmett is eight," I say finally. "He'll grow up here. After he comes of age, the four of us will decide what to do with the house."

The lines across Luc Valencia's brow smooth out, the corners of his flawless mouth turn up, and I remember his perilous dimples the instant before they reappear. My breath halts at the sight.

Dammit.

"In that case, Miss Delacroix, what do you think about moving forward with the renovation?" He's grinning now, just a little, but it feels like sunlight on my face.

Wait, what is he asking?

"Move forward?"

He nods. "I haven't seen it, of course, but the plans and my father's notes suggest your kitchen is pretty outdated. Even if you don't take appliances and décor into consideration, the wiring and plumbing are probably barely keeping up with your needs."

I press my lips together and say nothing. He's right. We can't make a smoothie, brew a pot of coffee, and run the toaster at the same time without tripping the breaker. And the décor is circa 1980. All subway tile and honey oak cabinets. Pretty much straight out of Steven Spielberg's *Poltergeist*— except the chairs don't move by themselves.

But that kitchen has been the heart of this home as long as we've been here. I doubt the twins even remember the rent house we had when they were little, and Emmett has never lived anywhere else. Sometimes, I still feel like I can come through the garage into that kitchen and find Mom at the stove, fighting with one of the burners.

Now I'm the one trying to finagle the safety lighter with one hand while cranking the gas with the other just to boil a pot of pasta.

Yet the popping sound of that crappy stove is the sound of Mom. And home. And family dinners. What would it feel like for that to be silent too?

"I don't know," I hear myself say.

I realize I'm clutching my elbows, my go-to self-soothing stance, and Luc Valencia is watching me again like he has no idea what to say.

I get that a lot lately. I'm almost used to it.

He narrows his eyes on me. "Would you…" He hesitates, and I blink to let him know I'm listening. "Would you consider letting me take a look and going over the plans with you?"

Now I double-blink. "What? You mean right now?"

The dimples are back. *Christ Almighty.*

"Well, I'm here now," he says, stating the obvious in a way that is cuter than it should be. And then he has the good grace to look abashed, and dammit if that isn't cuter. "If now is good for you."

I worked this morning and basically just walked in the door before he pulled up. I'm still in my scrubs. Tuesdays are surgery days, so I hope he doesn't notice the light brown stain on the front of my top because it isn't blood. It's canine anal gland musk from the sacculectomy I performed. If you've never smelled the contents of a canine anal sac, count yourself lucky. The odor is just this side of lethal. I scrubbed the spot with alcohol after the surgery, but if he gets too close, he'll probably still smell it.

On second thought, maybe I want him to smell it. One whiff, and he'd keep his distance for good.

"Sure, I guess now is fine."

He nods. "Let me just grab the project board from my truck."

I watch him go, dragging my eyes over the broad expanse of his back and the tight nipping in of his waist. It isn't until I see him pull the large board with paint samples, pieces of tile, and pictures adhered to it that I come out of my daze.

"Come on in." I turn and mount the steps, snapping for Clarence to join me, but when I reach the front door, I halt. I look back at him over my shoulder, chewing on my bottom lip.

"Something wrong?" he asks, those dark brows drawing together.

I nod, picturing the state of the kitchen. "I wasn't expecting anyone. The kitchen's a mess from breakfast," I explain in a rush. "Getting three kids and myself out the door in the morning isn't always easy."

Those brows relax, and I could be wrong, but I may see a twinkle of amusement in his eyes. Is he laughing at me? Judging me?

And so what if he is? If we actually decide to redo the kitchen, and this guy is in my house for months on end, what's wrong with him thinking I'm a rude slob who wears *Eau du Dog Anus* and has an attack Great Pyrenees? He certainly won't look at me the way he did last night.

"I've seen worse than a lived-in kitchen." His tone is as dry as paper.

"You're right," I hear myself say. Why am I still talking? "A few dirty dishes and a bit of dried scrambled egg isn't all that scary."

"Especially since I don't have to clean it up." As he says this, his mouth quirks and a dimple dances on one cheek.

It takes me a good three seconds to realize I'm staring at the dastardly dimple, and then I turn on my heel and practically sprint toward the kitchen.

I could take him past the stairs and through the so-called dining room, but old habits die hard. We never used the formal dining room, opting instead for the farmhouse table in the kitchen. In fact, in recent years the dining room was where my parents kept the treadmill and a spare TV. So instead, I lead him from the foyer past the entrance to the master suite and Dad's study on our left and through the family room.

"This is a great house," he says, and I turn to find him taking in the fireplace, the French windows, and the original wide-plank flooring. "Folk Victorian. When was it built?"

I stop moving because he's standing still, head craned back, taking in the bones of the house. "In 1901."

He lifts a hand and points to the wall right where the family room ends and the kitchen begins. "There used to be a wall here," he says, sounding certain. I'm surprised. My parents tore the wall down even before we moved in, making a clear view from the kitchen table to the family room fireplace. I barely remember the wall's existence.

"That's right," I say. "Mom said she didn't understand why the two rooms were ever separated."

"To make heating and cooling easier," he says, almost absently as he eyes the ceiling. "Back before central air, it was easier to heat small rooms in the winter, and in the summer, you wanted to keep the heat in the kitchen from the rest of the house. Whoever took down that wall did a really good job leaving a smooth transition."

I smile. "That was Mom. She worked in interiors, and she did a lot of projects, updating the house over the years." He may not be able to hear the pride in my voice, but I can. God, I miss her. "She always said she was going to hire someone to deliver her dream kitchen. She said she couldn't be responsible for that kind of disruption to the household day-to-day."

Valencia gives me a wincing grin. "Kitchen renovations are pretty disruptive."

Stifling a sigh, I wonder just exactly how much more disruption the Delacroix clan can handle. And would it even be worth it?

Oblivious to my doubts, Luc moves past me to the middle of the kitchen before executing a slow three-sixty. Finally, his eyes land on mine.

"Dios mío. It's like the set of every John Hughes' movie ever made."

His accented Spanish and my breathy laugh catch me off guard. "Something like that."

Don't start flirting, Delacroix.

He sets down the plans and the board on the kitchen table, which still bears Emmett's cereal bowl featuring a few soggy Frosted Flakes. I pick up the bowl and his near empty orange juice glass and quickly ferry them to the sink.

I hear Valencia's footsteps behind me. "That stove looks older than me," he mutters.

"You'd think it would know how to behave by now," I say, giving the bowl and glass a quick rinse. I'd set them in the dishwasher if it were empty, but that was another chore I didn't have time for this morning.

He chuckles under his breath, and I turn to find him peering beneath the burners. "Having trouble lighting it?"

I dry my hands on a dishtowel. "Yeah, mostly that front burner on the right."

"The one you need the most," he says almost to himself. His eyes meet mine as he taps the enameled surface. "Mind if I take a look?"

I shrug. "Knock yourself out."

He lifts the cooking grate and sets it aside. Then he peels back the little metal cap in the center of the burner, leans over, and inspects the ring. I step closer to try to see what he's looking at. "The base looks clean..." He squats down so he's eye-level with the stovetop. Then he turns to burner knob to light it. As usual, the igniter pops, but the burner refuses to light. He kills the switch before the kitchen can fill with natural gas. "You might have a bad igniter."

"But it's sparking," I say, squatting down beside him, eyeing the stubborn burner. "If it's sparking, it should light, right?"

He inhales to respond... and I see the moment it happens. He smells me.

Or rather, not me, but the evidence of the anal sacculectomy I'm wearing on my scrubs. But the way his eyes cut to me with sudden horror, it may as well be me, not my clothes. A full-body blush assaults me.

Why did I think this was a good idea?

"That's not me," I hear myself say.

Valencia looks away, giving me his profile. He clears his throat and nods. Oh my God. Are his eyes watering?

"Good to know." He rises and takes a not so discrete step to the right. Presumably out of sniffing range.

My face burns like I've moisturized with Tabasco. "I swear, it's not me," I say, almost pleading. "It's... from a patient."

He raises a fist to his mouth and coughs against it. I'm not sure, but he might be trying not to gag. "O-Okay," he rasps. When he clenches his jaw, I know he's trying not to gag.

"Oh, Jesus," I mutter, roasting with embarrassment. I take

three steps backward, guessing that my rising body temperature isn't going to help matters. "I should go change."

He clears his throat again with obvious force and shakes his head. "No. I'm good." His face is red now too, but I know he can't possibly be embarrassed. Can he? He looks like he's fighting a smile, but it's a lost cause. "So... uh... are you a nurse?"

"No." I frown. "I'm a vet."

He looks genuinely surprised, and he blinks at me with confusion. And my humiliation gladly steps aside to make room for affront.

"Why would you assume I'm a nurse and not a doctor?" I ask, cocking a hand on my hip.

My question seems to stun him. Yeah, there's no way he's looking at me like he did last night. Not now. Never again. And that's exactly how I want it.

I just wish I didn't feel this clenching in my stomach. Like I've missed winning the lottery by one number.

He stares at me for a second, surprise turning to challenge in the narrowing of his gaze. "You don't look old enough to be a doctor."

Damn. That's a good answer.

My chagrin must show on my face because his expression softens just a little. "Besides, when my dad was in the hospital, it wasn't the doctors who did the dirty work," he says, tipping his head in the direction of my fouled top.

Another good answer.

I bite the inside of my lip because he doesn't need to know I think so. "With animals, a lot of it is dirty work." But then I have to give credit where it's due. "I'll admit that my techs probably have it worse than I do most days."

"Just not today," he says under his breath.

Laughter ambushes me.

He smirks. "So if you're telling me that smell isn't human, all I can say is *Thank God.*"

I laugh harder. Wait. What am I doing?

Shit! Flirting alert!

The thought is like a fire alarm. I clear my throat and pull myself together. "So the stove," I say, brushing wisps of hair off my flushed face. "Is it an easy fix?"

My about-face seems to sober him too because he wipes the smile off his face and turns back to the range. "One way to tell for sure," he says, squatting down again. "Could you turn off the lights?"

Turn off the lights? That's a little weird.

"Um... why?"

He taps the top of the range with an index finger. "To check the spark from the igniter. If it's blue, it should be good, but if it's yellow or whitish, then you know the thing's busted."

"Oh." Who knew? "Okay." I reach forward, moving quickly so my German Shepherd Ass-scented scrubs don't violate him, and I flip the switch over the sink. Then I cross to the wall and turn off the overheads.

He twists the knob, and the popping sound fills the room. The flash is small, but even from where I stand against the wall, I can tell it's white, not blue.

"Huh," I utter, impressed with his know-how. "But would it really be worth fixing if we decide to redo the kitchen?"

He shakes his head. "No, but if you decide not to renovate, fixing it will make your life easier."

Just like that, I wonder why Mom never thought to call someone out to take care of it. Then again, it's also pretty minor. An aggravation, yes, but I don't lose any sleep over it.

There are plenty of other things to lose sleep over.

This thought, the way my skin still feels the electric tingle of laughter and charged attraction, and the sudden darkness of the room, make for too much stimuli. I need a break. I flip the lights back on.

"If it's all the same to you, I'd like to go change before we look at the plans," I say, already backing toward the living room. I gesture to my shirt, but my next words are meant for more than just that. "I don't think I can handle this."

A ghost of a smile quirks his mouth. "Sure. Take your time." The slope of his shoulders and the looseness in his well-favored limbs tells me he means it, and I'm grateful. Both for the reprieve and for his patience.

With a nod, I turn, cross to the front of the house, and dash upstairs. In my bathroom, I carefully peel the disgusting top from my body, regretting there's absolutely no time for a shower. Hell, there won't even be time after he leaves. Tuesdays after my shift are for the weekly grocery run. And then it'll be carpool, snack time, homework, and then time to fix dinner.

At the sink, I scrub my hands and wrists since this is the best I can do at the moment. I hear myself sigh and catch my reflection in the bathroom mirror. Really, it's the burgundy lace bra that catches my eye, the way its deep color seems to tie together the pink fairness of my skin and the red of my hair. It's pulled up in a ponytail this morning, but now slipping out in wisps around my face, my bangs no longer the neat curtain over my forehead but tousled from hours of wrangling animals and sweating through surgery.

With the color still high on my cheeks, I look like I've just left someone's bed. The only evidence to the contrary is the knotted drawstring low on my belly. On a whim, I pluck at the bow with still wet fingers, and the scrub bottoms gape open. The fabric dips just enough so I can see my matching burgundy lace undies.

I may be relegated to the life of a nun for the next ten years, but that doesn't mean I have to wear granny-panties.

I put on sexy underwear almost every day. And shopping

for lingerie is a definite guilty pleasure. I like the way it looks. I like the way it feels. And I like the way I feel when I put it on in the morning and when I undress at night.

Sexy underwear is like a secret weapon. Really, it's like a secret multi-purpose tool. A kind of morale-boosting Swiss Army knife. Good for building confidence, positive body image, and inspiring hope.

I've always liked lacy bras and racy panties, but these days, they mean something more to me. They are a little reminder of the truth. Smokin' hot underwear says, *You're sexy even if there isn't a man in your life.* It says, *Maybe the only balls you'll touch for a decade will be the ones you snip off cats and dogs, but you've still got it.* It says, *This part of you that you can't share with anyone? It hasn't died.*

"Stop feeling sorry for yourself," I scold my reflection.

I shuck the scrub bottoms and leave them in a puddle on the floor of my bathroom. A moment later, I'm dressed in a pullover and jeans, ready for my trip to the store as soon as this guy leaves.

Before I reach the kitchen, I hear the rustle of papers. He's talking as I walk in. "So last time this kitchen was updated, it was sometime in the eighties," he says, studying the plans. "The vision your mother had fits the age and original decorative style a lot more naturally."

At the mention of Mom, I feel a little quickening in my heart. Not like the bottomed-out faintness I had earlier, but excitement. He's about to show me something from my mother. Something new.

Without warning, tears blur my vision. I clutch the frame of a dining chair, trying to hold back the feeling.

But then it hits me.

When is this ever going to happen again? When I'll get to lay eyes on something she meant to show me? To have a new memory of her to add to my very finite collection?

Probably never. And if this is it, if this is the last time I get to share something new with my mom, I want to feel every minute of it.

So I let the tears fall.

Nothing else is at hand, so I grab the wadded up paper towel Harry left on the table this morning and wipe my cheeks, determined to be unashamed. I've apologized for dissolving into tears a dozen times in the last five months, especially at the beginning.

I don't think I can apologize anymore.

Hell, if it bothers Bob the Builder, he can add it to my growing list of unattractive traits. Sarcastic, stinky, slovenly, sobbing psycho.

But when I let my gaze fall on the plans, I forget all about repulsing Luc Valencia, the chores ahead of me, or apologizing for grieving.

The two-dimensional kitchen rendered on graph paper might as well be drawn in Mom's hand. Every detail is so her —so us—it's like walking into her hug.

My watery gasp makes him look up at me, but I don't take my focus from the inked image of Mom's dream kitchen. I feel rather than see him avert his gaze, but out of the corner of my eye, I can't help but notice his hands as they grip the edge of the table with obvious strain.

But I have no time for his discomfort. I'm too busy catching tears with the stiff, scratchy paper towel and wishing Mom were here to see her ideas on the page.

A moment later, when Valencia speaks, his voice is low, careful. "I'll just leave these here," he says, and then I hear the creak of leather and the whisper of paper against paper. "My number's on the card. Call if you want to go through with it."

At first, I can only nod, but when he turns and heads for the front door, I call out. "Wait." I force myself to face him. He's standing in my living room, all loose-limbed ease gone.

He looks as taut as a bowstring, his expression tense and guarded.

Some men just can't handle tears. *Just like Carter,* I think with a stab of bitterness. But I share my words anyway. "Th-thank you for these," I tell him, my voice catching just a little. "I don't know yet what we'll do. It'll have to be something we all want, but thank you. She would have loved them."

Chapter Five

LUC

I feel like a *cabrón* leaving her to cry alone, but the only way I know to stop a woman's tears is to pull her into a hug—and apologize if the tears are my fault. It works with Mami and Abuela. With all my cousins, Aunt Lucinda's four daughters. My girlfriends back in high school.

In the four years we were together, I never once saw Ronni cry, so I wouldn't know if it works on her.

But the thought of wrapping Millie Delacroix in my arms feels as dangerous as running into a burning building.

First of all, she's a client—or she could be—and you don't hug clients. Secondly, the last half hour has been an exercise in self-control. Giving in to touching her would have been a bad idea. The moment she put her hand in mine I wanted to hold on. When she led me inside, all I could think about was laying a hand on the small of her back. When she cleared the table, I strangled the urge to take the dishes from her. Carry them for her.

At the stove when she bent next to me, I wanted to breathe in her scent, the one the afternoon breeze had carried to me in the soccer stands yesterday. Strawberries and summer.

What you got was exactly what you deserved, I tell myself, chuckling at the memory as I fire up the truck.

A vet. She heals animals. That's so cool.

My chuckle mellows into a grin. "Yeah, she let you have it when you asked if she was a nurse," I mutter aloud, backing out onto St. Mary Street when I get a break between cars. I pop the truck back into drive and give Millie Delacroix's killer folk Victorian one last look.

She's as fiery as her hair is red. Prickly. And soft. She seemed to get pissed when I asked if she was selling the house. And then she blew me away when she said the decision to renovate would have to be unanimous. Hers as well as the kids'.

Would I do that? Would I leave something that important up to Alex to decide?

Hell, would I be able to handle raising him? Not to mention two others. And that little one only eight?

"Jesucristo." I cross myself, my prayer half for Millie Delacroix and half for myself. May God help her, and while he's at it, may I never have to be in her shoes. I love my little brother, but raising that kid would be the end of me. Hanging out with him is one thing. Making sure he's fed, has clean clothes, and, shit, doesn't kill himself after he gets a driver's license is something else entirely.

She must be scared out of her mind.

I come to a stop at the intersection of St. Mary and Johnston Street with one thought in mind: I'd really like to build Millie Delacroix a kitchen.

"How's Jorge and Inez?"

Cesar Luis Herrero Blanco has been my best friend since August of 2003. In a sea of white faces, he was the only other

Mexican-American in Mrs. Brumsfield's sixth grade home-room. We didn't seek each other out, though we'd probably clocked each other before the tardy bell had even rung. But when Mrs. Brumsfield pulled out her seating chart to pair up the class at the fifteen two-person tables, guess who I was partnered with in the back corner?

Cesar and I have joked over the years that we owe our friendship—and even our very lives—to a xenophobic history teacher who smelled like licorice. While her choice to lump us at that table might have been small-minded racism, if I knew where Mrs. Brumsfield was today, I'd send her a fruit basket.

"You know," I say with a shrug and take a bite of my shrimp *patacon*. I grabbed a smoothie after my meeting with Millie Delacroix, but that was like seven hours ago. I'm so hungry I could eat a beer can dipped in ketchup.

And *Patacon*, the Latin cuisine hole in the wall on Bertrand, is a favorite. I savor the bite, the salty-sweet plantain patties, the smoky etouffee shrimp, and the ripe tomatoes, sighing in satisfaction. I swallow and answer Cesar's question.

"Papi's hobbling around on his cane, griping about how I'm ruining the business. Mami's feeding him every carb known to man, deep fried and sprinkled with powdered sugar—"

Cesar's ill-timed laugh interrupts me. He's mid-bite around his *arepas*, and the result is messy. Laughing, I offer my goof of a best friend a napkin. He wipes butter sauce from his chin, shaking his head.

"I can't take you anywhere."

He chews and swallows, eyes narrowed into laser beams. "This place is one of my accounts. If anything, I'm taking you."

Cesar works for Waitr. He started out as a driver when the company first moved into Lafayette. He slid right into middle management as soon as he graduated with a degree in business. Cesar is good at what he does, and that company is expanding every day, giving UberEats some serious competition. Cesar is going nowhere but up.

I'm happy for him. And proud.

"She still busting your balls about Ronni?"

I take another bite and roll my eyes. "You should have heard her yesterday at Alex's soccer game."

The words summon an instant memory. Not of Ronni, my ex, but of Millie Delacroix. Looking away from me in those bleachers.

She couldn't look away from me today. And I sure as hell couldn't stop looking at her, try though I might.

Cesar shrugs, his expression knowing. "You should just tell her the truth."

I wash down a bite with a gulp of Canebrake, shaking my head. "*Mami* and Ronni's mom are close. If I tell her Ronni slept with that fuckwad boss of hers, it won't go over well. You know my mother."

He snorts. "Uh, yeah." Cesar takes a pull from his beer before leaning forward and pointing the neck of the bottle at me in accusation. "Every time we got in trouble in high school, she fussed at *me*. Even if it was your idea."

I grin in spite of myself. "What can I say? Neither of her boys can do any wrong."

"Please," he insists, holding up a hand. "I'm eating."

I smother my laugh with the last bite of my *patacon*. *Damn, that's good.*

Cesar narrows his eyes at me. "But why would you care? I mean, Ronni's the one who cheated. You'd never pull shit like that. Unlike when we were kids, this time," he holds up a finger to single out the incident, "you didn't do anything wrong. What's wrong with people knowing that?"

I wince. "What's wrong with people knowing my shit? My mom? Her mom? *Your* mom? Every Chicano in town?"

Cesar's look is dry as sand. "For the record, *my* mom also thinks you can do no wrong."

I grasp onto this. Anything to change the subject. "I've always admired Delores's wisdom."

Cesar's wadded up napkin hits me in the face. He gives me the evil eye while I laugh, and to make sure the subject is dead, I poke at his soft spots.

"So, how was your *date?*"

He scoffs. "It wasn't a date, and you know it."

I nod. "Only because you haven't grown the balls to ask her out yet."

Cesar has been ass over eyeballs crazy about one of his clients for a good three months. She owns a sandwich shop near the university, and he stops in for lunch to check on her every Tuesday and Friday.

His eyes cut to his empty plate. Cesar pretends to be absorbed in the task of picking up crumbs with the tip of his finger. "Masie is a client. You know that's forbidden fruit."

Fruit that smells like strawberries and summer...

"Tell me about it." The words, heavy with meaning, are out before I know it.

Cesar's head snaps up, his eyes alert. "Say what?"

I shake my head too quickly, and my best friend gives me the side eye. I take a casual sip of beer.

"You got a desperate housewife who needs a stud finder?"

Canebrake almost comes out my nose. I splutter and cough while he laughs. *"Dios mío,* Cesar," I rasp, fighting for breath.

Cesar shakes his head. "I can't take you anywhere."

Chapter Six

MILLIE

"So that wall," Harry says, pointing to the one that separates the kitchen and formal dining room but keeping his eyes on the plans, "would be gone, right?"

"Yes." I nod, but he's not looking at me. "And that's an island where the wall is now, and there would be a breakfast nook at the bay window." I tap on these details in the design, the last one so sweet and irresistible, I want to become a two-dimensional version of myself and curl up on its cushioned window seat. It would be like getting the coveted booth at your favorite restaurant instead of one of the square tables adrift in the middle of the room.

"Mom would have loved that breakfast nook," Mattie says wistfully. She's standing behind Emmett, peering down at the plans from over his head, her hands on his shoulders. I'm glad she's touching him, bracing him. I'm trying to gage all of their reactions, but I can't study all three of them at once.

When my eyes flit to Emmett, he's running his fingers over the tile samples on the project board, and I see his nose wrinkled in confusion. "What's a nook?"

Harry shrugs. "It's like a hideaway."

Emmett's eyes round. "In the kitchen?" He sounds so mystified, I know he's picturing something out of a story book, like a secret passageway or a trap door.

"It's not hidden," I explain. "It's just a place that is sort of tucked aside."

His gaze turns accusing and he aims it at Harry. "Then why did you say *hideaway* if you can't even hide in it?"

Harry rolls his eyes. "I said *hideaway* because that's like the definition. Look..." He pulls his phone out of his back pocket and drums the screen with his thumbs. *"Nook: a corner or recess, especially one offering seclusion or security."*

As one, we look back at the drawing of the little alcove. *Seclusion or security.* A little safe place for the four of us to gather. It looks so cozy. I can picture us there on Saturday mornings. Playing *Spontaneous* on Sunday nights. Tucked in right where Mom wanted us to be.

My throat closes on the thought, but I bite the tip of my tongue until the threat of tears passes. I don't want my feelings to influence my brothers and sister.

But if I hadn't already made up my mind, it's made up now. I want this remodel. And it's not just because this is the kitchen Mom wanted. Yes, I want to see it through for her.

But I also want it for us.

I want its cozy, welcoming embrace. I want the morning light as it will shine in from the bay window and fill the kitchen. I want to sit at the nook's table with a book and wait for Emmett's bus. I usually only have about fifteen minutes between the time I get home with Mattie and the time when his bus shows up, but that's now how I want to spend those minutes. And for this to be the spot where I sit with him to do his homework, listening to the sound of Mattie practicing piano.

"And we can afford this?" Harry asks, still scrutinizing the plans. I smile at my brother's caution, his concern for our financial welfare.

"We can. It was already earmarked in one of the savings accounts," I explain. "I just didn't know what it was for before now."

In the beginning, the paperwork had been staggering. Accounts, policies, portfolios, fund statements. In my old life, I'd only had a checking account that Mom and Dad bankrolled. I was still in vet school, and they put money in my debit account every month so I could cover rent, utilities, groceries, and spending money. That's all I'd ever had to worry about.

Mom and Dad's lawyer and their financial planner both met with me after the memorial to help me make sense of everything, but even with their help, I was overwhelmed. My Uncle Gill, Mom's oldest brother and a CPA, came in for a weekend about a month later, and he helped me set up a Mint account so I could see everything in one place. We put as many bills as we could on automatic draft, and we created a schedule so that the rolling balance from the life insurance payout would stay in a money market account and only make a deposit into our expense account once a month.

By and large, that means I don't have to think about the details all the time. Quarterly updates are good enough. But last night, after Luc Valencia's visit—and after the grocery run, the homework rodeo, and a dinner of homemade chili and cornbread—I sat in the living room while the kids watched *Milo Murphy's Law* on the Disney Channel and went through the various savings accounts again.

Sure enough, one of them was labeled *KIT RM BGT.* I hadn't given it any thought before, but now that I've seen the plans and the bid, I think this probably stands for "kitchen remodel budget." I certainly can't fathom what else it might stand for, and, after all, I know from talking to Mom that she was planning for this.

"Honestly," I tell him because I don't want him or the other two to worry. "Even if they hadn't set money aside for it, we could still afford it."

Harry's eyes meet mine, and he nods. "Then I say we do it." He casts his eyes around the kitchen. "The way I see it, this room has been needing an update since we moved in."

I hold my breath. If Harry's for it, my money is on Emmett being on board too. I look at Mattie. She's biting her lip.

"We don't have to make any decisions right now," I say, hoping to reassure her. "If we decide to do this, it's going to be pretty disruptive. I don't want anyone to feel like they were rushed into making a choice they didn't really want."

Mattie still looks worried. "How long will it take?"

I've poured over the plans, but I don't know for sure. Three months? Six? I don't want to scare anyone with the worst-case scenario, but I don't want to mislead them either.

"It'll take months," I say, meeting each of their eyes in turn. "I just don't know how many." Harry's expression is neutral. Mattie frowns a little, considering. Emmett looks impressed.

"Months?" he asks, eyes bugging. "Like until summer?"

Surely, it won't take that long. Will it? "I think it'll be done before summer's here, Em."

His face screws up in confusion. "Will we still be able to eat in here? And make food?"

My gut tightens. This is the reality. "Well, for some of it, yes, and for other parts, no."

They're all watching me. This is something, too, I've had to get used to. So many times over the last five months, it's been just like this. The three of them staring up at me, looking to me for the answers. Watching me for a clue on how to behave, what to do, where to go.

Sometimes I want to look back at them and shout, *What the hell are you doing?! You shouldn't be looking to me? What do I know?*

But then who would they look to? There's no one I can turn to for all the answers, and that's an awful feeling. They're too young to feel that way. So I keep my mouth shut. I have to pretend I know what I'm doing long enough for them to grow up and realize no one knows what they're doing.

"I've given this some thought," I explain. "We'll be able to keep using the fridge and microwave even if we have to move them, so we can always make cereal, sandwiches, and frozen meals. But we'll be eating a lot of takeout."

And just like that, all three of them relax.

I narrow my eyes at my siblings. "What? Is that a good thing?"

Harry and Mattie attempt twin deadpan looks in a way that make their twinness unmistakable. But Emmett grins outright.

"We like the nights when we have takeout," he says innocently.

"Emmett," Mattie hisses, glowering at him.

I put my hands on my hips. "What does that mean? The nights we have takeout?" I pin each with a glare. "As opposed to the nights I cook?"

No one speaks, but Harry and Mattie both give Emmett gimlet-eyed stares, as though daring him to open his mouth. My little brother may be young, but he's not dumb. He ducks his chin, making himself look like he's five instead of eight, and shakes his head.

"Well?"

I'm not the best cook in the world. I get that. But I'm not horrible. Am I?

The twins exchange a glance, and by some tacit agreement I can't decipher, Mattie is elected spokesperson.

"Millie, we love it…" Mattie swallows visibly, and I know for certain she's in the middle of a lie. "when you cook."

"Oh, yeah?" I say, folding my arms across my chest. "What's your favorite? The best thing I make?"

The twins' eyes lock again, looks of caution and warning pass between them.

"Your pancakes are really good," Emmett says, head bobbing with enthusiasm. I don't need a polygraph to know he's speaking the truth.

"Pancakes."

Missing the flatness of my tone, he nods, delight sparking in his blue eyes. "I could eat 'em every day."

I raise a brow. "Thank you for that, Emmett," I say dryly. "But Bisquick really gets the credit for pancakes. I just add water to the Shake 'N Pour bottle."

Without turning his face from me, his gaze flick up to the twins, a sure sign he's realizing he should have kept quiet. His lower lip buds as he looks at the floor.

"You make really good sandwiches too," he says so low it's hard to hear him. But we do hear him, and the twins seem to ripple with unspent laughter. I gust a sigh.

Pancakes and sandwiches.

"So I'm a lousy cook," I say, aiming this at the fourteen-year-olds. "Thanks for telling me."

Mattie's jaw drops and Harry puts up his hands in defense. They speak at once.

"You're not a lousy cook—"

"We didn't say—"

But it's Emmett who steps up and hugs me around the middle. "You're doing your best, Millie," he says. "We know."

I hug him back and try not to feel like a total loser. I *have* been doing my best. Trying to make the dishes Mom used to make. Her roast, rice, and gravy. Her lemon chicken. Her shepherd's pie.

Except I don't have any of her recipes. She never wrote any of them down, and, dammit to hell, I never asked her to. I didn't even bother to try to make a home-cooked meal when I lived in my apartment during vet school. Between classes, cases, and studying, there wasn't time, and if I really had a craving for something of hers, I just asked Mom to make it and came home for the weekend.

Most nights, if I didn't get something at the caf, I made a salad, or a grilled cheese sandwich, or an omelet. Or I got takeout. Not exactly the stuff of culinary school.

So I've been trying to recreate her recipes. I'll look them up online and pick ones I think have her same general ingredients, and then I just tweak as I go, trying to steer the flavor toward what I remember of hers.

But I guess I've been steering us off a cliff.

"Maybe if we redo the kitchen, I could use that time to take a cooking class," I muse aloud. Harry and Mattie's expressions freeze, but Emmett, still hugging me, has his back to them, and he nods so hard, I think he'll give himself whiplash.

Harry rubs his chin with the pad of his thumb where he thinks he's starting to grow a beard. "It's not a bad idea," he says with a noncommittal shrug.

I look at Mattie. Her lips are pressed together to hide her smile, but I can tell she likes the idea. "Sis, what do you think?"

She gives a little head tilt. "If that's something you want to do, go for it."

I'd love them even if they were total turds. But I adore them for not wanting to hurt my feelings. I wish I could hug all three of them, but Mattie and Harry just stiffen when I try. I get it. It's not me. It's the age. And maybe it's because that was Mom's job, too.

To hug us every day.

But Emmett still needs hugs. He craves them. So I squeeze him tight enough to be squeezing all three.

STEPHANIE FOURNET

And then it hits me. The kitchen. They're all on board. At least I think they are.

"So you... So we're going to do this? Remodel the kitchen?" I ask, checking each of the faces I love above all others.

"Yes," Mattie says.

"Yep," Harry adds.

Emmett smiles up at me. "It'll be fun."

I snort. "It'll be fun for about five minutes, and then it'll be a pain in the butt," I say. They're all smiling now, so I smile back. "But I think we'll be happy with it once it's done."

None of them looks the least bit hesitant. That's probably because they don't really get what we're signing up for, but then again, do I even know? Yet, for reasons I don't really understand, I want this too. This project. This chance to make something new.

"Okay. I'll call the contractor tomorrow."

Chapter Seven

LUC

I PULL UP TO THE LAMBERT'S HOUSE. IT'S THURSDAY, FIVE minutes before noon, and not one member of my crew is here. No cars. No trucks. No Hector.

"Sonofabitch."

If no one's here, it means Hector, the site manager, left for an early lunch. And the rest of them followed.

No question about it. This is Hector's third strike. Yeah, everybody knocks off early for lunch now and then. But not two days after the boss gets on them for not being where they need to be.

I have to fire him. It won't be the first time I've done it, but it will be the first time it's my call. And firing people—firing anyone—sucks ass.

"Shit." This is so not in my Daily Three. Not Finances. Not Motivation. Not Fitness.

I grab my phone from the cup holder, and I'm about to search for Hector's number when it rings. It's a 337 number I don't recognize.

"Luc Valencia," I answer.

"We're ready."

My abs twitch. That voice. I shouldn't know it, but I do. It's her.

"Miss Delacr—"

"It's Millie," she says in a rush. "Please, call me Millie." She sounds nervous. Maybe a little keyed up. I can hear her breath.

For a second, I go still, listening to the sound. And then I swallow and return to sanity.

"You've decided?"

"Yes," she says, excitement clear in the word. "We're ready. The four of us are agreed."

I smile, imagining that. Her and three kids talking it out. A unanimous decision, if what she told me was true.

And I'd bet payroll it is.

"Good to hear," I say, ignoring just how glad I am she called. She's a client. Just another client. "We can get started Monday if that works for you."

Silence.

"Monday?"

I frown. "Yeah. Is that too soon?" I listen, but there's nothing. Not even breath. Is she holding it?

Breathe, I want to tell her.

"N-no... it's not too soon." She says this, but something's off.

"Is Monday a problem?"

"No... It's just I—" She pauses, and this time I do hear her breathing. I lean back against the headrest, listening.

An insistent voice in my head speaks up, *She's a client. We don't listen to clients breathing.*

I open my eyes. When did I close them?

"What is it?" I prompt, peering through the windshield, checking to make sure none of my guys have shown up on site.

"I-It's stupid. For some reason, I just pictured you starting tomorrow," she says, sounding embarrassed.

I sit up straight, surprised. "You've already packed up? Set up your temp kitchen?"

"Huh?"

It's my turn to be silent because I don't trust my voice. My face is split with a huge ass smile, and I'm afraid she'll hear it. I clear my throat and pull it together.

"Um, Miss Del—"

"Millie," she interrupts.

"Okay, Millie." I say her name and smile again. How did she end up with such an old fashioned name? But maybe it suits her. She has a lot of responsibilities for someone so young. And it's different. I don't know anyone else named Millie.

I sweep these thoughts aside and focus on her kitchen. "We can't get started until everything—all of your dishes, cookware, furniture, everything—is cleared out," I explain, picturing the new footprint. "The first thing we're going to do is rip out the cabinets and counters."

"Oh shit," she mutters. "I... didn't think of that."

I'm glad she can't see me because my grin would probably piss her off. "So do you need the weekend to do that?"

She groans. It would be sort of cute if she didn't sound so overwhelmed. And miserable.

"We're *not* ready, Mr. Valencia."

"Luc." My name comes out soft, and I clear my throat again and speak with more force. "Call me Luc."

"Well, Luc, we won't be ready for Monday," she says, disappointment heavy in her voice. "We've got too much going on this weekend."

A light bulb goes off. "Soccer tournament Saturday." Mami mentioned it Monday night.

"Yeah, and piano recital Sunday." From her weary tone, I don't think she's looking forward to either.

I rub my forehead and think about the other jobs I have waiting in the wings. Maybe I could shuffle around a small one to give her a few weeks to get ready. I reach for the laptop beside me.

"Just give me a sec..."

"Sure."

I cradle the phone between my head and shoulder as I type, but even though the speaker is not pressed directly to my ear, I don't miss a loud chorus of barking that mutes the background music of Millie's breath.

I chuckle. "You at work?" I ask, scanning over my waiting list.

"How'd you guess?" she asks dryly.

"Here's one." I open up the plans for a closet makeover. That'll take three weeks. Four tops. "What if I shift some jobs around and get back to you next month?"

She gasps. "What?! No! Oh, please, no." She sounds almost desperate. "We're all looking forward to it. I-I still have tonight and tomorrow night. I'll get it done."

I frown. I can picture her doing it. Standing on a stepladder in her scrubs, taking down platters and Pilsner glasses from the highest cabinet. By herself.

I have the urge to offer to help her. And as soon as the impulse strikes, I really, *really* want to.

But she's a client. *We don't listen to clients breathing and we don't offer to help them pack up,* the voice reminds me.

But this time, I argue back. *What about the remodel we did for the guy with the spinal cord injury? Making his house wheelchair accessible?*

Papi had made sure the guy and his young wife didn't have to worry about moving furniture, picking up toys in the kids' rooms, or emptying closets as we outfitted the whole house with wider doors. We'd done it all.

Yeah, but his skin didn't make you think of ice cream flavors. And it's NOT on your Daily Three.

"I just need to find enough boxes…" I hear her voice trail off, and I come back to my senses.

I have boxes. Plenty of boxes in the warehouse. The ones for light fixtures and ceiling fans are probably the size she needs. I could drop them off on my way home…

Stop.

"Ah!" she exclaims. "Pay dirt. Tons of boxes in the supply room. Good God. Who needs this much catnip?" She's talking to herself. I grin. It's a lot sweeter than the way I talk to myself.

Sounds of scuffing and shuffling have replaced sounds of barking dogs. "Schedule us for Monday, Mr. Val—I mean, Luc. We'll be ready." Then her voice drops, but I still make out the words. "Even if I have to pull an all-nighter to do it."

I LEAVE Red's Health Club a little after six, my muscles rubbery after circuit training and heavy after the sauna and shower. I needed it, both the beating the workout gave me and the vaporizing heat.

Firing. Hector. Sucked.

The guy had the nerve to act surprised. Even after what happened Tuesday. Even after I recounted the list of screw-ups —costly screw-ups—he'd made under Papi.

He'd scowled and told me I'd never be the boss Papi was. And when he said it, I knew what this was all about. Him not wanting to take orders from me. The boss's son. Who's now the boss.

And that sucked too. Because I've sensed a little of that from all the guys, the way their eyes cut to each other when I come down on them or make them redo sloppy work. The *yes, sirs* with just a hint of attitude in the *sir*.

They may not know I never asked for this. Never asked for

Papi to get sick and retire early. He sure as hell never asked for diabetes. Papi has a gripe about nearly every call I make, but I know part of that comes from being sidelined before he was ready. And I know him. I don't even need to pick up the phone and ask him what he would do. Every call I make is with him in mind.

Papi put everything he had into this business. When he finally got his green card, he worked three jobs, seven days a week, to finish building the capital to buy the equipment he needed to strike out on his own. It took him two solid years. And then he busted his ass to build a reputation based on efficiency, honesty, and affordability.

When I started working with him at seventeen—which was when he could actually afford to pay me—he told me we had to work harder than all the white contractors. *People here look at us and expect us to be lazy,* he'd said. *They'll try to catch us cheating them or stealing from them. We can't just be good enough. We have to be great to be good enough.*

I've been doing this almost ten years, and while our clients are hiring us because they've heard of our reputation, their neighbors are always watching. Waiting. We still have to be great to be good enough.

So, yeah, I can be hard on our guys. And maybe I'm being harder on them than Papi would have been. Because if he had to be great to be good enough, then I have to be frickin' perfect to be great to be good enough. Because he's watching, and I can't let him down.

And I'm not stupid. Nobody's perfect. I fuck up too. And I try to balance being a hardass with giving credit where it's due. That means keeping my eyes open. Which of the guys is doing a stellar job? Who needs to be singled out and patted on the back? Who needs a raise? Who's going to take Hector's place as site manager?

I toy with this last question as I walk to my truck. The Lambert's job definitely needs a manager, and I can't do it. I move around too much. Before firing Hector, my plan was to put Miguel, Sam, and Donner on the Delacroix job with Miguel as manager. All three of those guys are careful and don't need much looking after—even Sam, who's just nineteen.

Until I can hire someone new full-time, I'd probably be better off leaving Tony where he is at the Sterling's, moving Miguel to the Lambert's, putting a temp worker to follow Donner's lead at the Delacroix's, and checking in on them and helping out as often as I can.

I reach my truck and spot the half-dozen boxes I'd pulled from the warehouse this afternoon. Millie Delacroix said she had plenty of boxes, but I pulled them anyway.

Don't go over there. We don't see clients at night without an appointment.

The voice is right. I might make a night time stop at a new construction site or a home the owners have moved out of for a major renovation, but I don't disturb families after dark unless I need to meet with a homeowner to go over plans or changes and they can't fit me in during the work day.

But I hear Millie's voice, and it's even louder than the one in my head. *We'll be ready...even if I have to pull an all-nighter to do it.*

It's almost as though the truck drives itself.

THAT MONSTER of a dog is barking from inside before my boots even touch the ground.

This is a mistake, the voice warns. Ignoring it, I slam the truck door and pluck two of the boxes from the bed. The front door opens as I approach, and the bear dog steps out, still barking, but he doesn't charge me the way he did Tuesday. He just walks to the edge of the porch and barks up toward the moon, just two or three great bellows.

Behind him, Millie's brother, the young one, stands in the

open door, staring. I approach with the boxes, but I stop at the foot of the steps under his suspicious gaze, letting the dog sniff me, and I see the moment the boy's eyes narrow with recognition.

"Hey, you were at the game the other night," he says, almost accusing.

I nod. "I was." What's his name? Evan? Eric? "I'm Luc, and I'm going to be working on your kitchen. Is Millie home?"

He blinks, surprised, but then his expression turns bored. "She's in the shower."

I'm mounting the steps, but at this I halt. She's in the shower? The knowledge grabs me by the throat. To swallow... breathe... speak, for a moment, is impossible.

Go. Leave the boxes and go, the know-it-all voice commands.

But I don't. I can't explain it. I know I should. I should just drop the boxes, tell the kid to give them to his sister, and come back Monday with the crew.

The words just won't come. Not those words, anyway. Instead, different ones open my throat.

"Has she started packing the kitchen?" As soon as I ask, the urge to push my way inside and start helping her with the task has me gripping each box with shaky force.

The kid shrugs. "She started, but—"

"Emmett, who are you talking to?" The female voice has me looking past him, but it isn't Millie. It's her sister. For the life of me, I can't remember her name either. At least I know Emmett's now.

But when she steps up behind him and sees me, her eyes widen. "You're Alejandro's brother," she says, a little breathless.

I crack a smile. "Yeah, I'm Luc." I tuck one box under my arm and step forward to offer my hand. She takes it, but her gaze moves behind me, searching, looking hopeful.

Is she looking for Alex? *Puta madre. She has a crush on my brother.*

My smile widens. "I'm a contractor. We'll be doing your kitchen remodel."

Her eyes come back to me, alight. "Does Alejandro work with you?"

This has me smothering a chuckle. "Not yet. He'll work with me this summer though."

"Oh." Clearly, she's disappointed. Her gaze sharpens and a blush climbs her cheeks. She doesn't have her sister's stunning red hair. Hers is a cinnamon brown. But she's cute. Really cute. Alex should count himself lucky. If he knows... "I'm Mattie. Can I help you with something?"

She's going to take the boxes and send me on my way. I should be relieved. A part of me *is* relieved. But another part wants to see Millie.

Who am I kidding? All of me wants to see Millie.

"I brought these to help with the packing." I hold out the boxes, and she takes them, thanking me.

"There's more in the truck." I turn and head that way, resolving to hand over the rest of the boxes. Yeah, I want to lay eyes on Millie Delacroix, but what good could come of that?

None at all.

Maybe one of my Threes tomorrow should be Dating. It's been a couple months since Ronni and I split. This redhead is the first woman to catch my eye since then, and that's probably all this is. A sign that I'm ready to get back out there.

Carrying back the load of boxes, I'm relieved. This is an issue I have the power to address. I climb the steps wearing a self-satisfied grin and stop dead. Emmett and Mattie are gone.

But Millie, wet hair framing her face and spilling over her shoulders, stands in the doorway dressed in a long-sleeved crop top and drawstring pajama pants.

Relief—along with all the moisture in my mouth—vanishes.

I only let myself take in the expanse of bare skin at her midriff for about .3 seconds, but *Dios mío. Demasiada belleza.*

But it's what I see in her eyes that does me in. She's surprised—and confused—to see me. Yet beyond that, she looks tired. Faint smudges of fatigue paint the fair skin beneath her eyes. Dressed in her pjs, her hair still wet, she looks soft, unprotected, and bone tired.

I don't even think. My mouth just opens. "What can I do to help?"

Chapter Eight

MILLIE

MAYBE IT'S SEEING LUC VALENCIA ON MY FRONT PORCH. Maybe it's his words. Maybe it's standing in the open doorway with wet hair on a November night. But the tiny blonde hairs on my arms stand on end, and my nipples pebble under my pajama top. And then I do the stupidest thing I've ever done. Ever.

I look down.

Yep. My headlights are on. High beams. Shining right at him.

And, of course, because I've looked down, so does he. I know because it's like a jolt of electricity shoots through his body, and he says something in rapid Spanish. Turning a shade of red somewhere between fire-roasted tomato and old timey barn, I swiftly cross my arms over my chest and brace myself to meet his gaze.

When I do, it's terrifying. I'd expected him to at best look embarrassed—not as embarrassed as I am—and at worst to be leering, giving me a wolfish grin.

But he's scowling. His frown is downright menacing with

that scar notching through his left brow. Why the hell does he look so grumpy?

He shakes his head, and his expression eases. Just a little. He's still frowning. "You're finished with the kitchen already?"

"I…" I glance down at the boxes in his arms. Is that why he's pissed? Because he brought me boxes and he thinks I don't need them? If so, that's messed up, and he'd be wrong anyway. I don't have enough. "I'm not," I say, swallowing as I recount the barest of scratches that I have put into that monster of a job. Who knew Mom had so many dishes? And crystal? And appliances? "Not even close."

My tone sounds suspiciously like despair, so I clear my throat. "That's why I had to take a break," I blather on, shrugging a shoulder in the direction of the stairs. "A cold shower wakes me up better than anything else. I'm about to dive back in."

He's still frowning, but he looks more confused now than annoyed. "But you're in pajamas," he says, almost absently.

Now it's my turn to frown. Like it's any of his damn business. What's he doing here anyway? If I hadn't already crossed my arms over my chest, I'd do it now with a flounce. "Yeah, so after I work until I collapse, it'll be one less thing I have to do before I face-plant on my bed."

He blinks, drawing back a little, and I think maybe my words came out a bit too snippy. We stare at each other, and I'm pretty sure I'm giving him the same uncertain look he's giving me. I have no idea what the hell I'm supposed to say to him now, but I'm not about to be the first to look away. That's for chickens, and I won't spend the next three to six months letting this guy think I'm a chicken.

Luc raises his armload of boxes, and I think he's about to hand them over and get the hell out of Crazy Town, when the hint of a smile lifts the corner of his mouth. "I can help knock that out. I brought boxes."

"Wh-what?" I stammer. He steps forward, and I can either let him crash into me with his bunch of boxes or I can move aside and allow him in. I move aside. "Wait. You don't need—"

He walks past me toward the living room. "Yes, I do."

I follow, my bare feet slapping on the wood floor. "This isn't your responsibility. I can handle it." I grab his arm, and we both stop.

Arm? Did I say *arm?* His bicep has to be made of cedar.

Luc swings his dark gaze to me, skepticism hard in his eyes. I let go.

"You're doing this by yourself?" he asks, his eyes snapping to Mattie and Emmett on the living room sectional. Mattie's surrounded by books and papers. Emmett holds his Nintendo Switch, but they are watching us, silent and wary-eyed.

I scoff. "Yes. I'm the adult."

Mattie has an AP Bio test tomorrow. Harry is at a friend's working on a world geography project, and Emmett is only eight. I'm tempted to tell Luc this, but what business is it of his? I don't owe him an explanation.

His brow quirks as though he's debating the truth of my last statement. With a subtle tilt of his chin, he indicates my clothes, and I know exactly what he's thinking, the bastard.

What kind of adult is already in pjs at six-thirty at night?

Luc shakes his head. "This isn't a one-person job. You need help. I'm already here," he says, matter-of-factly. "Let's get to it."

Thirty minutes ago, I was dead on my feet, but now I feel like I could go thirteen rounds with this guy without taking a break. *I* need help?! How dare he?

"I. Do. Not. Need. Help."

He rolls his eyes. "Fine. I'm not helping you. I'm helping me," he says with a slight bow of concession. "If the crew and I get here Monday morning, and the kitchen isn't ready for demo, it'll cost me money in wages and push us off schedule."

I scowl. "But it *will* be ready—"

"Have you set up your temporary kitchen yet? Moved your fridge? Your microwave? The table?"

This brings me up short. "N-not yet."

"Do you have a dolly for moving the fridge?"

I press my lips together. "No."

"I have one in my truck," Luc says with a glint in his eye. "Would you like to borrow it?"

I try to picture moving the refrigerator by myself. Could I even manage it without the thing crushing me flat? I honestly hadn't even thought of moving it. Maybe Harry and I could handle it together, but what if he got hurt?

Luc is watching my face, and I'm probably turning green in front of him because as he waits for my answer, his eyes soften.

"I'm being an ass," he says.

I swallow and stand as tall as possible. "You kind of are."

His mouth quirks and cue The Dimples.

Goddammit. I don't want to, but I crack a smile.

He cocks his head to the side, but the look in his eyes is sincere. "If I say I'm sorry, will you let me move your fridge and pack up some of your stuff?"

I sigh. What are my options? Death by refrigerator or life as the object of pity. Let's face it. I'm already an object of pity to virtually everyone I know. Why does it matter if this gorgeous contractor thinks of me as his charity case?

I clench my teeth. Because it does matter. I don't want him to feel sorry for me. But like I've said, getting what you want is overrated. Right now, I have to go with what I need. And fuck all if I don't need some muscle to help me move that goddamn fridge.

Begrudgingly, I nod. "Deal." So, this is what crow tastes like. I prefer chicken.

The smile he gives me—*avec Les Dimples*—makes my lungs empty when they should fill, and I sound like an asthmatic.

"Millie?"

"Y-yes?" My God, why does my name sound so good when he says it? It's a terrible name. The worst name ever. It's—

His stare practically stakes me in place. "I apologize for acting like an ass."

"O-Oh, it's okay. You don't have to apol—Oh, wait, this is you saying sorry," I blither. I don't know if I've ever blithered before, but blithering I indeed am.

STOP BLITHERING!

AND STOP THINKING OF FORMS OF THE WORD "BLITHER!"

Luc's top teeth sink into the flesh of his bottom lip in a way I'm sure means he's trying not to laugh in my face.

I need a bra. And shoes. And a shirt that covers my stomach. If he's going to help me with all this shit, and I'm going to continue to make a fool of myself, I need to at least be decently clothed.

Without removing my arms from over my boobs, I raise one index finger and turn on my heel. "I'll just be a minute."

He nods, grinning. "Great. I'll just go get that dolly."

IT TURNS out moving a refrigerator is more involved than it sounds. *Cleaning out the refrigerator* is actually the first step in the process. I did not know this. Luc did.

And guess what my life *before* didn't prepare me to do? Yep. *Clean out the refrigerator.*

It has been five months. Five months since my parents died. Five months since I moved back into this house. And I have not once cleaned out the fridge.

Sure, I've thrown stuff out that was taking up too much space and tossed things that I've noticed looking... well...

ancient. But large-scale culling of expired salad dressing and mold-growing sour cream and—

God help me. What the hell is that?

A mushroom panini? Someone's liver?

"What the hell is that?" Luc asks over my shoulder. He sounds afraid. I should have worn gloves. And a mask. And a hazmat suit.

"Ignorance is bliss," I declare, and drop the thing in the garbage. To my mounting humiliation, the bag is almost full.

"How much more is in there?" He peers over my head. What remains is, at minimum, identifiable. Eggs. Lunch meat. Cheese without blue spots. Apples. Celery. Avocados that aren't doubling as water balloons. And milk I bought Tuesday.

But the dearth of old food means that suspicious and, frankly, alarming stains are visible on the shelves and crisper drawers.

"Okay," Luc says in a choked voice that makes me think he's fighting his gag reflex. Again. "Got any spray-on bleach?"

My spirits lift. "Yes. Plenty."

He nods. "Right. Put everything you're keeping on the counter, and spray all in there," he says, grimacing and waving a hand to encompass the fridge's innards. Then he nods to the trash. "I'll take this out. Then we'll move the fridge."

He's doing me a favor. I get that, but I just can't help it. "Bossy much?"

If his face were an egg, I've just cracked it. He stares at me, surprised, and then his eyes narrow. But maybe it's the curling lashes. Or maybe it's the almost imperceptible tugging at the corners of his mouth, but I know for sure I haven't offended him.

But he doesn't take his eyes from me when his voice pitches low. "Twenty-four seven."

And now I'm the one who is stunned.

With that, he cinches the red ties of the garbage bag, yanks them into a knot, and lifts the thing out of the trash like it weighs no more than a Kleenex.

"Trash bin is in the garage," I say, giving him a helpful nod to the side door. I'm proud of myself. My words sound completely steady—as if that low rumble in his voice didn't just cause a seismic event in my lady parts.

But it did. The ground shifted. Pebbles scattered. And boulders threatened to break free.

I gulp a few lungfuls of air and step deeper into the cavity of the refrigerator, letting its artificial cold tame the blood that has rushed to the surface of my skin.

By the time Luc comes back inside, every shelf and drawer in the fridge is awash in Clorox spray, and I am in a fierce battle against a sticky brown stain that I hope is congealed maple syrup.

"Where's your temporary setup going to be?"

"Just inside the living room," I say, gesturing over my shoulder. "We can move the table in there, and I have a stand for the microwave. I just don't know where I'll put the dishes I'm going to leave out."

Luc gives me a confused look. "What do you mean?"

I blink at him. "The one's we're going to use."

He gives me a slow shake of his head. "You shouldn't leave any out."

"Why not?" I ask, frowning.

A kaleidoscope of responses passes over his face. Surprise. Curiosity. Amusement. Each morphing quickly into the next without any one holding sway. His mouth opens and closes. I catch sight of the crooked incisor as his dimples emerge. "Millie, where are you going to wash them?"

I turn to point to the sink and stop midway. "Oh."

To his credit, Luc just sniffs when he could double over at my stupidity. Why is there never a convenient hole to crawl into when you need one?

"You have paper plates? Plastic utensils?" he asks, smiling.

My face makes a big to-do about trying on shades of red. "No, but I'll get them."

"Some people set up a basin by an outdoor faucet to wash dishes, but it gets old." Luc shrugs. "That might be worth it if you barbecue a lot and you have tongs and basting brushes to wash."

I've never barbecued anything in my life. My dad's gas grill is on the back deck, and, honestly, I wouldn't even know how to light it. But Luc doesn't need to know that.

I press my lips together and nod. "Good idea."

It's after nine when Harry comes home, starving, as usual. He strides into the kitchen, finds me packing dishes into boxes with a strange man, and blinks at me.

"What's for dinner?"

I'm wrapping a juice glass in newspaper. Boxes, empty and full, cover the kitchen floor. I give Harry a long look. *"Hi Millie. Who's our guest?"* I say, doing my best Harry impression with exaggerated politeness.

My brother gives Luc a sidelong glance, but he does it wearing an abashed grin. "Hi Millie," he drones, his deepening voice sounding nothing like my impersonation. "Who's our guest?"

With a hand covered in newsprint, I gesture to the man who has been helping me for the last three hours. "This is Luc Valencia. He's our contractor."

Luc steps forward, hand extended. "How's it going?"

"Nice to meet you." Harry shakes his hand, looking at him more closely. "Valencia?" he asks with emphasis.

Luc's smile is easy, and even though I'm ready for The Dimples, they still hit me like an electric charge.

"Yeah, my brother Alex is on your soccer team."

Harry's eyes go wide. "No way! Alex is your brother? Man, he's a *beast!*"

Luc chuckles. "Thanks, but he's not the only one. I've been to a few of your games," he says, looking impressed. "Starting goalie? You've got skills."

The sight of my little brother puffing with pride has me riveted. Did he just grow taller right before my eyes?

"Oh... thanks," he mumbles, but he looks ridiculously pleased. He clears his throat and glances back at me. "So, is there any food?"

"You didn't eat at Connor's house?"

My guess is Harry is going to be a defense attorney one day. He looks at me doubtfully. "I didn't say that."

I roll my eyes. "What did Mrs. Owens serve?"

"Meatloaf... with mashed potatoes and peas," he says. "I had seconds."

"Well, no wonder you're still hungry," I tease, but I was prepared for this scenario. "Pizza's in the oven."

"Thank God," he mutters and steps over the three packed boxes that block his path as if they are just cracks in the sidewalk. The oven door gives a squeaky groan as he wrenches it open, revealing the two pizza boxes. "Yeah, Papa John's. What kinds are they?"

"One's Garden Fresh and one's Ultimate Pepperoni." He removes each and sets them on the stovetop. I brace for the complaints I know are coming, but I pinch a sheet of newspaper and grab the next glass, determined to keep working.

"Of course there's like a thousand slices of veggie left and only two with actual meat," he grouses.

"You were at Connor's," I remind him tiredly.

He reaches up and opens a cabinet, only to find it empty. Harry looks back at me, clearly perplexed. "Um, no plates?"

I wave a hand to indicate the boxes crowding the kitchen floor.

"I'll just eat over the box," he says, transferring two of the unpopular Garden Fresh slices to the near empty box of pepperoni. "I have two more chapters of *Les Mis* to read for tomorrow. I'm gonna take this upstairs." He high steps over the boxes, moving toward the door.

"Please don't leave that box in your room overnight," I beg. "It'll attract vermin."

Clarence has been stretched out on the floor, keeping watch since Luc and I have been working, but when he sees Harry leaving with food, he scrambles to his feet to follow.

"Clarence will catch any vermin," Harry says, grinning.

"Please, Harry. Please bring the box down." I'm still trying for politeness, but I hear the edge in my voice. I'm his sister. I'm his guardian. But I'm not Mom or Dad. What can I really do if he doesn't listen to me? I have to pick my battles, and if we start butting heads now, what'll it be like when he's sixteen and driving?

Harry's eyes roll skyward. "Fine," he drones. "I'll bring it down."

"Thank you, Harry."

My brother grumbles something under his breath, but then proves he still has some manners when he turns to Luc on his way out. "Nice meeting you." Harry leaves with Clarence at his heels, the dog's black nose tipped up in the air, following the alluring scent of pizza.

It's all I can do not to heave an exhausted sigh, but I don't need Luc Valencia to pity me more than he already does. My guess is he has an opinion on the little vignette he's just witnessed, but I don't really want to hear it.

That's another thing I've had to get used to since assuming the role as guardian of the household. Other people's opinions. What I'm doing right with my siblings and what I'm doing wrong. Usually, it's what I'm doing wrong. As soon as people know our situation, all they want to do is dispense advice. At the doctor's office. At Mattie's piano recitals. At school. Emmett's school counselor is particularly vocal.

So I keep my eyes firmly fixed on the newspaper I'm stuffing into the last juice glass. But I can hear Luc employing the Sharpie on the box of coffee mugs, and out of the corner of my eye, I can see the leg of his jeans and steel-toed boots.

I've never really appreciated how good jeans and steel-toed boots look on a guy.

I appreciate it even more as a solid two minutes pass, and Luc hasn't uttered a word.

And then the unmistakable grumble of an empty stomach fills the kitchen. It's so loud I actually jump.

I shoot him a concerned look. He's unloading the spice cabinet into a box on the counter and soundly ignoring my stare.

"Would you like some pizza?" I offer, realizing with a belated pang of guilt that I should have offered him something long before now. We've been at it for hours, and I'm sure his caloric needs far outweigh mine. I mean, you don't get muscles like that without consuming some serious fuel.

"I'm fine," he says, waving a hand in my direction, but still not looking at me.

With a shrug, I get back to work until his stomach roars again less than a minute later.

"When was the last time you ate?"

"Earlier," he says, but this time, he glances over his shoulder at me, his eyes inscrutable.

I move to the sink to wash the ink from my hands. "How much earlier?" I'm standing closer to him, and he abandons his task to face me.

"Lunch." He says it almost like a dare. *I dare you to hassle me to eat.*

I scoff. He has no idea that I hassle people about eating properly three times a day. Just no one as big as he is. I dry my hands before opening the still-warm oven.

"You haven't had dinner. You've got to be starving," I say, pulling out the box. "There's still half a pizza in here."

"Which you are saving for lunch tomorrow." Amused certainty plays in his dark eyes, but he doesn't openly smile.

I blink. "How did you know that?"

Luc chuckles. "It was just a guess, but why else would you get a large veggie pizza if your brothers and sister don't like it."

"But—I—" My mouth opens and closes, but he's right. I was saving some of it for lunch. Then inspiration strikes. "I'll only eat two pieces. There are four left. You should take two."

His eyes narrow, but now he is grinning. "Then you could have it for two lunches."

I pull a face. "I'd be sick of it by then." It's true, but I'd probably eat it anyway. I mean, Saturday is going to be crazy. It'll be a mad dash to get all of us out of the house for Harry's tournament. Two pieces of stale pizza could be my breakfast.

Screw it. We can get donuts on the way to the soccer field.

I give him my best level stare. "I really can't let you pack one more spice jar on an empty stomach."

Laughter takes him off guard, and holy shit. It's better than chocolate cake. It's better than a foot massage. It's better than dewormed puppy kisses.

And for the record, a kiss from a dewormed puppy is the only kind of puppy kiss I'll accept. Advice to live by.

Luc laughs, and I know for sure I'm total crap at cooking because it's the best thing I've ever made in this kitchen. By a long way.

The sight of it makes my stomach muscles sashay like they are "New Orleans Ladies." Unable to speak, I do the only thing at my disposal. I open the pizza box and thrust it toward him.

His awesome laugh turns into a wry smirk. Luc leans toward me, and for one shocking moment, I think he's going to plant a kiss on my cheek, but he's just reaching past me to tear a napkin from the roll mounted under the counter.

"Unlike Harry, I'm not going to eat over the box," he says, drawing back and then claiming a slice. Luc takes a bite. Watching that is almost as good as watching him laugh. I forcibly tear myself away, putting the still open pizza box on the counter and blithering a bit more.

"I'll just put two of these into a Ziploc," I say, awkwardly narrating my actions. "Good thing we haven't packed these." I raise the box of gallon size bags like I'm a marching band conductor.

Shut up, Millie. Just shut up!

Leaving the biggest for him, I pack up two slices of pizza. I'm certain that tomorrow over lunch I'm destined to be reliving this moment and having inappropriate thoughts of Luc Valencia.

And then it hits me. Tomorrow is one thing. Monday is something else. When the work actually starts, is he going to be with the crew? And what time are they going to get here every morning? He's the only kitchen contractor I want to go braless in front of.

Wait. That didn't come out right.

He's the *last* kitchen contractor I want to go braless in front of.

No. What I mean is *I DON'T WANT TO GO BRALESS IN FRONT OF ANY MORE CONTRACTORS!*

There. That's better.

I give a decisive nod to my internal monologue, except my nod is external, and it's the movement that pulls me out of my head—and my head out of my ass—to discover Luc watching me with a slight frown of concern, mid-bite.

"I—uh—zoned out for a minute there."

He bites, chews, and swallows, but even through these actions I can see the corners of his mouth tipping upward. "Really? I didn't notice."

I hear the irony in his voice, but even that is delivered gently. He's teasing, but he's not mocking.

And I'm embarrassed, but I'm not offended. Still, "I have a lot on my mind."

His smile fades. Those dark brows draw together. "Yeah," he says. "That I've noticed."

Chapter Nine

LUC

I beat the crew to Millie's on Monday morning. It's no accident. But it's also not to see her. I successfully avoided running into her at the soccer field on Saturday. Mostly because I only stayed for half a game and I stood on the sidelines the whole time I was there.

Mami was not happy about it.

But I wanted to be the first one here today because Donner, Sam, and the temp, whoever he is, don't make up my ideal team. The thought chafed at me all weekend. This is a chance for Donner to prove himself and be promoted to site manager, but I don't want his lack of experience to cause any problems for Millie and her family.

They have enough problems already.

So I'm here. Parked in the driveway with my travel mug of coffee at 6:45 a.m. I told the crew to be here at seven. And, yeah, maybe that's because I want to give Millie as much time as possible to get dressed in the morning. My guys don't need to be anywhere near that.

The memory of her in that pajama crop top gives me no peace at all.

The smooth plane of ivory skin. The well of her navel, the sight of it both shocking and tempting. My lips want it. All of it.

It's easy enough to imagine my hands gripping her hips and tugging her to my mouth. I know her hands are soft, so she must be incredibly soft there.

Tap tap tap.

My eyes fly open. Millie is standing at my driver's side window, smirking. *Jesucristo.*

"Taking a nap?" she asks through the glass.

Fuck.

I heard nothing. Not the front door. Not her approach. See what I mean? No peace at all. And there's no way I can step out of my truck just now, so I roll down the window.

"Not sleeping," I grumble, but would it really be so bad if that's what she thought I was doing? It's better than the truth. I hold up my cup of coffee and take a scalding sip. "Waiting."

Despite my concerns, she's dressed, though not in scrubs. The yoga pants and sports hoodie give her full coverage, but they cling to her in a way I know I'll be seeing again in my masochistic mind.

Disgust with myself leaves me scowling. I need to think of something else. I pull my eyes away from her to see a sleepy looking Emmett coming up behind her. He's practically dragging a backpack behind him the thing is slung so low over his shoulder. "Off to school?" I ask him.

He just glares at me. The kid looks grumpier than I feel. My eyes flick to Millie. She lifts her brows as if to say, *tell me about it.*

"Case of the Mondays," she says under her breath. Her tone is light, but the look in her eyes is anything but. She's been here before. Too many times.

"Why do I have to go to school when you get to stay home?" Emmett drones.

She turns to him, and I watch her inhale through her nose, gathering herself, the line of her jaw tense. "Come on, Bud. You already know the answer to that." She tilts her head toward their SUV parked in the open garage. "Let's get in the car. We don't want to be late."

"Don't care if I'm late," Emmett mutters, but at least he moves. Sort of. His feet drag like they're weighted.

Millie brings her gaze back to me, and I don't miss the hint of embarrassment in it. "Harry and Mattie already caught the bus. No one's inside except Clarence," she says, nodding toward the house. "But I put him in my room in case your guys don't like dogs."

I shake my head. "Not a concern. They can deal. We work in your home, not the other way around," I say, echoing a message my guys have heard me say a thousand times. House rules come first. You don't like a homeowner's dog, cat, music, mother-in-law, soap opera, you keep it to yourself and keep working.

The side of Millie's mouth curves up. "Good to know. Anyway, I'm off today. Heading to the gym, but I'll be back in a couple of hours. The kitchen door is open," she says, pointing to the garage.

I watch her go, reminding myself—a little late—of my Daily Three: Training, Communication, and Professionalism.

"Professionalism," I say aloud as soon as her driver's side door closes. "Work on that, Valencia."

Donner pulls up as soon as Millie drives away, and Sam and the temp, a smiling guy named Joey, show up just before seven, but still on time. I'm glad Millie has left garage entrance open for us. The temp looks tame enough, but I don't need him traipsing through Millie's house, taking notice of the Delacroix's stuff, all of which is top of the line. Potty Time is delivering a port-o-let this morning, so the guys should have no reason to leave the kitchen to venture further into their house.

I lead them inside and they take in the kitchen while I tape the permit to one of the panes of the big bay window.

"The upper cabinets come out first. Skip the one over the range hood," I tell Donner. "That way we don't have to shut off power or water until later. Strip everything down. Crown molding and all."

Donner nods. "Got it, boss."

"Now the waste bin's not gonna get here until tomorrow, so put a tarp on the lawn and pile everything there for today. Keep it neat."

"Will do," Sam says. Joey just smiles.

I keep my eyes on him until the smile shrinks. "Yes, sir," he says.

Good.

And then Clarence decides to make his presence known. Three pairs of eyes snap to the ceiling. Even from upstairs, the unholy racket threatens to shake the house down.

"Good God," Joey mutters.

"That's Clarence," I say, a new appreciation forming for Millie's beast of a dog. "He'll eat your face if provoked, so don't provoke him."

This comment is directed at the temp, whose eyes go wide. Donner and Sam exchange uncertain glances.

"I'm gonna check on our other crews, but I'll be back before lunch." I don't need to spell it out that I expect them to still be here when I return. Even though I've said nothing about Hector's termination, everyone seems to know the what and why.

MILLIE'S GARAGE is still empty when I get back at ten-thirty. I'm both relieved and disappointed. I push the feelings aside and take note of the debris pile on the tarp in the Delacroix's front yard. Not a ton, but not a bad start either. Walking into the kitchen, I find Sam and Donner, both standing on counter-tops, working drill-drivers. Only two upper cabinets remain, one over the range hood, and both of these have had their doors removed. By the looks of it, Joey has been assigned hauling duty.

"It's going okay?" I ask. Donner looks back at me and drags an arm across his forehead.

"No drywall," he says, and I know what this means. The house is old, the walls all center-matched, which means everything drilled into the walls is going through solid wood.

"Your drills holding up?"

In answer to my question, Sam pulls the trigger on his, and the bit spins with a *vroom*. But I notice the way his biceps are shaking. Keeping the drill lifted for a couple of hours is taking its toll on his arms. Sam may be nineteen, but he's not much bigger than Alex.

"Hop down and hand it over," I tell him, gesturing toward the drill. He doesn't argue when I climb up and take his place. "Flip the light switch on the hood so we can cut the power, eh, Sam?"

"Sure thing." Sam turns on the light over the stove. "Where's the breaker box?"

I've lined up the bit with one of the remaining screws and toss my head toward the back of the house. "In the laundry room."

I barely have time to pull the trigger before I hear him. "Whoa!"

I lower the drill. All of us turn in his direction. "What's the matter?" I call.

"Uh…" Is Sam's squeaked reply.

I swing my gaze to Joey. "Go see if he needs help," I tell him, but with what I have no idea. Joey takes off.

"Ooh! Come to Papa!"

Wrong. Something is wrong. I leap to the ground and head to the laundry room, Donner at my heels. I reach the doorway to find Sam slack-jawed, Joey grinning like a rabid hyena, and a drying rack dripping with lingerie.

Millie's lingerie.

At our approach, Joey reaches out a hand and comes within an inch of a ruby red bra cup trimmed in black lace.

"Do. Not. Touch. That." The words are bitten off. The temp drops his hand, and it's only when he faces me and his eyes widen that I realize my teeth are bared.

"Out."

The laundry room empties without a word—a good thing since I'm ready to commit murder. And I'm still holding a drill, which I'm pretty sure could be used as a deadly weapon.

I set the drill on top of the washing machine and close my eyes, willing rage, lust, and anything else testosterone carries to settle in my blood. But behind my lids, all I see are jewel-toned panties and bras, sexy and suggestive.

The breaker box is in the wall. Directly behind the drying rack.

I drag a palm down my face, eyes still closed. *Professionalism,* I remind myself. I open my eyes and stare fixedly at the wall as I walk forward. I grab the rack by its hinges and set it aside, ignoring the swaying and fluttering of its contents in my field of vision.

The gray door of the box is cool under my fingers and pulls open with a squeak. Luckily, someone—Millie's father or mother, perhaps—has left a strip of masking tape beside each switch with a location label. *Upstr Bath. Mstr BR. Frt Porch.*

I flip the one that says *Kit Lts.*

"Overhead, boss. Hood's still on." Donner calls.

I move the switch back and kill the next one. *Kit misc.*

"That's it!" This time, Sam answers.

I close the breaker box door and stand there for a second,

my hand palming the cool metal. Averting my eyes, I turn and grip the rack again. I've just got it back in place when I hear the whisper of silk and the rasp of lace against leather.

I look down. A thong—the sexiest fucking thong ever made —rests on the toe of my left boot.

Sweat breaks out across my brow.

Made entirely of smoke blue and pale blue lace flowers, there is so little to the garment that it might as well be stitched together with air. I stare at it. How can something that barely exists threaten my sanity?

I shake off the thought, bend down, and snatch it up. Without warning, the memory of Millie's bare midriff assails me, and I smother a groan. Was she wearing these that night? Just behind the drawstring knot of her pajama bottoms?

The urge to fist the scrap of fabric and stuff it into my pocket is staggering.

Do not put that in your pocket, my voice of reason orders.

To which a darker, sinister voice replies, *what about my mouth?*

"Madre de Dios."

And it's as if invoking the Virgin Mother's name reminds me where the hell I am and what I'm doing. With a flick of my wrist, I sling the thong back onto the rack with its fellows, stalk out of the laundry room, and shut the door behind me, only just managing not to slam it.

"Take down that hood." Without another word, I'm headed outside to my truck. The November air hits my face with a welcome chill. I should be back inside, taking part in the demo. Ripping out cabinets and smashing subway tiles would be the best thing for me right now.

But the last thing I want is company.

I lean back against the door of my truck and put my head in my hands.

"Get a grip, Valencia."

And this is how Millie Delacroix finds me when she pulls into her driveway. I straighten up and rake my fingers through my hair as she parks in the garage, but it's too late. She steps out of her Infinity wide eyed and looking worried.

"Luc? What's wrong? Did something happen?"

I snort. Luckily, she's too far away to hear it. The sight of her has me gritting my teeth. She's going to walk into that kitchen, and all three of those guys will be picturing her wearing nothing but peek-a-boo lace.

I know this because that's all I'm picturing, and I'm trying like hell not to. I feel the hot tightening in my throat I felt Thursday night when she answered the door. Doesn't she know better not to come to the door at night dressed like that? I could have been anyone.

Donner, Sam, and that fuckwad Joey could be anyone. Hell, even though Donner and Sam have worked for me for months, I don't know what they're capable of. And they know where she lives. They're about to know what she looks like.

Millie stops in front of me, frowning. She's changed since this morning, her hair is blown out, her fresh lipstick the color of fall leaves, a dark, russet red. And I wrestle the urge to shake her.

"What is it?"

My teeth are still clenched, and I force myself to relax my jaw. *Professionalism.*

"The drying rack," I say flatly. "You might want to move it for the time being."

She blinks, eyelashes, I now notice, the color of nutmeg. And then her eyes fly open wide. "Oh God." Her hand slaps over her mouth with a *smack.* "And you?... Oh *God!*"

Crap.

The heat of my temper plummets. I wanted to warn her, not humiliate her. She's covering her face with both hands now and the parts I can still see are bright red. On impulse, I step toward her and then step back.

"It's okay—" But it's not. "It's not like—" But it is. "I just want you to be careful."

Slowly, her hands drop, and she stares at me in confusion. "Be careful?"

I nod. The less said the better.

"What do you mean? *Be careful?*"

Chapter Ten

MILLIE

HE LIFTS ONE SHOULDER AND DROPS IT, EYEING ME WITH caution now. "Stereotypes exist for a reason."

My gaze narrows. I don't know any stereotypes about sexy panties. "What stereotypes?"

That scar in his brow twitches. "About construction workers."

Is there a stereotype about construction workers and underwear? I shake my head. "I don't get it."

Luc rolls his eyes, clearly frustrated. "In every movie ever made, what happens when a beautiful woman walks by a construction site?"

"She gets cat-called," I say.

Wait a minute. Am I the beautiful woman in this scenario? Did Luc just imply that I'm beautiful?

I ignore the thought when he throws his hands up in exasperation. "Exactly."

I frown. "You want me to be careful," I repeat his earlier comment, "because you think I'm going to be cat-called for leaving *my* underwear to dry in *my* laundry room."

He shrugs. "Basically."

My spine straightens and my shoulders square. "So it's up to me to make sure I don't get sexually harassed in my own home, is that it?"

Luc's posture stiffens. "I didn't say that."

"Oh, but you did."

"That's not what I meant—"

"You said I might want to move my drying rack," I say, ticking off his points on my fingers. "You wanted me to be careful because stereotypes existed for a reason, implying that the location of my drying underwear might invite sexual harassment. You're saying now that's not what you meant to communicate?"

During this little speech, Luc Valencia has gone rather red in the face. "I'm saying—"

"Because if any one of your workers sexually harasses me—"

Did I say red? The look that overtakes Luc's face is black as pitch. I've seen hurricanes less scary. "If any one of my workers sexually harasses you, he will be out on his ass, Miss Delacroix. I'll see to that."

A smile breaks across my face. "Then I think you should be having this conversation with your staff, not me." I bat my eyelashes at him because I can't help myself. "And we've already established that it's Millie."

If we were cartoon characters, this would be about the time when my over-the-moon gorgeous contractor would have steam coming out of his ears. His nostrils flare.

"Millie," he growls my name through clenched teeth. "Do you lock your doors at night?"

I know exactly where this is going. I sigh in resignation. "Of course I do, Luc."

A wicked smile quirks his mouth. He thinks he's got this argument in the bag. I hope he can handle disappointment well. Whenever he lost an argument with me, Carter would pout for the rest of the day. It was so annoying.

Wait. Why am I thinking about Carter? Luc's not—

"So you take measures to protect yourself against victimization."

"I do," I say, nodding emphatically. "The difference here being that I don't have a contractual relationship with burglars, and I do with your company. Therefore, I expect professionalism."

Luc's mouth falls open and his eyes bulge. *"Professionalism?"* He's staring at me like I've just slapped him across the face. Then his mouth and eyes close at the same time. I watch him press his lips together and frown. He raises a hand to his brow, and to my surprise, he laughs.

I have no idea what's going on. He laughs with his eyes closed, his head hanging, and it's the most disarming sight in the world.

"Professionalism," he says again, almost to himself. Then he straightens up, drops his hand, and grins at me. "I've been an ass again. Please accept my apology."

I grin back. "Apology accepted."

Carter never used to apologize. He'd just sulk for a few hours and then pretend like nothing happened.

STOP COMPARING HIM TO CARTER! HE'S NOT YOUR BOYFRIEND!

It's all I can do not to palm my forehead, but that would look really dumb right now. Instead, I turn and point to the pile of dismantled cabinets on the lawn.

"It looks like you guys have been busy."

The Dimple Twins emerge. And now it's all I can do not to titter and wave, squealing *Hey, guys!*

"A little."

"Can I see?"

"Sure."

Luc gestures for me to proceed ahead of him. I do, stepping into the garage and moving past the car. Even from here, I can smell a change, as though wood particles, dust, and memories fill the air. I mount the steps and walk into the kitchen, catching my breath at the open air where cabinets used to hang.

A guy with a stringy ponytail and a Slim Jim moustache is carrying the oven hood toward me. He sees me and winks.

"Scoot that loose caboose to the side, sugar," he says, leering. "Unless you want me coming at you hard and fast."

My jaw drops.

"Excuse me?" The question isn't mine but Luc's. I turn back to see him filling the doorway, glowering like an avenging angel. Aside from Slim Jim, two other guys stand in the kitchen, and they are both watching the scene unfold, bug-eyed.

"Give me that." Scowling, Luc gestures toward the metallic hood in Slim Jim's arms.

"Hey, I got it," he says casually. "No problem."

"Oh, there's a problem," Luc affirms. "Hand it over."

Drawing back with a look of shock, Slim Jim thrusts the contraption into Luc's ready arms. Then Luc angles his head toward the open door.

"Your services will no longer be needed. I'll see you out."

"*What?*" Slim Jim's eyes bulge. "I didn't do nothing."

Luc shakes his head. "We're not doing this here. Outside." The way he says this leaves little room for misinterpretation. That and the hunk of metal Luc's holding as easily as if it were a box of cereal and not a major appliance must make Slim Jim think twice because he stalks out the door with a muttered, "*Shiiiit.*"

Without looking at me or the other guys, Luc follows and makes a point of closing the door behind him. I glance at the other workers, but they quickly jerk their gazes away, getting back to ripping out cabinets.

Did that really just happen?

I want to ask the question out loud, but I'm too stunned to form the words. Are these guys all buddies? Did they just watch their friend get fired? Are they afraid they'll get fired too? Is this my fault?

The idea of heading upstairs and hiding in my room with Clarence is more than tempting, but I turn and beeline to the laundry room instead. I stop when I see the lion's share of my lingerie collection. It's exactly how I left it last night after putting everything through the delicate cycle, but instead of looking like regular laundry on a drying rack—like it has every other Sunday night of my adult life—the display looks lurid. Pornographic.

Shameful.

Red-faced, I yank an empty basket from the shelf above the washer and launch bras and panties into it.

"Goddammit," I hiss, a knot forming in my throat.

"You don't have to do that."

I wheel around to find Luc standing in the doorway, jaw tense, hands balled into fists.

"Apparently, I do." The drying rack is half-empty, and I rip a black Cosabella bralette from the back rod and whip it into the basket.

For the fraction of a second, Luc's eyes follow the arc of the bralette. And why shouldn't they? It's beautiful.

And it cost $85, I remind myself a moment too late. I glance into the basket to make sure the precious garment survived the launch intact.

When I look up, his eyes are fixed on me, but I'm too mortified and too furious that I'm mortified to face him, so I turn my back and continue—with more care—to collect my lingerie.

From behind me I hear the door of the laundry room close, and for a moment, I think he's gone, leaving me alone with my searing emotions.

"Are you okay?"

My breath leaves me in a huff, and I turn back to glare at him. Luc stands in front of the door, watching me. I ignore his question. How the hell would I answer it anyway?

"Did that asshole come in here?" I ask.

The muscles in Luc's jaw stand out and disappear under his skin. "It doesn't matter."

"That's a yes. That's why he said I had a loose caboose, isn't it?" I don't need him to answer. I grab the last thong and bra from the rack and toss them into the basket. A laugh that feels like sulfuric acid climbs my throat. "Loose caboose. The irony is hilarious."

When I realize I've said this aloud, I look up. Luc's brows are drawn together. I can't tell if he's confused or concerned. But why would he be concerned? I'm sure talking to me is confusing as hell.

"Sorry I cost you an employee," I mutter.

"That guy?" Luc's face contorts with disgust as he throws a thumb over his shoulder. "That guy's a temp. Today was his first and last day working for me."

I blink at this news. I inhale through my nose and feel marginally better. "And the other two?"

He must hear the apprehension in my voice because his face softens. "Donner and Sam work for me, and they'd never behave like that." I watch his throat work as he swallows. "That should never have happened. I'm very sorry it did."

I give him a tired look. "It just proved you ri—"

"No," he says, shaking his head and taking a step closer. "No. I was out of line to say anything at all. This is your house. Your laundry room. Your laundry. It has nothing to do with me —with us," he adds quickly.

I shake my head. "No, I should have put it away this morning. I would have come home, seen it, and been embarrassed no matter what you'd said." This is the truth. I was mortified when he mentioned it in the driveway. It seems I'm destined to be mortified whenever I'm around him.

He arches a brow. "There's a difference between being embarrassed and being intimidated. You shouldn't be intimidated in your own home." He holds my gaze, and as he does, I realize I was both embarrassed and intimidated.

But I'm not anymore.

He's quiet. I'm quiet. We stare at each other.

No. It would be more accurate to say *we watch each other.* The skin on my cheeks goes hot again, but this time it's not from humiliation or rage. I clutch my wicker basket to my chest.

"I-I'd better go put these away and let Clarence out," I stammer.

As if my words are some kind of starting gun, Luc jumps back, grasps the knob, and whips the door open. He holds it open and ushers me past him, and I don't hesitate. I practically dart from the room, but when I move past him, I fill my lungs and inadvertently catch his scent as I do. Fresh sawdust. Spicy sweat. Warm skin.

And out of the corner of my eye, I see him tense as if he's holding himself still.

AT TWO O'CLOCK, the skies open. Because the forecast shows rain until midnight, soccer practice is cancelled. I get a notice from the team app on my phone, and despite his size, Clarence is a big baby when it comes to storms, so I take him with me to pick up Mattie and Harry.

"What are we gonna do for dinner?" Harry asks as soon as he's inside the SUV.

I suppress a sigh. He already knows the answer to that. "I made gumbo last night. We're having leftovers." It was our last night cooking in the old kitchen, and everyone helped.

"Oh, yeah," Harry mutters, sounding less than enthused.

Okay, so, yeah, I might have used a little too much jarred roux. The broth might have been a little heavy. Emmett even used the word *greasy*, but it was edible.

"Gumbo is always better the second day," I say.

"Maybe we should wait a third day," he says under his breath. Mattie snickers from the backseat.

"Hey, now," I warn, but even though the joke is at my expense, I still chuckle.

"What else is there to eat? Like right now?" Harry the Walking Stomach asks.

"You mean like for a snack?"

I see him nod out of the corner of my eye.

"Um cereal, sandwiches, apple and peanut butter. The usual."

His long-suffering sigh fills the cab.

"If you're not hungry enough to eat an apple, you're not hungry," I say, echoing one of Mom's favorite after-school mottos.

"And you're not Mom."

I grip the steering wheel. It's like I've been punched in the throat. Mattie's eyes in the rearview mirror are as big as sand dollars. I see her glance from me to Harry, worry etched on her sweet brow.

The light at Cajundome Boulevard turns red, and I stop. The only sound in the car is the drumming rain and the rhythmic squeegee of the windshield wipers.

I test the waters. "Harry..."

But my brother stares fixedly out the side window, jaw set, arms crossed over his chest.

He's angry. I need to just let him be angry. I curse the stupid cold front that's coming through because if he were at practice, he'd be working some of this off. Yeah, he'd come home hungry—ravenous even—but he'd feel better.

When I pull onto the driveway, I note Luc's truck is gone. This shouldn't depress me further, but it does.

"Whoa," Mattie says as we pass the debris pile on the lawn.

"Yeah," I say. "Brace yourselves. It looks different already." I glance at Harry as I come to a stop in the garage to see if this elicits any reaction.

Nope. He's out of the car and slamming the door before I even kill the engine.

Mattie takes her time gathering her backpack, purse, and lunch box. "He didn't mean it," she says softly.

I take a breath, wanting to tell her something reassuring. That I'm fine, and his bombshell didn't just crush my spirits, but I'm not that good of an actor.

"I know," I say on a sigh.

Mattie opens her door. "You coming in, Millie?"

I don't look back at her. "In a minute. I'm going to wait out here for Emmett's bus. I've got the golf umbrella."

"Okay," she says, slipping out of the SUV.

"Take Clarence with you, would ya?"

"Sure." She calls the dog, and it's only when I see the kitchen door close behind them that I let my head fall to the steering wheel.

I really, really don't want to cry today, so I take a few sharp inhales and exhales and then dig my phone out of my purse and tap the third number on my favorites.

"Loftin Veterinary Hospital, this is Kath." I like everyone at the clinic, the techs, Dr. Loftin and his wife Sarah, but I've bonded with Kathleen Morvant. We haven't hung out beyond work, but we eat lunch together almost every day. And we talk. A lot.

"Hey, it's Millie."

"Hey, I thought I recognized the number," Kath says, a smile in her friendly voice. "What are you doing calling in on your day off?"

I give a thready laugh. "Is it a day off? I think being at work would be a lot easier."

"Ohhhh," Kath draws out the word, her voice rising like a soap bubble. "What's wrong?" Her ready compassion makes me smile. It was the second thing I noticed about her, how attentive and gentle she is with clients whose pets are sick or dying. The first thing I noticed was that she seemed to have a new book every day.

Kath is the first new friend I've made since moving back. My two best friends from vet school, Grace Stolworth and Abbie McKenna, both moved out of state when we graduated. Grace went home to Tallahassee and took a job at a clinic with a vet who's semi-retired, and Abbie got her dream job at the St. Louis Zoo. We try to keep in touch. They know what I'm going through, but the distance makes it hard, and our lives are undeniably busy.

And maybe it's wrong that I'm reaching out to Kath, because I know that unless she's dealing with a client or on the phone, she likely isn't all that busy. A lot of the time she's sitting at the front desk, she has her nose in a book. But what do I know? Maybe she was in the middle of something important.

"Is this a bad time?" I ask, wincing at my own selfishness.

"Hmph. You know it's never a bad time, ma love." Kath calls everyone *ma love.* "What's going on?"

I sigh and then tell her about Harry. I'd love to also tell her about this morning and the underwear fiasco, but that conversation will require tequila, and I haven't had a drink in months.

Not since—

But I shove that unbearable thought aside and focus on a woe I *might* actually be able to deal with.

"If there's anything I know without a doubt, Kath, it's that I'm not Mom. I'm not even *trying* to be her. That would be…" I grip the steering wheel with my free hand and watch my knuckles go white. "Well, that would be a joke—"

"Oh, c'mon, Millie," Kath scolds gently. "Give yourself some credit. I'm sure you're a lot more like your Mom than you realize, who sounds like she was awesome, by the way."

"She was awesome." I close my eyes and picture her, hold her in my mind. The ache of it clogs my throat, and tears burn my eyes. I blink them open, wary of letting the tears fall. Emmett will be home soon. "So awesome," I rasp.

"You're awesome too," Kath says softly.

I clear my throat. "Huh, well, I don't know about that, but I'm doing the best I can," I say, forcing the words out. "I know he's just a kid, but I wish Harry could see that. I wish they all could."

"He sees it, Mil, trust me. Kids don't miss much." Kath has a six-year-old son named Daniel. He's on the autism spectrum, though most people wouldn't know it to look at him. Not until they get to know him or see him in a situation with too much stimuli. Kath, of course, is great with Daniel. But she's had lots of practice. Her husband Jake is offshore twenty-one days a month.

"I just wish he understood that I'm not trying to be Mom. I just want to respect her and Dad's wishes. Raise the kids the way they would have."

"Wellll…" She stretches this word out too, and the lilt of her voice lets me know she's about to impart a hard truth. As kind and compassionate as she is, Kath has no problem telling it like it is. As far as I'm concerned, that's a winning combo.

Friendship jackpot material. "You can't raise them the way your parents would have."

"I know. I'm not them. I just—"

"No, it's not that you're not them. It's that your lives are not the same ones anymore. You can't compare the life y'all had with your mom and dad to the one you have now. This life is on a totally different path."

I frown at this. "I disagree. I think it's up to me to keep it on the same path."

Kath's laughter on the other end of the phone has me shifting in my seat. It's like someone's plucking the baby hairs on the back of my neck one at a time. I let go of the steering wheel and scratch my neck in agitation.

"Millie, it can't be the same path. It's like the multiverse theory." Kath is a science fiction addict. She can talk about time paradoxes and causality loops and the rise of the machines all day. "All the possibilities that can exist do exist, but distinctly. Separately."

"So, you're saying there's a universe where my parents didn't die in a boating accident, and they're raising my sister and brothers as if nothing happened?" I hope for all our sakes that this is true. The thought of one happy Delacroix family out there somewhere gives me a warm glow in my chest.

But I wonder if in that universe I'm still with Carter. And if I'm still carrying his baby. If so, I'd want to warn that Millie. *He's not what you think. You're better off without him.*

"What I'm saying is, if so, the universe we're in, right here, right now, it's uncharted territory, no longer connected to that universe where the accident never happened. They split off. Irrevocably."

Irrevocably. What a shitty word.

"You can't possibly raise your sister and brothers exactly the way your parents would have. The lives they're leading, even the world they're living in isn't the same." Even though she speaks firmly, her words are cushioned with compassion. It's the only thing that makes listening to her manageable. "They have struggles and scars they never would have had before. Your job is to help them survive this and adapt."

Survive this.

A cold chill trickles down my back. Helping them to survive and adapt sounds so much less promising than raising them the way my parents would have.

But it also sounds more achievable.

"Yeah, but what about my parents' values? Their wishes? Their standards and rules?"

"Hmmm," Kath muses into the phone. "I don't know. Let me ask you something. If your parents had known that they'd die so young, do you think it would have changed the way they raised all of you?"

Her question wallops me over the head. I've never considered it. "Y-yes. It would've had to."

"In what way, do you think?"

I open my mouth to say I don't know, but it isn't that I don't know. It's that there are too many ways to count. If they had known with any kind of certainty that they'd be gone, they would have raised us to be more self-sufficient. But at the same time, they would have wanted us to be able to rely on each other. They would have taught us practical things. How to cook. Manage our money. And they would have wanted us to be whole. To comfort ourselves. To believe in ourselves.

But they would have made time for fun, too. And the making of memories. So, in the end, maybe it wouldn't have been all that different from the life my parents had given us, unwittingly trusting that the future was theirs. Not so different, maybe just more concentrated. More deliberate.

Survival. Adaptation. Fun. Memories.

Is that what I've been offering?

We're surviving, sure. And we're adapting because what

other choice is there? I don't know how much fun we're having. And I'm not sure the memories we're making are the kind we'll treasure later on.

I heave another sigh. "In ways that would have focused on the most important things," I say, feeling like an idiot for not realizing this sooner. I mean, I've picked my battles, but I haven't picked my parties, so to speak. "Is it really going to be the end of the world if Harry eats junk food after school instead of an apple and peanut butter?"

"I doubt it," Kath says, chuckling. "But there's probably room for compromise there too. Maybe take the kids grocery shopping and let them each pick a mix of healthy and crappy snacks for the week. When the crap is gone, they have to eat the good stuff until you go back to the store again."

I sit bolt upright. "Kath, that's a great idea," I practically shout. "Because then I won't be the bad guy. They'll have to self-regulate."

"It gives them ownership. We do the same thing with Daniel, except it's with bath versus skip nights. He gets two skips a week, and the rest of the nights, he has to take a bath."

"Does he ever skip two in a row?" I wrinkle my nose at this, hoping I never have to go here with Emmett.

She laughs at this. "He did the first week we tried it. He hasn't since. He doesn't want to have to take a bath five straight nights."

"I like it. I—" But I stop mid-sentence when Mattie charges outside, looking as mad as a wasp. "Hang on, Kath." I quickly glance at the dash to check the time and make sure Emmett's bus isn't about to pull up.

2:55. I've still got a good five minutes.

I roll down the window just as a pissed off Mattie approaches. "What's wrong, sis?"

"They're ripping out the stove. Do you know how noisy that is?" she fumes. "I can't practice with noise like that."

"Kath, I gotta go," I say, knowing she just heard all of that. Mattie wasn't going for subtle.

"I hear ya, ma love. Hang in there. You're doing great."

"Thanks, Kath. Thanks for everything."

"Anytime, love."

I disconnect the call and give Mattie my full attention. "Maybe it won't take that long. You're not practicing yet, are you?" She usually doesn't start for another hour.

Mattie's shoulders sag, but her eyes widen with worry. "No, not yet, but what am I going to do if I can't practice?"

Ladies and gentleman, my sister The Fretter.

"Mattie, honey, this isn't a problem yet. We don't even know if it will be a problem." I try to keep my voice from betraying any frustration. Maybe I should have kept Kath on the phone. She might have been able to help me with this one too. "How about we try to solve it *if* it becomes a problem."

Mattie's jaw drops and she looks at me like I've just confessed to a pastime of smothering puppies. "But I can see it *being* a problem. Why not be proactive and help me find a solution *now?*"

And there it goes. The last vestige of my patience. "Because, Mattie, I can only deal with the problems that actually do exist—and then not even all of those." I'm not yelling. I don't yell at them. But I do sound a bit like a teakettle. "If I have to find solutions for all the things that *could* turn into problems, I'm gonna lose it!"

Her eyes grow even wider, but I'm pretty sure it's because of my outburst, and I'm about to apologize when her eyes cut to the right.

Emmett's bus!

In a panic, I turn back to grab the golf umbrella, but that's when I see through the back windshield it isn't the bus, but Luc Valencia's dark shape cutting through the downpour at a dead run.

And I have to admit, it's quite a sight. Both him running through the deluge and Luc standing outside my car, black hair slick with rain, gray T-shirt plastered to his sculpted chest.

"Ladies," he greets us, panting just a little. "Can I help with something?"

Chapter Eleven

LUC

Damn. I meant to get back here before Millie came home. After what happened this morning, I feel like I should be around until she's okay with Sam and Donner. But when the lightning started, the crew at the Sterling's needed help packing up equipment, and that held me up.

But as I look at each Delacroix sister, it hits me I've interrupted something. The way the younger one is glaring at me, I'm pretty sure it has to do with the kitchen demo. "Is there a problem?"

"No, it's fine—" Millie stops, eyes fixed behind me. "Shit. Emmett's bus." And then she's pushing the QX80's door wide and wrestling with a giant green and white umbrella.

"Here, let me," I say reaching for it.

She's struggling to get both herself and the umbrella out of the cab at the same time, and I grab it.

"I'm already soaked."

"But—" She gives me an exasperated expression and lets go. I take off down the driveway, rain like a hail of bullets pelting against my already drenched clothes. I reach the bus as the door flaps open, and I deploy the umbrella just in time for Emmett to hop underneath it.

He looks up at me under its green and white shelter. "You're pretty fast."

I grin down at the kid. "Where do you think *mi hermano* gets it?"

Emmett smiles, but as he does, the rain lashes both our pant legs. "We should probably get inside before we drown."

Before my eyes, the kid's smile collapses. He stares at me, saucer-eyed, for three whole seconds, and then he takes off running.

"Hey," I call after him, giving chase, thrusting the umbrella ahead of me to keep him covered. It's a bad job, and we both splash into the garage dripping.

Emmett crashes into Millie, wrapping his arms around her middle and burying his face in her stomach. I glance at Mattie, baffled, but she looks just as confused as I am.

"What's wrong, buddy?" Millie asks softly, stroking her little brother's wet head. He just shakes it, refusing to pull away. She looks up at me, frowning. "What happened?"

I shake my head. "I-I have no idea. He was fine, and then he just—" *Flipped out. Freaked out. Lost it.* These are the words that come to mind, but I don't think they'd be too helpful.

She dips her head to his. "Did something happen at school?"

He shakes his head again, and I see his arms tighten around her. And Millie seems to give up searching out the cause and just squeezes back, wrapping him up in her arms, swaying, just a little, from side to side.

It looks like it would feel really nice.

I see the kid's shoulders ease, comfort making its way through his body. But then she kisses the top of his head and turns to lay her cheek against it, and I see the worry pressed to her brow. And it makes me wonder.

Who holds *her* tight? Whose arms does she run to?

Her eyes meet mine. I realize I'm staring and quickly look away. Groaning, squeaking noises are coming from inside the house, so I excuse myself and head up the steps. Inside, I find Donner and Sam walking the old Kenmore stove toward the door like a couple of idiots. The noise is grating.

"Dios mío, use the dolly, would you?"

Donner shoots Sam an *I told you so* look, and Sam ducks his head.

"It's in the trailer," he says, sheepishly.

"So go get it."

My two guys exchange glances again before Sam releases the oven and turns to go. I hold up a hand.

"Wait. What am I missing here?" I demand.

"Nothing, boss," Sam says, looking guilty.

I shake my head. "That's not the answer I'm looking for." I glance at Donner, but he's giving Sam an expectant look. "Somebody better fill me in."

"It's my fault," Sam says, his chin dipping lower. "Donner told me to get the dolly. I said I didn't want to because I'd get soaked." His eyes seem to take in my drenched state, and he winces. "I said we'd walk the oven out and wait until the rain let up to move it out of the garage."

I nod, getting what he's saying, but I'm not happy about it. I look at Donner.

"Explain to me why that decision goes against the way we do things?"

Donner blinks at me before opening and closing his mouth. "Um…"

I press my lips together but manage not to scowl. This is a teachable moment. I look back at Sam.

"Put the customer's comfort first. Waltzing a stove across the room not only sounds like the world's coming to an end, you risk scratching the floors." I hold up a hand again before either of them can interject. "I know the Delacroixes will be refinishing the floors. But good practice is good practice. Sam, if you don't want to get wet, bring a slicker to work."

"Yes, sir," he says with a ready nod.

I shift my focus to Donner. "Don't forget. If I'm not here, you're in charge. So anything that goes on while I'm gone lands on you. If anyone on your crew forgets that, you remind them."

Donner goes red in the face, but he squares his shoulders and nods, accepting both the responsibility and the dressing down. "Got it, boss."

I see he does have it. At least for now. But he needs more grooming, which means I need to make sure I'm here as much as possible for the next couple of weeks. Especially since I'm not about to let another temp get anywhere near Millie.

"I'll get that dolly," Sam says, and then wastes no time scuttling out the door.

The Delacroixes have been in the garage this whole time, and when they come through the door right after Sam heads out, I see why. Mattie leads the way, but Emmett still has his arm hooked around Millie's waist, and he's rubbing tear-reddened eyes with a fist.

And then the situation goes from bad to worse as the kid looks at the job we've done.

"Oh, no..." His wail goes straight through my gut. Emmett's eyes fill with horror and fresh tears as he takes in the ugly emptiness that has replaced the comfort of his family's kitchen. He flings himself back into Millie's embrace and yells at the top of his small voice. *"I WANT MOM!"*

If the sound of his cry punched me in the gut, the pain in Millie's face nearly takes out my knees. Grief, helplessness, and, worst of all, guilt, are all there in her eyes.

I jerk my gaze away from her to Donner and mouth one word. *Out.*

He doesn't hesitate, and I follow him past the three of them, now tangled together. I'm on the top step when Emmett's agonized question freezes me mid-stride.

"Why? They both knew how to swim? Why did they have to drown?"

Oh, fuck.

"We should probably get inside before we drown."

I'm a fucking idiot.

I grip the doorframe, debating if I should walk away or turn back and apologize. Walking away would give them privacy. Who am I to intrude on their pain? I'm about to descend the steps, when I take one look over my shoulder at Millie.

She's clinging to her brother and sister, like she's trying to hold them up. Hell, she *is* trying to hold them up. All of them. Even the older brother who's nowhere in sight. And she's barely getting by.

I can't let her clean up my mess.

I turn, step back inside, and drop to one knee. "Emmett," I say softly.

With his face still pressed into Millie's shirt, he opens one scowling eye. "Go away."

Ouch. Who knew an eight-year-old could make you feel sick to your stomach?

"I will once I apologize." I meet Millie's eyes with a quick upward glance, and she's frowning down at me in red-eyed confusion. Then I look back at her little brother. "I am so sorry. I had no idea what I said would hurt you."

The eye is still scowling, but he blinks twice, listening at least.

"What did you *say?*" Millie asks, sounding stricken.

I look up and have the sudden realization that her scowl is identical to Emmett's. That, and my current position down on one knee is an ideal one for having my teeth kicked in.

"I'm sorry, but when I met Emmett at the bus, I said we'd better get inside before we drowned." Her eyes snap wide like I've struck her. "I should have been more careful."

This is what makes me an idiot. Not that I didn't know how his parents died, but that I even mentioned dying to a little kid who just lost the two most important people in his life.

Pendejo.

Upsetting a client is the last thing I want on any given day. What I've done to Millie and her family today alone should carry some jail time as far as I'm concerned. Too far from good enough. Miles away from great. Galaxies from frickin' perfect. And everything I've fucked up today is even worse.

Because it's Millie.

I look back at Emmett, but my words are for her. "I want to promise two things, Emmett. One: while we're here, I'll make sure no one says anything upsetting to you, your sisters, or your brother." His scowl is gone, but I still have his full attention. Millie and Mattie's, too, for that matter. "Two: I'm going to fix your kitchen so that you and your family love it so much. You'll love everything about it. Just give me some time."

Emmett takes a deep, shuddering breath, but he isn't crying, and he's not looking at me like I'm a monster.

"Does that sound good to you?"

His lips pinch together, bunching to the side. He shakes his head.

"No?" I ask, a shock running through me. He's eight. Isn't he too young to hold a grudge? No matter what, the opinion of an eight-year-old never seemed so important to me. Not even when I was eight. "Well, tell me, what else can I do?"

Emmett says nothing for a good five seconds, still tucked into Millie's embrace, watching me. *Santa Maria, Madre de Dios, ayúdeme.*

"I don't like surprises," Emmett says, eyeing me with steady focus. "Even candy or parties. If something good is going to happen, I want to know."

He looks up at the stripped and scarred walls of his gutted kitchen. "If something bad is going to happen, I want to know." He swings his gaze back to me. "I want to know what you are going to do every day."

I bite down on my grin, a quick glance at Emmett's sisters tells me I'm not alone. I nod. "I can do that. At the end of every day, I can tell you what we've completed and what we have planned for the next day," I promise my new boss. "If you're not here when I leave for the day, I'll write you a note."

This, *Gracias a Dios,* makes him smile.

"Sound good, *jefe?*"

Emmett frowns. "What's that mean?"

I grin. "It means *boss.* We got a deal?"

Beaming, he nods.

"Let's shake on it," I say, offering him my hand.

He peels an arm away from Millie's waist and puts his small hand in mine. I squeeze, and he squeezes back with surprising strength. And then I get to my feet.

Aware that the three of them are still watching me, and Sam and Donner are waiting patiently in the garage—hopefully unable to hear everything that's just happened—I glance at the kitchen and then at my watch. *3:27.* It's been a long ass day, but it ain't over yet.

I look at Millie and then back at Emmett. "There's more work we have to do today." I glance back at Millie and hope she can read the question in my eyes. *Should we call it a day? Start fresh tomorrow?* "The next things on the list are pretty big."

I look around the kitchen again, stomach tensing. He's not going to like this.

Emmett blinks up at me. "What's next?"

I reach back and scratch my neck, nervous. "We need to, uh, break up the tile and then remove the lower cabinets.

The whites around Emmett's pale blue irises bloom. He looks at the white subway tile on the countertops and back-splash. "How do you break it up?"

I narrow my eyes in a wince. "With hammers and sledge-hammers?"

My eyes have been on Emmett, but beside him, Mattie's jaw drops. "You're doing this *now?!*"

I shrug. "After we take out the dishwasher." But I look to Millie. *Are we doing this now?* She meets my gaze and bites her lip, shrugging back.

"Can I help?"

We all turn to see Harry standing in the entrance between the kitchen and living room. He's wearing a wicked smile as he surveys all the perfect white tiles.

Emmett's gasp collides with Mattie's outraged *"What?!"*

"I want to help too!" Emmett shouts, raising a hand and bouncing on his toes. "Pick me! Pick me!

No. No. No. No. No, my voice of reason chants. Visions of lacerations and lawsuits swim through my mind.

Millie is still biting her lip, but there's a hopeful glint in her eyes.

Jesucristo, hope looks good on her.

"Only if you wear gloves and goggles."

The boys cheer, though Harry's sounds more like a roar.

"And promise not to sue me."

Mattie turns accusingly to her sister, turning up her palms in annoyance? "Really? *Really?* What about piano?"

That hope disappears just as quickly as it rose, and Millie gives her sister a pleading look. She swings her gaze to mine, eyes hesitant.

"What's wrong?" I ask.

She looks torn, and no wonder. By the looks of it, she's being pulled in three directions all the time.

"Mattie has a piano lesson at five-thirty, and she's worried about the noise," she says, apology in her voice.

"We'll be long gone by then." I look at Mattie when I say this. "Demo for another hour and then clean up until five."

The girl presses her lips together, clearly still concerned. "Yeah, but I have about an hour of homework to do before that."

"You can work in your room," Millie says, as though this is covered ground.

The teen cocks her jaw, giving her sister an accusing glare. "It's still noisy even up in my room. Have *you* tried to read about Neoclassicism in the middle of a demolition?"

Millie seems to steel herself before responding, but it looks like it's going to take whatever's left of her strength and patience to do it.

And I don't want to watch that.

"You're right," I say, responding before Millie can. All eyes swing back to me. "It's going to be really loud and throughout the whole house. Construction is loud."

Mattie shoots her older sister a *See. I told you so* glare.

I raise my hand as if I could block it. "But I have noise cancelling headphones in my truck. Would you like to borrow them while you do homework?"

The sisters give me matching looks of surprise and then speak at the same time.

"You don't have to do that."

"Do they really work?"

I grin and answer Millie first. "I want to do it." Even though I hold her gaze for just a second, letting it go is harder than I'd care to admit. I force myself to look at Mattie. "You won't believe it. I use them all the time. Wanna give them a try?"

Mattie gives me a reluctant smile, and it's great. But, *Dios mío*, it's nothing like the smile her big sister lays on me. A man could demolish ten kitchens on a smile like that.

Fifteen minutes later, after scouring the supply trailer and my truck, I've found enough goggles and gloves for every Delacroix. Yeah, Emmett's nearly reach his elbows, but it's all good. And outfitting them with mallets and hammers is no problem, though Harry insists on using a sledgehammer.

"Go for it, kid," I say, handing it to him.

The five of us fill the kitchen, staring down at the pristine white tile that spans the workspace. I've given Sam and Donner a ten-minute break. I don't think any of Millie and her crew are going to take interest in this job much longer than that.

Harry palms the butt of the handle. "I can hit it as hard as I want?" he asks, a defiant jut to his chin.

Maybe I'm wrong. He looks like he could smash the whole room if I let him.

"You can hit it as hard as you want, *amigo.*"

With a subtle nod and a narrowed eye, he surveys the U-shaped counter space. Then he hefts the sledgehammer and rests it on his right shoulder.

"I call this side," he says, eyeing the long arm of the counter closest to their kitchen table.

"Then I call that side," Emmett pipes up, pointing to its opposite.

Mattie turns to her big sister. "You want to take either side of the sink?"

"Sure," Millie says with decision. She's grinning and wearing the safety goggles I gave her. She looks adorable. Those goggles never had it so good.

Without another word, Harry heaves the sledgehammer and slams it against the counter. With a great, clanking crash, tile chips fly everywhere.

The Delacroixes share a collective gasp at the jagged hole in the countertop. Not to be outdone by his older brother,

Emmett bashes the surface in front of him. And it's like someone fired a starting pistol. Hammers and mallets fly with a fury I've never seen in a kitchen demolition.

Smash. Crash. Crunch. Shatter.

I stand the hell out of the way and just watch—a little in awe. Harry raises the sledgehammer and roars, bringing it down with teeth-rattling force. In the next instant, Mattie and Emmett take up the cry, Mattie's pitching to a scream as she pounds with her hammer, Emmett sounding more like a panther's cry.

This goes on, Emmett trading his animal sounds for a karate-style *Hi-ya!* with each strike.

And beneath the sounds of screams, bellows, smashing, and shattering, Millie is laughing. My eyes land on her. Sure, she's bringing down her mallet, popping tiles like one would pop bubble wrap, absently and with her eyes on her brothers and sisters. Laughing her ass off.

For the first time, she looks loose and relaxed. Her hips sway as she turns from watching Harry and Mattie on her left to Emmett on her right, her legs almost giving as she laughs. It's like she's dancing.

She wears dark washed jeans. They hug her neatly. And I swallow with the certainty that beneath them is just enough silk and lace to kill a man.

Chapter Twelve

MILLIE

"She needs to wear an e-collar."

It's Saturday. I don't usually work Saturdays, Dr. Thomas does, but she's at a wedding, so I'm the one to see what the four-year-old Catahoula mix has done to the near perfect cruciate ligament repair I performed on her Thursday. The incision is a good five inches long. I closed the muscle and subcutaneous tissues with monofilament sutures and the epidermis with staples, one of which has been licked clean off. The distal aspect of the incision is gaping slightly, but at least the underlying sutures are still intact.

Naturally, my patient's name is Millie. The only other Millies I know are either eighty-year-old ladies or dogs.

"The Cone of Shame?" her owner, Mrs. Louise asks, wincing. "She's going to hate that."

I nod. "She *is* going to hate that. At first. This time tomorrow, it'll be just the way things are," I say, keeping my tone kind but firm. "Otherwise, she's going to open this up all the way instead of just licking out one staple, and then we'll really be in trouble."

Mrs. Louise blanches at this. "Okay. I'll keep the cone on her."

"And let's make sure to stay on top of the pain medicine. Are you giving her the Tramadol every eight to twelve hours?"

Mrs. Louise winces again. "She wasn't whining or anything," she says meekly.

I stifle a sigh. "A dog won't tell you when she's in pain," I explain. "The most she'll do is lick, pant, or pace. Whimpering or whining is a liability in the wild. Animals just don't do it."

I run my hand down Millie's sleek back, admiring her beautiful tricolor coat. Her back and head are black with a dusting of brown on her ears, and her belly and legs are white with hundreds of black spots. She's a beauty. "Our girl here had the doggy version of ACL repair surgery two days ago, Mrs. Louise. That's painful."

"Oh, Millie!" Mrs. Louise gushes, bending down and hugging the dog around her neck. "I'm so sorry, baby."

The dog pants, tipping her head up, looking happy. I don't care what anyone else says, dogs smile. With open mouths, with closed mouths. All the time. And they're the most forgiving creatures on earth. Deny me pain meds after surgery, and I'd tear your throat out.

Of course, I don't say this to Mrs. Louise.

The sad truth is she's doing her best. Some pet owners don't do shit. They let their dogs get heartworms. Let their teeth rot out. Or let them limp around on a torn cruciate ligament, which Mrs. Louise clearly didn't do.

She just didn't know any better about the pain meds.

"With the collar, the Tramadol, and kennel rest, she's going to be just fine," I say, wanting to reassure her, but making sure the points sink home.

"Thank you, Dr. Delacroix." She nods like she's got it. "Millie's so lucky to have you."

The dog seems to understand because she turns her golden

Kind of Cursed

brown eyes up to me, grinning. I let her sniff my fingers before scratching her under the neck. She's so sweet, I smile back.

I shouldn't do it, but I've got to know. "What made you name her *Millie?*" She might know it's my first name. I just have an *M* stitched to my white coat. *M. Delacroix, DVM,* but the business cards at the reception desk give my first and last names. And Exam Room 3 has my degrees on the wall. *Mildred Agatha Delacroix.*

Yes, my initials are *MAD.* With a name like Mildred Agatha, what else could I be? You'd think Mom and Dad would have known better, but no.

She titters. "Oh, I named her after my great aunt Mildred," she says, her eyes almost squeezing shut as she smiles. "She never married. Never had children. But she was just so sweet, and she always had dogs when we were growing up."

My smile slowly shrinks. A spinster aunt. Of course. Exactly what I'll be once Emmett and the twins are grown.

"Is Millie short for Millicent?" Mrs. Louise asks, sounding hopeful.

Millicent isn't great, but it's leagues better than Mildred. I shake my head. "No. I was named after my great-grandmother Mildred."

Everyone has always called me Millie. The first day of kindergarten, I came home in tearful hysterics because that was when I'd learned—along with everyone else in Miss Wilcox's class—that my name was Mildred.

What were my parents thinking? I wonder for the millionth time?

Mildew. Mil-dred-ful. Moldy Mildred. Silly Millie. Smelly Millie.

I've heard it all. I was rarely smelly, and I know I was never moldy, but it didn't matter. Mom and Dad knew how much I hated the name—and for the record, I still hate it—but they never apologized.

It's keeping with family tradition, they'd said. *It means "gentle strength,"* they'd said. *You'll grow into it,* they'd said.

But I haven't. I told Mom as much after the last time I had to go to the DMV when I turned twenty-four.

"Grandma Mildred was my favorite person in the world when I was little," Mom had said, wearing a wistful smile. *"And now you're one of my favorites. It's perfect for you."*

She'd taken me to lunch at Bread & Circus Provisions for my birthday when I'd recounted the embarrassing story of sitting in the waiting room next to another Mildred. One who was ninety-two and was denied her renewal because her vision was too bad.

Mom had laughed and laughed at the story. Not because the other Mildred couldn't drive, but because I could always make her laugh with my stories.

God, I miss that.

"She must have been very special to you." Mrs. Louise pulls me from my grief daydream.

"Hmm? Oh... no... I never knew her," I say, blushing at my lapse. "I was just thinking—"

If I say *about my mom,* my voice will crack.

"—about something else," I manage, hoarsely. I've never cried in front of a client, but I've had a couple of close calls. The first euthanasia I did at the clinic when I watched an eleven-year-old girl say goodbye to her very best friend. My grief rose right up to the surface at the sight of hers, recognizing a member of my new tribe. The time a woman about my age casually mentioned going to New Orleans for Father's Day.

Both times, I'd made it through the appointment before falling apart in the bathroom for a good ten minutes.

Mrs. Louise is our last appointment today. I can fall apart when she's gone.

But by the time we get an e-collar that actually fits poor Millie, the crisis has passed. Even so, Kath notices.

"You okay?" she asks, locking up the side exit.

I nod. "Just thinking about my mom."

Kath's mouth pinches in sympathy. "Is it the kitchen again?"

"What?" I asked startled. "Oh, no. Since Monday, it's been good."

I'd filled her in on Emmett's meltdown and the smashfest. I still couldn't bring myself to talk about the lingerie debacle. But the rest of the week went a lot more smoothly. The four sets of noise-cancelling headphones we got at Best Buy Tuesday afternoon have proven to be a good investment. At least no one can say the renovation is interfering with homework.

And Luc has been there every afternoon.

But he won't be there today.

My stomach gives a little plunge of disappointment at this thought, and I scold myself for it. Of course, he's not going to be there today. It's Saturday. And I shouldn't feel disappointed anyway. Why should I feel disappointed that I won't see my contractor until Monday?

I hope I see him Monday.

I give my head a violent shake.

Kath frowns at me. "You sure you're okay?"

I snort a derisive laugh at myself. "Nothing outside of the usual crazy."

She smiles and shrugs. "Oh, well, if that's all." Then she bites her lip. "I wanted to ask you something." Her voice is lower, more cautious. David, one of our techs is still here, sweeping up in the back but the rest of the office is empty.

"Yeah?"

"Jake and I wanted to invite you and your family to our house for Thanksgiving."

Thanksgiving.

At first, it's like she's speaking another language. Because Thanksgiving means Mom, Dad, Harry, Mattie, Emmett, me —sometimes Aunt Pru and Uncle Bill when they aren't on yet another cruise—and Mom's traditional menu. Cranberry-beet chutney, cornbread dressing, butternut squash and kale gratin, and, of course, roast turkey. And for the last four years, the twins and I have been responsible for the desserts. Together, the day before Thanksgiving, we make three pies: pear, apple, and pumpkin.

Thanksgiving is less than two weeks away, and I haven't thought about it once. Because how can there be a Thanksgiving without Mom and Dad?

I stare at Kath, my lips parted, unable to speak. And she's watching me, patiently. Compassionately. And not at all like I'm an imbecile.

"You don't have to give me an answer right now—"

"Kath—"

"It'll just be me, Jake, Daniel, and my in-laws, and we'd love to have you," says my sweet, kind-hearted friend.

"I-I… I'll have to ask the kids," I say, knowing already this is going to be hard. All of it. The holidays are going to suck, and somehow, I've got to get us safely through to January 2nd. *How the hell am I going to do that?*

But we have to have Thanksgiving somewhere. It's not like our kitchen is an option—even if my cooking didn't inspire mutiny. And we're not about to have our first Thanksgiving without Mom and Dad in a restaurant.

I take a deep breath and accept yet another reality check.

I force a smile. "If they're all on board, could I bring some store-bought pies for dessert?"

Kath laughs. "Store-bought pies are my favorite."

I'm about to ask her if she wants to grab a coffee before

heading home when my phone rings. It's Harry. Probably wanting lunch.

"Hey, Harry. What's up?"

"Are you on your way home?" His voice is tight, and I hear a noise in the background.

"Not yet. What's wrong?" I ask, frowning.

"Um…"

My spine tingles, and I'm on full alert. "Harry, is everyone okay?"

"Yeah. Yeah. We're all good. It's just the kitchen—"

"What's going on in the kitchen?" The noise in the background gets louder. It's like… a *rushing*. "Are you washing clothes?"

"No, there's a leak," Harry says.

"What?!"

Kath's eyes go wide at my shriek, but I'm on a mission. Purse. Keys.

"What is it? What's wrong?" she asks, following me to the back office.

"What's leaking?" I ask Harry at the same time.

"Um… I think it's the pipe where the dishwasher used to be?"

I grab my purse and keys from my locker and head for the back exit. I throw a desperate glance over my shoulder. "Kath, I gotta go. Can you lock up?"

But she's already fanning me away, bouncing on the balls of her feet. "Go. Go. Don't even worry about it."

And then I'm out the door, sprinting to the Infiniti. "Is there a shut off valve?" I climb in, throw my purse on the seat and punch the ignition button. The car revs to life and *ping… ping… pings*, patient but insistent that I put on my seatbelt, even though I'm already backing out of my parking spot, sending gravel flying.

"I don't know." Harry's voice comes through the car's

speakers, and I ditch my phone in favor of the seat belt. Chemin Metairie Road is clear, but I hesitate at the stop sign anyway. There is no fast route home. All three ways I could go will take at least twenty minutes.

"Shit." I make a left, opting for Ambassador Caffery Parkway, judging it's the route where I'm least likely to get a speeding ticket. "Harry, you have to look. Go up to the wall. Look for a little knob or a lever to turn."

Through the speakers, the sound of water gets louder, like I'm driving through a car wash. I press the gas, picturing this geyser flooding the kitchen.

"Harry? Tell me what's going on," I prompt.

"Um…"

"Words, Harry. I need words." Why isn't he saying anything? What is it with teenage boys? When he was ten, he'd never shut up. Now, he only talks to complain or ask for food.

"I don't see anything."

"Shit." I take the forced right and get over to make the U-turn to head north again. The main shut off is outside in the front yard somewhere. But I've never had to find it. "Where's Mattie?"

"She's…"

I pound the steering wheel, biting down on my full repertoire of curse words. "Harry," I growl through gritted teeth, swinging into the northbound lane and gunning the accelerator. "Where's Mattie?"

"She's talking to Emmett, geez," he says, clearly affronted. "You sound demonic."

"Because you're not communicating. Tell Mattie to grab a bath towel, wrap it around the pipe, and put pressure on the leak while you go outside and look for the shut off."

The light at Verot School Road turns red and I nearly drop the F-bomb. A moment later, Mattie's shrieks eclipse the sound of rushing water. Harry must set the phone down because I'm treated to the distant sound of the twins arguing.

"It's freezing!"

"Hold it tighter, Matt."

"YOU hold it. I'm getting all wet!"

"Millie said for you to hold it. I have to find the shut off outside."

Mattie protests, but I can't make out what she says. The light at my intersection finally turns green. By the time I get home, everything in the house will be floating.

"So where's the thing?" Harry asks, clearly picking up the phone again.

"I don't know. Outside *somewhere*. Wherever the water meter is? Close to the street probably?" Then inspiration strikes. "Luc probably knows where it is. Keep looking. I'll call you right back."

I disconnect before he can respond and voice command my phone to call Luc Valencia, grateful that Mom's Infiniti has a lot more bells and whistles than my old Mazda. The call rings twice.

"Millie?" Luc's voice surrounds me on all sides. He sounds surprised.

"Hi. I'm sorry to call you on a Saturday." I hope he won't block me for this, but I'm desperate. I know I *sound* desperate. "But do you know where our water main shut off is? We've sprung a leak."

"Where?"

"In the kitchen," I say cringing. "Where the dishwasher was."

"¿Cómo?" Disbelief overrides the word. "The shut off is by the street on the south side of your property. But you'll need a trumbull. I'm on my way."

"A *what?*"

"A trumbull. The T-shaped screwdriver tool to close the valve," he says. And then I hear the sound of a car door slamming—in his case, it's probably a truck door—and then the unmistakable sound of an engine roaring to life. "I'm on my way."

"Me too."

"Where are you?" he asks, confusion in his voice.

"I just left work. I'm on Ambassador by Chuy's." I say this as I pass the restaurant and cringe. Will he think I said Chuy's because he's Latino? As if the only landmark he would know on this side of town is the Tex-Mex chain?

"A-and B.J.'s Brewhouse and Buffalo Wild Wings," I add, stammering.

"You hungry, Mille?" Luc asks, sounding even more confused.

"Um… No… Just pointing out landmarks on Ambassador." Like an idiot.

I hear him sniff. He's probably laughing at me. Again.

"Well, I'm on Colonial. I'll be there in five minutes."

"Okay," I say, letting out a breath.

He disconnects before I can thank him. He'll get there at least ten minutes before I will. And he'll know what to do.

He's on Colonial? That's not far. Just on the other side of West Congress. Is that home?

It's Saturday. He was probably visiting his girlfriend.

The thought catches me off guard, and I bristle. The bristling catches me off guard too.

"Damn." I give my head a quick shake. "It's okay if he has a girlfriend. You're not interested anyway."

Maybe saying the words aloud will make the idea sink in.

"You are not interested."

Except Luc *is* interesting. Watching him work is supremely interesting. And not just because of his P.P.

And, no, I do not call man parts *pee-pees*. P.P. is my mental shorthand for *Phenomenal Physique*. And Luc definitely has one. Whoa. Does he ever. Every day this week when I've come home to find him working—measuring, hammering, sawing, so much *ing*-ing—I've scolded myself:

Millie, stop staring at his P.P.

You don't need P.P.s.

LOOK AWAY FROM THE P.P.!

Even without the P.P., Luc is interesting. He knows what he's doing and he means what he says. I mean, that's refreshing, right? Like Alpine-spring-water kind of refreshing. And I've been to Switzerland. You can swim in *and* drink from Lake Lucerne. That's pretty damn refreshing.

And speaking of water, my kitchen is currently filling up with it, and he's just dropped everything to come to our rescue. That's some service right there. And, sure, he—or one of his guys—capped the pipe, so it shouldn't be leaking, and maybe it's their fault it's leaking, but he didn't just tell me how to fix it and hang up. Hell, some people wouldn't even take the call on a Saturday.

He has integrity.

I saw that the first time he came over. When he wouldn't just take our deposit and run. And I've seen it every day since. The way he treats his workers. The way he treats Harry, Mattie, and Emmett.

The way he treats me.

He's interesting, all right. I just can't afford to be interested.

I pull up at the house fifteen minutes later to find the twins, both drenched, talking to Luc in the front yard. Clarence is making figure eights around the twins and Luc, wagging from all the excitement.

Emmett, I notice, is nowhere to be found.

Clarence is there to greet me when I open the driver's side door. He's wet too. To prove this fact, he gives a canine full body shake, sharing some of the fun with me.

"Great. Thanks, buddy." I pat his head and walk toward

the three of them in the yard, comparing their expressions. Mattie, no surprise, looks nervous. Harry eyes me warily.

Luc is trying not to smile.

"What?" I demand.

The twins glance at each other. Oh jeez. What now?

"Is someone going to tell me what's going on? And where's Emmett?"

Harry and Mattie shift their weight on their feet in identical movements, and as one, they look at Luc.

I sigh and bring my gaze to him. "What?" I repeat.

He reaches into his pocket and pulls out a white, cylindrical piece of plastic and puts it in my hand.

"What's this?" I ask, noticing that Mattie is biting the corner of her lip and Harry is clenching and unclenching his right fist.

"That's a quick-connect end cap," Luc says, extending a finger to turn the object over in my palm so I can see the open underside and a black rubbery-looking stopper within. "You use it to cover a pipe you want to eventually reconnect again. It saves you from soldering or having to cut pipe later."

I blink and look back at him. "So did it just pop off?"

Les Dimples appear in his cheeks, but Luc firms his lips and they hide again. "No," he says, that voice of his going soft. "These are easy to install and easy to remove. Somebody popped it off."

My stomach drops. "Emmett."

His eyes wince, but he nods. "I don't think he *meant* to flood the house," Luc says, taking the cap from me again. "Apparently, when he disconnected this, the water pressure sent it flying, and it shot into the living room and under the fridge.

Up close, I can see the muscles in his face struggling for composure. It's costing him everything not to laugh.

I don't think he meant *to flood the house.*

I brace myself. "How bad is it?"

He wrinkles his nose. "I'm going to get a shop vac from the warehouse. The good news is your floors in the kitchen and living room are cypress."

"Oh shit," I gasp. "There's water in the living room?"

He presses his lips together. Beside me the twins give each other that look again.

"I'm gonna—" Harry starts.

"We're gonna get some towels," Mattie finishes, and before I can respond, they sprint toward the house.

"Oh my God." I bury my face in my hands, needing the world to go away for a few minutes.

A big hand lands on my shoulder and squeezes it. "It'll be okay."

His touch is solid and strong, and I can feel its warmth through my scrubs. I'd like to lean into that warmth.

Instead, I step back, letting his hand fall from me. I rake my fingers through my hair, pulling strands from my ponytail. I look up to see Luc frowning.

"It really will be okay," he says again, this time so gently.

"But why would he do that?"

Luc looks at the house and then back at me. He shrugs. "Because he's a kid."

I sag on an exhale. "That I can't fix."

A grin brings back the dimples. "Yeah, but we can fix the mess. You should probably go talk to Emmett though," he says, grimacing. "I think I heard wailing. But I'll be right back with the shop vac."

I sigh, nod, and turn to go, but then stop. "Thank you, by the way," I say, feeling extremely grateful, and also irredeemably pathetic. "That water would still be flooding the house if you hadn't come."

One corner of his mouth lifts, and his lips part as if he's about to speak. But then he closes his mouth and firms his jaw. "Glad I could help."

This wasn't what he was about to say. Somehow I know this. I don't know what he would have said. I don't know why he didn't. But he wanted to tell me something else, and I can't help the sudden wish to know just what it was.

I watch him. He watches me. And it's not awkward. It's… *charged.*

His eyes are such a dark brown. Like solid earth. As though anyone could look into those eyes and feel sure-footed.

"I'll be right back."

It's the third time he's said that. He turns and heads for his truck, moving with purpose. I watch him start the engine and reverse out of the drive.

When he's gone, I turn toward the house and come face-to-face with two thoughts.

Number One: Knowing he's coming back is the only thing that makes walking inside bearable.

Number Two: Number One scares the hell out of me.

Chapter Thirteen

LUC

I'M BACK FROM THE WAREHOUSE WITHIN TWENTY MINUTES. I might have broken the speed limit on University Avenue. Just a little.

The scene in Millie's kitchen is much how I left it. Plus saturated towels and a teary-eyed Emmett.

And the air in the room isn't just damp. It's heavy with tension. I set the shop vac down and push it ahead of me, the noise of it announcing my presence and making all the Delacroixes look up from their individual clean-up stations. Millie and Emmett are on their knees with towels, and the twins each have a mop and bucket.

"I brought an industrial fan too," I say, hoping a little good news will lift the mood. But Emmett just sniffles from his corner of the kitchen.

"Thank you," Millie says stiffly.

I don't know what I missed, but judging from the way Mattie and Harry keep their gazes to the floor, it couldn't have been a lot of fun. No surprise. There's standing water in here. Some of it ran past the threshold into the living room, and it looks like most of that has been sopped up, but the mess is going to take a while to set right.

Still, it's like I've won the World Cup.

When I got Millie's call an hour ago, my heart thumped so hard I thought she could hear it. It felt like I'd been caught. As though she were calling to give me hell for waking up this morning sweat-soaked and moaning her name. As though she'd seen a live feed of my dreams.

It didn't matter that I was ashamed. It still made my day to see her name on my phone.

Yeah, I'm in trouble. I have to stop thinking about her—stop *dreaming* about her—but right now, she needs my help, so for today, that's what matters. The fact that I'd rather be here than anywhere else is beside the point.

I plug in the shop vac. "You guys can stop with all that," I say and point to the wet-dry vacuum. "This is going to take care of almost all the water."

Millie stands, the set of her jaw tight. "We're all responsible for this mess, so we all need to help clean up."

My brows draw together. How is *she* responsible for this? But she's not looking at me. She's glaring at her little brother.

"Emmett, is there something you want to say to Luc?"

The eight-year-old hesitates, ducking his head but then he looks up. He can only hold my gaze for a moment before he glances away. "I'm sorry I played with the pipe plug." His eyes meet mine again for just an instant. "I didn't know this would happen."

"How could you *not* know?" Harry snaps beside his mop bucket. "It's a plug and a pipe. Duh."

"Harry—" Mattie starts.

"And where were you?" Millie asks, turning her tight expression to the older Delacroix brother. "You were supposed to be watching him."

"Not just me," he fires back, scowling.

"No, not just you. Both of you were in charge, so both of you bear some responsibility."

"What do you expect?" Mattie asks, closing ranks. "We can't literally stare at him for five hours while you're at work. *You* don't stare at him the whole time you're home. This could have just as easily have happened on your watch."

On your watch. It sounds like they're at war.

But by the look on Millie's face, I can tell she feels like it did happen on her watch. And Emmett's head hangs so low, his chin is practically on his chest. I shouldn't be witnessing this, but I can't keep quiet.

"Let's all remember this was an accident," I say, and the way each Delacroix head whips toward me, I think they all forgot I was here. "This was an accident, and we'll fix it. No harm done."

Millie blinks and her face softens, some of the tension and guilt leaching out of it. Her chest rises and falls with a swell of breath. "Tell us what to do."

That I can handle.

"You can pick up the towels and put them in the wash," I say to Millie and then turn to the twins. "You guys can dump the buckets outside and wring out the mops while I show Emmett how to use the shop vac."

The twins look relieved, and Emmett's eyes bug with the excitement that only a child could have for operating a shop vac. But it's Millie's expression that turns my blood to liquid fire.

She looks at me like I'm the best thing that's ever walked on two legs. *Dios mío,* I could get used to a look like that.

It's hard, really hard, to turn away, but I do, motioning to Emmett. He hurries over. "This is a special vacuum for water. You know you can't use a regular vacuum on water, right?" He nods, still wide-eyed. "Good. You want to hold the nozzle while I steer? You can slurp up all this water."

"Yeah. Cool," he says. I've kept my eyes on him, aware that the twins have gone outside. Yet Millie is still watching us.

Watching *me?*

I don't turn to check, but the thought tickles the back of my neck, sending goose bumps all down my arms. The urge to move closer to her makes me squeeze the handle of the shop vac until my knuckles go white.

I let go and hand Emmett the nozzle. "Okay. Let's start in the corners. A house this old is never perfectly level." I flip the on switch and the roar of the shop vac gives me refuge. Not from Millie. From myself. From this tension that just might pull me in two.

She's a client, I remind myself as I watch Emmett try to wield the giant hose. He jabs the nozzle into a puddle and looks up at me in silent wonder when it disappears.

"Whoa!" he shouts over the shop vac.

I nod. "It's powerful," I yell back.

Millie moves then and my eyes track her. She's smiling as she leaves the kitchen, headed for the laundry room.

She pulled away when you touched her in the yard. Don't even think about it.

But I am thinking about it. Sometimes, it's all I think about.

I force myself to focus on the eight-year-old, who is now attacking puddles like they are enemy Pokémon.

A couple of hours later, the floors aren't exactly dry, but drying, and with the blast from the industrial fan, they should be totally dry in an hour or so. Emmett found the chore entertaining for about ten minutes. The twins each took a turn and then, with ninja-like skill, disappeared, so at the end, it's just Millie and me.

"The wood isn't going to warp?" she asks as we shut off the vac for the last time.

I shake my head. "Nah. Cypress resists warping. Think about UL's Cypress Lake," I say gesturing in the direction of the university where the student union overlooks the oversized pond. "Those trees live in water. You really couldn't have had a better wood under the circumstances."

"You went to UL?"

The way she's smiling at me, I can't believe I ever thought she was some *fresa* Ice Princess. But that's what I'm used to. All of Valencia & Sons customers are at least middle class. Some of them are crazy rich. And many, rich or not, let me know in unspoken ways they out-class me and my crew.

The way they talk without making eye contact—or avoid face-to-face meetings altogether—seems to reinforce who is doing the serving and who is being served. Upstairs/downstairs shit. It doesn't matter what I'm charging them and what that must suggest about how much I make or what my net worth might be.

It's nothing jaw-dropping, but I do okay.

If I felt like it, I could say it's because I'm Chicano. But it's not just that. If someone is going to look down their nose at me, they'll do the same to the white guys on my crew or the subcontractors I hire now and then. Maybe it's because we work with our hands. Maybe these customers think we're uneducated. Or stupid.

We're not.

Not even the guys on my crews who've never finished high school. You can't be stupid and wire a kitchen hood. You can't be stupid and float sheetrock. You can't be stupid and plane a door. All of these things take care, attention, and knowledge. And if you do them wrong, a house could fall down around your ears or burst into flames when you aren't looking.

But whatever they think, when clients won't get off the phone while talking to you, won't look up, won't use your name to address you, I don't care what century it is, you feel like a servant.

Millie looks me in the eye. Not only does she use my name,

but she knows Sam and Donner's names, and she uses them. I've never seen her in this house with a phone in her hand. Not around me. Not around the kids.

That's got to be a conscious decision, right?

All these thoughts pass through my mind as I answer her question.

"I went to UL freshman year to save money, and then I transferred to LSU where I graduated," I say. And then because I want to know, "Where did you go to school?"

"I spent two years at Tulane on the pre-health pathway, and then I got accepted to LSU's vet school." Her smile grows as she tips up her chin. "We both finished at LSU."

"Go, Tigers." Stupid, but what else could I say? That she has a D.V.M. while I just have a B.S.?

Millie tilts her head to the side, wearing an amused look. "You have to admit, as a mascot, tigers are way better than a swell of swamp water or an irate French descendant."

I frown. *What the hell is she talking about?*

At my expression, she laughs, her hips swaying just a little. "Think about it. Tulane's mascot is the Green Wave. After some dumb song from 1920? Why?" she asks, her voice choppy with laughter. It makes me smile hard. I've only seen her laugh a couple of times. It's not something she lets herself do too often. But when she does, her body loosens. That line that seems to live between her brows disappears, and she just... *shines.* "And what is a Ragin' Cajun, anyway? I don't think anyone knows because at UL games, they trot out a bulldog named Ragin."

Before I know it, I'm laughing, and she's not even finished.

"Seriously, as an ethnic group, are Cajuns really known for their raging? I don't think so. All our stereotypes center around music, food, beer, and Boudreaux and Thibodeaux jokes."

Dios mío, she's funny when she's not carrying the weight of the world on her shoulders. I laugh until a thought brings me up short.

I'd like to shoulder some of that weight.

The image grips me and won't let go. Me wrapping an arm around her, wedging a shoulder under that burden she carries around, and giving her some breathing room.

Some laughing room.

And even though I want to, I can't laugh anymore. I grasp for the first thing that comes to mind. "Are you Cajun?"

She arches a deep red brow. "Do I look Cajun?"

You look angelic.

I hope I hide this thought behind a look of skepticism. "Are we still talking stereotypes? Because if I had to pick, I'd say Irish."

Her smile gleams. "My mother's maiden name was Bailey."

I want to ask if her mother was a redhead like she is, but she looks so happy right now. I don't want to mess that up.

"Do *I* look Cajun?"

This sets her off, and she's laughing again. "I don't think either of us makes the cut."

I chuckle. "I'm too brown, and you're not brown enough."

This seems to sober her, and she straightens up, covering her mouth. "I don't think—I didn't mean—"

I shake my head to stop her. "I know I'm brown. It's not a secret," I tease, wanting her to know she's done nothing to offend me. In demonstration, I hold out my forearm just inches away from her lily-white hand. "Pretty obvious."

As usual, she has on a long-sleeved T-shirt under her scrubs. Without a word, she pulls up the sleeve and lines up her forearm next to mine. Not touching, but close. The difference is crazy. Like whole milk next to maple syrup.

The blonde peach fuzz rises from her skin, invisible except for where the light hits it just right. It looks crazy soft. Because

I have to, I lean in and let the length of my arm touch hers. I feel those light hairs whisper against my skin, and I hold my breath so I can't make a sound. Because she doesn't pull away. Because her skin on mine looks better than anything I've seen in a long time. Because it *feels* better too.

"Bronze," she says, her voice hoarse and almost inaudible beneath the whir of the giant fan. I glance up to find her gaze fixed on our arms, her lashes low.

"What?" And because I've been holding my breath, I sound choked, thirsty.

"It isn't brown," she says, almost absently. "It's bronze." And the way she says it makes me think bronze is her very favorite color.

I swallow, heat erupting over every inch of my skin. My bronze skin.

God, I want to touch her. All over.

She's. A. Client. No. Touching.

But before I can pull my arm away and break our connection, she wraps her other hand around my wrist, making me go stock still.

Millie looks up into my eyes, and I realize that everything— absolutely everything—has changed. I don't know how. I don't know when. But the look in her blue eyes—afraid, but hopeful —tells me all my rules are no good here.

"Is this okay?" she asks, her voice shaky.

Dios mío. She's asking permission to touch *me.*

And any quality I had resembling control—restraint, civility, sanity—snaps. My arm in her grip hooks low around her back. My left hand cups the back of her head before bringing her mouth to mine, and I groan louder than the giant fan.

I kiss Millie Delacroix like it's my job. Like she is my Daily Three. Millie. Millie. And Millie.

Her mouth opens under mine, and the only thing sweeter than this sweetest of welcomes is the feel of her hands. One still clutching my wrist behind her. The other gripping tight to my hair just above my nape, pulling me closer.

Telling me I'm not the only one.

She. Wants. This. Too.

My tongue sweeps over hers, and she rises up on her toes, making a little squeak. Of effort? Of urgency? What other noises does she make? I want to know. I want to learn her language. I tilt my head, bite her lower lip, and suck it into my mouth. She gasps, a sound that fires straight to my balls. When I release the sweet flesh, she bites and sucks mine in return, and I'm the one making noises.

"Sagrado..."

We inhabit a new world. Nothing from the old one remains. Not the laws of physics. Not gravity. Not even the rotation of the earth. And long gone is the rule of not touching Millie.

I will touch her morning, noon, and night, I promise myself, the first decree of this new world.

I will make sure she laughs every day. This isn't just a promise; it's a constitution. What could be a more perfect union?

My lips seal over hers again, and when her tongue pushes into my mouth, eager and seeking, my first impulse is to drag us both to the floor, but somewhere in the attic of my brain, there's a dusty cardboard box that holds a reason for why this isn't a good idea. I don't open the box. I don't even climb the stairs to the attic. I just nurse her tongue in my mouth and lead her like we're dancing, moving her back until we smack against the wall.

Ah, that's it. Her kitchen. Her home. Her family. They're all here. That's why I can't take her on the floor this minute.

I will lay her down where we can be alone.

But for now, I just want to taste her and hold her as long as I can. Feel her pressing, clasping, claiming me. Millie is kissing *me.* How long has she wanted this? I would have given it the first day I laid eyes on her. Whatever she wants, she can have.

I will give her anything she wants.

But time is against us. A light has flicked on in that attic. Any minute now, one of the kids will come searching for her. Wanting food. Needing help. Asking for a ride to a friend's. I've heard it every day.

I will answer.

I will help shoulder her load.

Adding more decrees, building this world from the ground up, I break the seal of our mouths to kiss her jaw, the hollow beneath her ear, down her neck. Millie tastes like salt and summertime. Like sea breeze and ambrosia salad.

And there's not enough time. Not nearly enough.

I will make time for her.

Unable to get enough, I keep kissing her neck. Her lips graze my ear, and the sound of gasp drives me mad.

"Oh God," she whispers.

Yes, she's right, I think. *I will praise God for this.*

"Oh God. What am I doing?"

I freeze.

And then she's panting, pulling away. At first, I hold on. She's afraid. I don't know everything about her, but I know she's afraid. Something like this scares her. I just have to reassure her.

"I'm sorry," she says, looking down. "I shouldn't have—"

"It's okay," I tell her, grinning. "We both want this."

Her gaze jumps to mine then, her eyes wide and stark. "I don't want this." She pulls back harder, and this time I let her go.

"Millie—"

"I *don't* want this." She steps to the right, freeing herself from between me and the wall. "Things would happen… Things I don't want."

Does she mean me? That I would do things? I narrow my eyes at her. "Nothing would happen that you didn't want."

Her face is flushed, and I can't tell if it's from arousal or anger. Or both. Hell, right now I feel both.

She shakes her head, eyes a blazing blue. "Trust me, Luc." Her voice has gone throaty, and she wears a bitter smile I've never seen. "You don't want this either."

Before I can open my mouth to tell her she knows shit, Millie is gone.

And I am in this new world alone.

Chapter Fourteen

MILLIE

Before Saturday, there were two things I absolutely refused to think about. The last moments of my parents' lives and the last day I was pregnant.

Before Saturday, my memory cooperated. It kept my brain, and, therefore, my heart, safely cocooned away from those stories so I could deal.

But I fucked up.

I tried to add one more memory to the vault—the look on Luc's face when I pushed him away—and I broke the whole damn thing.

I bolt up in bed. Wide awake at 2:37 a.m. Heart racing. Pits sweating. Sure I've heard Mom calling Dad's name.

And even though I'm awake, I'm right there. Smack dab in the middle of my personal nightmare.

The best the Fort Myers Coast Guard could tell, based on Dad's injuries and the blood spatter on *The Eloise II*, the boom caught him on the back of the head and sent him overboard. Unconscious. In the middle of a thunderstorm. With night falling. And seventeen-foot seas.

The investigative team said they weren't sure how Mom

ended up in the water, but I am. She went in after him. I have no doubt about that. She didn't waste any time. She pushed the emergency button on the DSC-equipped radio and didn't wait to talk to anyone. The Coast Guard got the distress call with their position—nearly twenty miles offshore—but by the time the crew from Fort Myers located them, it was too late.

Did you know you can drown while wearing a life jacket? It's true. If you're unconscious and face down, it doesn't take long. That's what happened to Dad. He wasn't dead when he hit the water. The coroner's report was clear about that. Water in his lungs proved he had drowned.

Just like Mom.

She hated wearing a life jacket. I suspect she only did it when any of us were on board to set a good example. Every time I remember her putting one on, she'd make a face like she'd eaten something sour. Half the time, she wouldn't even secure the clips, saying that made her feel like she was being smothered.

Even after having the four of us, Mom was a gravity-defiant D cup. It probably did feel like being smothered.

But she had to have on her life jacket if she went in after him. It would have been crazy to jump in that water without it. I can't believe she'd do that. I refuse to believe it.

Yet she wasn't wearing one when the Coast Guard found her. Eleven hours after they found Dad.

It wasn't on her, but her hot pink life vest wasn't on the boat either. She couldn't have jumped in without it. She didn't jump in without it.

My guess? She didn't have it strapped on. When she went in after Dad, there was no time. She was probably beside herself with panic. Jumping in. Calling his name. Watching his lifeless shape bob and disappear between every crest and trough.

This is what I can't bear to think about. Her fear. Her helplessness. Her knowing that their lives were in her hands alone.

Did she take off the jacket, thinking she'd reach him faster if she could just swim unencumbered?

When I picture that, I can't get enough air. The first time I did, the day after we got the news, I hyperventilated and started seeing stars. Carter made me breathe into a paper bag. It was from Meche's Donuts. It smelled like sugar and Bavarian cream, and as soon as I could breathe, I puked on his shoes.

Carter had been grossed out, though he tried not to show it. He'd been wearing a weird tightness around his eyes since we got the news about my parents. I thought he was worried about me. About me and the baby. It wasn't until weeks later—after the miscarriage—when he told me he was leaving that I realized it wasn't just tightness.

He'd looked trapped.

One in five pregnancies ends in miscarriage. But only women who've lost a baby know that stat by heart. Another statistic is that miscarriage risks drop dramatically after a fetal heartbeat can be detected—at about six to eight weeks.

I miscarried at eight weeks. Five days after I heard my baby's heartbeat.

Four weeks after I found out I was pregnant.

Three weeks after my parents died.

Two weeks before Carter left.

Saying that the end of May and the beginning of June were shit for me would be true, sort of, but shit isn't scary.

Everyone can do shit.

Those weeks were a hell of a lot scarier than shit.

Before June 11th, I thought nothing could be scarier than learning my parents were gone and I was supposed to see Harry, Mattie, and Emmett into adulthood as their guardian. But waking up on that Monday morning in blood-soaked pajama bottoms and that unmistakable, deep inside cramping was the most terrifying free-fall-into-despair feeling I have ever, ever known.

I knew. Even before I was fully awake, I knew I was losing the baby. But I woke Carter, screaming that I needed to go to the hospital, unable to accept what was happening.

Aunt Pru was still with us then. She was already up and making coffee when she heard me. I'll never forget the look on her face when she saw the bed sheets, my legs. The grim sorrow I saw in her eyes was unbearable. I knew that pain and more was waiting for me, and I couldn't face it. I had to look away.

She stayed at the house with the kids while Carter took me to Lafayette General. We didn't have to wait. They took us right through. Carter held me while the ultrasound tech searched and searched for that rapid *pow-pow-pow-pow* we'd heard just days before.

And then Carter had held me the rest of the day as I lay in my bed, grieving in triplicate. Mother. Father. Child. Grieving for generations.

But even as he held me, he was comforting *me*. He wasn't devastated. He kept saying *I'm sorry… I'm so sorry, Mil.* Just like he'd said over and over about my parents. Like it wasn't also his loss. His baby.

He never said, *Maybe it's for the best.* Thank God. I might have killed him if he had.

But looking back, a part of me already knew I was losing him too. Carter couldn't take it. The instant family. The endless responsibility. Those were his exact words. *"I can't take it, Mil. I can't deal. This is too much to ask of me."*

I hadn't asked. We'd been together less than a year. But it had been good. I'd believed my love meant as much to him as his did to me. I was wrong.

And now? This place in my life? This new position at the helm of my family? Navigating through yet deeper seas of grief?

I was in it alone.

And holy fuck, why would the look on Luc Valencia's face after I pushed him away make me think of all that?

My pulse has slowed. The sweat on my skin has cooled so much it's making me shiver. I should just pull the covers up again and try to go back to sleep, but who am I kidding?

Sleep isn't coming back for me tonight.

Clarence is propped up on his paws, sphinxlike, watching me.

"Wanna go outside?" I whisper.

His ears perk and he does a kind of canine double-take. This usually isn't an offer I make in the middle of the night.

"C'mon," I say, sliding my feet off the bed. Hesitation gone, he jumps down and watches, wagging patiently while I put on fuzzy socks, slippers, and wrap up in my robe. I'm already cold to the bone.

Downstairs, the house is hushed behind the quiet hum of the heater. The only lights are the ones from the porch and the street lamps shining through the windows, making tall shadows on the floor. Passing through the living room, I go to the French doors that lead to the back porch, disarm the alarm, and head outside with Clarence.

The night is cold, sharp against my skin. Clarence lopes down the porch steps and into the shadows of the back yard. His white coat makes him visible even behind the ligustrums that line the back edge. I know his routine. He'll do a perimeter sweep, lifting a leg here and there, before deciding his territory is secure and he can go back inside. This will take a few minutes, so I sit on the cushioned outdoor settee and wait.

I concentrate on the cold air against my face, seeping

through my clothes, filling my lungs. When I do that, it's easier to keep at bay the thoughts that drove me outside. And it works.

For a few minutes.

But when Clarence has finished his business and we go back in, I see his paws are damp. Little pieces of leaf debris and dirt speckle his white feet. I tell him to stay, and head for the laundry room in search of a towel.

Of course, that brings Luc to mind.

I can't enter the kitchen or the laundry room without thinking of him.

Honestly? I don't even need to be near those rooms. He hasn't been far from my thoughts all week.

His kiss. His *kisses*. Nothing has ever turned me on like that. And I don't just mean sexually.

I mean ON. Lit up. Electric. In motion. *Alive.*

And, yes, turned on the other way, too. A lot. Picture *turned on a lot* and then turn it even higher. Way, way past eleven. Break the fucking dial.

Even after thinking about it for six days, I still don't know how I let myself go there. Maybe the hours cleaning up the kitchen wore me down. Or maybe it's his unfailing kindness. The sight of him teaching Emmett how to use the shop vac made my bones feel like melted chocolate.

The next thing I knew, we were alone. And touching. Then I *asked* to touch him.

What the hell is wrong with me?

Where did I think that would go? Touching him leads nowhere safe.

Memories fire through my hippocampus in rapid succession. Two lines on a First Response pregnancy test. Carter's quickly masked look of terror when I told him. The way the orbit of our lives shifted when my parents died to center around my brothers and sister. The way that shared orbit broke apart entirely just weeks later.

No matter what I felt—and I felt it in every cell—kissing Luc was reckless and weak. If I know nothing else, there are two things I'm certain of:

1) The Family Curse is real. If I sleep with a man, I will get pregnant.

2) If I get pregnant, Luc won't be able to deal. Me and my life just ask too much.

So that time-stopping, life-altering kiss? It'll just have to be a warm memory. A *really* warm memory. Which is good because it's going to have to last me a long time. The kiss—kisses—won't be repeated.

Even if I wanted that to happen again—

Scratch that. Of course, I want it to happen again. It was Luc. Touching him… tasting him… crushing myself against him… It was as if the soundtrack of my life was a dial tone, briefly interrupted by "Ode to Joy."

But it won't happen again. Even if I allowed it. Even if I initiated it. The look on Luc's face when I left him after that kiss made it clear I'm never getting that close to him again.

Now he barely even looks at me. We've exchanged maybe two sentences face to face all week. Whenever I walk into the kitchen or the part of the living room that's open to the kitchen, if he notices me, he keeps his eyes trained on what he's doing.

Or he finds a reason to go outside.

I think he saves any questions he has for when I'm at work because the only real exchanges we've had are through texts.

And, honestly, that's a relief. I don't know if I could bear to talk to him. If I've hurt his pride, I'm sorry.

If I've hurt his feelings, I'm even sorrier.

As Clarence and I climb back upstairs, that's a thought that stops me in my tracks as it has again and again.

Did I hurt Luc?

The impulse that made me pull away was all about protecting myself. And thus protecting Harry, Mattie, and Emmett. And I'll admit, at first, that's all I could think about. But after my heart stopped racing and my hands stopped shaking, I kept seeing that look of shocked confusion in the dark, wide open pools of his eyes, and the thought of hurting Luc hurt me too.

What I did was selfish. To run away without explaining was selfish. And cowardly.

Maybe that's why I can't sleep. Part of the reason, anyway.

But bringing it up now would be so *awkward*. Yet if I don't bring it up, how are we going to get through the next three or so months of this job? That'll be even more awkward.

I close the door of my bedroom and flop back on my bed with a groan. Clarence jumps up beside me and sniffs my head. Deciding that my distress is not life threatening, he lumbers around in a circle, shaking the entire bed before he lies down with a sigh.

Tomorrow is Saturday, and Harry has a nine a.m. game. I know Luc's going to be there because I heard Emmett asking him after school yesterday. Maybe I can find a minute to explain. And, of course, that won't be weird at all.

You see Luc, there's this family curse...

I'm sorry, but I can't kiss you because I'll get pregnant...

I have to keep a vow of chastity for the next ten years...

Then again, maybe I can just buy him some popcorn and pretend like nothing happened.

"Can I get a Coke?" Emmett asks as we walk toward the bleachers. He's leading the way, carrying a blanket. Mattie's got a second blanket and an insulated cooler. I'm holding yet another blanket and our three bleacher chairs. It's cold and we're going to be here a while.

"Buddy, it isn't even lunch time. And I brought hot cocoa."

In front of me, I watch his whole posture sag as if he's a marionette. "But I had a Cha Cha Moo Moo at breakfast."

Harry had to be here at eight-thirty, and since an ideal hot breakfast was not going to happen at our house, we were all at Hub City Diner at seven this morning. A Cha Cha Moo Moo is just chocolate milk, but Emmett loves saying *Cha Cha Moo Moo*.

He said it at least thirty times at breakfast, chanting it as a cheer before Harry threatened to give him a murphy lock. I thought this was a wrestling move, like a half-nelson or a head lock. It turns out I was wrong.

Harry informed the table that it is an irreversible wedgie. Emmett stopped chanting.

"I told you when you ordered we were bringing hot cocoa to the game. Drinking chocolate milk at breakfast was your choice," I say, trying to use reason with an eight-year-old.

"It's not called chocolate milk. It's a Cha Cha Moo Moo," he argues back over his shoulder, reminding me why using reason with an eight-year-old has its drawbacks.

"Whatever it's called, it was your choice to order it despite my advice. No Coke."

Emmett gives a wordless whine as we approach the stands. The game won't start for another half-hour, so there are only a few bundled figures in the bleachers. My eyes fall on the broad-shouldered one sitting alone on the third row. Even with the hood on his sweatshirt up, I know it's Luc. I don't think he's seen us yet. It's only a matter of time, there are so few people here, but if we can climb to the top of the bleachers without him looking this way, then maybe I can avoid an awkward encounter for the time being.

Maybe by half time, I'll have found the courage to talk to him.

But Emmett has other plans. *"Cha-Cha-Moo-Moo-Cha-Cha-Moo-Moo-Cha-Cha-Moo-Moo,"* he chants, exacting revenge for my Coca-Cola denial.

"Make him stop," Mattie groans beside me.

"I don't think I can," I confess, wondering if this hill is worth dying on. I certainly can't give him a murphy lock.

Emmett reaches the aluminum steps that join the bleachers, and he starts marching, stamping his feet in rhythm. *"Cha-Cha-Moo-Moo-Cha-Cha-Moo-Moo."* He pitches his chant louder to be heard over the clanging of each step, and of course, everyone in the bleachers, including Luc Valencia, turns to look.

Great.

"Hey, Luc!" Emmett stops his *Cha-Cha-Moo-Mooing*, his hand shooting up in a wave. He looks back at me excited. "Luc's here. Let's sit with him."

I freeze, horrified. "Buddy, maybe we shouldn't. It's his day off. He might—"

"But he's by himself!" Emmett's voice probably carries all the way to the visitor stands, and he takes off running toward Luc's spot.

"At least it got him to stop that stupid chant," Mattie says, passing me up before climbing the steps.

I stand there for a second before I make myself look at Luc. His eyes meet mine for just an instant, and then he's focusing on Emmett. He puts on a smile, but there's no dimple in sight.

Oh God. The last thing he wants is to sit with us. Sit with *me.* I need to put us out of our misery.

Emmett runs right up to Luc and plops down beside him. I open my mouth. I have to do something.

"Hey, buddy, Luc might be saving seats for his family." I point to the top of the bleachers. "Let's go sit up there."

Emmett's eyes follow the line of my finger to the top. "But it's gonna be windier up there," he says, and he's probably right. We've only been out of the car for a few minutes, but already his cheeks are pinking with cold. Then, to my growing horror, he turns to Luc. *"Are* you saving seats for anyone?'"

Luc's smile grows just a little, but not enough to reach his eyes, and not nearly enough to bring out *Les Dimples.* "Nope. Y'all can sit."

"Yes!" Emmett hisses in triumph, looking back at me. "See? Luc wants us to sit with him."

If I had a free hand, I'd palm my face. Instead, I mutter an *okay* and busy myself setting up our bleacher chairs. I try to plunk Emmett's down just a little further away from Luc so my baby brother isn't practically in the guy's lap, but Emmett just hops up and slides the seat right next to Luc before bouncing into it.

He immediately starts jabbering away, talking first about how cold it is. Then about Japanese Macaques who take baths in hot springs to warm up, and wouldn't it be great if we could watch the soccer game from a hot spring? And then he asks if Luc has ever been to Hot Springs, Arkansas.

"Stop swinging your legs," Mattie interrupts, trying to make Emmett be still. I strategically placed her bleacher chair next to Emmett's to give Luc as much distance from me as possible. Even so, I can still hear his and Emmett's whole conversation, which Luc is contributing to—Lord, bless him— whenever Emmett gives him the chance.

If Luc hates me now, I'm grateful he still treats Emmett with patience and kindness. Beyond grateful, really. I steal a quick glance in their direction and feel a surge of warmth in my chest. Emmett thrives on Luc's attention, and when I look over, Luc is chuckling at my little brother's description of geothermal springs and fumaroles, whatever those are. A dimple marks Luc's left cheek, and I relax a little. If he were only smiling or laughing to be polite, it wouldn't be there. Whatever Luc thinks of me, he likes Emmett. And it's no secret Emmett worships him. I'm relieved to see I haven't screwed that up for either of them.

"Ugh!" Mattie growls at Emmett through gritted teeth. "You're driving me crazy. Be still!"

Emmett looks up at her, surprised, I can tell, but not contrite. "Don't blame me. It's the Cha-Cha-Moo-Moo."

Mattie scowls. "Don't start—"

"*Cha-Cha-Moo-Moo-Cha-Cha-Moo-Moo,*" he chants, swinging his legs in time with each cha and moo.

Mattie fists her hair by the roots. *"Grrr."* She reels to face me. "You *have* to switch places with me or I'm going to punch him."

"Mattie..." I attempt to cajole.

She just glares. "Switch or I ditch."

My head jerks back at this. "What?"

"Switch with me, or I'm out of here."

I stare at her, stunned. "Mattie—"

"Seriously, I don't see why I have to sit here freezing my butt off on a Saturday morning—the first day of Thanksgiving break—when all of my friends are still asleep. Switch with me or I'm calling an Uber."

For a moment, I'm speechless. This is my little Mattie? Mattie The Worry Wart? Mattie The Peacemaker?

Mattie, who's going on fifteen and has more than enough reasons to be angry with the world, I remind myself.

"Sure. I'll switch with you," I say softly, pitching my voice several decibels lower than hers, hoping to disarm her. But she jerks out of her seat and elbows past me as I move. My eyes meet Luc's for a split-second, but he glances away before I can shoot him a look of apology.

So I sit. My sister stews on one side of me. My brother rides his sugar high on the other. And beside him, the guy whose face I nearly kissed off a week ago won't even look at me.

And the game hasn't even started yet.

Chapter Fifteen

LUC

Millie doesn't want to be sitting here. It's written all over her face. And why would she? I might maul her again.

"I don't *want this."*

She'd said it twice. Made that damn clear. The look in her eyes had felt like a guilty verdict. And I *was* guilty. I broke every one of my rules with her in the span of three minutes. Everything about professionalism. Boundaries. Respect.

Restraint.

A part of me wishes she would fire me. Then I wouldn't have to come face to face with my failure every day. My failure to be the man I thought I was.

The other part of me is so damn glad she hasn't.

Because I'm not sure when it happened, but I need to see her. And if I don't see her, I need to know she's okay.

Right now, she's just three feet away from me. So I know she's okay. Stressed out, as usual, but okay. So I don't *have* to look. I just want to.

I'm gripping the metal bleachers, ready to bend them like The Incredible Hulk I want to look so bad. Thank God the game is starting. Thank God for Emmett. That kid is a killer distraction. He can talk my ear off for the next hour and a half if he wants to.

And I know if he's talking to me, he's giving her some much-needed peace. Which means I'm giving her some peace. I don't know when this happened either, but I'd give her anything she wanted.

"I don't *want this."*

I have to believe her. Not believing would disrespect her, and I won't let anyone disrespect her. Least of all me. But when I close my eyes and let myself fall back into that kiss—and I have about a thousand times—I know what I felt.

Certainty. Clarity. Unity.

In that perfect, self-contained three minutes of history, we wanted the exact same thing. That time—that world—may not exist now, but it existed then. It was real. I didn't imagine it.

If I don't believe that, I think I'll lose my shit. Because I was there. And if that wasn't real, nothing is real.

So I have to hold these two opposing beliefs—Millie didn't want it and Millie did—in my head. Every waking minute of the day. Because if I don't, I'll either lose my mind or lose control.

"I need a piss," Emmett announces, bouncing in his seat and jerking me from my fucked up thoughts.

"Emmett!" Millie practically chokes. "Language."

"Sor-ry," he says, sounding anything but sorry. "I need the bathroom." He gets to his feet.

"I'll go with you," Millie says, moving to rise.

Emmett scowls. "No, I'm not a baby."

"Of course, you're not a baby, but…" Millie's words dry up, and her gaze flicks to mine. A tell. She doesn't want to lose Emmett as a buffer.

I stand. "I'll take him." I'll take him to the bathroom, and then I'll go stand on the sidelines. Leave her alone.

Emmett's face falls. *"You* think I'm a baby?" he accuses, sounding betrayed.

"No, *jefe,* I just…" Now *my* words have dried up.

Mattie shoots to her feet. "Well, I actually need the bathroom." She looks down at her little brother, all pissy attitude gone. "Will you be a gentleman and escort *me* to the bathroom."

Emmett screws up his face, but when she moves, he follows. "Why do *you* need an escort to the bathroom?"

"Just come with me, okay?" They move down the length of the bleachers, their argument hanging in the air behind them. I can't help but feel Mattie's doing this on purpose. To leave Millie and me alone together.

I chance a quick glance at Millie, and she's frowning at her lap.

I want to tell her I'm sorry. Not for the kiss. I'll never be sorry for that. The memory of it is my most valuable possession.

But I'm sorry I've made her uncomfortable. I pray I haven't made her afraid.

That thought spurs my tongue. "I'm sorry——"

"I need to apologize——" she says at the same time.

We look at each other. Really look at each other for the first time in a week. She looks miserable. I'm sure I do too.

I shake my head. "Don't apologize. *You* did nothing wrong." I will bear all the blame. All the shame. None of that will touch her.

Millie's eyes pinch at the corners like she's hurting. "I didn't really explain."

I keep shaking my head. "You did. You said enough." *Please don't say it again. I know you don't want me.*

Now she's shaking her head. "No. I didn't. You don't understand——"

"I do."

STEPHANIE FOURNET

She holds up a hand, looking irritated. "You *don't*. My family—" She stops. Closes her mouth and presses her lips together. "I have to think about my family."

From where I sit, all she does is think about her family. Who thinks about her? I want to ask, but bite back the question.

"The four of us are all I can deal with right now."

So, no room for me.

I want to argue that I could help her deal. I'd be good at it. She could lean on me. I could be her brick wall.

You sound like a fucking coño.

I grind my unspoken promises between my teeth. Swallow them down.

Instead, I apologize for my real regret. "I never meant to scare you."

Her eyes flash, a little of that ire I've seen sparking in them. "You didn't scare me."

You ran.

I don't say it aloud, but maybe she reads it in my face because she looks away, eyes going to the game that I'm sure neither one of us has even seen one play of.

"You don't scare me."

She could have said it like a challenge. The way she challenged my assumption that she was a nurse. The way she challenged my stupid cock-up about her lingerie. But she doesn't say it like that.

Her voice is feather soft.

If I don't scare her, then maybe she feels safe around me. Without even thinking, I sit up straighter. Not just to shed the shame I've carried all week, but to be her safety.

Her protector.

I don't take my eyes off her profile, so when the corner of her mouth curls up in a smile—showing up like a friend I never thought I'd see again—I don't miss it.

"Do I scare *you?*" she asks.

My laughter feels like a presidential pardon. I lean my head back and laugh clouds of relief into the cold air.

She turns to me, grinning, but waiting for the answer.

"Honestly?" I say when I can speak. "You scare the hell out of me."

Her eyes light up like this is the best news she's had in years. "Good!" she says, laughing too.

A moment later, the sound of Emmett and Mattie arguing makes her turn to track their approach. But she looks back at me, quick and nervous.

"So, are we good?" she asks, then bites the corner of her mouth. The mouth I want to kiss now more than ever.

I bite the corner of my lip, mirroring her. Remembering the moment I took her lip between my teeth. Remembering the moment she bit back. Remembering everything that was unsaid but so clearly spoken in those moments. But I get it. I can't have her. And that sucks. But she doesn't hate me. In fact, I'm pretty sure she likes me.

And that's fucking fantastic.

"Yeah, we're good."

Her brother and sister come back, but this time, Mattie sits beside me and Emmett is on the other side of Millie.

"Alejandro is looking good out there," Mattie says, watching the field.

Since I haven't taken my eyes off Millie, I don't miss the way she sits up, ramrod straight.

"He sure does," I reply, but I wouldn't know. I haven't been able to concentrate on the game at all, and the scoreboard is no help: 0-0. At least the Lions are holding the Rams at bay.

"His offensive game is amazing," Mattie says, sounding awed. "So intense."

Millie watches her sister with hawk-like attention, but Mattie appears clueless.

I've forgotten all about Mattie's crush on my brother. "Do you two have any classes together?"

At my question, Millie brings her bird of prey glare to me. I answer it with a wordless *What?* Her mouth tightens like a purse string, and she narrows her eyes, *Stop it!* her clear reply.

Mattie sighs. "No, but he has AP Bio in the lab right before I do," she says with a kind of dreamy regret.

I'd offer to introduce her to Alex, but I like having my head firmly attached to my neck, and the look Millie is giving me is all the warning I need. But I don't understand.

Millie telling me she has no room in her life for a relationship is one thing. I don't like it, but knowing what she's dealing with, I can accept it. But what's wrong with Mattie crushing on my brother? They're both good kids. Smart. Talented. Focused. I don't mean I want to see them eloping, but why get all worked up about an innocent crush?

I reach into my back pocket for my phone because I have to know.

Me: Is it because we're Latino?

Maybe this is something I shouldn't be asking, but if this is the reason, it would be better to know now. Know the situation for what it really is.

Back in high school, I wasted time once with a white girl who was all kinds of sweet. She laughed at my jokes. Flirted back. Gave me all the green lights until I asked her out. And then Mary Catherine Turner told me her father would choke her to death if she dated a Mexican.

I will never forget it. We were sitting on a bench under the big oak tree in the quad. Right here at Lafayette High. I bet I could leave the bleachers and find the exact spot in less than ten minutes. It was junior year. School had only started a couple of weeks before. The day was hot and damp, even under the trees. But when she said that, I felt a splash of cold hit my face.

I'm American, I'd told her. *I was born here in Lafayette.*

She'd smiled, but it was the way you smile at a little kid. With pity. Then Mary Catherine Turner put her hand on my knee and squeezed. *We can mess around Friday night at my house. My parents have a bridge tournament. They'll be gone for hours,* she'd said, her smile turning wicked. *You just can't tell anyone.*

I'd stood up. My legs moved as I walked away, and the rest of me did too. But it felt like I'd left my stomach right there on that bench.

I didn't even hit on another white girl until college and that was after a few of them had hit on me.

Millie doesn't have a father's disapproval to worry about. But if she has her own biases, it'll hurt—I'm not gonna lie. It'll hurt like a mother. But I already know how to walk away from that.

Millie's phone *pings,* and I keep my eyes on the game, even though all my attention is on her.

She gasps. I don't move.

Mattie turns. "What's wrong?"

"Nothing," Millie says, tapping on her screen. "Just a miscommunication with a friend."

My phone vibrates.

Millie: GOD, NO!

I let my lungs move. I've been holding my breath without even knowing it.

Jesús, María, y José. Gracias. The relief makes me swallow. Realization hits me like a wave. If Millie had been another Mary Catherine Turner, I would have left more than my stomach this time.

"You have friends?" Mattie asks with ironic surprise. I tune into the sisters' conversation, all thought of Mary Catherine Turner evaporating.

My phone vibrates again.

Millie: How could you even think that???

At the same time I read this, Millie *tsks.* "Of course, I have friends. Don't tease."

Mattie huffs. "You never spend any time with them."

Me: Sorry, but it wouldn't be the first time.

I look over after I hear the *ping.* Millie glances up from her screen and our eyes meet. Her brows knit before she looks down.

"Well, I'm busy," Millie defends, typing. "My friends understand that."

Millie: That's terrible. I'm sorry.

"You should make time for them," Mattie says. "You'd be happier."

I bury a smirk. I really like this kid.

Me: So, what's wrong with Mattie liking Alex?

"I'm happy," Millie says. I know she's read my text when she makes an exasperated sound.

"You don't sound happy." Mattie observes.

Me: She's right.

It's everything I can do not to grin like a fool right now.

Millie: Mattie's too young to be thinking about boys.

I arch my brow over Mattie's head. *Seriously?* Millie looks at me and scowls.

"You don't look happy, either." Mattie says. Then she gasps. "Wait. You're not texting Carter, are you?"

My spine goes rigid.

"Of course not!"

Me: Who's Carter?

"Good," Mattie mutters.

Millie ignores my question, but, from what I can see, her shoulders have tensed.

In the weeks that I've been working at the Delacroix's, the only other adults I've seen at the house have been Mrs. Chen, Mattie's piano teacher, or parents dropping off or picking up the kids or their friends. Nobody coming to visit Millie, and definitely no Carter.

"Anyway, you should go out with your friend. Who is it, by the way?" Mattie asks, casually. "Someone at w— *GO! GO! GO! ALEJANDRO!*" Mattie's on her feet, cheering with everything she's got, and I focus on the soccer game just in time to see my brother nail a kick right past the Rams' goalie.

I'm up—along with everyone else in the stands—clapping, cheering, calling his name. At the same time, it's like the clapping and cheering is someone else's, and my complete focus is Millie's. I'm so aware of her. The tension in her body. Her distraction. The way she's cheering too, but really just going through the motions. Like I am.

"Oh my God. He's amazing," Mattie gushes, still standing, still clapping, her pretty face flushed. Alex is slapping a few of his teammates' hands when he looks up into the stands for me. I pump a fist, but his eyes slide right off me onto the fourteen-year-old vision to my left. He waves at her.

Mattie waves back, squealing as she does.

We sit, and I take up my phone again.

Me: I think someone forgot to tell her.

Millie: Tell who what?

Me: Mattie. That she's too young to notice boys.

Millie leans back just behind Mattie's back and silently snarls at me. She hardly needs to go to the trouble of hiding it. Her sister can't take her eyes off my brother.

I give her a grin that might just be a little wicked. Her eyes drop to it and shift just a little to the right. They soften.

Is she looking at my dimple? My smile strengthens. For a moment, I just enjoy watching her watch me.

And then her phone rings.

She looks down, reads the screen, and answers.

"Hey Kath... Yeah?" Millie frowns. "Oh *no*. That's terrible."

This brings Mattie out of her Alex-haze. "What's wrong?"

Millie holds up a hand to her sister. "No, no, of course... You have to. I totally understand." She says this and then bites her lip, giving Mattie and Emmett each a quick glance. "We'll be fine. Don't worry about that for another minute... Take care, Kath. Safe travels... Right... You too. Bye."

"What's wrong?" Mattie asks again, sounding worried.

Millie places a hand on her back. "Everything's fine. That was just my friend Kath."

"The one you were texting?" Mattie ask.

Millie shoots me a quick glance. "Uh... No. The one at work. The one who invited us for Thanksgiving."

Emmett tunes in at this, looking up at her. "Are we still going to her house?"

Millie puts her other arm around him. Now she's essentially holding both her brother and sister. "I'm sorry, buddy, but no," Millie says, squeezing him to her. "Her mother-in-law broke her ankle, so Kath and her family are going up to Monroe so her mother-in-law doesn't have to travel with a cast."

Emmett blinks. "I have a question."

"What is it, bud?"

"Is it wrong if I'm glad we don't have to go there for Thanksgiving?"

Millie gives a flustered laugh. "I thought you said it was okay if we went to Kath's?"

Emmett shrugs, his lips pressing together, but he says nothing.

"What are we going to do now?" Mattie asks, the worry still there in her voice but less acute.

Then Emmett's eyes widen. "Can we go to Grub Burger instead?"

"We're not having Grub Burger for Thanksgiving," Mattie says sharply.

I'm really starting to appreciate the way Millie's kid sister thinks. They are absolutely not having Grub Burger for Thanksgiving. Not if I can help it.

"We'll figure it out, guys," Millie says, rubbing each of their backs. "*I'll* figure it out."

Me: Have Thanksgiving with my family.

I hear her phone, but she takes her time picking it up, easing her touch from her brother and sister first. When Millie reads the message, her eyes bug. She looks up at me and back at her phone.

Millie: We couldn't. But thank you. That's very kind.

Her text makes irritation churn in my gut.

Me: I'm not doing it to be kind. My family would love to have you.

I know this without asking. Our house is always full on Thanksgiving. Abuela, Mami, Papi, Alex, me, Aunt Lucinda, my cousins, and their husbands and kids. Friends and the occasional neighbor. The stray Valencia & Sons employee.

My family isn't here today because the cold is hard on Abuela and Papi, but if Mami were here, she'd be falling over the bleachers to extend the invitation. A client family and a teammate of Alex's? Kids who just lost their parents? *Santa María*, she'd push me out of the way to invite them to Thanksgiving.

Millie: Thanks, really. But it's going to be a tough holiday. Maybe best to just have Whole Foods cater it.

She's right about one thing. It is going to be a tough holiday, but that doesn't mean she needs to heat up her Thanksgiving dinner in the microwave.

Me: The offer stands.

Millie shifts in her seat, and I can tell she's resisting the urge to just turn and talk to me. She looks back at her phone.

Millie: Why are you doing this? The last thing I want is people taking pity on us.

I fight a smile. Yep. That would be the last thing she'd

want. It's one of the reasons I can't stop thinking about her. She's so damn tough. Unbeatable. And at the same time, she's so soft. Gentle. Fragile. I want to get between her and anything that might take a swing at her.

Me: Who did you tell Mattie you were texting?

I watch the side of her mouth curl up.

Millie: A friend.

Me: Exactly.

Chapter Sixteen

MILLIE

I<small>T SHOULDN'T, BUT THE WEEK OF</small> T<small>HANKSGIVING CATCHES ME</small> off guard. The clinic will be closed Wednesday, Thursday, and Friday for the holiday, so instead of taking my usual day off on Monday, I agreed to cover for Dr. Thomas so she can enjoy some vacation time.

That's easy enough since the kids are home and no one needs to be ferried to and from school. But being home means they're bored. Which means they text me all day long. It goes something like this:

Emmett (on Mattie's phone): It's me. Emmett the Great. Can Trevor come over?

Me: No, your greatness. I'm not there. See if Trevor can come on Friday. I'll be home all day.

Emmett (on Mattie's phone): But what am I supposed to do today???

Emmett (on Mattie's phone): Are you there?

Emmett (on Mattie's phone): Why aren't you answering???

Eleven minutes later:

Me: Because I was with a client. Don't forget I'M AT WORK.

Emmett (on Mattie's phone): You don't have to shout. Sheesh!

Twenty-three minutes later:

Mattie: Emmett needs his own phone.

Me: He's too young for a phone.

Mattie: He keeps bugging me to play on mine. It's driving me nuts!

Me: Tell him he can borrow Harry's for a little while.

Two minutes later:

Harry: Emmett is NOT borrowing my phone. He locked me out the last time he did.

Harry: Also, can Alex come over?

Harry: Why aren't you answering???

Thirteen minutes later:

Me: Seriously? I'm a vet. I'm at work. Why do you think I'm not answering?

Me: Alex who?

Harry: Alex Valencia. Luc said he could pick him up at lunch.

Me: No.

Harry: Why not?!

Me: It's just not a good idea.

Harry: It's a great idea! We could practice kicks and blocks in the back yard. Emmett can watch. Mattie can watch. Everybody wins!

Me: Not happening. No friends over while I'm not home.

Mattie: Why won't you let Alex come over???

Emmett (on Mattie's phone): Yeah??? Why not???

And so on.

By noon, I have a headache. I vow to myself that the next holiday break, I'll either have to take off work on the days the kids are home or sign them up for some camps or classes so they have something to do while I'm gone.

I treat a Calico cat with a UTI, a King Charles Spaniel with a yeast infection in her ears, and prescribe Metacam for a ten-year-old boxer with arthritis in his hip.

By five o'clock, my throat burns when I swallow, and my ears are ringing.

When I get home, Luc's truck is still in the driveway, but Sam and Donner's vehicles are gone. I go in through the kitchen, expecting to find Luc cleaning up from the day's work, but the space is empty.

Last week, the crew started taking out the wall between the kitchen and the dining room. It was a messy job, so they taped up plastic sheeting to seal off the kitchen from the living room and the dining room from the foyer. Today, the sheeting is down, and the only sign the wall ever existed is the raw outline on the ceiling, sidewalls, and floor.

I'd half expected the whole house to topple down and the room I'm sleeping in to come crashing into our old dining room, but Luc explained the wall wasn't load-bearing. When I asked how he knew, he gave me a dimpled smile and said he knew because it ran parallel with the floorboards. He showed me where the joists were and how Mom had used a wall beam when she knocked out part of the wall between the kitchen and the living room all those years ago because that wall *was* load bearing.

I guess if the house didn't fall down from what Mom and Dad did back then, what Luc is doing now won't bring it down around our ears either. And I'm starting to be able to see what the finished product will look like, especially now that I have a clear view all the way out the bay windows from the spot where our kitchen table used to be.

What I don't see are my siblings or Luc.

"Hey guys?" I call, moving into the living room. It's empty, and the TV is off, which is almost unbelievable.

No answer.

My guess is they've all gone upstairs to collectively sulk in their rooms since I haven't given in to any of their demands. But then where's Luc?

I'm about to head toward the stairs when I hear muffled laughter and Clarence's bark.

I turn, and through the French doors, I see all four of them, Harry, Mattie, Emmett *and* Luc in the yard, playing soccer. Clarence is trying to join in, running circles around them and barking. Twilight is all but gone, but the floodlights from the porch illuminate their play, and no one notices when I step outside. Not even Clarence.

By the looks of it, the twins are one team and Luc and Emmett are the other. No one's really defending a goal. They're all just jostling for possession, kicking and chasing. The real contest seems to be between Luc and Harry, but as I watch, I see that as defenders, Mattie and Emmett aren't making it easy for either one of them.

Even if the teams weren't evenly matched, it wouldn't matter. Their smiles are like beacons. Great lighthouse smiles calling me ashore.

In a stealth attack—probably thanks to his size—Emmett snags the ball from Harry, and Mattie whoops in surprise. They all laugh. Emmett makes a deft kick to the far side of the yard, apparently into the imaginary goal, and Luc roars in triumph.

I get a moment to watch them all. Beaming. Breathless. Happy. My heart bobs like a buoy, floating effortlessly for the first time in months. And I feel everything.

This is exactly what they need.

I love this.

It won't last.

And as that thought plunges my heart back into dark waves, Clarence lifts his head, spotting me. He barks a greeting and bounds toward me, surprising everyone. I bend down to pet him, hoping to hide all the emotions—so stinkin' many of them—on my face before anyone can see. I swallow against the lump in my throat and feel a deeper soreness there.

"C'mon," Luc pants, beckoning everyone toward the house. "Let's say hi to your *hermana.*" I've gotten so used to his subtle accent, I almost never notice it anymore. Except when he slips into Spanish. And then the sound of it shapes his words in a way that reminds me of his kiss.

Don't think about that now.

As a body they climb the porch steps, panting, flushed, and all smiles. That is, until Luc focuses on me.

"You okay?"

I nod. "Yeah, fine," I say, but the pain in my head is now cinching in tight.

"You look pale," he says, frowning.

Harry snorts. "She always looks pale."

Luc's frown etches deeper. As always, the scar in his brow makes his frown look scary, but I now recognize the look in his eye as concern.

I wave it away. "Just a long day." I tear my gaze from his and take refuge in Emmett's beaming face. "It looks like y'all were having fun."

"It was the *best!*" he cheers, collapsing against me in a clumsy hug. I have to brace myself to keep us both upright. He's getting too big for this.

"What's for dinner?" Harry asks. "Can we have Cane's?"

The thought of getting back in the car to pick up dinner is nearly enough to bring tears to my eyes. And that's not normal. It's probably time I faced it. I'm coming down with a cold. Probably from freezing my butt off all Saturday morning at the soccer game.

"We can have Cane's tomorrow night," I promise. "Tonight, I need something that delivers."

It's just a cold. I'll feel better tomorrow.

WHEN MY ALARM goes off at six-thirty Tuesday morning, I keep my eyes shut and swallow. Then whimper. My throat feels like

I've chugged a shot of broken glass. I'm pretty sure there's an SUV parked on my forehead.

"Dear God," I plead with whoever's listening. I slap my alarm to kill the fiend and press my hand over my eyes. My skin feels sandpapered. My bones have to be swollen. There's no other explanation for this full body ache.

I keep my eyes shut and assess what's possible. Advil is possible. Taking two will make me feel better. A shower. A shower is definitely possible. And coffee. Yes, I can handle coffee. It's my friend.

Breakfast is not possible. The thought of chewing and swallowing anything solid makes my stomach shrivel. And a smoothie is out of the question. Too sweet. Too cold. Definitely too cold. I shiver under my sheets and quilt.

So in that order, Advil, shower, coffee, I make it out the door. I'm wearing my gray thermals under my scrubs and my fuzzy socks stuffed into my sneakers, so I'm not shivering anymore.

I can do this.

If I have to pull the chute and call Dr. Loftin later today, I'll do it. But, for now, I can do this. I'll feel better once the caffeine kicks in.

I fire up the Infiniti, crank up the seat warmers, and take a sip from my travel mug. It's a close call, but the hot coffee is just a little less stabby than swallowing the Advil. Maybe if I keep taking small sips, the warmth will ease my throat, and I'll feel better.

I sip at every stop light and tell my myself each one feels better than the last. The trouble with that is I'm a terrible liar. Even I don't believe me.

"Dr. Delacroix, you look like sh—" David Webber, our nineteen-year-old vet tech clamps his mouth shut. His eyes bug. "Sorry. Are you okay?"

"I'm fine." I say the words, but they're little more than air. I clear my throat, wince, and try again. "I'm fine. Just a cold."

His brow goes up while his chin goes down. "You sure about that?"

I ignore him and walk over to the kennels. "How's Leopold?" The two-year-old black lab mix looks up at me glassy-eyed. He's in the middle of treatment for heartworms, and his owner brought him in, lethargic and vomiting yesterday. He probably threw a worm from too much activity. We put him in the ICU cage for a few hours yesterday, gave him twenty-five milligrams of Acepromazine to calm him down, and kept him overnight.

"A little wobbly on his feet this morning, but I walked him, and he peed, drank water, and ate all his breakfast."

"Can't ask for better than that," I say, opening the kennel door. Leopold picks up his head and blinks sleepily at me. "That Ace is pretty potent, isn't it buddy?" I actually envy the big guy. A sedative and the prospect of being trapped in bed sounds pretty good right now.

Fat chance of that.

As if he's rubbing it in, Leopold gives a spectacular yawn, and his tongue curls up like an upside-down question mark. I check his vitals. Heart rate, respiration, gum color, and then just rub his side for a few minutes.

"Call Mr. Mouton and tell him Leopold can go home today, but I recommend a half dose of Acepromazine every twelve hours for the next week," I detail. "I'd like for him to come in Tuesday or Wednesday for a recheck."

I close the kennel door, note my orders on Leopold's chart, and let Hailey, who's filling in for Kath, know I'm ready for our first appointment. And the day rolls on.

At one o'clock David catches me asleep at Dr. Loftin's desk, my forehead pillowed under my hands. I sit up too fast and the room spins a little.

"You should go home, Dr. D," he says gently. "Hailey and I can cancel the rest of the appointments for today."

I shake my head, and then wince, regretting it. "I'm good." I just meant to sit down for a minute during our lunch break. Looks like a minute turned into thirty. "Who's up next?"

By three, I can't drink any more coffee or my stomach will turn inside out. I've switched to the lemon ginger tea Kath keeps in the break room, but my throat feels like I'm swallowing flaming arrows one after another.

Ellen Degeneres comes in at four with an abscess. Not Ellen Degeneres the comedian. I may not be feeling well, but I'm not hallucinating. This Ellen is a cat. One who has recently had her ass kicked. Judging by the swelling on the dorsal aspect of Ellen Degeneres's shoulder, it happened in the last couple of days. It's not foul yet, so we should be able to get away with a good irrigation and a course of antibiotics.

Point of fact, cats are not good patients.

Ellen Degeneres is no exception. David wraps her in a towel and gently holds her head down on the exam table so neither of us gets bitten.

Another point of fact. A cat bite is serious business. If a cat bites your finger, and you don't treat it IMMEDIATELY, you can kiss that finger goodbye.

Ellen Degeneres hisses as I shave the area around her puncture wound.

Mrs. Hartley, her owner, gasps. "I had no idea it was that bad."

"Puncture wounds don't bleed much," I say to reassure. "You got her in early. I don't think she'll need surgery."

"Surgery?!" Mrs. Hartley wails. I don't look up. Instead, I just try to move quickly. Ellen Degeneres's hisses have turned into yowls as I irrigate the abscess with sterile saline.

By the time I give her an injection of Metacam to help with inflammation and prescribe the Clavamox, Ellen

Degeneres is growling at me from inside her crate, and David is frowning at me.

"You okay, Dr. D?"

The floor beneath my feet rolls. It reminds me of being on the deck of the *Eloise II*, and I think of my parents.

Mrs. Hartley, who's only a little younger than Mom, puts her hands on my cheeks. "Child, you're burning up with fever."

I try to step away from her touch and bump into the exam table. I want to tell her I'm fine, but I'm supposed to be a medical professional. "I'm probably contagious," I say instead. She drops her hands.

I lean against the wall. I hear David tell Mrs. Hartley that Hailey can check her out and someone will call tomorrow to follow up on Ellen Degeneres. But honestly, I'm not sure if he really says that or if I think he should say it. They leave.

David comes back with my purse and keys. Hailey walks in behind him.

I frown. "Who's next?"

"No one's next," David says.

I look at the clock. It's only four-twenty. We should have three more appointments before we close.

"Dr. Loftin said to cancel the others and close up," he explains.

I blink. "He called?"

David and Hailey exchange a look that reminds me of the twins. *Co-conspirators,* I think. Hailey looks back at me.

"I called Kath. She called Dr. Loftin. He called and told us to cancel."

Mutiny. I think I've only thought the word, but by the look on both their faces, I might have said it out loud.

"Can I give you a ride home, Dr. D?" David asks.

Too many thoughts are coming at me to process. No more appointments? They called Kath? Dr. Loftin closed the clinic without even talking to me? I swallow to stall for time, but it's like drinking a Molotov cocktail.

The thought makes me laugh. "Drinking a Molotov cocktail," I say, giggling.

And then David is escorting me out the back door of the clinic. I'm arguing—or I think I'm arguing—about how I can drive myself home. *I'm a veterinarian, for Christ's sake,* as if this has any relevance.

It's just a sore throat.

I don't argue long, mostly because I fall asleep before we even reach Ambassador Caffery Parkway. I can't really help it. Right now, life is just better with my eyes closed.

When I hear Clarence's bark, I startle awake. I open my eyes to see him sniffing my vet tech from the open car door. We're parked in the driveway. It's nearly dark.

"Easy, boy," David says, sliding out of the vehicle and letting my Great Pyrenees sniff his knuckles. Clarence recognizes him from the days he comes with me to the office and licks David's hand in greeting.

"Who are you?" Luc's voice cuts through the dark, and he stalks out of the shadowed garage. I have the urge to call him on that harsh tone of his, but I'm just so tired.

The driver's side door closes. Male voices seesaw just outside of the car. And then Mattie is standing in the open passenger door.

"Millie, what's wrong?"

Her worried look sends a shot of adrenaline through my veins. I sit up straight. "Nothing. I'm fine." But my voice is scratchy, my sinuses congested. "Just a sore throat."

"You should be in bed." She reaches across me and undoes my seatbelt. "C'mon."

"But—" I look over at the two men on the other side of my car, each giving the other suspicious stares.

"Hailey's on her way," David says. "One of us can stay—"

Luc shakes his head. "I'll stay."

What the hell?

"C'mon." Mattie tugs me out of the car as another set of headlights swings onto the driveway. I look over to see Hailey's blue Kia. She must be here to give David a ride back. They didn't need to go to all that trouble.

"No one's staying," I say in as clear a voice as I can manage. It sounds like a rusty swing set. "I'm fine."

Hailey kills the Kia's engine and pokes her head out the window. "What's the plan?" she asks.

It's cold out here. I'm shivering already, and I just want to lie down, but I have to hold it together long enough for all of them to see this fuss is not necessary.

"The plan is everyone goes home. I go to bed," I say. "All I need is a good night's rest."

"You sure Dr. D?" David asks.

"I'm sure. Thanks for the ride, but I'm fine." I force myself to meet his, Hailey's, and Luc's eyes in turn. "I'm home now. It's all good. The rest of you should go home, too."

I turn to walk away. I hope it looks like this is the end of the discussion, but really, I just need to get inside. I need my bed.

"Goodnight, Doc," Hailey calls.

"Feel better, Dr. D," David says.

"I have some cleanup to finish," Luc mutters.

I manage a goodnight and climb the steps into the kitchen with Mattie and Clarence at my heels.

"Can I get you something?" she asks, the familiar fretting tone in her voice.

"Where are the boys?"

"Upstairs. I was practicing before my lesson when I saw that guy drive up in your car."

It's Tuesday. Mattie has her lesson. The boys are home. Am I forgetting anyone? No. What am I forgetting?

It's too hard to think. My head is pounding. I'm thirsty, but my throat is on fire. I need to lie down. The twins and Emmett are home. That's all that really matters. I head upstairs but Mattie follows me. She fires question after question at me, but I can't answer just yet.

I reach my room and see exactly what I need. Bed. Even as I crawl across its welcoming surface, I know there's something I'm forgetting. Something else I should be doing, but I can't even.

Just a few minutes...

Chapter Seventeen

LUC

I LIED.

I told Millie I was staying to clean up. I'm not. I finished that twenty minutes ago. I was just killing time until she got home so I could see her before I left.

She has worked until five this week. I'm not used to it. I like it better when she comes home at noon. In the last few weeks, I've rearranged my routine so that I'm at the other job sites early to be here when she is.

It's the best part of my day.

And now that she's home, looking like someone who's escaped the ICU, I don't want to leave. Not until I know she's okay.

I head back inside after Millie's coworkers are gone and close the door against the night. I hear steps descending the stairs, and I look up to see Mattie.

"How is she?" I ask.

Millie's sister gives me a look of surprise. "I think she's asleep already. She must be really sick."

The urge to go up and look in on her is one I have to check with no small amount of restraint. I've never been upstairs. I don't belong there. But, right now, it's the only place I want to be.

I should just go and come back first thing in the morning. The only problem is I can't seem to make myself leave.

Mattie heads straight back for the piano where she picks up with her practice. I slink back to the kitchen because that's my territory. I look around for something to do, but any progress I could make would require the table saw or nail gun, and I don't want to wake Millie.

Not to mention, Mattie might kill me if I interrupt her piano time.

I'm about to park myself on a tool chest and answer emails when I hear footsteps thundering down the stairs. Harry.

With a great *thwack!* he lands at the foot of the stairs. "Millie?" he hollers.

I'm across the house in seconds. "Hey, hey, hey," I hoarse whisper, almost charging him. Harry steps back, eyes wide.

"Luc, what the hell—"

"Millie's asleep upstairs. She's sick."

He blinks and his brows lower. "Well, did she say when she'd be getting dinner?"

I suppress a growl. Hanging around Alex has reminded me that fourteen-year-olds are pretty selfish. They don't really mean it. They aren't trying to be *burros.* They just haven't figured out yet that not everything is about them.

"No, she didn't." I look at my watch. It's barely five-thirty. "Do you usually eat this early?"

Harry shrugs. "Around six. I'm starved."

I know from the time I've spent under this roof, Harry is either eating or hungry at all times. Just like Alex. Another trait of fourteen-year-old boys.

"Millie looked pretty bad. What do you want for dinner? I can get it for you."

His lowered brows leap. "You'd do that?"

I grin. Harry's a good kid, even if he is a little self-absorbed. "Yeah. That's easy."

"Aw-right," he says with a chuckle. "Cane's. Always."

The piano playing stops. Mattie turns on the bench. "We should get Chick-Fil-A," she says to her brother.

He scowls. "No. Cane's. Millie said we could have it tonight because we had Chinese delivery last night."

This I remember. Millie looked worn out when she made that call. I had asked her if she was okay, and she'd blown me off. I should have been paying more attention.

"Sorry, Mattie. Sounds like it's Cane's," I tell her. Then I turn to her brother. "What do y'all usually get?"

He points to himself. "I get the Caniac Combo. Emmett gets the Three Finger Combo, and Mattie gets the Sandwich Combo."

I look at Mattie to confirm this. She pulls a face but nods. "What about Millie?"

"She doesn't like Cane's. She usually gets something else," Mattie explains.

"Like what?"

Mattie's face goes blank. I turn to Harry.

"Well, don't look at me," he mutters.

I roll my eyes. "What about drinks?"

"Cokes. All three of us," Harry says with confidence.

I look back to Mattie to confirm. She bites her bottom lip. It's such a Millie gesture I almost grin.

"What?"

Her gaze shifts to her twin brother and she winces. "Millie usually makes us get waters."

"Then water it is," I say, starting to get a better idea of just how hard it is to be Millie Delacroix. Shit, it's got to be like walking a tightrope with these three. Give in on the fast food chicken. Hold the line on the sodas. Put up with their disagreements. Put what she wants aside.

Harry gives Mattie an ugly glare before turning to me. "Look, Luc, you can get us soft drinks this once. Millie's sick. She won't care," he argues. Admirably, I might add.

"Nice try, Harry." I glance at my watch again. Mrs. Chen will be here any second for Mattie's lesson. I jog to the front door and open it. Her white minivan is pulling into the driveway.

Damn, I'm good.

Now she won't ring the doorbell, Clarence won't bark, and Millie can keep sleeping.

I go through a checklist in my head of what I've seen Millie doing each night before I leave. I turn back to the twins.

"Harry, go upstairs and *quietly* tell Emmett he needs to *quietly* take a bath, and then you *quietly* feed Clarence." Harry opens his mouth, presumably to argue, but I adopt the tone I take with my workers. No nonsense AF. "No one is to wake up Millie. Are we clear?"

Harry ducks his head. "Yes, sir."

Behind him at the piano, Mattie, eyes wide, just nods really fast.

While I wait in the drive-thru line at Raisin' Cane's Chicken Fingers, I open the Waitr app on my phone and place an order for me and Millie at La Pagua. It may not be what she usually gets, but a dinner of deep-fried chicken strips, crinkle-cut fries, coleslaw and Texas toast is not what she's going to want, and I don't blame her.

I mean, it smells great, but it's the kind of meal that would have *Gym* top my Daily Three for a whole week.

And if I'm being honest with myself, I haven't been attending to my priorities the way I should the last few days. After Saturday's soccer game, I told myself I'd go out with Cesar, flirt with some girls at Red's, open up to the possibility of finding someone to take Millie off my mind.

It's what I should be doing. But hell if I want to.

Sure, I'd go to Legend's with Cesar to drink a few beers and watch a Saints game, but the thought of clubbing, of checking out someone who isn't Millie just holds no interest for me.

By the time I get back to the Delacroix's, Mattie's piano lesson is wrapping up, and all three kids—even Mattie—descend on the fast food like vultures. They don't seem too surprised when I tell them to eat at the table, so my guess is this is a family rule that Millie enforces.

Ten minutes later, Waitr arrives, and I come back from the front door to find all three of Millie's siblings piled on the sectional in front of *Gortimer Gibbons*. The table is still littered with gaping Styrofoam containers, plastic tubs of dipping sauce, chicken finger crumbs.

That's not gonna fly.

"Hey." The edge in my voice makes all three look up. My hands are full of takeout bags, so I point to the table with my chin. "Is that how you leave a table?"

They twist around and take in the table behind them. Mattie gets up first, but her brothers are quick to follow.

It shouldn't piss me off, but it does. Because if they leave shit like that all the time, then there's just one person in this house picking up everything. I remember my first day here. The mess in the kitchen. Is it like that every meal? Every day.

"Hey guys," I say, keeping my voice as level as possible, but I'll admit, it still might be a little scary. "From now on, you clear your place. Don't leave it for your sister to do. That's not cool."

All three of them nod.

"You're right," Harry says.

"Yeah," Mattie says.

"We'll be better, Luc," Emmett says, looking up at me like a stray puppy. "We promise."

I snort a laugh. Maybe they're just blowing smoke, but it

works. "I'm going to check on Millie." I turn and head for the stairs.

The staircase sweeps up to the second floor hallway, leaving me with six doorways to choose from. I go right. I'm not even sure why. It's as quiet as a closet up here, but I aim for the room at the end of the hall.

A few of the doors stand open. One is a bathroom, and another has to be Emmett's room. There's a stuffed snowman with a pointy head lying face-up on the ground. I think it's the one from *Frozen*. My cousin Natalia's little girl Sofie used to watch that movie on a loop. She had lots of the princess merch, but I don't think she had the stuffed snowman. On the floor beside it are some Avenger action figures. Iron Man. Captain America. Is that Bucky Barnes?

They make Bucky Barnes action figures?

I'm sure Emmett will tell me all about it later. I continue down the hall. The last door is open. A pair of teal scrubs dot the floor at the foot of the bed, and a Millie-sized shape huddles under the covers.

Even though I have food in hand and it's hot, I don't want to wake her. I just want to make sure she has everything she needs. I'll go as soon as I know she's okay. One step into the room, and I hear a jingle, and Clarence emerges from the far side of the bed.

His growl is so low, my ears barely pick it up, but it's enough. Grinning, I step back into the hall. So, no one sneaks into Millie's room without the Great Pyrenees's okay.

Works for me.

I'll send Millie a text. Let her know there's chicken tortilla soup in the fridge whenever she's ready for it. I'm about to turn to go when Clarence jumps onto the bed and collapses beside his mistress with a huff.

It's not gentle. It's not subtle, and no surprise, Millie stirs. She rolls onto her back with a deep inhale. For a split second, I consider ducking out of sight. Waking up to me standing in her doorway might freak her out. Friends or not, my place isn't in the bedroom.

But knowing I should go and actually making myself do it are two different things, and it turns out I suck at it.

As if Millie knows someone's there, her head pops up, and she squints at me. *Dios mío,* even though she's pale and sick in bed, she's so damn beautiful it hurts.

She lets her head drop back on the pillow, but she keeps her eyes on me. "Are you a dream?"

Not the question I was expecting.

I chuckle. "No. You okay?" I don't wait for her to answer, and I don't wait for her to invite me in, or worse, send me away. I step back into the room, and now that Millie is awake and acknowledging me, Clarence seems to have no objections at all.

I move around the far side of her bed and set the bags on her nightstand. She doesn't even look at them. Her gaze has tracked me, and she still looks pretty confused. Her eyes are glassy, and she's got the covers pulled tight around her like she's freezing.

"You okay, Millie?" I ask again because I'm not sure she even heard me the first time.

"What time is it?" She's frowning now, worry creasing her forehead.

"A little after seven. You slept a couple of hours."

Her eyes fly open. "Oh Jesus!" She tries to sit up but only makes it onto her elbows before wincing in pain. I put a hand on her shoulder.

"Hey. Hey. Not so fast."

Millie gives up, somewhere between sitting and lying, and rests the back of her head against the headboard. It looks really uncomfortable.

"I have to get up," she groans.

At first I think she needs the bathroom or she's about to be sick.

"I'll help you," I offer, moving my grip to her elbow. "What do you need?"

"It's getting late," she says, her voice raspy and weak. "The kids need dinner."

"Oh. They're good. They had Cane's."

She stills. "How? Did... Did Harry Waitr it?"

I narrow my eyes at her. "I'm going to forgive you for that because you're sick."

"What do you mean?" she asks, blinking. Then she seems to remember herself. "And I'm not sick. It's just a cold."

I snort. "You're unbelievable." She is. In every way. Millie can't let her guard down unless she physically collapses. Even when she does collapse, she denies it.

It makes me want to scoop her up in my arms and pull her into my lap. Tell her she can rest her head for five minutes. *Dios mío,* I've never known anyone who tries so hard.

"I got dinner for the kids." Then I point to the bag on her nightstand. "Waitr got dinner for us."

She scoots up a little higher on the headboard for a better view. It still looks pretty uncomfortable.

I lean over her and grab the spare pillow beside her. "Here. Let me help you."

A scowl crosses her face. It's like the very notion of letting someone help her makes her testy, but I ignore it and slide one hand behind her shoulder blades to ease her up, slipping the pillow behind her with the other.

"Do you think you could eat something?" I make a point of not asking if she's hungry. Admitting as much might seem like weakness to her.

Millie clears her throat, but she looks at the paper bag. Oh yeah, she's hungry.

"I don't know."

"It's just chicken tortilla soup," I say, rolling a shoulder like I don't care, "from La Pagua."

Her eyes widen and she sits up just a little higher. "Really?"

I bite down on my smile. Millie is not going to come out and ask for it. Somehow I know this is as close as she'll come to admitting she's hungry and the soup is calling her name. I reach for the first bag and unroll the top. Grabbing the container, I feel heat seeping through the cardboard. Good. It's still nice and hot. I hand it to her with a spoon before reaching deeper into the bag for the little wax paper pouch of tortilla strips.

I hold it out. "Want some tortillas?"

Millie swallows visibly and makes a face. "Maybe not just yet." But she doesn't hesitate to pry off the circular cardboard lid. Steam rises off the surface of the soup, and it's tangy, savory aroma fills the room.

"Mmm. That looks good," she mutters, poising her spoon over the soup. But she stops before dipping it into the broth and looks up at me. Her blue eyes, still glassy and tired, are round with awe. "Thank you. I don't know what else to say."

I let my smile loose. *"Thank you* is plenty." I'm not doing this for her gratitude. I'm doing it for my peace of mind. Making sure she's okay doesn't really feel like a choice.

Millie ladles a spoonful of chicken tortilla soup—minus the tortillas—and brings it to her mouth. She sighs, closes her eyes, and her whole body seems to melt a little as she savors the bite. I like the sight of that. So much I let myself just stare—until she swallows and wrinkles her nose in pain again.

"It hurts a lot?" I ask, frowning,

Shaking her head, Millie opens her eyes. "Probably just needs a little warming up. The soup will help," she says, and then she scoops up another bite. She doesn't wince this time, but I can tell it's because she's trying not to. Instead she braces for the swallow, and she may be fooling herself, but she's not fooling me. It hurts.

"Your throat has been hurting since last night?"

She answers with a shrug and takes another bite. Then she nods toward the bag. "Did you get something for yourself?"

I did, and I know she's just trying to change the subject, but she's eating, so I let her. "I got a soup for me and a steak milanesa, but if you want that too, you're welcome to it."

"No, this is great. You should eat."

I wasn't counting on being welcome to stay, but I'm not about to turn down the invite. I reach for the other bag and remove the soup container and spoon, leaving my foil-wrapped entree for later. I carefully peel off the lid, tear open the baggie of tortilla strips, and sprinkle them into the soup.

Millie watches with unmasked longing.

"You sure you don't want to put a few in yours? The soup will soften them up," I say.

She meets my gaze before looking back in her bowl. "I'm good."

Right. She's anything but good. I'd bet the business on it. My guess is Millie has strep throat. I haven't had it since high school, but that shit hurts like a mother. It also means she needs to see a doctor. But no reason to hassle her about that now. None of the walk-in clinics in town are open, but she's going tomorrow if I have to carry her.

I take a bite. "Mmm."

"I know, right?" she says hoarsely.

I grin. "Good. Just not as good as Mami's."

Amusement brightens her eyes. "Oh really?"

I nod. "La Pagua is great. Don't get me wrong," I say, stirring the cup. "Best authentic Mexican in town. Just not as good as her cooking."

"What's her best dish?" She tilts her head to the side, smiling. I think the soup might be helping a little. Some of the color has come back to her cheeks.

"*Mole poblano* is my favorite," I say, my voice coming out deeper at just the thought of Mami's *mole* sauce.

Millie blinks. "What's that? Like guacamole?"

I bite the inside of my cheek so I won't laugh. "No. it's nothing like that. It's a sauce made with like nineteen thousand ingredients—like Indian curry, except it's nothing like Indian curry," I ramble, feeling an excited fire stoke up inside me as I try to explain the greatest and most complex sauce in the history of Mexico. "No two *mole* recipes are exactly the same, but once you taste it, you'll know it no matter whose recipe it is. It's made with chilies—Mami uses three different kinds. And seeds. You can use pumpkin, sesame, peanuts, almonds, anise, tomatoes, tomatillos, and about a half-pound of chocolate."

She goes starry eyed. "Chocolate? Is it a dessert?"

I shake my head. "No, you pour it over meat. Mami usually makes it with roast chicken, but for *Cinco de Mayo,* Papi grills the chicken instead," I explain. I want to tell her Mami will serve it with turkey on Thursday, and that she should come and try it, but I already know how she feels about that.

"Alex likes it best with pulled pork. Kind of like a Mexican brisket."

"Mmm," she moans. "That sounds amazing." She takes another bite of soup, but I can tell just by the look on her face, it's not as satisfying as it was five minutes ago. Not after hearing about the magical *mole.*

"Mami's an amazing cook," I say honestly.

She looks at me. The light in her eyes has dulled a little. Her smile fades. "Just don't take it for granted," she says, her voice going hollow.

Oh shit.

I shake my head. "Millie, I didn't mean—"

She holds up her spoon to stop me. "I know. It's fine.

Just…" She pushes the corners of her mouth into something that can't even come close to a smile. "Just make her write down all her recipes and tell her how good it is every time."

Millie doesn't look away, so I don't either. I hold her gaze because she has to hold all of this every day.

"I will," I promise, and I mean it. My parents are getting older, and Papi's health isn't great. But I have them, and watching Millie try so damn hard every day lets me know just how lucky I am.

She breaks her gaze and looks toward her door. "So, the kids are okay?"

I nod. "Present and accounted for. Fed, and in Emmett's case, bathed."

Her brows leap. "Are you serious? Bathed? How did you manage that?"

"Don't underestimate me," I say with a grin.

"Hmph." She rolls her eyes and then takes another bite of soup. But she winces, wrinkles her nose, and sets the container on her nightstand. "I think I've had enough."

She's hardly had any. "Throat hurts that bad?"

She looks caught and gives me that shrug.

"You need to see a doctor tomorrow."

Millie shakes her head. "I'll feel better tomorrow."

I *hmph,* imitating her. "Do you have a fever?" I don't even wait for her to answer because I know she won't admit it if she does. I put down my soup on her nightstand and reach across for her.

My hands press to her cheeks. The touch should mean nothing, but as soon as our eyes meet, the memory of our kiss flames between us. All it takes is her face in my hands, and I'm in that moment. I can tell, in the open depths of her blue eyes, she's in it too. That lost world of ours still exists right where we left it. Right here.

The only thing that stops me from pulling her to my mouth

is the heat. Her face is hot. Really hot. I shift a hand to her forehead. Fever blooms.

"You're burning up," I say, frowning.

She tries to shake out of my touch, but I grip her shoulders. "Millie, you're really sick."

"I can't be sick. I'm f—"

My grip tightens. "If you say you're fine one more time, I'm going to get my *abuela* over here to give you her egg remedy."

Millie's brows drop into a glower, but she tilts her face and looks at me sidelong. "What's her egg remedy?"

"Trust me," I threaten, putting on my best poker face. "You don't want to know."

It's nothing more than a little Mexican white magic she used on me and Alex whenever we were sick. Abuela would take a raw egg and make the sign of the cross with it all over our bodies. Then she'd break the egg open in a bowl by our beds and construct a little cross out of toothpicks and set that on top of the exposed yoke. She'd leave it on our bedsides until we got better. Abuela once said something about how the sickness would go out of our bodies and into the egg. Crazy, I know, but she's my abuela. She gets away with anything.

The threat to call my grandmother must be enough because Millie sinks down into her pillows. "Fine. I'm sick. I feel like shit," she says, grumpily. "Happy now?"

"H-happy?" I choke, laughing. "No, *boba*, that doesn't make me happy."

She frowns. *"Boba?* What does that mean?" She bats my hands away from her arms, and I sit back, ignoring the sting her brush off delivers.

"I'll give you one guess," I say, but give her no time to respond. "Have you taken anything for the fever?"

Millie looks over at her nightstand, her brows knitting

199

tighter. I follow her gaze to the bottle of Advil. "Yeah…?" She drags out the word.

"Yeah?" I ask, picking up the bottle. "When was that?"

She purses her lips. "This morning and…" Her gaze drifts to the left as though she's searching her memory. "Maybe before I fell asleep. I know I meant to."

I set the bottle back down. "Have any Tylenol? Just to be on the safe side?"

Millie nods. "Bathroom cabinet."

I'm up and across the room. Her bathroom is small but neat. No stray lingerie, unfortunately. I grab the bottle of Acetaminophen, carry it back to her room, and shake out two pills into my hand.

"Here."

She pops them into her mouth and then chases them with a sip of water that makes her grimace. Seriously, it hurts just to watch her.

When she lies back against the pillow, she looks spent. As though the last twenty minutes with me took all she had.

"Get some rest," I tell her. "I'm taking you to a walk-in clinic tomorrow."

I expect her to put up a fight, but Millie just closes her eyes. "We'll see."

Shit. I'd like it better if she put up a fight. The fact that she doesn't means she probably feels even worse than I imagine.

I've never wanted to wrap someone in my arms more than I do this minute, but that's not allowed. Instead, I collect the food containers and takeout bags and head downstairs. Harry, Mattie, and Emmett are sprawled across all three sides of the sectional, but when I step into the living room, they all perk up.

"How is she?" Mattie asks, her green eyes pinched with worry.

"Under the weather, but okay." I keep my voice light. Not just for her, but for all of them. Mattie is the one who's most obviously worried, but her brothers are paying close attention, so I know they feel it too. And who could blame them? Without their parents, Millie is all they have. I don't have to see the tightness in their faces to know that at some point, they've all wondered what would happen to them without her. "She ate some soup, and she's resting now."

Emmett's face clears at this. "Are you going to stay with us?"

His question stops me in my tracks. I was planning to put the rest of Millie's soup in the fridge and tell them goodnight. Make sure they lock up behind me. Come back in the morning.

But I don't really want to leave. Not Millie. Not the kids. It's just not my place to stay.

I look to the twins. They're looking at me. Waiting for my answer? Do they need me to stay? Fourteen is old enough. I know Millie leaves them in charge now and then. But would it make them feel better if I stayed?

"We're just about to watch *Guardians of the Galaxy Vol. 2*," Harry says, holding up the remote. "Wanna join?"

The three kids are wearing the exact same expression. Cautious. Hopeful. *Hell, yes, I'm staying.*

"Hit play."

"Yay!" Emmett launches off the sofa cushions like he's spring loaded. He smacks the space next to him. "You can sit in Millie's spot."

Warmth floods my chest. "Sure," I say. "Just let me put this away."

When the credits roll two hours and fifteen minutes later, my bicep is just pins and needles. Emmett's sleeping head has been using it as a pillow for the last forty minutes. The other two are awake, but they seem just as relaxed as he is.

Looks like that's my cue.

I start to slide out from underneath Emmett's melon, trying not to wake him.

Harry shakes his head. "I have to get him upstairs anyway," he says to me. Then he leans over and puts a hand on his little brother's shoulder. "Hey Em, wake up."

Emmett whines in protest, but he turns his head and sets me free. I get to my feet.

"Anything I can do before I go?"

"Nah," Harry says, giving Emmett a nudge. "We're good."

"I'll be back first thing in the morning," I tell them, making sure I meet Mattie's always watchful gaze.

She nods. And then Emmett whines again, but this one comes out a little rougher. I turn to see him push Harry's hand away.

"Quit it, Harry," he complains, sounding cranky. "I don't feel good."

Shit.

The twins and I exchange glances.

"What's wrong, buddy?" Mattie asks, stepping closer.

Without opening his eyes, Emmett frowns. "My throat hurts."

Chapter Eighteen

MILLIE

I'M CLIMBING A GLACIER.

I've never done anything like this before. I have no idea what I'm doing. I've never trained or practiced. I just know It's cold, I'm tired, and I can't let go.

When I look up, it's just craggy ice as far as I can see. Like *The Cliffs of Insanity* in **The Princess Bride**. I look down, and there's nothing but clouds. If I fall from here, I'll just keep falling forever.

The pack I'm carrying is so heavy. The straps dig into my shoulders, and my back aches with its weight. I want to take it off, but there's nowhere to set it down. Just sheer ice. I reach above me for a handhold, but the next one is so far above my head.

I stretch up, bounce on my toes, trying to get the height I need, but it's not enough. I press my body against the wall of ice, lengthening out as much as I can.

It's so cold. I'm just so cold.

I reach and reach, but there's no hope for it. I wail in defeat, and the freezing air rakes my throat with cold.

Breathing hurts. I can't climb any higher. I can't get back down. Down doesn't exist anymore. All I can do is cling to the ice. But I can't stay here for long. I'll die out here.

And then I look down at my feet. The block of ice beneath them has grown slick. I've stood here for so long, the heat of my body has started to melt it from underneath me. And I know that what's holding me up won't last.

I'm going to fall. I'm going to fall. I'm going to fall.

"Millie."

I open my eyes. I'm shivering, curled into a tight ball. I blink at the darkness, sure I heard Luc's voice. Was it in the dream?

"Luc?" I rasp, feeling like a fool. What would he be doing here in the middle of the night?

Shadows move and a hand lands on my shoulder. I suck in a startled breath.

"It's just me," he says. "I didn't mean to scare you."

But I'm not scared. I'm relieved. Luc being here with me is so much better than hanging from the frozen Cliffs of Insanity. Even if my teeth are still chattering.

Luc's hands cup my cheeks. *"Dios mío,* your fever has spiked."

I groan. Every muscle, bone, and joint in my body has rebelled. Words seem out of reach.

Until Luc switches on my bedside lamp.

"Aah! What are you doing?!" I cover my eyes, but spears of light have already skewered them.

*"Shh...*You'll wake the kids. I'm getting you some medicine."

You'll wake the kids.

I unravel his words as I hear the snap of a bottle cap and the rattle of pills.

"What time is it?" I manage to whisper this time.

"A little after two."

"In the morning?" I ask, incredulous.

Luc's hushed chuckle brushes over me. "Yes, *boba.* Put out your hand."

I keep my hands to my eyes. "Turn out the light first."

Click.

I peel one hand away, and Luc catches it in his.

"Can't see a friggin' thing," he mutters, but I feel him press two tablets onto my palm, and then he closes my fingers over them, cupping my hand in both of his. "Take those. I'll hand you the water."

I obey and grope until the bottle meets my hand. Then Luc's arm slides behind my neck as he helps me to sit up. Swallowing is fresh agony, and the water sets my teeth chattering again.

"Is the h-heater broken?"

He lays me back on the pillow, cradling the back of my head. "No, *linda,* it's the fever." The side of the bed depresses with his weight. "Are you hungry? Do you need anything?"

A shiver runs through me. "I'm so cold."

His hand closes around my arm. "You're shaking. Where are extra blankets?" Luc starts to rise, but I grasp his wrist. He stills. The darkness makes everything unreal. Like a continuation of my dream. But I know I'm awake. I know, despite all logic, that Luc really is in my room. And I know that no matter the reasons I shouldn't be, I'm so glad he is.

My throat is on fire. My body aches like I've been knocked to the ground and kicked. Medicine and blankets are okay. But I remember what it felt like to be in Luc's arms, and all I want is for him to hold me. I just can't ask for that. Not after I pushed him away. Not ever.

I let go of his wrist.

"Millie," Luc whispers. He still hasn't moved. "Tell me what you need."

He's talking about medicine and blankets, right?

I turn on my side, facing him, and draw my knees up to get warm. I try not to shiver. "I'll be okay as soon as the fever breaks."

"Millie." He's still whispering, but I hear an edge of impatience. "Tell me what you need."

He must be crazy if he thinks I'll tell him I need him to climb into this bed and hold me. Besides, I don't *need* that. Sure, I want it *really, really* bad. But we all know how that song goes.

"Just sleep," I say. And, okay, fine. I sound about as convincing as a used car salesman, but I'm running a fever after all.

Luc grunts a sigh. *"Mujer obstinada,"* he growls, and the bed dips again. "Move over."

"What?"

But his body just crowds mine, so I scurry to the side like a maimed crab. Before I even cross the middle of the bed, one of Luc's arm hooks me around my middle and tilts me onto my side. He stretches out behind me and tugs me into him, spoon-wise.

At first, all I feel is shock. But then all I know is Luc. The length of his body pressed to mine. His delicious heat soaking into my freezing skin. His arm like an iron band across my stomach, caging me to him.

And my sigh is like the breaking of a dam. Luc feels so good I could weep. I nearly do. The ache in my throat doubles with it, and I can't speak. Can't thank him for giving me this gift.

Instead, I lay my right arm over his. He gives me a squeeze in response.

"Better?" he asks.

I'm not shaking anymore. This must be obvious. But the chance of sobbing as I draw breath is high, so I hold it and nod instead of answering. He can't see, but with my head tucked into the hollow beneath his chin, I know he can feel it.

How is it possible that he's here, holding me, right when I need to be held?

How is it that he knows exactly what I need—what we all need—every time? Whether we need to smash some tile or kick the soccer ball in the yard or eat chicken tortilla soup.

Or be kissed.

And how come, whatever we need, he just gives it?

Of its own accord, my hand squeezes his forearm. It's slight, but he nuzzles the top of my head in response.

How is it that he doesn't have a girlfriend?

At least, I don't think he does. Would he have kissed me? Be lying in bed with me if he did?

No. No. Definitely not. Not the man who fired a guy for talking about my loose caboose. That's not the sort of man who cheats.

Luc is a good man. He should be with someone who has all kinds of good to give back to him.

This thought does nothing to help the ache in my throat, but I swallow against it anyway.

"What are you even doing here?" I rasp.

He exhales, and I feel it in my hair. "I'll tell you in the morning. Go to sleep."

I realize he's probably exhausted. But as bad as I feel, I've been sleeping for hours. I'm wide awake. And what's happening now—me, lying in Luc's arms—will never happen again. So I want to savor it.

I lie here, taking it in. It would be wrong. I know it would be wrong to touch him after he falls asleep. Nowhere creepy like below the belt. I'm not a perv.

But his hands. The curve of his shoulder. The spots where his dimples hide.

I won't do it of course, but I get a heady thrill knowing I could.

But when he falls asleep, I am so going to turn over so I can look at him. Even in the dark, I know how beautiful he is. And if I can stay awake until the sun comes up, who knows how long I can look?

He's so beautiful.

For now, I'll have to content myself with the feel of him behind and around me. And that's pretty damn good, I have to admit. The steel of his thighs against the back of mine. His chest pressed to my spine. Luc's arm wrapped around me feels like it belongs there. Like I belong here.

I know I don't. But I can pretend for one night.

Pretend that I have this every night. And then I can remember it. The way I remember his kisses.

"Why aren't you sleeping?"

I jump like I've been caught stealing. My heart practically hammers in my nose. Has Luc been listening to my thoughts for the last ten minutes? I can tell now he has been awake. His muscles haven't relaxed. His breathing hasn't drawn out.

Definitely no snoring.

"Why aren't *you*?"

He makes a kind of strangled noise in the back of his throat. "Because." The wall of muscle surrounding me tenses.

I frown into the darkness. *"Because* is not an answer. Why?"

He heaves a massive exhale, the ultimate sound of resignation. "Because I'm worried about you."

My head jerks to look over my shoulder, but I can't meet his gaze. I shimmy around until I can roll over and face him. There's only enough streetlight to make out his shape. I can't even see the glint of his eyes. "Why are you worried about me? I'm fi—"

"Don't say it," he warns, and again, I'm reminded of the mysterious egg treatment. What the hell does his grandmother do? Does it involve eating a raw egg? Does exposure to salmonella cure colds and flus? Is it *worse* than eating a raw egg? Like some kind of egg enema? This may be one of those things I don't want to know.

But I do want to know why he's worried.

"Tell me."

He's quiet for a moment. I wish I could see him better. Still, I shouldn't be complaining. His arm is still around me. Our knees and feet touch. Being this close to him feels like floating in a pool on an inflatable raft. Sun warmed. All the time in the world.

"It's not like you."

I'm tipped off my pool raft. I have no idea what he's talking about. "Huh?"

It sounds like he's smiling. I want to touch his face, but I keep still. It's not too hard. My arms and legs feel so heavy anyway.

"It's not like you not to insist on answers."

He's right. I do insist on answers. From him. I have since the day we met. He must think I'm such a bitch.

Am I a bitch? Was I always a bitch? Or have I just become one in the last six months? The thought makes my eyes sting. I blink them mercilessly so they don't fill.

"I don't know what you're talking about," I lie. The words should sound defensive, but through the swelling in my throat, they just come out scratchy and weak.

"Yes, you do." He's laughing gently, but I still feel it through the mattress and where we touch. "You asked what I was doing here, and I told you I'd tell you in the morning. Any other day, that would never fly."

He's right again. I can't tell him that I'm just so glad he's here that it doesn't matter why. That I'd rather have him here than anyone else. Than any*thing* else. So I say something else instead.

"Why are you still here?"

Luc gives a knowing hum. "I'll tell you if you promise not to freak out."

I bolt up on my elbow. "Oh God, what's wrong?" My head spins and maybe I sway, but I ignore it.

The bed shakes with Luc's laughter. He cups the back of my head and eases it down to the pillow.

"It's okay." The way he says it makes me believe him. "It's just that Emmett's sick too."

"What?!" I try to jump up again, but Luc is ready for me, his arm a bracing weight against my efforts.

"He's okay, Millie," he croons. "We took his temperature: 100.3. We gave him some Children's Motrin, and he's asleep on the twin bed in Harry's room."

I absorb all of this. In my current state, it's a lot to absorb, and not all of it makes sense. "Why is he in Harry's room?"

Luc's arm relaxes. Now that I'm not a flight risk, he moves his hand up to my head and brushes my hair behind my shoulder. I'm not so addled that I don't recognize how good it feels.

"Two reasons. One, so Harry could keep an eye on him," he says, softly, his fingers idly brushing through my hair in a way that makes it hard to keep my eyes open. "And two, so I could crash in Emmett's room."

"You were sleeping in Emmett's room?" I ask surprised. Of course, he'd have to be sleeping somewhere. "Why?"

"To be close to you." My heart bucks like a rodeo bull, and then he quickly adds, "In case any of you needed something."

"Oh." It's all I can manage.

"I wasn't about to leave with both you and Emmett sick."

"No, of course not," I say dumbly. But it's not a matter of course. Who else would have stayed under the circumstances? All night? Sleeping in an eight-year-old's room after feeding and taking care of the whole family?

Not many people. Not Carter.

It's too much to ask.

I'd like to do something. Give Luc something. But the only

thing I have to offer right now is a fever and sore throat. He wouldn't want that.

He's lying on his side, facing me. I'm not going to kiss him. That would gross him out. And if it didn't gross him out, it would confuse the hell out of him.

I'm confused, and I still want to kiss him.

I reach up and touch his cheek. "Thank you so much."

Luc covers my hand with his, pressing it closer. I feel his smile. Somewhere under my palm, a dimple is shining in all its naked glory.

"It's nothing," he whispers.

"It's not nothing," I counter.

The smile under my hand grows. "Okay, *boba*, it's not nothing. It's something, but it's something I want to do."

I can't go anywhere safe with that, so I get prickly instead. "Why are you calling me *boba?* What does it mean?"

He chuckles. "It means a few things," he hedges, keeping my hand pressed to his face, "but the way I'm using it means *silly.*"

"Silly?" I frown. "What else does it mean?"

Laughing, he shakes his head, and my hand goes with it. "Don't ask. You'd just get mad."

I jerk my hand away. "Mad? What does it mean?"

He snatches back my hand—laughing harder now—and brings it back to his face, except it's not my hand now, but my fist, balled tight.

"I'm just going to look it up on my phone," I threaten.

"Where *is* your phone?" he asks, sounding like a know-it-all.

And this question makes me wonder. I have no idea. I remember David putting me in the car with my purse. I hope it's not still in the car. David parked in the drive, and I doubt anyone moved the car into the garage. Our neighborhood is beautiful, but there are car break-ins all too often.

I tug at my arm, but he doesn't even loosen his grip. "Where is my purse?"

"It's downstairs."

"Hmph." I let my arm go slack. We both know I'm not up for a trip downstairs just to get my phone to look up a stupid word. But then it hits me. Luc probably has his phone on him. I've seen him on the phone maybe a dozen times. If he has it on him, it's in his right front pocket, which right now would be the side that's toward the ceiling, not the one he's lying on.

My left hand is trapped under his right. I'm lying on my right side, but maybe...

I slide my right arm down, gliding over the mattress between us. "Are you going to tell me what else it means?" I might as well give him one last chance to come clean.

Luc snickers. "No. You're in a fevered state. You'll forget all about this in the morning."

That does it. "Fine."

My hand shoots down to his jeans in search of a bulging pocket. I find a bulge. But it's not his pocket. And that's definitely not a phone.

He jolts. *"Aah!* Millie, what the fuck?!"

In a clash of hands, torsos, and hips, I'm on my back, arms pinned above my head, a panting Luc on top of me.

It should be noted I'm panting too.

"What are you doing?" he rasps.

"I—just—sorry," I squeak. What *am* I doing? I can't even think of an answer, much less put words to one. All I can process is that Luc is on top of me. And if I thought spooning with him felt amazing, this is light years better.

Because that bulge that is assuredly not a cell phone is about two inches away from where I'd really, really enjoy it.

And, shit. Does he just carry that thing around? Fully loaded like that? All the time?

His face hovers above mine, and I know—though I can't

exactly see—he's frowning. Waiting for an answer. I owe him that.

"I'm sorry," I manage. "I shouldn't have done that. I-I was reaching for your phone."

"W-what?" His lungs constrict, and I feel the shock of it through my body.

I also feel incredibly stupid. "To look up the word," I admit weakly.

He stares down at me, not saying a thing. I have no idea what he's thinking. Probably about how much of an idiot I am.

"*¿Qué estoy haciendo?* You're sick," he hisses, and rolls off me. The loss of him is almost enough to make me whimper.

"I'm sorry," he whispers, still sounding out of breath. "I'll go."

I grip his hand. "Please don't."

I know it's wrong. It's selfish and inconsiderate. But the last thing I want is for him to leave. He's propped up against the headboard, staring at the ceiling. The hand beneath mine is stiff, thrumming with tension.

"You want me to stay?" he asks finally.

Shame washes over me. "You don't have to."

"I want to."

"I shouldn't," I admit. "But I want you to."

Luc's sigh cuts through the room. He sounds confused, frustrated, and it's my fault.

"I didn't mean..." I start, squeezing his hand. "I... I didn't know."

The tension leaves him, and he squeeze back. "You didn't know what?"

I gulp. How do I explain what I mean? Maybe it's better I don't.

"Say it."

"When I..." I'm so glad he can't see me. I'm probably turning every shade of red, "...grabbed you."

A laugh erupts, shattering the night, and then smothered laughter shakes the bed. Luc squeezes my fingers with one hand and covers his face with the other. He rolls toward me, so we are again face to face.

"Why do you think I couldn't sleep?"

"Oh!" I gasp, covering my own laugh. The urge to reach for him is so strong I give in halfway and touch his face again.

"And then you did that," he says, his voice so soft it's almost painful. "Touched my face."

I shouldn't. I shouldn't be touching him. I start to pull away, but again, he captures my hand and keeps it right there.

"Not yet," he whispers, and I can no longer breathe.

"Luc." I say his name as if it's a plea. A plea for him to understand.

"I know."

"You don't understand."

"I do." He sounds certain. The way he does when he talks about wood and granite. This is just another hard thing.

"But you don't," I whimper.

His thumb caresses the back of my hand. The one pressed to his beautiful face. How can a touch so small feel so wonderful?

"Tell me what I don't understand, *linda.*" His voice is a warm purr.

My body is a wreck of fever and soreness, and I never want this night to end. Luc is here. I'm touching him. He's touching me. I want him. He wants me. And it will never be better than this.

Then I know I am wrong because his left hand reaches across the distance between us, and he cups my cheek. I smile and I know he feels it. I move my right hand over his left hand at my right cheek, so now we are mirror images.

Now, it will never be better than *this,* and I need him to understand why.

"Luc, I want you, but I can't sleep with you," I whisper.

"Of course not," he murmurs. "You still have a fever."

I shake my head. "No, I mean I can't sleep with you. Ever."

I feel something run through him. Like a shock of stillness.

"Ever is a long time." I hear him swallow. "Just me? Is it just me you can never sleep with?"

I remember him asking at the soccer game if it was because of his heritage. I shake my head, almost frantic.

"No. It's anyone. I can't sleep with anyone."

Chapter Nineteen

LUC

I AWAKE BEFORE DAWN AND KNOW EXACTLY WHERE I AM. MILLIE is tucked to me, my arm draped over her waist. Her bottom snug against me.

My balls are going to ache all day, and I don't give a damn.

I learned a lot last night, and the most obvious is that lying next to Millie is not a great recipe for sleep.

Another is that when she's delirious with fever, she says some crazy shit.

When she started talking about never being able to have sex, I got a little worried about her. But then she started shivering again, asked me to hold her, and fell asleep in my arms.

Night has faded into watery light, and it falls on Millie's head, painting her deep red hair even darker. She sleeps still, but I can tell by her quick breathing and the heat she radiates that she still has fever. I've got to get both her and Emmett to a doctor.

Moving as slowly as possible, I lift my arm off her and reach into my pocket for my phone. It's ten until six. Later than I usually wake up, but not bad considering last night and how little I slept. Still, it's Wednesday, and I need to move.

All at once, the day's concerns pepper me like a hailstorm. I set the phone down, encircle Millie again, and close my eyes. The world can wait for two more minutes while I hold her and sort out my Daily Three.

Besides, who knows when I'll be able to do this again. If I'll be able to do this again.

Being this close to her, breathing in the summer sweetness of her hair, feeling the way her body seems to welcome the press of mine—it just feels right. This can't be the one and only time, right?

I want you, but I can't sleep with you.

If I let myself think about that one comment, I'll go mad. We're going to have to talk about that one some more, but not until she's better.

Take Care of Millie. That's priority number one today. I'm not gonna lie. Today isn't the first day it's made my three, but today, this one is going to drive everything else. In order to Take Care of Millie, I need to get her and Emmett to a walk-in clinic. Which means I need to make the time to do that, sooner rather than later.

Taking Care of Millie also means lightening her load. The kids are going to need breakfast, lunch, and dinner today. At a minimum. Last night, Mattie mentioned they were almost out of toilet paper. Who knows what else they need. I might need to call in reinforcements.

But Taking Care of Millie means protecting her privacy. Donner and Sam are going to show up soon, and I don't want to be up here when they do. I don't even want to be downstairs still in yesterday's clothes.

Which means I need to make a quick decision about my next two priorities. I prop my head up and look at Millie.

Fuck Two and Three.

For the first time in months, I can't even think of a Two and Three.

I need to move, but I can't quite make myself. Memorizing her profile in sleep—the way her hair spreads over her pillow, her spice-colored, down swept lashes, her alabaster skin—I promise myself this won't be the last time I see her like this. It can't be.

The promise is the only way I can get out of her bed. And getting out of her bed is the only way I can think clearly. I scan her room and find a notepad on her dresser. I scribble a message letting her know I'll be back by nine, and head out.

EVEN THOUGH IT'S only been about twenty-four hours since I last saw my apartment, this morning it feels… *barren.* Not just empty. Not just quiet. But destined never to be more than empty and quiet.

I'm used to spending precious little time here. It's a place to sleep, to eat a quick dinner after work or have a cup of coffee in the morning, but after one night at the Delacroix's house—a night that included a dinner run, a Marvel movie, and hours in Millie's bed—it feels like an abandoned cave, and I can't wait to get out.

Determined to be back before Millie can wake up and hatch any plans of her own to drive herself and Emmett to the doctor's, I shower and dress as fast as possible and make quick stops at the two other job sites, checking that everything is in order.

I pull both site managers aside at each location and fix an easy goal for the day. Jobs they can finish by noon. Or sooner. Tomorrow is Thanksgiving. For years, I watched Papi do the same thing for every major holiday.

It's only eight-thirty when I get back to the Delacroix's. Clarence greets me at the door, but despite the whine of the table saw in the garage, no one else is downstairs yet. Upstairs, every bedroom door is shut except Millie's. Hers is open just like I left it, but the bed is empty.

Right as I walk inside, her bathroom door opens, and Millie steps out—in the middle of pulling on her jeans.

"Christ!" I swear.

"Aagh!" she shrieks.

I cover my eyes, but it's too late. Blue on blue lace. *The* blue on blue lace thong I handled in her laundry room. Adorning her feminine valley. Disappearing into her jeans. For the rest of my life, I'll close my eyes and see nothing else.

"I'm sorry," I choke, gulping for air.

"What. The. Hell. Luc?" Her voice sounds like tearing paper.

I'm the biggest fuck up to ever fuck up. *Cabrón. Cabrón. Cabrón.*

"I'm sorry," I say again, still covering my eyes. "I was coming to check on you. I didn't think you were up."

I hope like hell her brothers haven't heard this. Or Mattie. Or Sam and Donner for that matter. Where the fuck has my professionalism gone?

"Your note said you'd be here by nine. I was trying to get ready." She sounds defensive, but, to my surprise, not really upset.

Blindly, I start walking backward. "I'll go wait downstairs."

"Well, I'm dressed *now*," Millie says, her tone comical. "Might as well open your eyes."

Deciding it's better to be a *cabrón* than a coward, I lower my fists. Millie is glaring at me, her hands on her hips. But she's holding her mouth tight, like she's trying not to smile.

"Relax," she says, giving in to the smile. "After all, I grabbed your pocket wrench last night."

I choke again. "M-my pocket wrench?"

Millie wrinkles her nose. "That doesn't really work does it?

Power drill? Nail gun? I was trying to go for just the right construction penis pun."

I convulse with laughter. *"Santa Maria,* you're delirious." I want to reach for her to check her fever, but I'm laughing too hard.

She shakes her head, laughing now too. "I feel like shit, but I'm not delirious." She rubs her head, turns, and sits down on the edge of her bed. "I wanted to take a shower, but I don't think I can stand up that long."

Without warning, I picture helping her in the shower, holding her in my arms while she washes her hair, and the laughter dies.

She moans, but not the way I'm about to, and collapses back onto the mattress. I go to her, sit by her, and put a hand to her forehead. She's hot. Still. How many days of fever does this make? Two? Three?

"Let's get you to the doctor's," I say softly. Her eyes are closed. Unwilling to stop myself, I trace the pad of my middle finger over her eyebrows. Their cayenne color leaves me unprepared for such softness.

In a slow sweep, my finger moves across her smooth forehead.

You are so beautiful.

I run my finger along her hairline where the richest red meets the fairest white. She sighs with a contentment I feel through my whole being. Because she lets me, I trail my fingertip down the elegant slope of her nose to the ripe beauty of her mouth.

Would she let me kiss her again? If she lets me trace the outline of her lips, could I kiss her again?

My tongue tells the tip of my finger what to do. Touch her right at the seam so she knows I want in.

Her lashes flutter, her lids lifting just enough so I know she's watching me. I feel my pulse everywhere. My chest. My throat.

The back of my knees. The tip of my finger. I wonder if she can feel it too.

"What are you doing?" It's not an accusation. She speaks softly in her hoarse voice, looking at me with just a hint of confusion.

I don't take my hand away. She can feel me. I want her to feel me.

"Planning to kiss you."

Her brows lift lazily. "But I'm sick."

"I still want to kiss you," I say with a shrug. She could have the plague and I'd want to kiss her. We still need to talk, but last night changed things. If nothing else, last night changed me. What I think is possible. And what isn't. Like not kissing her again.

I take her silence as assent, dip my hand to her chin, and tilt it up for me, giving her plenty of time to protest.

She doesn't.

Leaning over her, I brush my lips over hers. Softly. Patiently. Reverently. She is still sick. I'm not going to ask for too much or take advantage. Just let her know where my head is.

Where my heart is.

I press my mouth to hers, and Millie's breath catches. It's just my lips against hers. It should feel chaste. Tame. Instead, it feels like driving a Tesla. My blood goes from zero to sixty in 1.9 seconds. And when she touches my face, it's like I've upgraded to one of Elon Musk's rocket launchers.

And all of this velocity and heat is trapped within the borders of my skin, only allowed to pass into her where we touch. Lips. Hands. Faces.

Not enough.

My tongue is about to seek permission to call on hers when I hear a *thump*. Millie stiffens beneath me.

Thump-thump-thump.

"Shit," she mutters against my mouth, her other hand flattening against my chest. "They're up."

I admit it takes me a second to parse out what this means. And then I spring from her and get to my feet. I know without her having to say it. She would not want Harry, Mattie, or Emmett to walk in and see us kissing in her bed. For that matter, neither do I.

Down the hall, a door bangs open. Bare feet slap against wood. Another door in the hall. And then I hear the unmistakable knock of a toilet seat against a toilet lid.

Followed by the roar of retching.

"Oh fuck." Millie pushes up to sitting, but I wave her off.

"I've got it."

"But—"

I'm out the door before she can protest. Another retch emits from the bathroom, and I find Emmett hunched over the toilet bowl, white as paper.

"Hey, *jefe*," I say, leaning against the door frame. Emmett looks up at me, watery-eyed and shivering. And embarrassed. Can't have that. I nod at the toilet and the still clean floor. "Nice shot."

He doesn't say anything but coughs and spits into the bowl.

I reach for a clean washcloth on the shelf opposite the sink, wet it, and offer it to him. "Feeling any better?"

He nods, takes the cloth, and wipes his mouth. I don't need to touch him to know he's probably burning up just like Millie, but I put a hand to his forehead anyway.

"*Caliente.*"

He lifts his pale blue eyes to mine. "What's that mean?" he croaks.

"Hot. We need to get you and your sister to the doctor's." I drop my hand and point to the sink. "But not with puke breath. Rinse and brush first."

Emmett looks past me. "Did you throw up?"

I turn to find Millie behind me, holding her boots in one hand and looking the worse for wear from her trip down the hall.

"Not yet."

"I don't recommend it," her little brother says, and Millie and I both grin.

Emmett goes to the sink to clean up.

"You want to get dressed or go to Minute Med in your pajamas?" Millie asks him.

He rinses and spits. "Get dressed. I'm not a baby."

Millie's eyes meet mine in the mirror. My face says, *He told you.* Hers says, *Welcome to my life.*

If only she'd actually say those words out loud. I'd take her up on it.

Chapter Twenty

MILLIE

THE MINUTE MED IS LITERALLY THREE BLOCKS AWAY. I TRIED to convince Luc we could manage without him, but he refused to let me drive even that distance.

I was too tired to argue, so here we are.

The receptionist gives me two clipboards of paperwork to fill out for both Emmett and me, and we grab a row of seats in the waiting room, which is mostly empty. Only a couple of people are ahead of us.

"Let me help with that," Luc says, reaching past Emmett and grabbing one of the clipboards. "You fill in yours and *jefe* and I will do his."

I hold onto it for a second but then let go. I'm too tired to argue about this too, but it's more than that. It's just so dang sweet of him, and I don't know if I can handle it. The boundaries between us have seriously blurred since last night, and it's messing with my head.

I let him kiss me this morning.

It was pretty innocent as kisses go, but still. It must be the fever. My defenses are down. That's all. When I get some meds and feel better, I'll be able to fortify the walls.

Luc clicks the pen in his hand, bringing me back to the present. "Okay, Emmett. What's your full name and birthday?"

I turn my attention to the clipboard in my lap and start filling it in. Name. Date of birth. Address. Insurance information. Reason for coming in today. Medical history. I breeze through the questions until I don't.

Are you pregnant or breastfeeding?

No. No. And no. I mark an X over the no so hard, I almost tear the paper.

Have you ever been pregnant? If so, how many live births have you had?

I stare at the page until it blurs. I don't know if I can write it down and hold it together. How do you write *0* in the place where there should be a child?

Without warning, I'm blinking back tears, unable to move. Luc's questions for Emmett are no more than static. My head throbs. My throat aches. But it's nothing compared to the crushing in my heart.

"Hey." Luc is leaning past Emmett, his hand on my knee. "Everything okay?"

I swipe my knuckles across my eyes, nod, and flip the page. Why do I even need to answer those questions? I'm here for a fucking sore throat.

I clear my throat and try to get a grip, moving onto questions about my prescriptions. I'm signing the bottom of the second page when Emmett snort-laughs beside me.

"No?" Luc asks. "You don't have hemorrhoids today? Are you sure?"

My eyes whip to the two of them. Emmett is nearly doubled over in his seat, laughing, and Luc is frowning with mock seriousness.

"N-No," Emmett stammers in near hysterics.

"Hmm. What about flatulence? Are you flatulent?" Luc asks, pretending to check the form.

"Wh-what does that mean?"

"Gassy," Luc says, completely straight-faced. "Are you having excess gas?"

Like any eight-year-old boy, Emmett nearly comes apart at the seams. Sick or not, Emmett is a big fan of fart jokes.

I raise a brow at the two of them, but I do it fighting a smile. "Behave."

Luc turns his clinical frown to me. "What about you, Miss…" He pretends to glance at my form. "Miss Delacroix, which are you suffering from today? Constipation or diarrhea?"

Emmett is in danger of falling out of his chair.

I roll my eyes. "Are you finished with that?"

Luc unleashes The Dimples and hands me the clipboard. "Yes. You just need to sign the guardian parts."

I sign the forms, trying not to think too much about what I'm doing and why. Then I return the clipboards to the desk. A nurse opens the interior door and calls one of the other patients.

"How much longer?" Emmett says, now fully recovered from his fits of hilarity.

I look from Emmett to the other guy in the waiting room and back to Emmett. "There's still somebody ahead of us, buddy. That should be pretty obvious."

Emmett pulls a face. "I'm bored."

Of course, you are, I want to say. *You've been without entertainment for thirty seconds.* But somehow, I manage to keep this snippy comment to myself.

"Here, buddy," Luc says, reaching into his pocket. "Want to play Smash Road?"

Emmett's eyes go wide. "Yeah!"

Luc hands him his phone, and I want to kiss the man more than ever.

Luc gets up and paces around the waiting room, giving me a chance to check out his profile. And his butt in those jeans.

If I know anything for sure, it's that Luc Valencia is going to make some lucky woman very, very happy one day.

I stifle a sigh and pick up a magazine on the table in front of us. My eyes are just running over the pages when Luc sits down in the empty chair to my left. He manspreads so his right leg bumps my left.

I look over at him.

"You okay, *linda?*" he asks in a whisper.

I frown. "Does *linda* mean the same thing as *boba?* Because if so, the answer is no."

His teeth flash in a sudden smile. "You're so funny." Then he shakes his head and looks at me from under those curling lashes. "No. It means *beautiful.*"

My jaw unhinges. Before I can say anything, the interior door opens, and a teenage boy comes out. He goes to the guy waiting on the other side of the lobby, and they gather coats and keys. Then the nurse pops out again.

"Delacroixes?" she calls, eyeing us.

I stand. "Emmett, give Luc back his phone."

Emmett doesn't take his eyes off the screen. "But—"

"C'mon, buddy. It's our turn," I urge. I glance back at the nurse with a look of apology.

"Your boyfriend can come back, too, if you want."

My eyes must bug out of my head. "Oh, he's not my—"

"Yay!" Emmett cheers in triumph, clutching Luc's phone close.

I glance at Luc. His brows are raised, the scarred one make him look just a little wicked. As does the half-amused-half-cautious look in his eye.

"Buddy, I think that might be a little awkward for him," I say. When I glance back at Luc, he's smirking. I can almost read his mind. *More awkward than everything else?* This man has

227

smelled my stinky scrubs; viewed the inside of my dirty fridge; seen nearly all of my underwear; watched me cry; kissed me senseless; slept in Emmett's bed; slept in my bed; glimpsed me pulling up my pants; and witnessed my brother puking.

At the thought of it all, I blush to my roots. Yeah, maybe he's seen enough.

"C'mon, bud. It'll be quick."

"In and out," the nurse promises with a nod.

Emmett goes still. "Wait a minute," he says with suspicion, eyeing the nurse. "Are you going to give me a shot?"

Her poker face is terrible. "Only if it's *necessary.*"

Damn. Emmett has a thing about needles. It's understandable. I give injections nearly every day, and I'm still not jumping for joy at the prospect of being stuck by one. But Emmett has always hated shots.

And this is the first time without Mom and Dad that he's had to face one.

I look back at my little brother to find his eyes wide and his lips compressed. His gaze flicks to Luc. He's trying very hard to be brave. Emmett pulls in a deep inhale through his nose. I watch his chest rise and fall.

"I'm not a baby," he says under his breath, and I'm pretty sure he's saying this for no one but himself.

But bless his heart. He's only eight.

Emmett gulps and nods, looking resolved. "Luc, would you come back with us?"

Holy crap. What's he doing?

Surprise smacks Luc in the face, but he gets to his feet without hesitating. Then he glances at me. "I-If that's okay with your sister."

Now all eyes are on me, including the nurse who looks like she's about to run out of patience.

"I-I…"

Emmett steps closer and crooks his finger, beckoning me to bend down. When I do, he puts his mouth to my ear.

"I don't want to cry about getting a shot. That's for babies." He's whispering, but it's so quiet in the waiting room, Luc must hear it. "If Luc comes with us, I won't let myself cry. Not in front of him."

I hold Luc's gaze over Emmett's shoulder. Yeah, he's heard. His eyes are as soft as I've ever seen them. He gives me the slightest nod.

In for a penny. In for a pound.

I swallow my sigh. "Okay. Let's go."

The nurse looks relieved as she holds the door open for all three of us.

I'm sure I look the opposite as she motions me to the scale. "Okay, ma'am. You're first. Hop on."

Great.

I want to be all confident, body positive, and devil-may-care about Luc or anyone else knowing how much I weigh. The urge to order Luc to look away is almost more than I can master, but I do, toeing off my boots—hey, they're heavy—and stepping on.

But as it happens, after the nurse slides the chunky balance in place and taps the little weighted arrow until the beam levels out, she silently notes the number, keeping it private. I start to shiver a little as I step off the scale. I sneak a peek at Luc while I pick up my boots, but he has the good grace to be engrossed in studying Emmett's Smash Road progress.

I think I love him.

The thought sends me into such a tailspin I don't even notice what Emmett's weigh-in is and if it's normal or not.

Clearly, whatever virus or bacterium that has invaded my body has messed with my prefrontal cortex and likely amped up my amygdala. That's the obvious explanation because my logical, reasonable thinking is definitely not what it used to be, and my emotions—not to mention my sex drive—are throwing a rave.

Yep, nothing between my ears can be trusted until I crush this illness.

In the exam room, the nurse goes through her routine while I clutch my elbows against the chill. Q&A. Blood pressure. Temperature. Emmett and I both have fever, but mine is a little higher 102.6, compared to his 101.2.

"Dr. Singh will be right with you," she says before ducking out and leaving the three of us to stare at each other. So far, aside from the scale, none of this has been too awkward. At least it's a walk-in clinic, so there's no paper gowns.

I would have drawn the line at paper gowns.

"What?" Luc says, eyeing me funny.

Crap. Did I just say that out loud? Damn you, fever!

He's leaning against the empty exam table while Emmett and I languish on the chairs, but he straightens up and comes over to me. He bends down, searching my face. I want to grab him by the collar, yank him down, and mush his mouth against mine.

"Your eyes get glassy and you talk *loco* when your fever spikes," he says, his eyelids lowering as he studies me. "Did you take anything when you woke up?"

I don't even hear his question. He's too close.

"Back up, Valencia. My amygdala isn't the boss of me!"

His brows lift, his hand flattening against his slate-like abs as he laughs. "Wh-ha-ha-hat?"

"You heard me," I say, crossing my arms over my chest.

Luc shakes his head, amused.

Without warning, I want to cry. My bottom lip quivers and my eyes fill. What the hell is wrong with me?

"Hey." Luc isn't laughing anymore. He reaches forward and tucks a stray lock behind my ear. I put my hair in a ponytail today because I can't remember when I last washed it. I'm sure I look like a turd on roller skates. "You'll feel better soon. I'll take care of you until then."

My throat aches with the effort not to sob or sniffle. I force a nod and look down at my knees so I don't have to face Luc like this. I see his steel-toed boots step away and then return before he thrusts a tissue in front of my face.

Defeated, I take it and dab my eyes.

"It's okay, Millie," Emmett says beside me. "At least you didn't throw up."

The door opens then and woman in her forties with a lab coat and braid streaked with gray steps in. She takes in my current state and Emmett's pallor and addresses Luc. "What have we got here?" Her words are clipped, touched with an Indian or perhaps Pakistani accent.

Luc points to Emmett. "Sore throat, fever, vomiting. Started last night." Then he shifts to me. "Sore throat, chills, fever spikes, delirium, no appetite. Started probably Monday."

I blink, stunned at his account. I'd like to contradict him, but I can't. He's right.

Dr. Singh eyes me with pursed mouth. "Mmm. Not too good." She draws her stethoscope from around her neck and sets the earpieces in her ears, nodding to me. "You first."

She listens to my heart. My lungs. Shines a light in my nose. Checks my ears. Then I get the tongue depressor.

"Mmm. Very red," she says. "We'll swab it."

The nurse shadows her as she gives me a gag-inducing throat swab. Seriously, it's like I've tried to swallow a sword. The nurse takes the nasty thing to the back while the doctor swaps out her gloves and gives Emmett the exact same treatment, finishing him off too with a swab job.

"Shouldn't be long. Wait here." She leaves the room, and I clear my throat trying to shake the scratchy tickle. At least I don't feel like crying anymore.

"My money's on strep," Luc says, leaning against the table again.

I shrug. "Maybe. We're not coughing, so it's probably not flu."

The door swings open again.

"Streptococcus," the doctor says. Then she turns her pointed stare at me. "You shouldn't ignore a sore throat and high fever. Strep can develop into rheumatic fever, and if you get that, you'll have rheumatic heart disease. Not too good."

The nurse comes in with a tray bearing two syringes. Emmett gasps.

Dr. Singh looks at him and cracks her first smile. "These aren't for you, young man. They're for your sister."

"Both of them?" I ask, hoping the urge to cry isn't resurrected.

"Both," she says, and I'll be damned if she doesn't look happy about that. "That is, the penicillin you have to take. The cortisone is optional, but if you take it, you'll feel better by tomorrow."

"I want to feel better."

"Then two shots it is. Hip or thigh?"

"W-w-wait. Why doesn't he get one?" I jab my thumb at Emmett, who's now eyeing me like the traitor I am.

Dr. Singh smiles again. "You're worse off than he is. We caught his early. He gets the oral antibiotic. Hip or thigh?"

Since either one of those options require me to drop my pants, I point to Luc and Emmett. "You two. Out."

Emmett scrambles to his feet. "Thank God. I don't wanna watch."

Luc gives me a look of amused concern. "You sure, Millie? That cortisone shot is *fuerte*. I could hold your hand."

I shoot him a sour glare. "Go."

I have no idea what *fuerte* means, but it doesn't sound good. It's the nurse who does the honors while Dr. Singh scribbles out

Emmett's prescriptions on a pad. The penicillin is just a pinch. But Luc is right. The cortisone shot goes into my hip like a fiery lake through a straw.

"Sweet Jesus," I hiss, clutching the exam table.

When I join Emmett and Luc in the waiting room, I'm limping just a little.

Luc winces in sympathy. "I got one when I tangled with some poison ivy a couple of years ago. Burns like *El Diablo*."

I wave away his attention. "Worth it. I'll feel better tomorrow and—" I freeze.

Tomorrow. Tomorrow is Thanksgiving.

At the look on my face, Luc's brows shoot up. "What's wrong?"

I cover my mouth in horror. "Thanksgiving." My heart starts hammering in my chest. I recognize the symptoms of hyperventilation and sink into a chair. "I never—I never placed an order at Whole Foods."

I'd meant to do it Monday, but I felt like crap, and the day had been crazy with all of the kids' interruptions. Every free moment I had between patients I'd spent responding to their texts.

I look up at Luc. "Do you think I can place an order now and pick it up today?"

He just shrugs, looking completely unconcerned. "Maybe, but you're not going to."

I blink. "Why not?"

Les Dimples spring into action. "Because y'all are coming to my family's for Thanksgiving. Mami and Papi are already expecting you."

Emmett's eyes bug. Then he leaps into the air, fist held high. "Yes!"

"B-B-But…"

Chapter Twenty-One

LUC

"*Dios mío*, what are those?"

Millie is trying to lock her front door with a ginormous arrangement of flowers balanced on her hip.

"I can't go to your parents' house for Thanksgiving empty-handed," she says, turning her face away to avoid getting a mouthful of greenery. "That would be rude."

I climb the porch steps to unburden her as the kids race to my Tundra.

"Shotgun!" Emmett calls.

Someone's feeling better. I take the arrangement from Millie and call over my shoulder. "Not today, *jefe*. You three in the back."

He doesn't look back at me but drops his shoulders instead. "Awww."

"Not middle!" Harry shouts.

"Not middle!" Mattie echoes.

"Aww, *man!*" Emmett whines.

My eyes track to Millie who's dropping her keys into her purse with a look that clearly says, *Tell me about it.*

This woman. I swear. She has the patience of Job.

"How are you feeling?" I'm dying, *dying*, to touch her, but I don't. As much as I'd like it to be, this isn't a date. Of course, if it were, it wouldn't involve her siblings. Or my parents.

She nods her relief. "Much better, thanks. The doc wasn't lying about that cortisone shot."

I walk her to the passenger side of the Tundra just as the back doors slam shut. We have about three seconds of semi-privacy. I reach for the door handle before she can and stop.

"You look great," I say. And she does. Under her denim jacket, she's wearing a hunter green blouse that sets off her fiery hair and the vivid blue of her eyes. And I'm going to have a hard time keeping my eyes off those jeans today.

Millie looks great in scrubs. She looks great in anything. But scrubs don't do her hips and thighs justice like these jeans.

"Thank you." For all her stubbornness and spirit, Millie can't take a compliment without blushing. That goes with the hunter green too. "So do you."

The way her gaze sweeps over me, I realize she has never seen me cleaned up. Millie doesn't say more, but I pick up plenty when she swallows and takes a second look.

"You ready?" I ask.

Ooph. Wrong question. That just killed the mood. Worried eyes meet mine. "I can't believe I agreed to this."

Actually, I can't believe it either. It took some convincing, and not just from me. The rest of the Delacroix clan had to mount a pretty solid offensive with specific avenues of attack. *We'll get to be with Luc!* (Emmett's). *There will be kids there our age!* (Mattie's). *Mexican food!* (Harry's). I'm not sure if they ever really convinced her or just wore her down, but out of all the many things I'm thankful for, the fact that they did is what I'm celebrating today.

"It'll be fine," I promise. "It'll be fun."

It'll be a zoo, but I haven't mentioned that yet.

I open the truck's door before she can change her mind, help her in, and hand back the flowers.

I WAS WRONG.

It isn't a zoo. It's a circus. With at least one sideshow in every room of my parents' house. Papi and Uncle Raul are singing *"Cielito Lindo"* for Abuela, who sits in her glider, rowing back and forth to their serenade. As always, her glider is camped in front of the TV, which is tuned to NBC's coverage of the Macy's Thanksgiving Day parade. The TV's volume is somewhere between obnoxious and ear-splitting.

My cousin Felicité's two boys, Isaac and Ian, ages six and five respectively, fight on the sofa over what looks like pieces of a Happy Meal toy. I lead the Delacroixes past the serenade and the scuffle into the buzzing hive of the kitchen, where Mami, Aunt Lucinda, and all four of my cousins are talking over each other, stirring, tasting, grating, and basting. As soon as we walk in, Mami's hands shoot up like she's doing the wave. She rushes over, pushing Aunt Lucinda—who's filling circles of dough with pumpkin puree—out of the way.

"¡Bienvenidos! Welcome! Welcome!" she shouts, wiping her hands on her apron. She opens her arms, aiming to hug Millie, who looks terrified. But to my surprise, Millie hands me the flowers and—instead of bolting for the door—leans in, stepping into Mami's embrace, the back half of her torso disappearing behind my mother's bingo wings, the front lost in Mami's ample bosom.

"You must be Millie," Mami says into her hair. "Luca has told us so much about you."

I groan, but with all the noise in here, no one else can hear it. I've mentioned Millie to Mami exactly three times. Granted, yesterday morning's conversation about her and the kids was the most detailed, but I don't need Millie to think I'm more obsessed with her than I am.

She knows enough already.

Drawing back, Millie shoots me a surprised look. "He has?" I can tell what she's thinking, and I hope she can read my expression just as clearly.

No, boba. Nothing about underwear or kissing or sleeping in your bed. Or about how I can't stop thinking about you either. But she might have guessed that one already.

Mami still grips Millie's elbows, keeping her close. "All good, *Dr.* Delacroix. Very impressive for someone so young," she adds conspiratorially. I hold my breath. I told Mami about the family's situation, but I made her promise on her rosary she wouldn't bring it up.

"I'm Inez Valencia, Luca's mother, but please call me Nezzie. Everyone does." Mami turns to Millie's siblings and puts a knuckle to her chin. "Now, let me see if I remember. We haven't met, but I know Harry from the team." Without warning, she pulls him into a hug, releases him and captures Mattie. "And you're Mattie…"

When it's his turn, Emmett is ready for her, arms open wide. Mami laughs. "And that makes you Emmett." When she folds him into her arms, I catch the look on his face. Eyes closed, a dreamy smile lifting the corners of his mouth.

And my worries vanish. The Valencia's might be loud and pushy and coming out of the woodwork. But we also might just be what these four need today.

I close in. "Happy Thanksgiving, Mami," I say, leaning in to press a kiss to her plump cheek and hoping she knows I'm grateful. "It smells great in here. These are from Millie."

I hand her the flowers and she exclaims over them for a good thirty seconds. "Esme," she calls to one of my cousins. "Please put these on the dining table."

When the flowers are out of the way, Harry edges closer to

the island and points to Lucinda's tray. "What are those?" His worshipful tone charms my aunt, and she beams at him.

"These are my pumpkin empanadas," she says, folding over one of the stuffed dough circles and sealing the edges together with the back of a fork. "Or they will be after they're baked. I'm Aunt Lucy, and these are my girls."

Aunt Lucinda proceeds to introduce all my cousins, from oldest to youngest: Felicité, Natalia, Rosa, and Esme. Isaac and Ian run through the kitchen to the back door, Natalia's four-year-old daughter Sofie trailing behind them.

"We're going on the trampoline," Isaac shouts as he bangs into the screen door by means of opening it. The younger ones careen after him.

Mami turns to Emmett. "Would you like to go too?"

It's written all over his face that he does. He's older than the little ones. I wasn't sure if playing with them would clash with his motto of not being a baby, but he seems more than eager. He nods and looks to Millie for permission.

"Go on. Just be careful," she says. Before she can say anything else, he's out the door, tearing after the others.

Alex sweeps in from the living room. "Hey," he says in greeting. "Are the appetizers out yet?"

Both Harry and Mattie eye him as though he's the Holy Grail. Harry because he's asking about food. Mattie because he's Alex.

Mami moves around the island. "Come here, you three." They obey as one body, and she points out bowls and platters. "Take the guac, salsa, chips, and veggies out to the coffee table. Don't spoil your appetites, okay?"

Alex takes over, handing the bowl of guacamole to Mattie, the plate of veggies to Harry, and taking the salsa and chips. "C'mon," he says, and the three of them are gone.

Millie blinks after them, worry in the corners of her eyes.

She steps closer to me and drops her voice for my ears only. "Do you think—"

"They're fine."

Her eyes narrow now in annoyance. "You don't even know what I was going to ask," she hisses.

I arch a brow. Her eyes follow the movement, and for a half an instant, she just stares. I realize it's the brow the goalie from St. Thomas More split with his class ring. That was sophomore year—after I got past him in the state quarterfinals and helped the Lions advance to the semis.

Millie is checking out my scar. How about that.

"Yes, I do." I keep my voice low. "Mattie's fine. Alex isn't going to seduce her."

Horror rounds her eyes. She sneaks a peek at Mami before glaring back at me. "Shh! I don't want to offend your mom. She's nice."

My grin is wry. "We're all nice, *Doña Angustias.*"

She scowls. "Calling me names I can't understand is not nice, *coquin.*"

I chuckle under my breath. "What? Is that French?"

She nods with mock menace. "Uh huh. Doesn't feel too great, does it?"

I laugh outright. Because she's funny as hell. And because she's wrong. It feels amazing. Laughing with her. Being with her. It's the best. But I put my hands up in surrender.

"Okay. Okay. *Doña Angustias* is like a worry wart." I nod toward the living room. "The kids are there with my dad, my uncle, and my grandmother. We can go in with them, but I don't think they're short on chaperones."

Millie exhales through her nose. It sounds like she's still worried, but she can't really argue against three chaperones.

"Millie, would you like a margarita?" Felicité asks, holding up a pitcher.

With a look of what must be real regret, Millie shakes her

head. "I'm on antibiotics," she says, wrinkling her nose. "I wish I could."

The women in my family all burst into choruses of sympathy, offering her everything from guava juice to soda to iced tea. All the fuss makes her turn a pretty shade of pink.

I lean over and whisper in her ear, "If you just let them put something in a cup, they'll leave you alone."

"Tea would be great."

But I make matters worse when I pour it for her, and all— *all*—of my cousins tease and cat call me in two languages.

Luca tiene una novia.

Look at what good manners.

¿Por qué no me sirves un poco de té, primo?

Ooh, I think he likes her.

I expect Millie to look mortified, but she eats it up. Probably because it's at my expense. I tell them to shut up in Spanish, and the room erupts in feminine laughter. Millie's included. By the time I hand her the tea, she looks relaxed, like she's having a good time.

It's a good look for her.

"Can I help with anything?" Millie asks, peering around the kitchen, searching for a job to do.

I want to grab her by the hand and tug her into the den where it's quieter. Maybe we can shoot a game of pool.

But my cousin Rosa beats me to the punch.

"Want to pressure cook the tamales?" she asks Millie.

"Uh..."

At Millie's nervous expression, Rosa smiles. "It's not hard. I promise. They're already wrapped. You just have to layer them right. I'll show you."

"Sure."

And with that, Rosa pulls her to the other side of the kitchen. Mami sweeps her hands at me toward the living room.

"Go find your Papi. Talk to him about work. He misses it."

I grab one last look at Millie, who's carefully picking up a husk-wrapped tamale, and head back to the living room. But Papi and my uncle are no longer there. Mattie, Harry, and Alex are sitting on the couch—Alex in the middle of the twins —laughing and eating guacamole. The Thanksgiving Day Parade coverage still blares from the TV, but Abuela is dozing in her glider.

Papi and Uncle Raul are playing a game of cutthroat in the den. I grab a beer from the mini-fridge and crack it open.

"How's work, *sobrino?*" Raul asks.

I greet him with a handshake and nod. "Busy."

"Busy is good," he says.

Papi takes a shot, knocking in the eleven. "Looks like you've been busier than usual," he says, inclining his head toward the kitchen and Millie. The flatness in his tone catches my attention.

I take a sip of my beer, debating my response. "Not so much." I'd like to be a hell of a lot busier where Millie is concerned, but that's a thought I'll keep to myself.

"No?" Papi ask, stepping away from the pool table— limping as he does and using his pool stick as a cane—to let Raul take his turn. "You seemed too busy when you came in to even greet your *abuelita* and introduce your friend."

I keep my tone light. "I didn't want to interrupt the performance."

Papi raises a bushy, gray brow. "You sure you weren't embarrassed, *mijo?*"

I snort. "You and Raul didn't sound *that* bad," I joke. My uncle chuckles, and I grin to hide the twist in my gut. Yeah, I was a little embarrassed that at the exact moment I walked in with Millie and her brood, Papi and Raul were already singing to Abuela. That's usually a tradition that comes with dessert. After a few toasts at the dinner table. Maybe more than a few toasts. "A little early though, no?"

My father shrugs. "I saw you pull up, and I thought I'd give your guests a traditional Mexican song in welcome."

I tuck my chin. "So that was for them? Not Abuela?" The twist in my gut cinches a little tighter. Had he started singing then to make Millie and her family feel welcome? Or to make them feel different?

Another shrug. "Your *abuela* enjoyed it, I think."

His words are innocent, and his lips are turned up at the corners, but in a hard smile. A sarcastic smile. The way he used to smile at workers who had lied about being sick to miss work.

My eyebrows close ranks. "Papi, you should know, nothing's going on between me and Millie Delacroix, but I like her. A lot," I say, my gaze moving between his and Raul's. My uncle has the good grace to look uncomfortable. "I consider her a friend."

Papi's mouth bunches and turns down like a catfish's. He adjusts his grip on the pool stick. "Which is it, Luca?"

I blink. "Which is what?"

"Do you like her? A lot? Or are you friends?"

I cough and shake my head. Okay. He's got me there.

"Honestly, I like her, but friendship is all she's ready for right now."

"Mmm hmm," he says, nodding like this is what he expected.

I glower. "You have a point, Papi?"

His sarcastic smile slips. "She's white."

I nod. "Yeah, I noticed." Now, I'm the one wearing a sarcastic smile. I'd figured he'd have an opinion about this. I hadn't expected him to come out and say something. Millie wouldn't be the first white girl I've dated—if we were actually dating, which we're not—but she's the first one I've brought to a holiday dinner. Dating or no.

In fact, the only other girl I've ever brought to a holiday

gathering was Ronni. And I brought her to all of them. For four years in a row.

Papi's eyes become slits. "And she's a client."

This one hits me below the belt.

If he doesn't like me being with Millie because she's white, that's his problem. He'll have to deal with it. If he thinks I'm crossing a line because she's a client, well, he's not the only one.

"Like I said, she's just a friend." Who I've kissed. Twice. And slept next to. And seen in her underwear.

And I'd give my eyeteeth to do all of the above on a regular basis.

His sarcastic smile is definitely gone now. "You said she doesn't want you. You should leave her be—"

My skin erupts in heat, and almost without knowing it, I switch to Spanish. *"I said she's not ready for more than that right now. She's been through a lot."*

His brows lower and his hands open in concession. *"Mami told me. I was sorry to hear about her parents."* Papi crosses himself, and I know his words are genuine. I cross myself too, with a prayer for the repose of Eloise and Hudson Delacroix's souls and the peace and sustenance of their children. *"Just remember, that business still has my name on it. Be careful what kind of reputation you build with it. People aren't hiring you for that."*

I flinch at this. *"It's not like that, Papi,"* I say, scowling. *"And as for our reputation, nothing's changed. Nothing's going on and no one would know if it were."*

His brow shoots up in doubt. *"Your men don't know? They don't see you 'being friends' with this woman?"* Papi uses air quotes when he says this, and while his tone pisses me off, I can't lie. My stomach bottoms out a little because as discreet as I've tried to be, Donner and Sam have to have noticed something. And if they have, it's possible some of the other guys know it too.

But really, what would they have noticed? Me staring after

Millie? Me sticking around after they leave? Me making sure none of them sets foot in the laundry room to access the breaker box in case some of her thongs are lying around?

The best they'd be able to tell would be that I have a thing for her. Neither one of them know I spent the night Tuesday. Just Millie and the kids know that.

Shit.

The kids. Mattie and Harry are hanging out with Alex right now.

Papi's eyes narrow on me in scrutiny. *"You know how long it took me to get back into this country and start that business?"*

This, too, hits below the belt. *"You know I do, Papi."* And if he hadn't gotten sick, he'd still be running the show. Not me. And he never lets me forget it.

"So have a care with what I'm leaving to you and your brother."

His words burn like cinders in the pit of my stomach. I've had enough of this conversation. But I refuse to give him the last word.

"I'm taking care of it, Papi. But the business isn't the only thing I want to take care of."

Chapter Twenty-Two

MILLIE

I'm. Completely. Stuffed.

Luc wasn't lying when he said his mom could cook. So can his aunt. And his cousins. Rosa's beef tamales. Felicité's chili-lime butternut squash. Esme's cornbread. And, holy moly, his mom's turkey in mole sauce.

I thought nothing could be better than Aunt Lucinda's pumpkin pie empanadas, but then Luc and his brother Alex made me try them with a scoop of butter pecan ice cream.

The food has been great, but the hospitality has made this so easy. I love Luc's family's home. And it's obvious that this is the home of a builder. The kitchen is to die for, and even though the dining room beyond it isn't huge, the vaulted ceiling and arched windows give it an airy feel—despite the presence of two full tables.

Across the room at the kids' table, Harry looks like he's had a religious experience. He lists back in his chair, eyes glazed, looking full for the first time in months. Mattie is doe-eyed too, but that's because she's hanging on Luc's little brother's every word.

Emmett, on the other hand, is laughing. Luc's cousin

Natalia is teaching all the kids how to balance spoons on the ends of their noses. So far, she can get two of them going, but someone starts giggling as soon as a third one joins, and then spoons clang to the floor.

Everyone is smiling.

At least they are now. When we all sat down to dinner, Luc's shoulders rippled with tension, and the look in his eyes was as dark as a thunderhead.

It didn't last long. His father sat at the head of the table, welcomed me and the kids, thanked his wife, sister-in-law, and nieces for the feast, and then closed his eyes for grace.

In that moment, Luc's hand clasped mine in my lap and squeezed it while his father thanked the Almighty for our blessings. Luc's fierce grip made my heart flutter like a baby bird, all downy and off balance. Learning to fly.

I'd squeezed back.

He'd held onto it until it was time to eat, and then he tried to serve my plate as well as his, but his cousins gave him hell for it, making me laugh. He lost his dark look after that.

I lean toward him. "Thank you for this."

His eyes meet mine, those curling lashes stealing my breath for a moment. "You're so welcome, Millie."

If things were different—if they could be different—it would be the most natural thing in the world to lean closer and steal his kiss.

Flushed, I tear my gaze away and see that the kids are pushing back from their table, shedding their post-feast stupor like only kids can. Alex makes a furtive glance toward his parents and then beckons the twins to follow.

"Alejandro, where do you think you're going?" Nezzie asks, giving him the stink eye.

At his name Luc's brother freezes, wide eyed. He reaches down and picks up his plate and silverware. "I was just going to start clearing up," he says innocently.

Nezzie smiles. "That's what I thought, *mijo.*"

At this, Luc gets to his feet, as do Natalia and Felcité's husbands, Paco and Juan Carlos. Or Juan Carlos and Paco. I can't remember now who is married to whom. I rise too, and it's like I've overturned the table.

Lucinda flaps a hand at me. "Sit back down, *querida.* When the women cook, the men clean. Family rules."

"Oh." I drop back in my chair. "That's nice."

"C'mon, Harry and Emmett," Luc says. "We'll show you how it's done."

Harry bristles. "Mattie didn't cook. Why can't she help?"

"Because," Alex says, stacking Mattie's plate and silverware onto his and winking down at her, "this time she gets a free pass."

Oh Jesus.

Mattie turns pink, but her eyes follow Alex as though he just lifted her plate using Harry Potter's *Wingardium Leviosa* charm. Still, if he wants to be The Boy Who Lived, he'd better not touch my sister.

"You finished?" Luc asks, reaching down for my dishes.

I sit back, startled. "Oh, yes. Thank you." And, okay, yeah, maybe I watch him walk away like he's magical too. Have the men in Luc's family stumbled onto some kind of aphrodisiac secret? Does clearing the dishes make a man suddenly more attractive?

And an already attractive man suddenly irresistible?

Judging by the contented and appreciative smiles of the other women at the table, who sit back as their husbands clean up, I'd have to say yes.

Luc's mother turns to Mattie, who's now sitting at the kids' table by herself. "*Niña,* why don't you come join us at the big table?"

Mattie rises, gives a longing look toward the kitchen, but comes and sits across from me, next to Nezzie.

"What did you girls think of your first Mexican Thanksgiving, ah?" she asks us.

"O-Oh," Mattie stammers, blushing anew. "Everything was *really* good."

"So good," I add. "Thank you so much for having us."

Nezzie beams, clearly pleased. "You're welcome anytime."

Mattie smiles. "You're a really good cook. It's been a while since we've had a home-cooked meal like that—" My sister clamps her mouth shut, realizing what she's said. She looks to me. "I mean…"

"It's okay, Matt," I say gently and turn to Nezzie. "She's right. My cooking doesn't even come close."

And because it feels wrong not to, I look back at Mattie and add, "To yours or to our mother's."

As soon as I mention Mom, the rest of the table goes quiet. If I wasn't sure before, I am now. Luc's family knows about mine. They've all been so nice. I hope it hasn't been out of pity. But I suppose, under the circumstances, their knowing makes things easier. No one's asked why we're not spending the holiday with our family, and while I'm grateful for that, not talking about them doesn't seem right either.

As though she recognizes this, Nezzie's face softens. "What did your mother make for Thanksgiving?"

Mattie answers first. "Really good roast turkey with gravy and cornbread dressing and rice." She looks down in her lap. I can see she's smiling at the memory of it. Of course, when she looks up to me, her eyes are shining.

Mine are too.

"And this butternut squash and kale recipe I think she got from Martha Stewart ages ago," I add, dreamily summoning the memory. "It had heavy cream and parmesan and roasted garlic in it."

"Ooh," Felicité sighs. "I might have to make that next year."

My eyes go wide. "Oh, but your butternut squash dish was *divine,*" I say, hoping I haven't offended her.

She arches a brow in a way that reminds me of Luc. "Yeah, but yours sounds *devilish,* and I'm tempted."

We all laugh.

"You know," Natalia says, putting her elbows on the table and leaning forward. "I bet you could find that recipe online— if it really was a Martha Stewart one."

"Found it," Rosa announces, phone in hand.

"You found it?" I ask, a little breathless. I hadn't even tried looking for it. I just figured it was one of the many recipes Mom used to make that was gone for good.

"Roasted garlic...butternut squash...kale...nutmeg... heavy cream..."

"That *sounds* like it."

She passes me her phone. "Well, does it look like it?"

I check out the picture of a casserole dish filled with golden slices of butternut topped with breadcrumbs.

"That has to be it."

"May I see," Felicité asks. I hand her the phone, and she reads the recipe. "That doesn't look too hard. Maybe you and I could make this for Christmas."

"Wait, me?" I ask stunned.

Luc's cousin smiles. "Why not?"

Because you just met me? Because I'm a terrible cook? Because no one said anything about Christmas?

"Oh—Oh," I stammer. "You're all so kind..."

"I think it's a great idea," Nezzie says, smiling.

I give Mattie a quick glance. She looks as surprised as I must, but she's smiling too. Clearly, the idea of spending Christmas here sounds good to her.

Christmas.

Heaven help me. If the thought of how we'd get through Thanksgiving daunted me, Christmas is way, way beyond scary.

If Mom were here, she'd start decorating tomorrow. By Saturday, we'd have a tree.

Oh God. I need to get busy.

If this is really an invitation, maybe I should just accept. We've made it through the day without disaster. And it's been pretty fun. More fun than I thought the first Thanksgiving without Mom and Dad could have been. Of course, I'll have to talk to the boys. And Luc.

Christmas is a whole month from now. He might be totally sick of us by then.

I blow out a breath. "Thank you." I look around the table. All the women in Luc's family are watching me, near identical soft smiles on their faces. "We're so glad to be here today. I-I never would have expected—"

Nezzie covers my hand with hers. "Luc is very fond of you. All of you," she says. "What makes him happy makes me happy."

With those words, it hits me. Maybe Luc's family isn't being so nice because they feel sorry for us. Maybe it's simply because we are Luc's guests.

My heart swells a little at that thought.

Luc's grandmother—I don't even know her name; everyone just calls her *Abuela*—reaches across Luc's empty chair and takes my other hand. Her joints are knobby with arthritis, but her grip is still strong.

"Él es un buen chico. Luca tiene un buen corazón," she says.

A little panicked, I hold her gaze and then look around the table. "I'm sorry," I say in a hushed voice. "I don't speak Spanish."

The other women start to answer, but Mattie pipes up. "She said, 'Luc's a good boy,'" she says, giggling. "And 'he has a good heart.'"

"Oh," I gasp, nodding. "Yes… He is a very good man." I'm not about to call him a boy. He's a man. But she's right. He's a really good one. For a moment, I'd like to tell her everything he's done for me—for us—but I don't have the words, and one look at Luc's cousins, and I think better of it. They really like teasing him.

Before I can say anything else, Alex pokes his head back into the dining room, eyes on Mattie. "We're going outside to kick the soccer ball around. Wanna come?"

Mattie pushes her chair back so fast I'm afraid it'll clatter to the ground. She catches it in time and looks back at me and Nezzie, blushing. "Please excuse me."

And before I can reply, before she can even catch the concern on my face, she's gone.

She can't get pregnant playing soccer in the back yard, I reason. Even though I know that's true, I can't help the clenching in my stomach at the thought of Mattie dating.

Luc's grandmother pats me on the hand again. *"Alejandro es un buen chico tambien."*

This time, I don't need the translation. I put on a smile. "I'm sure he is," I say. But I've met fourteen-year-old boys. They want the same things sixteen and twenty and twenty-four-year-old boys want.

The real trouble is the girls want it too.

The truth of this becomes painfully obvious when Luc walks back in, drying his hands on a dishtowel. I've never before thought dishtowels were sexy, but, holy cow, watching it twist and strain under his dark hands has me picturing him gripping the bed sheets.

He smiles at me over the heads of his cousins still at the table. "Wanna go outside and watch the kids?"

Is he reading my mind? I rise from the table. "Let me just get my jacket."

The air is crisp, but it's not as bitterly cold as it has been the last few days. The custom-made touches I noticed inside the Valencia's home spill outdoors too. A covered patio with stone tile flooring is semi-enclosed by an outdoor kitchen with a fireplace, sink, and grill with lots of granite counter space. The lawn is deep, and the big kids have plenty of room to kick the soccer ball, while the little ones play on a netted trampoline in the back corner.

Luc leads me to a cushioned patio sofa, and I nearly collapse into it.

"I'm so tired," I say, yawning.

Sitting beside me, Luc cocks his head to the side. "Should we go? You're still recovering."

I shake my head, watching the kids. "They're having fun." It reminds me of the other night. Except this time Harry is paired with Emmett, and Mattie and Alex make up a team.

No surprise there.

I sigh. If I ever had the power to delay Mattie's first crush, I don't anymore. Let's face it. I probably never did. And it could be worse. If Alex is anything like his brother, Mattie will be one pretty lucky fourteen-year-old.

But then again, if he's anything like Luc, how is she going to be able to control herself?

"What's the matter?" Luc asks.

I jump, pulled from my worries, and find him watching. "Nothing… Everything's fine."

He rolls his eyes. "That word is your tell. If you use it, something's wrong." He pins me with his stare. "What is it?"

I tried to tell him the other night, but he looked at me like I was crazy. It *is* crazy. But frogs sometimes rain from the sky. That shit's crazy too, but it's still real. The Curse is real.

I sigh again, this time out of frustration. "I don't think I can explain it to you."

He's sitting right beside me. Our hips are almost touching. He leans back and rests his arm along the back of the sofa. Not touching me, but I feel his closeness, and I like it. I'd love to just lean in.

Touching him Tuesday night had felt all kinds of right. It had been a heady mix of need, fulfillment, and a long-lost comfort. I want more. Now that I've known it, I'm afraid I'll want it all the time.

He's looking at me now, humor in his eyes. Just a hint of a smile on his lips. I kissed those lips only yesterday. It had been so natural. Just like breathing.

"Try," he says.

For an instant, I think he's talking about kissing. Telling me to try to kiss him. I wouldn't even need to try. It would be so easy. What I'm *trying* to do is not kiss him. Not touch him. And still be near him.

Everything is better when I'm near him.

I open my mouth to attempt a response when the door behind us bursts open. "Isaac! Ian! Time to go!" Felicité shouts across the lawn. The three littles halt their bouncing for all of one second, glance at each other, and start up again. Felicité mutters something in Spanish under her breath. "C'mon, *niños*. I know you heard me. Sofie, you too. Nezzie has something for you."

The little girl stops jumping and clings to the net of the trampoline. "What she got, *Tia?*"

Felicité shrugs, all innocence, and turns up her palms. "I don't know. Why don't you come see?"

Little Isaac grips the trampoline net and puts his mouth inside one of its holes. "Why does Nezzie have something for her and not us?" he asks, scowling at the injustice.

His mother's forehead wrinkles as her brows raise, hamming up the mystery. "Maybe we should go ask her."

Bitten by the curiosity bug, the kids scramble out of the trampoline.

"Tell Cousin Luc and his friend Millie bye-bye," Felicité tells them as they shoot past us.

"Bye!'

"Bye!"

"Goo-bye!" Three small voices shout before they disappear inside.

Felicité blows out a gust of air. "The price for a quick exit will be the sugar rush from the cookies Nezzie gives them," she says, brushing her dark bangs out of her eyes. "I just hope they crash with enough time for a nap before we go to my mother-in-law's tonight."

"A nap sounds terrific," I say, nearly moaning with envy.

Felicité gives me a tired smile. "Doesn't it, though?" Then she stoops down and hugs Luc before turning and hugging me. "Good seeing you, Luc. Wonderful to meet you, Millie. And it's on. You. Me. We are totally making that butternut squash dish for Christmas."

The reminder startles me, and I blurt a nervous laugh while Luc eyes me in question.

When his cousin disappears inside, he tips his chin at me. "What was that about?"

I shrug. "Just recipe talk." I shake my head, dismissing the idea. "We can pretend that didn't happen."

His brows lower. "You mean you being here for Christmas? Yeah, no. We're not pretending that didn't happen," a grin spreads over his face, "because I'd love for you to come for Christmas."

Heat blooms beneath my cheeks. But a honeyed warmth also bubbles up in my chest. I want to tell him I'd love it too. That I'll look forward to it. But I have to be careful. Even though I want to be near him, I can't let myself get too close.

I nod. "I'd like that, but…" I watch him wait on my words. "We'll see."

He mirrors my nod. "We'll see," he echoes with acceptance.

"Good," I say, and then cover my mouth as I yawn.

"You really do need a nap."

I shake my head. "I'm okay." The kids are playing hard core now. Laughing. Shouting. Tearing across the yard. "I'm good for now."

Luc stands up and holds out a hand. "Come with me."

I don't move. "Where are we going?"

He closes and opens his fingers, beckoning. "Trust me. You'll like this. C'mon."

I do trust him. Better still, he's giving me a reason to touch him, and I've been jonesing for that since he grabbed my hand during the blessing. I place my hand in his, and his surrounding warmth is my immediate reward.

Then we're moving across the yard toward the trampoline. Not at all what I expected.

"I don't think I'm up for bouncing on that."

He grips my hand tighter. "No bouncing. I promise."

Luc mounts the steps, but sits on the top one and toes off his shoes. He nods at me, still holding my hand, though I haven't left terra firma. "Now you."

Eyeing him with suspicion, I sink down on the middle step and pull off my boots. When he slips in through the slitted opening, I follow, still skeptical. Crawling on all fours, Luc makes his way to the middle, and I have to say, I may regret climbing up here with him, but I don't regret the view.

When he reaches the center of the mat, he sits, leaning back on his hands, his legs stretched out in front of him. This is another view I don't regret. But I'm confused.

"What are we doing up here?"

He wears the slightest smile, but he looks rather pleased with himself. "You're gonna take a nap."

I blink. "Excuse me?"

He pats the springy black surface beside him. "Come here and lie down."

"Uh, no."

His brows pull together, but his smile only grows. "Why not?"

I open my mouth. Close it. "B-because." It's the best answer I can come up with at the moment. And then a better one arrives. "It'll look ridiculous."

He glances at the soccer game. "You think they'll care? Even if they do notice?"

I look back. No. They're all having too much fun. When was the last time I heard Emmett giggling like that? And Mattie? My God, she's beaming. Harry's out of breath, shouting directions at his brother. I watch them for a while, a bittersweet sting spreading through my chest.

When I don't answer, Luc shrugs. "I'll go first." And then he flops onto his back, the movement shaking the trampoline's surface and jostling me just a little.

Seeing him lying here in his wine-red dress shirt and jeans, his stocking feet making him look both sexy and unguarded, I feel a pull right in my middle. I answer it and crawl to him. But I don't lie down. That's just asking for trouble.

He smiles up at me and then looks past me at the sky. I glance up. The Valencia's yard is edged with tall pine trees, but from this spot on the trampoline, the sky is an unbroken blue. That thick blue light of fall that can turn to gray with just a shift in the wind. It's cooler out here than under the shelter of the patio, but I'm still not cold.

Which is good. Because if I were, the temptation to snuggle up to Luc might be more than I could handle.

But I try not to dwell on that. I just keep looking at the sky, letting my mind clear. A pair of geese pump their way across the endless blue with silent effort. Just those two. A mated-pair. They make me think of my parents. My lungs empty.

"You okay?" Luc asks.

I look down and find him watching me. "Yes," I say truthfully. Sometimes I can think of them, and it's peaceful. I'm not sad. Not angry. Not restless. Right now is one of those times. They don't last long, but I'm grateful for them. "Just relaxing."

"You could relax more—even sleep—if you'd lie down," he says and then closes his eyes. It's like a gift because now I can stare.

God, you are so beautiful.

"I'm good," I say, softly, because right now, I am.

How long could we be friends? I mean, are we really friends? Friends might take care of each other when one is sick, but they don't kiss. Not on the lips, anyway.

Luc's lips are too gorgeous. Sensual. Just shy of full. The deep blush of passion fruit. Soft, yet unmistakably male. Friends don't stare at each other's lips. How long will I get to do this?

Will he still want to spend time with me at Christmas? Or after the kitchen is finished? I know he's attracted. He knows I am too. How long until he gives up on me, knowing nothing can happen for years?

"Lie down, Millie," Luc says with his eyes still closed. "I can't sleep with you staring at me like that."

I nearly bounce out of the trampoline. "How did you—" Then I swat him on the shoulder. "You were spying on me behind your eyelids."

His laughter bounces us a little more. "I'm not sorry," he says, mischief in his eyes.

I go to swat him again—if I'm being honest, just to touch him—but he captures my hand. "It's mine now," he says, is voice low and teasing. He doesn't let go. And when I look back, the mischief is gone. "Lie down with me, Millie. Please."

It's the *please* that does me in.

I lie on my side, facing him. He turns toward me, our hands linked between us. My heart hammers so hard, I'm afraid it'll shake the trampoline.

"Just for a little while," I whisper.

He nods. "Just for a little while."

We stare at each other, neither one trying to hide it this time.

For a long moment, nothing else exists. Just him. Just me. We're a thousand miles away from anyone else.

His throat moves as he swallows. "Millie. Tell me what you're afraid of."

I don't want to have this conversation now. Not here. "What do you mean?"

Luc squeezes my hand. "Don't play with me," he says, and the way he says it, guilt congeals in my stomach like instant grits. "You know what I mean."

I tuck my chin. "You're right. I do." I shake my head. "But I can't explain it any better than I already have."

His brow screws up into a frown. "Let me see if I've got it straight." He's been holding my hand with his left, but he swaps it now, covering it in his right so he can prop up on his elbow and peer down at me. "You're attracted to me." When he says this, he squeezes my hand, and a shower of invisible sparks soar up my arm and go off like Roman candles in my heart.

"Yes," I manage, my mouth going dry.

"And I'm attracted to you."

The Roman candles go forth and multiply.

I lick my lips. "Okay…" Because what else am I going to say to that?

"But you can't handle a relationship because Emmett, Mattie, and Harry come first right now."

"Yes…" I hope he can hear the disappointment in my voice, because I sure can. "It's a little more complicated than that, but in a nutshell, yes."

He nods. "I agree they come first. They're just kids, and they're your family…"

The Roman candles turn into beeswax candles and start to

melt. Everything inside me—my heart, my resolve, my defenses —threaten to melt too. Why does he have to be so awesome? It would be so much easier if he were just some hot jerk.

But I can't even imagine him as a jerk. He's wonderful. So wonderful, he should be taken already. Married, for Christ's sake. And, wow, it's really easy to imagine Luc Valencia married. So easy, I immediately want to punch his imaginary wife in the boob. I *really* don't like the idea of Luc being married.

"And I can't help but— Why are you breathing like that? You all right?"

I'm panting. I stop and try breathing normally. "Um..." I can't tell him I'm psyching myself up to tit-punch his imaginary wife. That's a little crazy. Even for me. "Sorry... I'm listening."

His eyes run over me for a second, maybe making sure I'm not about to pass out or succumb to an asthma attack. "What I'm saying is I'm okay with that. More than okay."

"That's great, but—"

He squeezes my hand. "Let me see you. We both want to. We both agree the kids come first. And if the last few days have shown me anything, it's that there's room." He smiles and those blasted dimples come out.

"Room?" I don't understand what he's saying, but it might be the dimples.

"Room in your life for me."

Chapter Twenty-Three

MILLIE

OH, SHIT.

I just fell in love with Luc Valencia.

The truth of it hits me right between the eyes. More like a racquetball than a bullet. As though I should have seen it coming. It leaves me with the absurd urge to laugh.

The beginnings of a laugh escape me, and then I bite my bottom lip, trapping the whole of it—all of this inconvenient, irresponsible, sweeter-than-life love—before it can wriggle free. I can't let this out.

If things were different, yes. Of course. I'd set it free. I'd give it to him with both hands. No regrets.

Room for him in my life? If things were different, I'd assign him his own zip code.

But things aren't different. So this feeling must stay behind the lines, within my skin, inside my lips, deep down in my chest, folded into a box that beats the rhythm of my heart.

"Why do you look so terrified?"

I swallow. "It's complicated."

"Try me."

I sigh, but I don't try to pull away. I want to keep touching him. Keep looking at him. "You wouldn't believe me if I told you."

The left side of his mouth curls up in amusement. "Like I said, try me."

I put my thumbnail between my teeth and chomp thought-fully. Saying it out loud just sounds so stupid.

Chomp. Chomp. "What if I told you I was cursed?"

Luc sniffs, and his eyes narrow just a little. "What do you mean? Who cursed you?"

Who? I never thought to wonder about a who. Maybe no one. Maybe this is just the way things are for me and mine.

"Maybe *cursed* isn't the right word. Maybe *doomed* is better. What if I told you I was doomed?"

"*Doomed?* That sounds worse than *cursed*. What are you talking about?" Concern pulls his brows together. "Does this have anything to do with your parents?"

I shrug. "Well, yes, actually."

Shock ripples over his face. "With what happened to them? Did someone sink their boat? Are you in danger?"

I lay a hand on his chest, shaking my head, suddenly—and inappropriately—laughing. "No, no. Nothing like that."

He arches a brow. "Because where my family comes from, when you say *cursed and doomed*, there's a good chance the cartel is involved."

"Oh. No, okay. Maybe I'm using the wrong words. *Fated. Destined... Conditioned.* I don't know," I say, flapping my hand in frustration. "But I'm powerless against it."

"Against what?"

I press my knuckles against my mouth because saying it is so awkward. "Getting knocked up."

His brows fly up. "Excuse me?"

I cover my face since he's looking at me like I'm insane. What else would he do?

"I told you you wouldn't believe me," I moan behind my hands.

"Millie." He grips my wrists and tugs gently, but I keep my palms to my face. "It's not that I don't believe you. I don't *understand.*" The way he stresses the word makes it sound less judgmental. More like he really *wants* to understand.

I find the courage to lower my hands. Just enough to peek at him over my fingertips. Luc is watching me, eyes alert, curious. I see nothing in his posture that suggests he wants to pull away.

In fact, he's leaning in.

Maybe he really does want to understand.

I bite my lip. "The bottom line is… birth control doesn't work on me."

Luc frowns, blinking. "You mean you can't take the Pill?"

"Oh, I take it," I clarify. Without the Pill, my cramps are pretty bad, but Luc doesn't need to know that. "It just doesn't work."

"So, you have to use something else? Like condoms?" He shrugs like this is no big deal. Carter hated using condoms. Not that they did us much good.

I sniff a laugh. "Those don't work either."

Luc shrugs. "I know their only like seventy-percent effective, but with something else—"

"Nothing works. Not for me. Not for the women in my family."

Luc stares at me. Not like I'm crazy, but like I'm not making any sense.

"Luc, my parents had four kids. None of them were planned," I explain. "My grandmother—my mom's mom— had six kids. My great-grandmother had seven. All three of them went to the altar pregnant."

He looks unimpressed. "A lot of people go to the altar pregnant. Aunt Lucinda did. My cousins tease her about it all the time," he says with a grin. "And she has four kids just like your mom did. That's a typical Catholic family."

"We're not Catholic," I say flatly. "We're freaks of nature."

He chuckles, shaking the trampoline. "You're so funny."

"I'm not kidding, Luc. This isn't a joke." I roll onto my back, exasperated. "I'm trying to tell you why I can't be with you. Why I can't be with anyone."

I've kept my voice low, but I glance over at the kids to make sure they haven't heard this. Luckily, they're still completely enthralled in their soccer game.

Luc tucks his finger under my chin and turns me back to face him. His dark eyes are serious, soulful, yet one corner of his mouth teases up a little.

"I know you're not joking. It doesn't mean you aren't funny." His smile fades. "Tell me more."

"There isn't more. I just can't be with you." This isn't true. There's a lot more, but I don't want to go through it right now.

And I don't want to live through it again. Ever.

I swallow against the lump that rises in my throat. Nope. Not going there. Not today.

"No." Luc shakes his head. "That's not enough."

I screw up my face. "What's not enough?"

"That's not enough of an explanation."

I'm pretty sure my eyebrows shoot to my hairline. "Not enough?"

"No." He shakes his head. "You want to be with me?"

My mouth opens and the truth plops out. "Y-yes."

He nods. "You know I want to be with you?"

I bite my lip, feeling a thrill of nerves in my stomach. But I do know. He's made that very clear. "Yes."

Luc clasps my hand. "What you're afraid of? It could happen to anybody."

I squeeze his hand. "But that's what I'm trying to explain. For other people, it *could* happen. For me, it *will* happen."

"Millie." He says my name gently, but, make no mistake about it, condescendingly. *Les Dimples* show up, and for the first time since I met him, the sight of them doesn't turn me to goo. In fact, I'm pretty close to punching him in the face.

I pull my hand from his and make a fist, but I don't pound him with it. "You don't understand. Luc, my parents had Emmett *five years after my dad's vasectomy.*"

"*Really?!*" Luc's eyes are wide, but instead of looking horrified, he looks... *fascinated.*

I shake my head. "In 1968, my great Aunt Maureen flew to the Philippines to see my Uncle Brian who was serving in Vietnam. He had a three-day leave, but there was a typhoon and Maureen's flight from Hong Kong was cancelled, and she only made it to Manila to see him right before he had to report back for duty." I clutch Luc's collar and give it a little shake to make sure he's listening. "They spent thirty minutes together. *Thirty minutes.* Nine months later, my mom's cousins Bradley and Bernard were born."

Luc blinks, his dimples digging deeper. "That must have been some thirty minutes."

I thump his chest with the side of my fist. "You don't get what I'm telling you. This thing," I say, waving my hand up and down to indicate my general reproductive system, "defies all logic and limits of medical science. That's why I call it a curse."

He narrows his eyes at me. "So, solitude and celibacy are your only options?"

I go still because I really hate that those are my only options. "Right now they are."

Luc's lips bunch and he nods, slowly, like he's assessing me. "Until when?"

"Until Emmett's grown," I say with a shrug.

He nods again. "That's the first thing you've said that sounds crazy."

"Pfft." I give his shoulder a little shove. "You mean to say you don't think the Theory of the Curse is crazy?"

Luc traps my assaulting hand and holds it against his chest. Through his dress shirt, I can feel the steady thump of his heart. "It's *wild.*" The way he says it, *wild* sounds leagues better than *crazy.* "It's incredible, but I believe you. At least, I believe what you're telling me about this phenomenon in your family. I don't necessarily agree it's a curse."

His belief surprises me so much, I'm speechless at first. "Why not?"

"Well, who cursed you?"

"Huh?"

Les Dimples emerge. "A curse implies malicious intent. Did one of your ancestors offend a *bruja?*"

"A bru-ha?"

His laughter shakes us again. "A *bruja* is a witch. You said your mother's side of the family is Irish. Did your great-great-great granny slight a fairy or something?"

"Um, no. You're right. Maybe *curse* is too strong a word." I give him the side-eye. "What would you call it?"

Luc presses his lips together, considering. "Uh… *superpower?*" He grins.

"Superpower," I echo, unamused. "Now you're making fun of me." I try to pull away.

He chuckles but shakes his head. "No, I'm not." He squeezes my wrist, keeping my hand against his chest. "You said your family's productivity defied all logic and limits of science. Sounds like Spiderman."

I snort. "Sounds like that Mother Goose rhyme."

His face goes blank and then—"The old woman who lived in a shoe?"

"A shoe!" I bemoan, throwing up my hands. "She had so many kids, and they lived a frickin' shoe! *Why?*"

Luc loses it. He laughs like I've never seen him laugh

before. Red-faced. Eyes squeezed shut. Gasping for breath. He rolls onto his back, and because my hand is still trapped, I roll too. Half on top of him.

Everything about it is amazing. He is at least nine kinds of beautiful. And the way he feels? Twelve kinds of *aaah!*

This is way too close. Way too much. Because all I want to do is shift to the left so I'll be *all the way* on top of him. I prop myself up on my right elbow to gain a little distance. Luc's chest heaves, his lungs recovering. His curling lashes are wet with laughter's tears.

Did I say just nine kinds of beautiful? I must have miscounted. It's thirty, easy.

God, I love making him laugh.

His eyes lock with mine. He reaches up and sweeps my hair over my shoulder. "Come home with me tonight."

The world goes still.

Say yes. Just say yes, the wild part of me begs.

I draw in my bottom lip. "You know I can't do that."

His eyelids lower. "You can. The kids will be fine. I'll have you home before they wake up. I promise."

"Did you hear anything I just said?"

"I heard everything you said." He licks his lips, and I'm mesmerized. "Nothing you said meant that you can't come over."

"Wh-what?" Shocked laughter shakes from me.

Luc's hand curls around the back of my neck, and his thumb strokes the edge of my jaw. "Millie," he says gently, his voice softening. "You're a virgin. I don't have any expectations."

A jolt runs through me.

A virgin?

"What?"

"It's okay," Luc says, his thumb tracing the shell of my ear. "I mean it. I just want to be with you."

His touch is a dangerous distraction, but I manage to shake my head. "Luc, what makes you think I'm a virgin?"

He keeps up the gentle caress, but his eyes narrow. "Well, you didn't have to come out and say it," he says, smiling easily. "Everything you said. About your mother and your grandmother and your great-grandmother all going to the altar *embarazada*. And you're not—"

Luc's thumb stills. His gaze sharpens.

My heart trips over its own beat and kicks into a gallop. Yet I know the blood must drain from my face.

"Millie." His eyes go darker than I've ever seen. "What happened?"

My lungs fold in on themselves like an accordion. I glance back at the kids, still playing and then at the house, still full of Luc's family.

"Not here," I rasp, my throat conspiring against me even worse than it did when I was in the throes of strep.

With eyes as dark as midnight, Luc gives one sharp nod. "Time to go."

I don't argue. I *can't* argue.

He springs up and takes my hand, steadying me as we leave the trampoline. As we descend, Emmett and Harry streak past us, arms raised, clearly triumphant. Alex and Mattie, obviously not the victors, brace hands on knees to catch their breath. All four of them are beaming.

Luc claps for their attention. "Schedule your rematch because it's time to go."

"*Awww!*" Emmett's voice wavers with protest.

"But... we—" Alex tries, breathless.

"Do we... really have... to go?" Mattie pants, looking crushed.

I can't bring myself to answer, so I merely nod.

"Your sister has been sick," Luc says before pointing to Emmett. "And so have you. We should probably call it a day."

"But I feel fine," Emmett argues, moping.

"And we're not sick," Harry says, gesturing between himself and his twin.

Luc turns up his hands, smiling. "And thank goodness for that." Then he hooks his thumb toward the house, ignoring their protests. "Let's get going."

The kids are poised to grumble, but unlike when they disagree with me, they hold back. Even Alex, who looks resigned. I don't really know how Luc did it, but I might need him to teach me.

Inside, it takes a good ten minutes to say our goodbyes. Nezzie refuses to let us leave until each of us is carrying some kind of leftover. I shamelessly accept everything she offers. The kids loved the food, and the haul will save us from takeout for at least two nights.

When we approach Luc's truck, no one tries to call shotgun, which surprises me, but what happens when we pull into our driveway surprises me even more.

"Who wants to earn fifty bucks?" Luc asks, throwing the truck in park but not killing the engine.

The kids nearly shed their skins in their haste to respond, all shouting *"Me!"*

I narrow my eyes at Luc. He stays my hand before I can push the release button on my seatbelt.

"Good, because I have jobs for all of you." He has been addressing them in the rearview mirror, but now he turns around to face them, claiming their full attention. "All three of you are going to put this food in the refrigerator. Emmett, you're going to let Clarence out, and then at five-thirty, you're going to feed him dinner."

I glance at the clock on the display. It's a little after four now. When did it get so late?

"Harry, you're going to lock the doors now and after anytime Clarence goes out. Mattie, you are going to find something—inside—for the three of you to do. A game. A movie. You decide, but all three of you have to enjoy it together. No one gets to hide in their rooms—"

"But—" Harry starts, and Luc raises a hand to silence him.

"Fifty bucks. I'm not paying good money for nothing." He looks at each of them in turn. All three of their mouths stay shut. "Emmett, you need to take your medicine before dinner, and each one of you needs to eat a real dinner before you can have any of the leftover desserts."

Emmett blinks, his wheels clearly turning. "Where are you going to be?"

Les Dimples make a surprise appearance. "I'm going to steal your sister for a few hours."

I do a double take. "Wait, what?"

"Oooh," Emmett croons. I turn back to see him tilting his head from side to side, making a kissy-face.

"I didn't—"

"How will you know," Harry asks, narrow-eyed, "that we're all earning our fifty bucks?"

"Photographic evidence," Luc says without missing a beat. "Of everything. You're going to keep me updated with pictures all night."

"All night?!" Mattie's eyes bug and she gives me a nervous glance.

I shake my head. "I'm not—"

Luc raises his hand again. "I'll have her home by ten o'clock."

Mattie blinks twice, her nerves clearly easing.

But mine are just getting revved up. "I'm home now, and I don't plan on leaving."

"Does that mean we don't get the money?" Emmett asks, his panicked gaze bouncing between me and Luc.

I release the latch on my seatbelt. "I'm afraid so."

The twins pipe up at once.

"But—"

"Can't you—"

"Guys, would you give us a minute?" Luc asks, avoiding my stare. "Maybe just wait on the porch for a bit?"

"Sure thing, Luc," Harry answers, already opening his door.

"Yeah," Mattie says, following suit.

Emmett, stuck in the middle seat, takes his time. My little brother gives me his most earnest look. "I just want you to know that I want a chance to earn that fifty dollars. I know I can do it."

I open my mouth to answer, but I really don't know what to say. If I'm being honest, I don't understand what's going on.

"Just wait on the porch, okay, *jefe?*" Then Luc pulls out his wallet and takes out a card. "Here. My cell is on this. Share it with your brother and sister so you can text me."

Emmett takes the card. "Sure thing, Luc," he says, sounding just like a mini-Harry. He slides out Harry's open door and both doors slam shut, leaving me staring at Luc.

"What the hell is going on? Are you trying to bribe my siblings?"

Chuckling, Luc shakes his head. "No, I just want some time alone with you."

An arc of electricity zings through me, but I do my best to ignore it. "Luc, we've talked about this—"

"No, Millie. We haven't. Not enough." His smile dims. "Just give me a few hours. All right?"

I want to. I really want to. "I don't think I should."

Luc shifts in his seat. He doesn't move any closer, but I seem to feel him—his presence, his energy, his pull—stronger anyway. "Why not?"

I don't trust myself.

Instead of saying this, I blather. "I-it's Thanksgiving. I... I should be with them."

The corner of Luc's mouth twitches. "You're always with them. I'm paying attention, so I know."

The arc of electricity grows hotter.

He's paying attention? Why is that so sexy?

His eyelids lower to slits, but I feel his focus intensify. "Other than for work, when was the last time you left them for more than an hour or two?"

I blink. "I…" But my words dry up. The last time I left for any length of time was June 11th. The day I lost the baby. I was at the hospital for about six hours.

Somehow, I don't think this example will help my cause, so I say nothing.

"You need a break, Millie."

The urge to tell him I'm fine rises in my throat, but I stop this too. My go-to phrase is beginning to sound ridiculous even to me.

"I want to take you to my place. Just for a few hours. Will you let me do that?"

I sigh. I don't want to say no, but saying yes would be disastrous. "It's too risky."

"Risky?" Luc eyes me like I'm making no sense. "How could it be risky?"

I give him my best stink-eye. "I just told you. And if you don't believe me, that's not my problem."

One side of his mouth tucks back, the look of amusement and heat in his gaze a disarming combination.

"I didn't say I don't believe you," he says, evenly. "I'm just saying it won't be an issue."

I shake my head. "It's always an issue—"

He cuts me off. "But only if we have sex, right?"

The question stops me short. "Yes…" I say cautiously.

Luc's dimples emerge. "What makes you think we're going to have sex?"

My cheeks prickle and then ignite with heat. Why isn't there a convenient hole in the ground when you need one?

"I…" Am I going crazy? Weren't we talking about sex just a little while ago? About wanting each other? And, not unrelatedly, can someone actually die from embarrassment?

Luc's hand closes over my forearm. His eyes have gone earnest. "Don't get me wrong. I want that. But it's not happening tonight."

"It's not?" The words are out in the air between us before I can stop them. I've never sounded more stupid in my life.

Somehow immune or at least ignoring my stupidity, Luc leans in and brushes his lips to mine. My flaming face seems to diffuse throughout the rest of my body. If he's trying to reassure me that there will be no sex, this tender kiss probably isn't the best method.

"It's not," he whispers. "Will you come home with me?"

Chapter Twenty-Four

LUC

I PULL INTO MY DRIVEWAY AND KILL THE ENGINE, GLANCING over at Millie. I still can't believe she said yes.

"Is that your house?" she asks, pointing to my landlord's twenty-five-hundred-square-foot home.

"No," I say with a grin. "I don't need four bedrooms. I'm in the back."

We leave the truck, and I lead her to the gate that separates my place and my downstairs neighbor from our landlord's backyard. Millie sees the duplex and gives me a funny look.

"You rent?"

"Yeah," I say, taking her hand and leading her up the wooden stairs that line the side of the duplex. "Does that surprise you?"

She nods. "It does. Shouldn't a builder have a house of his own?"

I sniff a laugh. "One day, but right now this works for me." I slip the key into the lock and deadbolt and hold the door open for her. "No upkeep. No yard work. I'm not here all that much."

She tilts her head to the side, taking in my sparse furnish-

STEPHANIE FOURNET

ings and almost completely bare walls. "Now, that doesn't surprise me." Millie faces me again with a pretty, winged brow. "You work all the time."

"I like it," I say with a shrug.

"I like my work, too, but I wouldn't want to do it twelve hours a day." She drops her purse by the front door, and, for the first time, I realize my apartment is missing a coat rack or a hall tree or something. A place to put purses and coats and shit.

"Sit down," I say, gesturing to the couch. "Can I get you something to drink? Coffee?"

Millie sits but wrinkles her nose and crosses her arms in front of her chest. "I don't think I need any caffeine."

My brows lower. "Are you worried?" Now that I've asked, I can see she is. And I don't want her to be. She needs a break from all that. "The kids will be cool."

She shakes her head. "I'm not... *worried* exactly."

I take her in, her stiff posture. Her balled up fists. She's not worried. She's nervous.

I set my keys on the coffee table and sit next to her. Close, but not touching.

"I meant what I said. We can just hang out tonight. You don't need to be nervous."

Her cheeks go pink in the way that tugs at my ribcage, and she looks at me under her lashes, all embarrassed. "Gah! You're making it worse." Then she hides her face behind her hands.

I laugh—she's always making me laugh—but I get the idea that without the kids to worry about and fuss over, Millie doesn't really know what to do with herself.

"Stop thinking." I grab her by the wrists to ground her, but I don't pull her hands away. She can hide a little while longer if she wants to. "Just be."

She spreads her fingers and peeks through them. "Be how?"

I roll one shoulder. "Be here."

She blows out a breath and drops her hand. "I wish I could have a drink."

I have a bottle of wine that has been on top of my fridge for a good six months from when we finished a wine cellar for a client.

"Would one glass of wine be so bad?"

She tilts her head from side to side in silent debate. "Antibiotics are bad enough. No need to stress my liver more than it's already being stressed."

"Good point. How about some tea? My downstairs neighbor is kind of a tea fanatic," I say, dropping my voice just in case my neighbor, Hen, can hear me. "She's from England. She gave me some chamomile-lavender tea a couple of weeks ago because she said she could hear me walking around in the middle of the night."

Millie's expression softens. "Do you have trouble sleeping?"

I give her a half shrug. "I wouldn't call it trouble. I don't sleep much."

Her mouth tips up in a smile. "That doesn't surprise me either." But then she nods. "Tea sounds good."

I head to the kitchen, fill the electric kettle, and take down two mugs.

"You hungry, Millie?" I call.

"God, no." Then I hear her mutter, "I may never be hungry again."

I chuckle, but I check the fridge just in case she changes her mind. I have some leftover grilled chicken. I could make her a wrap or a salad. But after Thanksgiving dinner at Mami's, even that might be too much.

Having Millie there today felt so right. Holding her hand while we said grace. Pressing my knee into hers under the table. Clearing her dishes.

She felt like mine.

She feels like mine now. She hasn't even been here for five minutes, and my place feels more alive, warmer than it ever has. It's not homey at all, but maybe it can be a retreat for her. A place to get away and forget her responsibilities for a little while.

A place to stop being a guardian and just be a woman.

I'd like to give that to her. I don't really know what to make of her stories about her family—and birth control and babies. I said I believed her and I meant it. But I can tell she's scared. That's one of the reasons I assumed she was a virgin.

But if she's not, and she's already experienced this *curse*, as she calls it, then she's been hurt. Because she's alone, and there's no sign of a baby. Maybe that means she trusted someone and he let her down.

Dios, help her to trust me.

The water boils, and I fill our mugs. "Sugar?" I call.

"Just a little," Millie answers.

When the mugs are ready, I carry them back to the living room and set them down in front of her.

"Thanks." She grabs hers and blows over the top. "Smells good. Your neighbor must really like you." Millie grins as she says this, but she watches me closely, waiting for a response.

"She's friendly, I guess."

Millie keeps her eyes on me as she takes a tentative sip. "Should I be jealous?"

I want her to be jealous so bad I choke on the tea.

"Um…" I clear my throat. *"Are* you jealous?"

She presses her lips together to keep from grinning, her blue eyes blazing. God, she's adorable. And the sexiest woman alive.

She narrows her gaze. "What if I were? Hypothetically?"

¡Éxito!

I take a successful swallow of the tea. "Hypothetically or otherwise," I tell her, "I'd never give you a reason to be."

She blushes again, but before I can enjoy it, my phone buzzes. I check the screen to find an unknown number and three pictures. One of the open fridge with Mami's to-go containers clearly stacked inside, another of Clarence lifting a leg on a sago palm in the Delacroix's backyard, and other of Emmett pouring food into the dog's dish.

Chuckling, I show the phone to Millie. She takes it from me, smiling.

"That's from Harry's phone." She swipes through the pictures, shaking her head at the one of Clarence and the palm. "Photographic evidence. Ingenious."

I smirk. "I figured it was the best way to get you to accept my invitation."

She presses her lips together, considering. "It helped."

When she hands the phone back to me, I save Harry's contact. Having it might come in handy if Millie lets me stick around.

"You're really good with them," Millie says, her voice going soft.

"They're good kids."

She bites her bottom lip. "Alex is a good kid, too."

I nod. "But you're still worried about Mattie hanging out with him."

"I'm worried about Mattie and every boy on the planet," she says on a sigh.

I put down the mug and turn to her. "Does she know what happened to you?"

Just like that, the color leaves her face. "What do you mean?"

I lean back against the sofa cushions. We might be here a while. "On the trampoline you said birth control doesn't work for women in your family, right?"

She blinks and nods once. "Right."

"And you said you're not a virgin," I say, this time more carefully. "Right?"

I watch Millie swallow. "Right." The word is barely audible.

"So, th—"

"I got pregnant," she blurts, leaning forward and setting down her tea. A splash of dark liquid sloshes over the side of her mug onto the coffee table. "Shit—"

Millie moves to clean it up, casting around for a towel, but I reach out a hand to stop her.

"Leave it. Tell me what happened."

Her eyes are on the spreading spill, but her hands clench at her knees. She breathes for a moment, not speaking.

"I got pregnant last spring."

Last spring? I say nothing, but it feels like I've been punched in the jaw.

"I lost the baby in June."

"Jesucristo," I cover her clenched right hand with my left. Pain and loss tighten the lines of her face and wash away the bloom of her color. "I am so sorry, Millie."

And then it hits me. June. Her parents died in May.

"Oh, my God." I say it aloud in English. Slowly. And in Spanish to myself. *Dios mío.* Begging God to listen. To comfort the woman I love. To spare her suffering. To make me worthy of her trust. "I... I..."

But there aren't words for this. So instead of making sense-less noise, I pull her into my arms, and she falls into me, surrendering. Her body shakes with sobs. Heartbreak spills out of her, and it's like torture. Because there's nothing I can do. Nothing.

I don't need to ask. I know she's dealt with this alone. All of this. Anger burns through my skull and across my shoulders. Because there's a man out there who left Millie to manage alone. I'd pay money for ten minutes with him to show him what it's like when life kicks the shit out of you.

Millie cries in my arm, her small frame shuddering with each breath. When I key in on this, the anger leaches out of me. Because if there had been a man who deserved her then, he'd be holding her now instead of me.

The thought leaves me hollow. I think back to the moment I first saw her. Sitting behind me at the soccer field. I couldn't stop looking. She pulled me like the tide. She would have still been the one to answer the door that day I showed up with her mother's plans. I would have still been the one she hired.

I would have still seen her. Maybe not every day. But enough. Enough to admire her. Enough to want her. Enough to fall for her, and she'd be his.

Damn.

I will make it up to you.

"Te lo recompensaré," I whisper into her hair. And for a moment, I think I've gotten away with it, telling her what's on my mind without her knowing, but she sniffles twice and pulls back.

"You've got to stop doing that," she says, her voice husky with tears.

"Doing what?" I give her my best innocent look, but she just wipes her eyes and glares.

"Saying things I can't understand."

I shake my head. "I can't stop speaking Spanish. It's my first language."

Her wet lashes bat twice, and she sniffs again. "I don't really want you to stop," she says, looking surprised.

I frown down at her. "You just said—"

"I said you had to stop saying things I can't understand," she says, her expression clear, sure. "I think, sometimes, you'll say something in Spanish so I won't know what you mean."

She's got me there. But I keep my mouth shut to see where this goes.

Millie tilts her head to the side and looks to the ceiling. "I mean, half the time, I think you're just cursing or exclaiming—"

I laugh because it's true.

"But the rest of the time, I think you just don't want me to know what's going on inside your head."

I still. "You want to know what's going on inside my head?"

Millie's eyes glisten. "Yeah." She nods, sounding kind of awed. Maybe even surprised. Her smile lights a hidden place in my chest. "I want to know. More than I want to know anything else."

More than I want to know anything else.

That light in my chest spreads in all directions. It warms every cell. My arms encircle her, and I draw them in a little tighter.

"Let me show you what's inside my head," I whisper. I melt closer to her, moving slowly so she knows what's coming, giving her a choice, the chance to refuse. But she doesn't, and my lips land on hers like they've been called home.

At first, I just let her feel the heat she's given me. Her lips are cool, her face still damp from her tears. She sighs at the contact, and I know she can feel it. Heat builds, and then I part her lips with my tongue, taste their silken sweetness.

Her breath goes choppy. It passes over me, speaking words all its own, saying again what she's just spoken out loud. She wants to know.

She wants to know me.

And I want more than to know. I want to see. Hear. Taste. Touch.

Love.

I want to offer. Promise. Shield. Fulfill. Bind.

Give.

I want to love and give. Tonight. Tomorrow. Twenty years from now.

But I also want to keep my word. I don't want her to misunderstand me and think I've talked her into being here just so I can seduce her.

"Mmmm," I moan at the thought of seducing her. How delicious that will be. One day.

"Paciencia," I tell myself, breaking from her mouth. I lean back and stare into her eyes. Millie's pupils are dark pools ringed in sapphire blue.

She licks her lips, making my cock twitch, and swallows. "What?" she breathes. "What'd you say?"

"Patience," I tell her, wanting to etch in my memory the way desire paints her beauty. "I can be patient."

"You can?" Does she sound disappointed?

"I can," I promise.

Her chest rises and falls, and then she nods, seeming to recover and think better of it. "Good. That's good."

And then, as if she's trying for patience, too, she slips her arms from around my waist, smooths her hands down her top, and picks up her cup of tea.

Everything about it is so forced—so clearly *not* what she wants—I can't take it. I lift the mug from her grasp and meet her surprised gaze.

"I said *I* can be patient," I say, setting down the mug. "I didn't say you needed to be." I reach for her, my hands landing on her slender ribs, inches from her breasts, and I pull her to me. Millie lets out a startled gasp as her lips meet mine.

She doesn't protest or try to hold back, and when I open my mouth, her tongue finds its way in, as sweet and soft as apricots. Her hands claw into my hair, tugging me closer—as if we could be any closer without becoming one flesh. Her breasts crush against me with soft heaviness.

Millie wants me, and it's enough. It's all I need. I can be as patient as the moon.

I break the seal of our mouths and murmur into hers. "I'll give you anything you want." I've wanted to tell her this since our first kiss, but hearing the words, I know they aren't exactly right. I try again. "I want to give you everything."

Yes, that's it.

Our mouths join again, and she makes a plaintive sound, one laced with regret. She tilts her chin down just enough to speak. "I *can't.*"

I hold her tighter so she knows she's not alone and drag my lips to her ear. "You can." I lick the dainty, almost translucent curve of her ear, and she shivers against me.

"I told you…" she murmurs. My lips press against her throat, and I feel her swallow. "I'm powerless."

I let my teeth graze against the slope of her neck and shake my head. "No, Millie. You have all the power."

Her hands move to my shoulders, and she grips them. "But I'll—"

"I keep my promises, *linda.* Let me show you how good I am at keeping my promises." I glide one hand up to cup her breast and run my thumb over its hidden peak. Even beneath her top, and what I'm sure is a bra that is sexy enough to make me cry, I can feel her nipple, hard and tight, ready to be suckled.

"Gah—" Millie's head tilts back and my mouth claims the invitation, kissing the base of her throat. "You don't understand," she warns.

I chuckle against her skin. "Unless there's something you're not telling me," I let my teeth skim her collarbone, "all will be well as long as I keep my pants on."

Millie straightens and meets my eyes, looking at me like I've dropped English and Spanish for Swahili. "Wha—You—"

Holding her gaze so she takes in every word, I run my very

lucky thumb back and forth. "I said I keep my promises. My pants stay on. Yours, on the other hand..." I glance down to her lap and let an even luckier hand touch the arrow of denim between her clamped thighs. A shudder runs through her, and I hook my arm around her waist to steady her.

When I lay her down along the length of the couch, she doesn't resist. A cry, half distress, half desire, leaves her, and I lean over her, intent on answering both the distress and the desire.

My fingers meet at the top button of her blouse. "Let me show you," I tell her, plucking the button free as I press a kiss to her rose petal lips, "how well I can keep my promise."

Millie sighs, her hands gripping my waist. I can see and feel the battle waging inside her. Slipping free another button, I watch her close her eyes, a line etching between her brows.

"Let go," I whisper. "I've got you."

But I sound much more calm than I really am. Because as the fabric of her blouse parts, I find silk and lace the color of pewter. Elegant. Exquisite. Maddening.

"Tan hermosa." My thoughts rise in Spanish, but I rush to translate them for her. "So beautiful."

A small voice in the back of my mind advises me to take my time. Stroke her with the back of my knuckles right where lace meets skin. Ride the scalloped edge of her finery with the tip of one finger.

If only I had that kind of control.

I don't. I bury my face in her breasts and devour. I taste sweetness, a hint of sweat, and warmth. She is fucking delicious. I tug down her delicate cup until one breast bobs free. As soon as I see her tight, coral pink nipple, I have to have it. Greedy, I wrap my mouth around her and suck.

Millie gasps, arching her back. One of her hands moves back to my head, her fingers threading into my hair. The other fights to free the tail of my shirt from my jeans, and when it does, her hand sweeps up my spine.

Her touches spur me. I mouth, lick, suck, and nibble, feeling the quickening of her heartbeat against my lips.

"Luc... Oh my God..."

My name on her lips and the ache in her voice make my hard cock even harder, but my own need is nothing compared to the need to give this to her. To prove this to her. I free her other breast and love it just as well.

By the time I get to my knees, straddling her so I can reach back and slip off her boots—because boots have to come off before jeans can come off, and jeans are coming off—Millie is panting, eyes half-lidded.

Her second boot hits the floor. My eyes lock with hers. I grip her fly—

And her phone rings.

Chapter Twenty-Five

MILLIE

"Shit!" Struggling for purchase, my arms and legs pinwheel as I try to sit up beneath Luc. I yank up my delinquent bra and slap my mussed hair out of my face.

"What are you doing?" Luc asks, still straddling me, and, for some reason, not moving.

"Getting up. Getting my phone," I say, not snapping, but not far. *It's ringing, for God's sake.* "It's probably the kids. Can you let me up?"

"It's not the kids. They just texted."

I ignore him. "Let me up."

He raises a brow, but Luc plants a foot on the floor and is off me and halfway to my purse before I can scramble up.

He snags my phone, swipes the screen and puts it to his ear. "What's up, Mattie?"

I shoot to my feet, my heart in my throat. "What's wrong?"

Luc frowns. "Oh, Emmett. What's going on?... I'm answering Millie's phone because I was closer." His frown gouges deeper. "Why are you calling, *jefe?*"

I can hear the tinny squeak of Emmett's voice, but I can't

make out the words. Luc's face goes blank. But he doesn't look concerned. He looks... *annoyed.*

"Yes. I got your texts. Good job. Is that why you're calling? To see if I got your texts?"

I bite my bottom lip.

"Mmm hmm," Luc mutters, sounding unamused. "So, everyone is fine over there?"

The squeaks on the other end of the line are definitely affirmative.

Luc nods. "Okay, so I'm adding a stipulation. If you want your fifty bucks, don't call unless it's an emergency—"

"Luc!" I whisper-yell, advancing on him, reaching out toward the phone. "Give me that."

He blocks me with one hand, his renewed frown aiming down toward the floor. *"Why?* Because your sister deserves a night off. That's why."

"Give it to me," I hiss, batting away his deflecting hand and almost reaching the phone before he turns, giving me his shoulder. And then the next thing I know, his arm snakes out and snatches me to him. Our bodies press together, his right thigh notched between my legs. My chest crushes against him, my mouth at his collarbone, inches from the phone. I swallow a moan just in time.

"We clear?... Nope. I'm not mad at you, buddy. Neither is Millie." I open my mouth to speak, and Luc lifts his thigh, grinding it into me. Right. There.

"Yeah, *jefe.* We'll see you at ten." Luc pulls the phone from his ear, presses the red button with his thumb, and tosses it onto the couch. "And you say *I* work too much."

I shake my head. "That's not work. That's family."

He gives me the look that says *Please. Who are you kidding?* "You work harder at taking care of them in one day than most of my guys work in a week." He takes two steps forward, pressing into me and walking me back. "And you know I don't hire slackers."

That's true, I think, gripping his shoulders for balance. He takes two more steps. With each one, his thigh rubs me in the most sublime, distracting way.

I grapple for focus. "So, everything was okay?"

Two more steps. "Everything was okay, Millie."

"Did he want—"

"No." Luc shakes his head. "We're not talking about him." Two more steps. I feel the air around us change, hush somehow. "Once we cross this threshold, we're in a sibling-free zone."

"But—"

Two more steps and we're in his bedroom. I look over my shoulder at the king-sized bed. It's neatly made, the slate gray comforter smooth across its surface and tucked under two over-sized pillows.

"You make your bed."

"Every morning."

I look back at him. "Were you a Boy Scout?"

Luc shakes his head. "I'm a builder. The first thing I learned from Papi was that a foundation can't be sloppy."

The corner of my mouth tugs up. "Your bed is your foundation?"

He doesn't answer my smile, but his eyes narrow on me, amused nonetheless. "My morning routine is the foundation of my day."

This shouldn't be sexy. My God, why is this so sexy? He walks me to the foot of the bed. I know I'm about to go down.

I meet his eyes. "I'll mess up your foundation."

One brow goes up. "You have no idea."

He gives me a little push, and I'm flat on my back. Reaching down, he grabs my ankles. With one firm tug, my jeans slide off. When did he manage to unzip them?

At least my panties stay put. But judging by the look in his eyes, I don't think that state of affairs is going to last very long. I'm stretched out on Luc's bed in my panties, bra, and unbuttoned blouse. And Luc's standing over me, fully dressed.

I lift my hand and gesture between us. "This isn't fair."

He shakes his head, giving me a wicked grin. "Life rarely is."

He plants a knee on the bed, but I place a foot on his knee, stopping him.

"Wait. I'm serious."

The grin dissolves. "Me too. I told you. My pants stay on."

I shrug. "Well." My voice drops, my confidence choosing this moment to take a smoke break. I twirl the fabric of his comforter with a timid finger. "At least take your shirt off. I feel…"

His eyes narrow on me. "You feel what?"

I swallow. Okay. Why not go for it? "Exposed."

He unbuttons the wine-red shirt faster than I would have ever thought possible. Luc wads up the shirt and tosses it to the ground, and I'm gifted with the sight of his powerful chest and shoulders.

"Holy God," I mutter.

He laughs through his nose, those dimples absolutely slaying me.

Help me, God. I'm in real trouble.

Looking like a bronze idol to masculinity, Luc prowls up my body on hands and knees until he hovers above me, staring down into my eyes.

Really big trouble.

He's looking at me like he has something to say—not hesitation, but declaration—and my heart thumps even harder in my chest. His dark eyes flick to my bra and then back to mine.

"I can take it off quickly, or you can take it off slowly."

Damn. That's the hottest thing anyone has ever said to me. Ever.

I swallow. "Take it o——"

But I don't get to finish because Luc hauls me up into his arms and peels the open blouse off my shoulders before whipping it from me. And then—like a pro, like he could compete in the Olympics at it—he unclasps my bra from behind, and I'm topless.

Pretty much naked, in fact, except for the tiny scrap of lace between my legs.

Luc lays me down again, much, much more slowly than he pulled me up, his eyes moving over me. One hand braces his weight, the other lightly traces my side, as if he were outlining my silhouette. It feels amazing. But his gaze is too close. Too intense. Instead of squirming under its full power, I put my attention on him and decide at once that this is a brilliant idea.

I run my hands up his sinewed arms, over the hills of his biceps and shoulders. His flesh is hot and hard, but his skin is so smooth, I'm immediately addicted. I could run my fingers over him all day. All night.

He's so beautiful. So strong and good. No guy has ever taken me at my word. Not Carter. Not my two Tulane boyfriends I had before Carter, both of whom found dating a virgin exciting and, let's face it, probably challenging—until it sunk in that I planned to stay a virgin until I finished college.

Carter was my first, and while he was patient—at first—he never, not once, promised to keep his pants on.

So, before I can stop myself, I ask the one question I can't riddle out.

"Why me?"

From somewhere near my navel, his gaze sweeps up and locks with mine. *Oh boy.* I thought I felt naked and exposed before. That was nothing compared to this.

"You can't be serious," he asks, those eyes narrowing on me.

I swallow. "I am."

His brows draw in, that scar, and the look in his eyes taking his sexiness to lethal levels. "You're the strongest person I know. How you manage everything blows me away. You're smart. Funny as hell, and seeing you is the best part of my day."

Okay, yeah, that's a really good answer.

He lifts a brow. "Good enough?"

I nod.

Luc drops his mouth to mine, and I welcome his kiss. I open to take him in, but he pushes away.

"What?" I ask, undeniably disappointed.

"Why *me?*" His eyes brighten, a smile at their corners, but that's just on the outside. On the inside, somewhere between his corneas and his optic nerve, I see a shadow of doubt. A vulnerability that is all wrapped up in his hopes and fears about what I'll say. And that vulnerability makes me love him all the more.

I raise my hand and stroke his cheek. "You do everything with integrity," I tell him, speaking softly. "Whether it's reminding your guys about safety or leaving notes for Emmett so nothing surprises him, or making sure you wrap up before Mattie's piano lessons. You put people first and you keep your word."

The shadow of doubt fades.

"I'm a big fan," I add, grinning. "Good enough?"

Heat stokes his smile. His hand comes up to caress my cheek. *"Te miro y me muero de hambre."*

I have no idea what he's said, but it sounds divine. I lift a brow, waiting.

The way his eyes become slits gives me tummy flutters. "I look at you," he says, heat radiating from his body. "And I'm starving."

I suck in a breath.

"Every day."

I open my mouth to tell him it's the same for me, but his kiss silences me, his tongue overruling sound and sense. His body presses into me, heavy and powerful. One of his hands finds mine, and our fingers converge, interlace. My heart does a little pirouette at the intimacy of it.

For a stretch of untold moments, I lose time and place, the tide of Luc's kisses pulling me away. His free hand cradles my face, and it takes me a moment to realize nothing is stopping me from touching him. Exploring him. I run my left hand up his side, and his moan rumbles into my mouth. His skin is so shockingly soft. It amazes me that this softness has been there this whole time, hidden from the world under humble cotton T-shirts. Being allowed to touch him is like gaining entrance to some secret society, a chosen order. Who knew?

Mesmerized, I untangle my hand holding his and run both palms down his back. Luc arches, the motion settles his hips snuggly between my thighs, and his fly hits me just right. Just like his leg did when he walked me backward to his room, except now, there's no thick denim to blunt the touch. Just the gossamer thin lace, and I feel his surge like seismic activity.

He breaks from my mouth, shifting his attention to my jaw and neck. I melt beneath him, tension I've carried for I don't know how long unspooling muscle from bone. I'm so relaxed that when he takes my breast into his mouth a second time, the erotic shock of it sends me arching off the mattress.

"*Oh God.*"

At the sound of my voice, breathy and urgent, Luc grunts, sucking harder. Under his hot mouth, my heart stampedes. Of their own will, my hips tilt and sway, rubbing against him.

"*Me vas a matar,*" Luc mutters, switching to the other breast. I want to ask what it means, but I can't. Words have aban-

doned me. All I know is Luc's mouth. His body. And the pleasure he is drawing out of me.

I want him. I want him so badly.

If I were anyone else, I'd be begging to have him inside
me. As it is, my hands settle on his waist, his obliques taut
and coiled with power as he moves above me. My fingers
touch where the rough denim waistband meets the silken
aliveness of his skin. At his waist, I allow my hands to delve
deeper into his jeans, and a shudder runs through Luc that I
feel all along my body. He pulls free of my breast, shaking his
head.

"No," he says roughly. "Can't go there."

I blink and bring my hands back to his ribs. "Sorry. I just
want to touch you—"

Luc growls low in his throat, and I feel it deep in my sex.
"Not today." The look in his eyes is serious, flashing an iron
will. The fact that he's not allowing me to touch him makes me
realize just how much I want to.

God, I want to touch him. I want to make him feel good.

"I want to be the one who makes you feel good."

His eyes soften, as though my words have struck him somewhere tender. I actually can't believe I said them out loud, but I
don't want to call them back. It's the truth.

"Millie," Luc says, his voice as rough as sandpaper. "You
are."

And then he's kissing me again. Fierce. Hungry. I'm all in.
Matching his ferocity, his hunger with my own. And if I'm only
allowed to touch what he's bared to me, then I'm going to
make him feel me on every inch. My hands sweep over his
back, ride his muscles, play along this spine. He feels as beautiful as he looks.

I draw them over his shoulders, making just enough space
between us to reach his chest. And when my fingers find the
pucker of his left nipple, the desire to taste it nearly turns me

inside out. I break our kiss and scooch down, Luc's startled panting filling my ear.

His pecs are exquisite. Flat and hard like river stones. I could love them with my mouth for the next hour. But the moment the tip of my tongue meets his dark nipple, he jerks away.

Luc planks above me, eyes wide. "What are you trying to do to me?"

I swallow. "I just told you."

I prop up on my elbows to close the distance between us, and he pushes up higher, shaking his head.

"No. Lie back down."

I blink. "Are you serious?"

"Do I look like I'm joking?" The glint in his eye and that scar in his brow have never looked more severe.

I lie back down.

Luc drops his knees between my legs again, and then he surprises me by grabbing my wrists and hauling my hands up over my head.

"These stay here." Then he angles down over me an inch above my face. "This," he dips and plants a kiss on my mouth, "stays right here."

"But—"

Then I'm staring at the ceiling. I look down in time to watch Luc kiss my navel. I move to sit up or shimmy down, but his big hand comes up, lands right on my sternum, and pushes me down.

"Quédate."

"What's that mean?"

Luc kisses me an inch below my navel and doesn't look up when he answers. "It means *stay.*"

My skin flames. Maybe it's because of the command. Maybe it's because of what he's doing with his mouth. "I'm not a dog," I manage.

Luc shakes his head, the tip of his nose drawing lines low on my belly. It feels amazing.

"No," he says, nuzzling the lacy edge of my panties. "But you're a vet. Figured you knew the lingo."

"Puh!" I start to protest when his teeth close lightly over the stretched lace. The fabric does nothing to block the wet heat of his mouth. The next thing out of mine is a moan.

"Have I mentioned that I really like your—" he licks the gusset of my panties. The shock of pleasure runs straight to the crown of my head, "taste in lingerie?"

I make a noise, but it's hardly an answer. His mouth closes over the spot he just licked, and Luc sucks me into his mouth, panties and all.

"Jesus Christ," I whisper, because a whispered prayer is all I can manage. If I wasn't already soaking wet, I am now. And let's face it. I was already soaking wet for him.

"Mmmm." He hums against me, and each of the ten thousand nerves that exist only for pleasure hum right along with him. Luc hooks the drenched scrap of finery with a finger and tugs it down. My panties skim down my legs, and with a flick of his wrist, they sail across his room.

Looming above my sex, Luc's eyes, intent and hungry, lock with mine. His gaze flicks down before returning. "Are you giving this to me?"

Oh God. The question is so impossibly sexy, yet how can I answer?

I grip his comforter, trying not to squirm.

He tilts the scarred brow with a teasing slant. "Is that a *no?*"

I swallow. Lick my lips. Shake my head.

He shakes his head in imitation. "I can't hear you." His voice is low, liquid with desire and shot with baiting.

He lowers his head, and with one swift upward movement, licks my slit. My inhale is machete sharp.

"Millie…"

It's only when he whispers my name that I realize my eyes are screwed shut, and I'm staring at the back of my eyelids. I open them and meet his gaze, dark and smoldering. His expression is one of patience. And command.

"Do you. Give this. To me?"

My pounding heart should be bouncing me off the bed right now.

"It would be—" I swallow. "A lot easier… if you just took it."

Luc bunches his lips, as though considering. Then he shakes his head. "Can't do that. You see…" He dips his mouth again, this time licking me from thigh to thigh.

"Cocker Spaniel!"

Yes. Luc Valencia's face was between my legs, his tongue doing the very thing I'm *dying* for him to do. And I just called out the name of the prissiest breed of dog.

I hate my life.

And, no, Luc didn't just succumb to a case of spontaneous hearing loss. At least, not if the tensing of his jaw and the narrowing of his eyes is any indication. I can see he's not going to laugh at me, inches away from my pussy—which would be more humiliation than I could handle—but it's a near thing.

He takes his bottom lip between his teeth and sucks on it meditatively. "Let me see if I understand." His voice rumbles as he speaks, the breath of his words landing on my merciless arousal. "You can say *Cocker Spaniel*, but you can't say, *Yes, Luc, this is yours?*"

Good God. It sounds so good when he says it. *Yes, Luc! This is yours!* I scream it silently. But no sound leaves my mouth. How can it? What would that say about me? How would that align with the way I've lived? With the way I must live?

Instead, I nod. Because it's true. Saying just about anything is easier than saying that.

His eyes narrow, but with no lack of warmth. "Do you know how much I want you, Millie?"

The raw feeling in his words embeds in my bones. He wants me as much as I want him. I'm sure.

"I think so," I squeak.

He nods. "And you know why I need you to say it?"

Without even thinking about it, I do know. It's because of who he is. Because of what I love about him. His integrity. His promises. His need to prove himself to me.

"I think so," I say, emotion squeezing my own words. "I just... I just can't."

A thought brightens his eyes. "I have an idea," he says, his voice as rich and decadent as chocolate ganache. "We're going to talk about this later, but right now, I have an idea."

"Tell me," I demand. Because a girl can only take so much.

"Can you say *Sí, Luc, te doy esto?*"

I smile, not needing him to translate. They are the words I can't say on my own. But these are his words. His language.

Yes, Luc, I give this to you.

"*Sí, Luc, te doy esto.*"

Before the last syllable is out, he is on me, his tongue singling out the swell of my clitoris. He rides its slope. Sweeps its circumference. Multiplies its value. Until the sum of my cries echo through the room.

My climax is quick and obvious. But he doesn't stop. He moans against me as I come, his mouth—my God, that mouth!—rearranging my axis, setting me on another plane. I don't know if I can take more. The sensation is almost too much. Until Luc's left hand coasts up my belly and cups my right breast, and the pleasure stretches out, equalizing while building again. I feel his other hand squeeze my ass once before his fingers glide down the back of my thigh, his short nails grazing my tender skin.

He's awakening flesh no one ever sees, let alone touches,

and every cell in my body tingles with life. Before his fingers reach the back of my knee, they reverse course, and I'm sure he's calling in reinforcements. No one's tongue can keep up this pace. It's impossible.

I'm so certain of this that the feel of two fingers at my entrance sends a shock straight through me, and I let go of the comforter I've fisted in both hands. I trade the bedding for his hair as fingers slip inside me, triggering my tiny muscles to dance and quiver.

The man can build. And build. And build. Until the two fingers inside me say—the only way two fingers can—*Come here. Come now.*

And I come. Again. And again.

Luc's fingers are still inside me when I'm all wrung out. But he's kissing his way up my sweat-misted body. Lightly. Slowly. Like he's savoring every taste.

"*Rosado,*" he murmurs, kissing between my breasts. He looks into my eyes, and I swear, he looks so warm and satisfied, you'd think he was the one who just had three orgasms. He licks his lips. "Pink. Everywhere."

I blush, going pinker. I take his face in my hands, and he kisses me. The taste of myself on his lips makes me clench around his fingers.

His breath hitches, and his eyes meet mine. "That's so erotic." He sounds awed, so invested, it happens again. "My God, Millie."

A smile, lit by some megawatt internal joy, lights his face, giving me both dimples. But it's like he has X-ray vision. The power to see—and feel—just what he does to me. It's too much. Too one-sided.

After what he's just done to me, I am wide open, defenseless. I'd give anything to even the playing field. Balance the scales. I need to watch him come undone. Taste, see, and touch the way he feels about me.

And that thought makes me clench again.

"Holy cow," he marvels, propping his head on his left hand. "Do you have the strength for another?"

Before I can answer, he strokes me once.

"Gah! No!" I grab his wrist and free myself from him.

His chuckle shakes the bed. "Okay. Just want to make sure you're satisfied."

"I am," I say quickly. "Quite."

I don't tell him that no one's ever given me two *O's* in one go. Much less three. I grab the edge of the comforter and roll up in it like a burrito, facing him completely covered.

Luc quirks a brow at me. "Cold?"

"No." I don't offer him an explanation, but I'm only too glad to be able to hide a little after that wanton display.

His focus narrows. Lying on his side facing me, Luc settles a hand on my blanketed hip. "You do know," he says, his voice hushed. "There's nothing you could give me—or share with me—that I don't want."

When I don't answer, he hooks a finger over the top of the comforter at my shoulder and tugs gently, leaving me covered but making his intentions known.

"Everything you've got I want," he says, certainty ringing in his words. "Everything you want to give, I'll take."

It's my turn to arch a brow. "Except for what you just gave to me."

His eyes blaze before narrowing to slits. "Wicked woman," he growls. "I'd have to be dead not to want that. But that's not what tonight is about."

Guilt takes a bite out of me. "I didn't mean to tease," I tell him. Then with spirit. "I'm *not* teasing."

His gaze softens. Just a little. "I know. But if you haven't already figured it out, I keep my word."

I nod. "I've figured it out." And then, because he feels too far away, I reach for him and pull him into my blanket burrito.

He moans when his chest meets mine. "You're warm." Luc holds me against him for a moment, but then he stirs. "Let's do this right." Unwrapping me from my cocoon, Luc tugs down the blankets and gestures for me to crawl beneath them. His sheets are cloud white and look just as soft. I don't hesitate.

When Luc joins me, he takes me back in his arms. His heavy, gruff sigh sounds as content as I feel. This is bliss.

He presses a kiss to my forehead. "It's early still. We could rest for a while."

"God, yes," I say on a sigh. The day—the week, hell, the last six months—feel interminable.

With a hand on my hip, Luc cinches me closer to him, and I hook a leg over his thigh. We fit just right. The fingers on my hip move in lazy crescents. Back and forth. Back and forth. My eyelids wilt.

"I'm glad you're here," Luc murmurs. Darkness has fallen outside his windows, and the only light comes from a small lamp on his bedside, giving the room a cozy dimness.

"It's nice here," I say, turning an ear toward the quiet. It's *so* quiet. I stiffen. "You think they're all right?"

Luc gives me a lazy smile. "I'm sure they're great."

I nod. He's right. Of course, he's right.

But what if he's wrong? I picture my phone across the apartment on Luc's sofa. Would he be offended if I dashed across the house—naked—to grab it? Do I really want to dash anywhere naked? Will Emmett remember to take his antibiotic with dinner? He'll get a stomach ache if he—

Luc untangles himself from me, and in one fluid motion, he's out of bed and striding across the room.

"What are you doing?" I call after him.

"Getting my phone," he calls back, and a moment later, he fills the doorway, shirtless, clad only in his jeans, looking like an ad for American Eagle Outfitters. I only notice the phone in his hand when he's sinking back under the covers with me.

"Why?" I ask, as he unlocks the screen.

He stops what he's doing and looks at me, amused. "Because I could hear you worrying."

"You couldn't *hear* me worrying," I protest, but he probably could.

He quirks a skeptical brow. "I knew you wouldn't rest until we checked. Here." He angles the screen so we both can see. He has seven new messages. All from the kids. Three pictures. Four texts.

As soon as I see them, everything in me melts, but nothing more than my heart. I look over at Luc. He's watching me, and I wonder how well he can really read my mind. If he knew I was worrying about the kids, does he know how I feel about him? How I feel in this very moment when he's just demonstrated—again—how completely sweet he is?

"Thank you," I manage.

He shrugs. I could watch him shrug while shirtless every day of my life and twice on Sundays.

"You really are so good with them," I tell him again.

Luc gives a slow shake of his head. *"You're* really good with them."

I try to smile, but it doesn't quite feel like I make it. "They have fun with you."

"You think they don't have fun with you?" He's watching me closely. I'd consider hiding if there was anywhere to go.

"Sometimes," I concede.

He cups my face and sweeps a thumb over my cheek. "They need you. You make them feel safe. You're what keeps them grounded," he says, pressing his hand tighter against me so I feel grounded too. "Fun is extra. It's important, but what you give them every day is more important."

I let go a sigh. I know what he's saying is true, but Harry, Mattie, and Emmett deserve more than safe and grounded.

They used to have fun. They used to have happiness. We all did.

"You're doing the best you can," Luc says, clearly reading my thoughts again. "And it's better than anyone else could do."

"There isn't anyone else." The words are out before I can stop them. I hate how self-pitying they sound and shake my head to dispel them. "I didn't mean—"

His thumb strokes my cheek again. "There is someone else," he says, his voice dipping lower. "*I'm* here."

It's as though my body becomes my heartbeat. I can feel the heavy pounding in every cell. He can't mean that. He's only known us about a month. If I can't count on my aunts and uncles to be here for the day-to-day, if I couldn't count on my boyfriend—the father of my child—to take this up with me, how can I lean on anyone else?

"Let me help you," Luc says, his dark eyes boring into mine. "I can take care of the fun stuff for now."

He says this, and all I hear are two words. The most important two.

For now.

Chapter Twenty-Six

LUC

EMMETT HATES MONDAY MORNINGS, AND AFTER THE LONG holiday weekend—which might be the best four days I can remember—I can't say I blame him.

I learned something amazing Friday night. Millie is so affectionate when she's rested and relaxed. I took all of us, including Alex, to see *Frozen II*. (The big kids wanted to see *Joker*, but Millie put her foot down.) I bought the tickets, but Millie insisted on getting the snacks, which turned out costing almost as much, but I'm learning when it's worth it to argue with her and when it's better to let things go.

Movie snacks fall into the second category.

We took up most of one row in the cinema, and Emmett demanded to sit in between Alex and Harry. Before the previews started, I had the pleasure of watching my little brother do some quick maneuvering to put Mattie on his other side, that other side being the one furthest from me and Millie.

And, yeah, I might have spotted them holding hands during the opening credits. If they kept it up throughout the rest of the movie, I didn't notice. I was too busy, holding

Millie's hand in mine and feeling the slow caress of her thumb along my palm.

Afterward, we left The Grand, picked up Deano's, and ate pizza and played Unstable Unicorns in the Delacroix's living room. It was a blast. And the more the kids laughed and carried on, the more Millie melted against me. Played her fingers through my hair. Stroked my back.

Honestly? I don't think she was even aware of it, the way she kept her body in contact with mine. As though it came naturally. But I was aware of nothing else. It made concentrating on building my unicorn army damned impossible, but I'm not complaining.

And last night, after I made burgers on Millie's dad's grill, we all piled on the sectional to watch *Spider Man: Into the Spiderverse*—which was a lot better than I expected. Still, Millie fell asleep against my chest, her red hair spreading over me like it was staking a claim, her body trusting me with its weight.

I just need her to trust me with her heart. God knows she's called dibs on mine.

But it's six forty-five when I come through the kitchen Monday morning. I walk in to find Emmett moaning about going to school and Millie wearing a crease between her brows.

"Morning, guys," I say, hoping my presence will help Emmet buck up. He ignores me.

"Morning," Millie says weakly, meeting my gaze with an exasperated look. All the affectionate ease we've enjoyed this weekend has run for cover.

"Why did I have to get sick *last* week?" Emmett grouses over his Pop Tart. "Why couldn't I have strep *this* week?"

Millie's standing by the head of the dining table, looking sinful in workout tights and a fleece hoodie. She's bound for the gym after she gets Emmett to school. *If* she can get him to school. "Do we really have to do this today, Em? You just had a whole week off."

I glance at the coffee pot on the makeshift counter we set up weeks ago. The coffee's brewed, but Millie hasn't made her to-go cup yet.

"Yes, because I *hate* school. I want to be off *all* the time. Why can't I be home-schooled?"

Millie sighs. "We've been over this."

I grab the top take-away cup from the stack by the pot and fill it with coffee. I've watched Millie rush through her morning routine enough to know she takes it with six drops of stevia and a glug of Half-N-Half. I busy myself with this while the two of them argue. Upstairs, the sound of hurried footfalls thump overhead. Millie hears it, too, glances at the microwave clock, and holds up a hand to mark her place in her exchange with Emmett.

"Guys! Three minutes!" she shouts. The twins catch the bus in the mornings. They also tend to cut it close. Muffled responses that sound promising come from each twin. Millie turns back to Emmett. "Three weeks. You have three weeks until Christmas break. You can do this. I know you can."

"What if I stay home with you today and go the rest of the week?" Emmett asks.

"We're not negotiating," Millie says, shaking her head. "You're going to school."

I snap the black plastic lid onto the disposable cup. Footfalls clatter down the stairs, distracting both Millie and Emmett from their battle. I take the opportunity to approach her and press the cup into her hand. Her eyes meet mine, surprised.

"Bye, Millie! Bye, Emmett!" Mattie calls from the front door. We turn to see her wave. "Bye, Luc!"

I smile, glad to be included. "Bye!" Millie and I call in unison. The sound of Harry coming down the stairs like a boulder down a mountain almost drowns us out.

He lands with a great *thwack.* "Bye!" he shouts, tearing after Mattie. The front door slams as we hear the squeal of bus brakes and see the strobing yellow caution light through the front windows.

"Two down," I murmur. We're both still holding the coffee cup, fingers just touching. Still, it's the first time I've touched her since she kissed me goodnight on the front porch. I've missed her all night, so I'm in no hurry to break it.

"One to go," she whispers back.

"I can hear you," Emmett drones. "And I'm not going."

Millie deflates a little, but I speak up before she can reply.

"How about I drive you today, *jefe?*"

Both Delacroixes jolt at this.

"You don't have to do th—"

"You mean it?"

Emmett's half out of his chair, eyes wide.

"Yeah. We'll go whenever you're ready."

His chair scrapes back as he stands. "I'm ready."

Millie's mouth falls open. "Wha—" She stops herself, looks at me and then back at Emmett. "Go brush your teeth and grab your book sack."

"Okay." Emmett snatches up his paper plate and makes for the trash can, only scattering a few Pop Tart crumbs as he does. "Be right back."

And then he's racing for the stairs.

Millie's eyes meet mine. "I don't deserve you."

I huff a laugh because I think she's kidding, and when I realize she's not, I grab her. "What do you mean?"

She shakes her head, her blue eyes wide with what looks like sad recognition. "You're too good. I should cut you loose for your own sake, but I don't know if I can."

Her words twist my gut like a pipe wrench. She's still holding the coffee, so I take it from her and set it down before I grab her again and drag her to me.

"Cut me loose? You think you don't deserve me? I don't

deserve *that.*" I'm sure she hears the edge in my voice. I'm not angry. Just afraid of what she could do to me.

"But it's too—"

"It's fucked up is what it is."

She blinks, startled. "What do you mean?"

"You thinking about dumping me because I want to help you."

Millie stares at me for a second. Then she closes her eyes and exhales. "You're right. I'm just…"

I'm gripping her upper arms, but now I ease my hold and stroke her. "You're just what?"

She opens them again. "Scared."

Any tension—and all fear—drains right out of me. She's scared. More scared than I am. I already know this. I shouldn't let it rattle me. "I'm sorry."

She shakes her head. "You're not the one who should be apologizing. *I'm* sorry."

I watch her face. She looks contrite, conflicted, and completely miserable. I give her a wry look, hoping to make her smile. "Was that our first fight?"

She wrinkles her nose, looking at me like I'm crazy, but at least the corners of her mouth turn up. "We fight all the time. We fought the first day you came over."

I laugh. She's right. "I meant our first fight as a couple."

Her brows leap. "Oh. I mean… Are we—Did we—"

"Yes." I grip her arms again. "We are. And we did."

Color rises to her cheeks because we're both thinking of Thursday night and the time alone we haven't yet been able to duplicate. I'd pay the kids again if Millie would let me, but she's forbidding it. For now, anyway. I know I don't really need to pay them. At least not fifty dollars each. They'd accept less to follow the rules and keep us updated, but Millie's hesitant to leave them again so soon.

I'm sure that's true. But I also have my suspicions that she's a little afraid to be alone with me again.

I, *Dios ayúdame*, find it hard to think about anything else.

So, it's no wonder when I let my hands glide down to her hips. The way her tights cling to her curves is maddening. I grip her ass with both hands. Millie gasps when I tug her against me. By the way her eyes widen, I know she feels it.

Feels how I want her.

I brush my lips over hers, and they part. My tongue is seeking hers when she whispers, "Emmett will be down any second."

I lick her bottom lip. "We'll hear him."

Acknowledging the logic in this, she relents and opens for me. Our lips meet, tongues reuniting after the too long night. She tastes like heaven. I want to slip a hand down the back of her tights and discover just what kind of bewitching *lencería* she's wearing today.

I keep an ear trained on the stairs. Is there enough time? Enough time to reach down between us, tuck my hand into her panties, and find her eager little pearl? *La joya.*

I'm imaging having her scent on my fingers all day when the kitchen door opens behind me. We spring away from each other, and I wheel around to find Sam, slack-jawed and going pale, standing in the doorway.

"Sorry, boss! Donner said to be here for seven o'clock." He gulps and drops his gaze to the floor. "The cabinets are being delivered."

I spare Millie a quick glance. Her knuckles are pressed to her lips. She's beet red. But I can tell her fist is hiding an embarrassed smile. She doesn't look pissed.

I breathe a sigh of relief just as I hear a door upstairs. Emmett.

"You're right," I say to Sam. "They should get here first thing. Glad you're on time. But it never hurts to knock."

Sam sniffs and hooks a thumb over his shoulder, gesturing to the driveway. "Sorry. I saw your truck, and I…" He shuffles his feet and chances a peek at Millie. "Sorry, Miss Millie. It won't happen again."

I look back at Millie to see her drop her hand and straighten up, trying to command her smile. The blush is a lost cause. "It's okay, Sam. No harm done."

I raise a brow at her that Sam can't see. No harm done? I was seconds away from petting the unicorn for fuck's sake.

Emmett makes it down the stairs, skipping the last two and landing with his own *thwack*, though nothing as loud as his brother's.

"I'm ready!" he shouts.

"Coming, *jefe.*"

"I'm right behind you," Millie says, grabbing her coffee. "See ya, Sam."

Sam, who's still standing at the door staring at his feet, nods. "Mmm hmm." The poor kid looks traumatized. Maybe I should let him know he's not in trouble, but that can wait until later. Right now, Emmett needs to get to school.

I'M on my way back from Woodvale when Miguel calls. It's barely 7:30, so I know immediately something's off.

"What's wrong?" I answer.

"Injury," he says, cutting right to the chase. "Nico slipped of a ladder."

I wince. "How bad is it?" I ask, rerouting and changing lanes so I can head south and get to the Lambert property.

"Ankle hurts. Might be a break. Might be just a sprain."

I sigh. "I'm on my way. I'll take him in." I make a right on Johnston Street. "How'd it happen?"

This time Miguel sighs. "Ladder was slippery. Condensation from the fog this morning."

"Damn," I curse under my breath. "Did he perform a safety check?" Before any task, my guys are supposed to check their equipment and surroundings for potential hazards.

"No."

My jaw clenches. "And did you?" It's the site manager's job to do a sweep of everything to check for safety issues each shift.

"I did, boss, but I missed it."

Either Miguel is telling me the truth, which means he did his sweep, but did it too fast or half-assed, or he's lying, and he didn't do it at all.

"Send me a picture of today's safety sheet."

"Got it right here," Miguel says, his voice even. If he's lying about the check, he's covering his ass pretty well.

"Be there in ten."

I get to the site, tell Miguel to document what I need to complete the report for worker's comp, and help Nico into my truck. We get to the Orthopedic Urgent Care on Ambassador just as they open, so once Nico fills out the paperwork, they take him right in.

When my phone rings and I see it's Papi, I'm not the least bit surprised. He and Miguel have been tight for years. The guy probably called him out of habit. Or guilt.

"Hey, Papi," I answer, getting up from my waiting room chair and heading for the exit to take the call outside. "Miguel call you?"

"Of course he called me," he says, sounding irritated. "When were you going to call me?"

I roll my eyes. It's ten minutes after eight a.m. Most people are just getting to work. "I was going to call after Nico got checked out. But, believe it or not, I've got it under control."

"Oh, you've got it under control?"

I step outside, frowning at his obvious sarcasm. "Yeah,

Padre, I do." I know I shouldn't get defensive, but I can't seem to help it. "I got Nico to the clinic for X-rays and treatment, I followed up with Miguel, and he's filling out an accident report. What else do you want?"

"How about you keeping your dick in your pants when you're on the job?"

For a moment I turn to stone, and then adrenaline streaks through my veins like venom. "What did you say?" The question comes out a growl, rumbling up from a place inside me both ancient and bloodthirsty.

"You heard me. And you know what I'm talking about." Condemnation. Disappointment. Flashbacks of cracking a granite countertop when I was sixteen wash over me, and the fact that he's talking to me like I'm a kid kindles anger.

"I know what you *think* you're talking about." A vision of this morning and Millie's sweet kiss flickers through my mind. Sam blabbed. That's no surprise. But Papi's accusation is. "But you shouldn't be talking at all. I'm seeing Millie Delacroix. That's my business."

A harsh laugh cuts over the line. "Not when you're staining the name of *my* business."

Too many objections rise in my throat, leaving me speechless. I fill and empty my lungs, fighting for control. "First of all, Papi, it's *our* business." I hear him draw breath, about to object, and I cut him off. "Don't misunderstand me. I know you built it. Single-handedly. I watched you do it."

Saying this aloud makes me soften toward him. Just a little. But he's pissed me off, and he's got to deal with it now.

"But we've worked together for years. The name on our business card isn't just yours. It's mine too."

While he's still the owner, Papi transferred operations to me when he nearly lost his leg. He was in ICU for two weeks and then in the rehab hospital for six, tending a wound that just wouldn't heal—that still hasn't completely healed. Just one of the reasons diabetes sucks so bad.

"So why you treating it like garbage? Sleeping with your *gringo* clients and setting a bad example for your brother?"

I see red.

"Papi." His name cracks like bone. I'm squeezing my phone so hard I could crush it. I hear footsteps, and glance up to see a woman wearing a look of alarm steering her young son around me. The boy cradles his arm in a sling, and he looks afraid. Not of the clinic. Of me.

I turn and stalk toward my truck. "Do not. Talk. About Millie. Do you understand me?"

He makes a noise in his throat. "So now that you're the boss, you think what your Papi has to say doesn't matter?"

I exhale and try to get a grip on my anger. This is where all this bullshit is coming from. Me running the business. Me taking over when he was in the hospital, fighting to keep his leg—and his life. Me doing exactly what he asked me to do to keep the business afloat. Keep his workers employed, his customers happy.

He's never once thanked me. Sometimes it feels like he *blames* me.

"Papi, you can say whatever you want to say about the business. Tell me I'm a shitty boss and every fuck-up is my fault. Whatever you want," I growl. "But you don't speak about Millie Delacroix unless it's to say how fucking amazing she is."

Then, for the first time in my life, I hang up on my father.

———

AN HOUR LATER, I drop Nico off at his apartment. The ankle is badly sprained but not broken, and the doctor gave him a cold gel pack, a brace, and orders to stay off it and keep it elevated for a few days.

I want to be back at Millie's when she gets home from the gym, but I can't get Papi's words out of my head. And I'm ready to wring Sam's neck. My guess is he told Donner, who is in a GroupMe with the other site managers. I already know they gossip like a bunch of seventh grade girls. And if it's not about who's banging who, then it's about what kind of mood I'm in.

Donner probably thought he'd nailed both categories.

Except I'm not sleeping with Millie.

And as much as his call galled me, I couldn't bring myself to say that to Papi. But the truth doesn't belong to him. Or Sam. Or Donner. Or anyone else.

But what's also true is that I'm dying to be inside her. I'm dying to look into her eyes as I lose myself in her. I'm not going to lie to myself. I want the release. I want to chase her climax with my own. Bring her to that event horizon with my whole body.

But more than that, I want to join. To share. To couple with her. I want to be as close to her as two people can possibly be. I want to be one with her.

And when I think that the last man inside her was someone else—someone who hurt her—I'm ready to shred something.

I want to be the last man inside her.

This is where my head is when I pull up to the Sterling house. I'm just this side of feral. The crew is installing Tyvek wrap, and I swear, if I see even one trip hazard or safety violation, I'm going to lose my mind.

But nothing is out of place. Not even one Wrap Cap nail. Tony, the site manager, must know to stay on my good side today. As I inspect the site, I feel eyes on my back. Anyone could see they've been talking about me. They know about Millie. They may not know her on sight or know who she is, but they know what Sam walked in on this morning. They know the boss is seeing a client.

I honestly don't know what's worse. That the guys and Papi think I'm sleeping with Millie or that they're wrong. I feel like a hair trigger landmine. I should just go to the gym and work out until I can't think. Or go home and take matters into my own hands. But my bed offers me no peace. Not since Thursday when I made Millie come. My sheets still smell like her.

After barking orders at Tony, I climb back into my truck and drive to the only place I want to be. Millie's Infiniti is parked in the garage, *gracias a Dios.* I enter through the kitchen door and find the room crowded with custom cabinetry. By the looks of it, Sam and Donner have measured and marked and measured again, making sure each piece has been made to our specifications. Sam is busy drilling pilot holes. Donner is balancing a level against the wall, double checking his marks.

Things look good. I should be happy.

But I'm not.

Both men turn when I shut the door. "Hey, Luc." Donner's eyes widen slightly at the sight of me. Sam actually takes a step back. Maybe my eyes are glowing red. I wouldn't be surprised if I've sprouted horns and a forked tail in the last hour. *El Diablo* has nothing on me.

"Take the day off."

Donner blinks. Sam grips the drill in his hand and it revs, startling him.

"What's that, boss?" Donner asks, eyeing me with alarm.

"Leave. Don't come back until tomorrow."

"Okay, uh…" Donner uses the level in his hand to point at their tools. "We'll just clean u—"

"Now. You'll get paid for today," I say, just in case this is a concern. Judging by their wary looks, it's not. "Come back tomorrow morning."

Eyes on me, Sam sets down his drill.

"And fucking knock," I tell him.

Sam flinches. "Right, boss." Then the kid practically skitters out of the kitchen.

When Sam clears the door, Donner starts to move, just not quite as fast as his assistant.

I wait until he reaches the door. "Donner?"

He looks at me over his shoulder. "Yeah, boss?"

I shake my head. "Best not to share this with the others."

Donner's face stiffens. Then he nods. "Got it, Luc. Sorry."

He pulls the door closed behind him, and I take the two steps toward it and flip the bolt. As soon as I do, I hear Millie's step on the stairs. By the sound of it, Clarence is descending with her.

I cut through what's now the front of the kitchen and watch her descend the last of the steps. She's barefoot in a gray, floral print sweater and black leggings. Nothing fancy. Everything I want. The deep V neckline of her sweater beacons my mouth. The contours of her leggings command my hands. She's in my arms before she's off the stairs.

Millie gasps her surprise against my lips, letting me kiss her for just a few seconds before breaking off. "Luc," she whispers. "They'll hear us."

"They're gone," I say, kissing her again as the unmistakable sound of Sam's Toyota firing up revs just outside. "I made them go."

"*What?!* Luc, why—"

"I need you." But the words aren't enough, so I take her mouth again. Her fingers fist in my hair. It drives me wild. If it were allowed, I could take her on the stairs.

But I know the rules. I've accepted the rules. But after this morning…

Our teeth clash. My tongue glides over hers, showing her again everything it knows how to do. I grip her tight ass with one hand and snake the other under the sweater and beneath the cup of her bra. When I pinch her nipple, Millie's breath jackhammers.

"What…" she pants against my cheek. "What's happening?"

I want the stiff peak of her nipple in my mouth, under my tongue. The neck of her sweater is a willing accomplice. My lips move to the top of the breast I'm fondling, and I kiss the blushing skin.

"Luc?" She kisses my temple. My hair. "What is it? Why'd you send them away?"

I succeed in bringing one coral nipple to light and swipe it with the tip of my tongue. "I need to make you come." And then I take her in my mouth. Her knees give, but I'm ready, shifting the hand from her bottom to the small of her back.

"Oh, God, Luc." Millie is a soprano. I've never heard her sing, but her moan is high, airy, and light. Angelic. I hear heaven as I suckle her.

"Upstairs… bed… please." Each word is an exhale, a desperate sound I recognize. I shift my hands back to her ass, mount the first step, and take her with me. Millie's legs go around my waist, she clutches my shoulders, and up we go.

I don't hear Clarence behind us, but I kick her bedroom door closed just in case. Then, holding her in one arm, I lock her bedroom door for good measure.

This belongs to no one else.

The reminder of this morning—Sam, Papi, the gossip and assumptions—makes me growl. I pitch us onto the bed. "I need to make you come," I say again, sounding like a beast.

"You *need* to come," Millie whispers, tugging at my shirt.

"No," I grunt, but I let her pull off my shirt. I know she needs this. My skin on hers. I slip her out of her sweater. It was hiding a pale pink satiny bra, the color of her blush. It blends against her skin like a chameleon. I moan. "You're going to kill me."

She shakes her head. "No. Let me help you." Her hands drop to my fly, but I cover them with mine.

"Not yet," I rasp. "I need to—

"I heard you the first time," she says, managing to pop the button on my jeans. "But it's my turn."

She doesn't understand. How can I make her understand? "Please." I move my hands to the waistband of her leggings. Millie doesn't try to stop me. In fact, she lifts her hips, and I tug them down, taking the pale pink thong with them.

She's got my pants unzipped and is pushing them halfway down my hips when I grab her wrists and drag them up by her shoulders.

"Please," I beg, locking eyes with hers.

She blinks up at me. Her gaze softens and a little crease appears between her brows. "Luc, what is it?"

I shut my eyes. "Nothing, I—" But before I can put anything into words, she has tugged her right wrist free, and she's cupping my cheek.

"Luc, my darling," she says, gazing up at me, her eyes full of longing and concern. Her *darling* lands somewhere soft inside me. It hits me then that what I need—what I've been restless and edgy all morning, hell, maybe even all my life—is for her to love me. "Tell me what's wrong."

Dios la amo. God, I love her.

I can't say this to her. I know Millie. She'll run. It'll freak her the fuck out. But this is what drove me here. What is driving me now to bring her to orgasm with my touch. Show her without words how I love her. Prove to her. To everyone. To me. That she is mine. This isn't something empty. This isn't what anyone else assumes.

"This is real," I say instead.

Her eyelids flutter and a smile slowly spreads over her face. Her thumb strums up and down my cheek. "And that upsets you?"

"No," I say, exhaling a laugh. I cover her hand with mine and close my eyes, loving the feel of her touch against my face. She's held me this way a few times now. The first time was that night in her bed when she asked me to hold her. I took it as a sign that she liked me more than she was ready to admit.

Is that what she's doing now? Does she like me more than she's ready to say? Love me, even? Are we both trying to show each other that it's safe?

"This is ours," I promise her. And I know I'm promising myself. Reassuring myself that none of the rules and obligations—none of the expectations I've lived under for years—apply here. Anyone else can say what they want, think what they want. It can't touch us.

As long as she is mine.

"Ours?" Millie asks, the look in her eyes searching, almost hopeful.

"Yes, *mi amor*, ours." I reach behind her and unclasp the bra before slipping it from her. Then I kiss each breast, letting the desire to be inside her wash over me. Through me. It's everything. And I accept the agony of it.

"I am yours," I say, moving my mouth to hers. "You are mine." I kiss her. "This is ours."

Millie drinks my kiss, and then I feel her free hand slide between us. She closes around me before I can stop her. "If this is ours, then we need to share."

Chapter Twenty-Seven

MILLIE

LUC'S BODY SHUDDERS ABOVE ME, HIS EYELIDS DROPPING HALF-mast. That's the only thing about him half-mast. The silken brick of his erection is as startling as if I'd reached down there and grabbed a handgun.

I stroke him, and he hisses, raising his hips as though to draw away, but I don't let go. "You heard me. We have to share."

Luc's eyes are closed now, and he's biting his bottom lip. Against my knuckles, his lower abs are rock hard. Just like the rest of him.

"Relax," I whisper, stroking again. "God, you even feel beautiful."

He groans, but I know I've won when he collapses on his side, and I roll toward him so we're facing each other, my hand freer now to do exactly what I want. But if I'm going to get to do this, I want him bare. As bare as I am.

"What do I have to do to have you naked in my bed?"

His eyes spring open. In an impressive flash of masculine thrashing, his jeans come off and land on the floor. I didn't even have time to let go. Not that I would have now that I've finally got my hands on him.

But now there's too much to look at, and my hand is in the way, so I let go and trail my fingertips down one gorgeous thigh. Dark skin. Darker hair. The curls at his sex are as black as kohl. I run my fingers up through them and hear the catch in Luc's breath, but my senses are too enthralled to pay full attention. His hair here is coarser than the mass of dark silk on his head, but it's still softer than I expected. I trace one curl with my index finger, and his cock leaps. At his sides, Luc's hands ball into fists.

Smiling, I look up and meet his stare. "I'm fascinated."

Luc's teeth clench, making the muscles in his jaw stand out. A strangled sound rises in his throat, and I watch him swallow, the masculine mechanics there so lovely too. I stretch up and kiss the column of his throat, gripping him again as I do.

His moan hums against my lips. I can't stop smiling.

"I should have known it would be like this," he croaks.

I draw back to meet his gaze, stroking him lightly from base to tip. "Like what?"

His eyes lower to slits. "Torture."

"No," I whisper, drawing out the word and timing my downward stroke to match it. "Not torture. I'm not teasing."

The brow with the sexy-as-hell scar arches. "Then what are you doing?"

A minute ago, he called me *mi amor.* That means *my love,* doesn't it? Is that what he means? Or is it just an endearment, meant to show feeling but not... I want to tell him the truth, but I don't think I can. Buying time, my hands slide down and I cup his balls gently. He hisses again, but he doesn't move. Doesn't try to stop me. He's surrendered, trusting me completely.

He does trust me completely. He has from the start.

My hand rides up the length of him again. "I'm… l-loving what's mine," I say, my voice trembling just a little.

Luc's nostrils flare, and his chest heaves. But he says nothing. My mouth goes dry. I lick my lips and look away, my heart racing.

Abort. Evasive maneuvers.

I squeeze him, my gaze on the erotic beauty in my hand. "Y-you did say this was mine," I say, trying to make the words light and meaningless.

Then his hand is covering mine. "Yes." His voice is fathoms deep. He glides my grip over him pumping once, but then he lifts my hand off him. I look up, confused. When my gaze lands on his, it's like he's seeing straight into me. And it's terrifying.

But then he settles my hand over his heart. "And this is yours, too."

The look in his eyes makes my breath leave me all at once.

"What about yours, Millie?" he asks, the corners of his mouth turning up.

"W-what?" Let's face it. I've always been a chicken shit.

His smile grows. "Are you trying to tell me you love me?"

Oh God.

Why do I have to be such a chicken shit?

"Because I loved you first," he says, sounding so cocky.

My jaw drops. "Nuh-uh!"

Chin to the ceiling, eyes squeezed shut, Luc laughs wildly. I don't think I've ever seen anyone so happy. It would be adorable if I didn't want to punch him. Only because I feel like an idiot.

Laughing, he rolls on top of me, pushing me onto my back. I feel his laughter everywhere. And maybe I don't want to punch him anymore, but I bury my face in the crook of his neck, still embarrassed.

"*Nuh*—" He cracks up again. "*Nuh-uh?* Wha… What does that mean?"

I growl, but it sounds more like grinding gears on a garbage truck. Luc has fits all over again. His arms slide under my back, and he squeezes me so tight.

I don't want it to, but it feels so good.

I squeeze him back and bite the bullet. "It means *I* loved *you* first," I say into his shoulder.

He makes a humming sound I adore, ducks his head, and searches for my mouth. I turn to meet his kiss, but he doesn't linger.

"Not possible. I wanted to take you home at the soccer game. The first time I saw you in the stands."

I shake my head. "I saw you first, walking with your dad and your grandma. It was so cute." I force myself to look up at him. "You looked so big and strong and gentle at the same time. I had to make myself stop looking at you."

His dimples are shining down on me now. I reach up with both hands and palm them. "These were my undoing."

"What?" he asks, frowning just a little.

"*Les Dimples.*"

He laughs again. "*Les Dimples?* I don't think that's technically French." He's smiling above me. His happiness is so big. It's so big, it tugs at my happiness. Asking for it to come out and play. But I can't let it go.

"Millie?"

"Yeah?"

His smile softens and he squeezes me again. "I love you."

My whole body tenses. I know he feels it, but he doesn't stop smiling.

"It's okay," he says. "You don't have to say it back."

"Oh, God, Luc."

I love you. I love you so much.

STEPHANIE FOURNET

Why can't I just say it? I can say I loved him first. I can say I'm loving what's mine. Why can't I just say *I love you?*

What if I give him my heart and he leaves me? Or worse?

For a moment, I think of my mother. Of what I can only believe was the last decision she ever made. To jump into that water and go after my father.

This feels like just as big of a leap—and maybe one that will be just as doomed.

"Millie. I get it," he says, looking peaceful. "I already know."

I blink. "You do?"

He nods. "I was having a shitty morning. A really shitty morning. And it was because I needed this. I needed you to know." He shrugs. "And I guess I needed to know, too."

Guilt squeezes my heart.

He must read my face because he shakes his head. "It's okay. You already made me feel better. Like you always do. It's one of the reasons I love you."

I bite my bottom lip. "You make me feel better too." *Can you hear me saying* I love you? My eyes sting. I blink them hard.

"I love you, Millie."

I shut my eyes, trying to keep from falling apart.

Luc brushes his lips against my ear. "Let yourself feel it," he whispers. "I love you."

Then I hear him. *Let yourself feel it.*

So I do.

Luc Valencia. Just told me. That he loves me. He loves *me.*

My stomach balls up like I'm in a plummeting elevator. Because I don't deserve him. Because I love him back. So much. Because I want this more than anything. Because letting myself feel his words is a shortcut to letting my heart get the shit kicked out of it.

"Luc?"

"Yeah, *linda?*"

I swallow. "I'm a chicken shit."

He presses his lips together and tries not to laugh. Instead, he shakes his head. "No, you're not."

"No, I am," I say, my brows climbing. "And I just think it's fair you know. You're in love with a chicken shit."

This time he does laugh. And the ball in my stomach softens a little. God, I love making him laugh.

He shakes his head again. "You're the bravest person I know."

I snort, an emission I immediately regret. Snorting while naked is never a good idea. "If I'm the bravest person you know, then you know a lot of chicken shits."

But by the time I manage to say this, we are both laughing. It becomes hysterical. Unstoppable. The ball completely dissolves and then I really feel it.

I feel what it means to have Luc's love.

It's big. I can't touch it or see it, but I know it's big. And it's solid. Solid enough to hold my weight. And my fears.

And it's warm. God, it's warm.

So warm, I want to draw it up inside me. I want to be one with it.

I want to be one with him.

I watch as he catches his breath, the laughter finally abandoning him. He's looking down at me, dark eyes shining, and the look in them makes me feel like I'm the most important person in his world.

Which is a damn good thing because even though there are three people who have to be pretty damn important in mine, I suddenly have no doubt that I can make room for one more.

"Luc." I capture his face between my hands again. I leave room in the valleys between my thumbs and index fingers so I can see his dimples.

"What, *mi amor?*" This time, I feel this too. His words tickle through my chest and land on my heart like goose down from a pillow.

That same heart pounds, picking up speed as I take a deep breath. "I love you, too."

And then he's kissing me, more words filling the air as though the pillow has succumbed in a pillow fight.

"*Te amo... Te amo más que respirar...* Millie, my God, I love you... *Eres mía, ¿me oyes?...* Mine, I tell you."

"Ours," I gasp, snatching breath where I can. "This is ours."

He groans in pleasure when I echo his earlier words. And with his groan, Luc tilts his hips, and I feel the branding heat of his erection on my bare thigh. I blink my eyes closed as sensation washes over me. Because, suddenly, it isn't *his erection* or *my thigh*. It's him and me. Not pieces and parts that can be named and separated.

No more separation.

The urge to be closer to him opens me. My knees fall wide, and he settles into the cradle of my hips.

Luc's breath rasps when his sex presses against mine, his hard length connecting with my slippery stem of nerves.

"Millie..." Luc's voice is both hoarse and deep, a rumble of warning hidden among the consonants and vowels of my name. I hear his warning, and a part of me tells me to heed it. To pull away. To play it safe.

But that niggling voice can't compete with the chorus of body, heart, and soul that calls for him. For us.

"I need you." I hear the words leave my mouth, and every part of me—even the tightly wound voice of protest—knows this truth.

"Millie..." The warning note is gone, replaced by one of pleading. "I can't... I can't say no if you're saying yes." His hips roll, and I swear it's involuntary, but mine echo the movement, grinding into him as though fated for nothing else. "I'm not strong enough to hold back."

In this moment, I'm not torn. I have no internal debate. Just this one possible path. "Then let go."

His breath leaves him. Luc kisses me, devouring me as though I've become air, and blood, and life itself.

One of his hands slips between us, and I gasp at his expert touch. I close my eyes, but when I feel him lean to the far side of the bed, I open them to find Luc reaching for his jeans. One-handed, he plucks his wallet and flips it open. I know exactly what he's doing, and a voice inside me, one that's neither panicked nor unsure, whispers.

It won't matter.

But I say nothing. Because the time for words is over. I run my hands down Luc's torso, wanting them to speak for me. My fingertips glide over the sensual terrain of ribs and muscles as he caresses me. His fingers leave me. Impatient, I palm the sides of his waist, feeling his taut strength. Now that he is this close, mere inches from me as he rips open the condom and rolls it down over his imposing erection, I can't believe I've been able to resist him as long as I have.

It feels like we were always destined to be here. Right here. I watch him grip himself at the base, and I know that nothing could be more natural than joining with him. It is as inevitable as the rising and setting of the sun.

I look up to find him gazing down at me, his pupils inky black pools. The head of his sex brushes the petals of mine.

"Are you sure, Millie?" His voice trembles with what I know is the effort to hold back. But I don't want him to hold back. We can't anymore.

"God, yes."

With my hands on his waist, I feel his breath still as he enters me. My eyes are on his face, and his look of sublime torture leaves me transfixed. Because I must, I wrap my legs around him, my heels landing on the backs of his thighs. He closes his eyes as he sinks slowly into me, and I want to watch, but I can't keep still. My back arches at his exquisite invasion, my hips impatient to bring him into me. All the way in.

He moves with such maddening slowness that my fingers become claws. I reach for the rock hard anchor of his buttocks and clutch him to me with a thrust that tears a cry from both of us.

Like a bolt of lightning, pleasure sears my every nerve.

Luc draws back, the friction of his retreat rapturous, but at the same time, not enough. Not nearly enough. I haul him back, needing him deep inside me. Needing him as close as he can get.

"Luc." It's almost a wail.

At my plea, Luc finds our rhythm. Rapid. Pounding. Dizzying.

Shocks of pleasure rock through me as his hips piston, his glutes firing beneath my palm. Sweat mists our skin, the heat we build igniting blood and breath.

"Luc," I call his name, more urgent this time. Trying to claim this moment as the sum of all my hopes. Wishing I could let him know that this is all I want. To be with him. To be joined with him.

"Eres mía… Eres mía," he pants. And as the pulsing of my climax converges, gathering like a summer storm, I think I catch his meaning.

Mine.

Mine.

"Eres mía," I echo in his tongue, clinging to him as I break.

At my words, Luc's eyes blaze before his lashes flutter, his whole body going taut as he crashes into me with almost brutal desire. With each thrust, I am thrown back into waves of ecstasy. For a timeless span, it seems it will never end, and I welcome this fate, doing my best to hold on as Luc's release shakes us both.

We're both panting, trembling, when his arms slide beneath me to cinch me tight to him. His pounding heart sends coded messages to mine. I wrap my arms around him, and my nose seeks his neck, loving the scent of his sweat mixed with our ardor.

I kiss his neck and lap his earlobe, making a shiver run through him. Luc moans, and I smile at the sound.

He pulls back just enough to meet my gaze. His face is flushed, and he's smiling, but his eyes search mine.

"You okay?"

I nod, my grin irrepressible.

His hand settles against the side of my face, and he traces his thumb over my left brow so gently. "No regrets?"

"No regrets." It's the truth, and I'm glad of it. I know better than to think too much about the future, but the universe might give us a few months before The Curse—or *superpower*—as Luc calls it, strikes. Carter and I were lovers for a few months before—

I shove the thought away. My mind should be nowhere but here. I focus on Luc's dark eyes.

"No regrets," I say again.

He lowers his mouth and plants a kiss on my forehead. "Good." Then he flashes a grin, his dimples winking devilishly. "Any chance we could do it again?"

"W-W-What? Now?"

Luc laughs. Inside me. Against me. Around me. And all of a sudden, the thought of doing it again now seems downright recommended.

"Not now, *boba*." His smile softens, but he eyes me with no little heat. "Soon. But not now."

"Soon would be good," I say, feeling color rise to my face.

After what we just did, I don't understand why I suddenly feel shy, but I do.

Luc sees my blush, and he kisses me once on each cheek. He reaches down between and draws himself from me. I blush harder.

"Don't move," he tells me as he rises from the bed, cupping himself. I'm treated to the sight of his sculpted backside, male perfection caste in bronze as he strides to the bathroom.

The door closes with a soft click, and I stifle a squeal. I can scarcely believe where the day has taken us.

"*¡Maldición!*"

The sharp word echoes from the bathroom, and I prop up on an elbow. "Everything okay?" I call.

Silence.

"Luc?"

"Yeah… Yeah… The floor's just freezing."

I smile, unable to help picturing him naked, standing on the white tile floor, that is, indeed, freezing this time of year.

"That's why I wear fuzzy socks," I call.

I hear water running.

"*¡Ay ay ay!*"

I try to smother my laugh. "The water's freezing too." I get to my knees, tug down the covers, and slip beneath them, hoping Luc will be up for a cuddle. Surely, he will. Right? It's our first time.

Honestly, I'm hoping he'll want to cuddle every time. I try for a moment, but I can't really picture anything better. And I have a couple of hours before I need to pick up the kids…

The door opens and Luc steps out in all his glory. All thoughts of kids and carpool are obliterated.

But Luc's looking down, his brow knit just a little.

"What's wrong?" I ask, tensing.

He looks up at me, his face clearing. "Nothing."

I bite my bottom lip. "You sure?" I ask. "Do *you* have any regrets?"

He crosses to the bed, lifts the covers and slides in beside me. At once, I'm dragged into his embrace, and he kisses me solidly on the mouth. Luc pulls back and looks me in the eye.

"Believe me when I tell you that was the single best moment of my life."

His eyes are clear, his brow smooth. I melt a little.

"Mine too."

Chapter Twenty-Eight

LUC

CESAR EYES ME OVER HIS MUFFULETTA. "THAT'S A WEIRD-ASS story, Luc."

"You're not helping."

My best friend puts down his sandwich and wipes his fingers on his paper napkin. We're sitting at a corner table in Chris's Poboys, and I've just told him everything. About Millie. The Curse—even though it's *not* a curse. And what happened yesterday. I've tried to keep my voice as low as possible so we don't snag the attention of any of the other lunch patrons. Like Cesar said, it's a weird-ass story.

And I don't know what to do.

"So, do I tell her?" The thought makes my fried oyster poboy congeal into a greasy ball in my stomach.

"That it broke?" Cesar gives me his best *are-you-crazy-amigo* look. "What good would it do? It would just make her worry until she gets her period."

I push my plate away and shut my eyes. I already know this. Millie will freak. It'll send her into a tailspin. She may even throw something at me.

But keeping it from her feels wrong.

"Besides..."

I open my eyes to find Cesar leaning over the table, giving me a shit-eating grin. "Condoms are for fucking pussies."

I glare at him. "That joke was old when we were juniors in high school."

He just chuckles and picks up his muffuletta. "It's still funny. And you look like you need a laugh." He bites into the sandwich.

"I'm not laughing."

Cesar rolls his eyes. "Look," he says, talking around a mouthful. "I'm not trying to be a dick. Really." He chews and swallows. "I can tell you care about this girl—"

"Love her," I correct. "I fucking love her."

His eyes narrow on mine like he's seeing me for the first time. "Wow."

I frown. *"Wow* what?"

Cesar shakes his head. "In all the years you were with Ronni, I don't think you ever came out and told me you loved her."

A small shock runs through me. Not at the truth of his words but at the contrast they draw. "What I felt for Ronni doesn't even come close. Nothing does."

He gives me a gentle smile. "I'm happy for you, *hermano.*"

"Yeah. Me too," I say, nodding. "And I don't want to fuck it up."

"Right," Cesar says, frowning now. I can see I have his full attention, and he's done joking around. "So, what would telling her do? You think she'd want to take the morning after pill or something?"

My eyes bug out of my head. *"¡Puta madre!"* I hadn't even considered that. I stare at Cesar, and he stares back. "I have no idea."

I sit back in the chair, shaken. Would Millie want that? When she told me that she'd lost a baby, I could tell by the pain in her face it was a baby she'd wanted. But that baby belonged to another man. That Carter asshole. She'd wanted Carter's baby.

But would she want mine?

A sudden ache in my middle hollows me out. What if she doesn't? I shut my eyes. Because on the other side of that hollowed out ache is a longing I can't even let myself touch.

I want to give Millie babies.

I want her to want my babies.

I grip my forehead and rub it with violence. "Fuck," I mutter.

"Talk to me, *compañero*," Cesar coaxes, his serious gaze softening with concern.

I shake my head. "I have to tell her."

He rears back, scowling his surprise. "You'd let her do that? Take that pill, I mean?"

It would fucking gut me to do it, but I can't admit that out loud. My mouth already feels like it's full of ashes. "I'd have to give her the choice."

"But I thought you said you loved her?" he asks, incredulous.

"I do."

Cesar shrugs. "So why not just wait? If she turns up *embarazada*, marry her."

The temptation to do just that is an anaconda coiling around my chest. I give a brutal shake of my head. "No. She's had almost no choice since her parents died." I think about everything she's already committed to. Everything she's given up. Ten more years of raising her siblings. I can't be the one who takes any more free will from her. "Whatever happens has to be her decision."

Cesar picks up his phone, and I study him with a frown. After swiping and tapping for a few seconds, he meets my eye and shows me the Google search results for the morning after pill. "Well, you have about three more days to tell her."

I DON'T SLEEP Tuesday night. I wanted to talk to Millie—in person—but the Lions had an away game in Barbe. An hour away. Knowing the late night and the demands of getting everyone home, fed, and finished with homework would have meant that we probably couldn't have talked until nearly ten.

That isn't how I want this talk to go.

The team has a home game tonight, and it starts at four. It'll be done by five-thirty, so maybe we can talk by eight. I've already asked Millie if I can come by, and she invited me to join her at the game as soon as my crews finished up.

I'm not gonna tell her no. Like ever.

By the time I get to the field, the sun has set, and the game is underway. Mami, Papi, and Abuela are sitting in the stands next to the Delacroixes. It's cold, so I'm surprised to see them, but when my mother and grandmother spot me approaching, their knowing smiles tell me all I need to know.

They aren't here to watch the game. They want a front row seat to Millie and me.

I kiss Mami and Abuela on the cheek and give my father a stiff nod. He nods back, but we haven't spoken since I hung up on him. Mami's eyes narrow at our chilly greeting, but she says nothing. If she wants an explanation, she's going to have to ask him. I couldn't explain his attitude if I tried.

"You're not too cold, Abuela?" I ask in Spanish.

She shakes her shawl covered head. She raises her arms under the blanket wrapped around her. *"Inez me compró calentadores de manos de Academy."*

Mami nods and translates for Millie's benefit. "I got her

some hand warmers from Academy," Mami says, then reaches for her giant purse. "Would you three like some? I have extra."

Millie smiles at my mother. "No thanks. We're—"

"I'll take one!" Emmett says, leaning across Millie with an outstretched hand.

"Here you go, *hombrecito,*" Mami says, handing one over before eyeing the Delacroix women. "You sure you don't want any?"

Wearing the same exact demure grins, Millie and Mattie shake their heads and thank her.

Mami looks up at me. "Here. We saved you a spot," she says, patting the bleacher between her and Millie.

I nearly snort. Of course, she wants me to sit between her and Millie. All the better for her and Abuela to hear everything we say.

"Thanks, Mami," I say, with just a hint of sarcasm. "What would I do without you?"

She huffs. "Never find the right girl..." she intones in Spanish. "Never get married. Never give me grandchildren..." I've got to hand it to my mother. Her sense of timing is uncanny.

"Who said anything about the right girl?" Papi mutters in Spanish. It's not loud, but Mami, Abuela, and, *me cago en Dios,* Mattie all snap their gazes at him.

"Suficiente, Jorge." My voice is soft but my meaning is anything but. Papi doesn't even look at me.

Seething, I sit next to Millie.

"Hi," she says softly.

"Hi."

She lowers her voice. "You okay?"

At first I don't say anything, my anger at Papi and the dread I carry for the conversation to come blot out almost everything else. And then I look at her. Her eyes are wide, watchful. She's hanging on my every word. And I've given her —the woman I love—just one.

Cabrón egoísta.

"Just a rough couple of days. I'll tell you about them later," I promise, giving her a half-hearted smile.

Millie lifts the edge of her stadium blanket and drapes it over me, enveloping me in her warmth. Most of the anger and even a little of the dread die away. Under the blanket, I reach for her hands and squeeze them tightly in mine.

"I'm sorry," I whisper. "I don't mean to be a *cascarrabias.*"

A smile breaks over her face. "What's a *cascarrabias?*"

In spite of everything, I smile. She can always make me smile. "A grump."

She wrinkles her nose, her smile growing. "I kind of already knew you had a grumpy streak," she teases. Then she gives me a little shrug. "I kind of already love it."

Sweetness pours through me like warm honey. *Nuestro Padre, please let her love me the way I love her. Let her want me. If it is your will, let her want my babies.*

Her face sobers as I watch her. "Luc, why do you look so sad?" She squeezes my hand.

I shake my head, squeezing back. "Ignore me. Let's watch the game."

Checking the scoreboard, I see the Lions are down by one. "What did I miss?"

Mattie snorts. "The same thing Harry missed. A kick by one of Jesuit's strikers."

"Ouch," I say, eyeing her with newfound respect. "Kind of harsh, Matt."

"I calls 'em likes I sees 'em," she says, not taking her eyes off the game. Or, more to the point, not taking her eyes off Alex.

"Exactly, why should she go any easier on him just because he's family?" Papi chimes in.

My teeth clench. These words are meant for no one but me. Millie must feel my body stiffen because beneath the cover of the stadium blanket, her thumb gently strokes the back of my hand. I've told her a little about what it's been like to take the reins from Papi when he was so reluctant to give them. He would have kept working for another twenty years if his body would have let him.

When he went into the hospital, his options were to put me in charge, sell the business—which wouldn't have amounted to much more than the equipment, especially after settling what we still owe on two small business loans—or close up shop and declare bankruptcy.

I've understood from the start that I'm the least of three evils.

If he could go back to work, I'd happily step aside. If only to get him to shut the hell up and stop resenting me.

All the more reason to give Millie this choice. I already know what it feels like to be someone's backup plan. And for them to hate me for it.

That's the last thing I want from Millie.

Chapter Twenty-Nine

MILLIE

THE LIONS LOST, AND EVERYONE SEEMS TO BE FEELING IT.

Harry's in a foul mood because of the missed kick. Mattie looks wounded, and I think it's because Alex didn't talk to her after the game. I tried to tell her he probably wasn't feeling very sociable after his second penalty flag. And Emmett is just feeding off his brother and sister.

The one who worries me the most, though, is Luc. He's been sullen and brooding since he showed up tonight.

Come to think of it, something's been a little off since Monday. Since we made love.

And. What. The. Hell?

I was there. It was spectacular. Unparalleled.

Not that I have much of a frame of reference.

But even without that, it was incredible. Cosmic. Otherworldly. I couldn't have been the only one who thought so. In fact, while we cuddled, he'd said it was, and I quote, "the single best moment of my life."

I'm sure those were his exact words because I think they're now tattooed in a place of honor on my soul.

So why does he seem so distant? And, I can't be sure, but

I'd swear he was totally pissed at the game. Though I'm pretty dang sure it wasn't at me.

But he says he wants to talk, and it makes me nervous. And I've got enough to be nervous about in my life.

Still, Luc does us a solid by picking up Judice Inn burgers after the game so we can come straight home. I send Harry up so he can shower first. Maybe it'll help put him past the loss. Emmett feeds and plays with Clarence, and Mattie is finishing her homework when Luc comes in with dinner.

Emmett is about to nosedive into his when I stop him.

"Hey, buddy, let's wait for Harry and eat as a family, 'kay?"

He slumps. "But I'm so hungry."

I'm about to negotiate with him when Luc cups an ear and cocks his head at the ceiling. "I don't hear the shower," he says, then gestures toward the stairs. "Why don't you go up, *jefe*, and tell him grub's here. Let's see how fast you can do it."

Emmett perks up. "Time me."

Smiling, Luc digs his phone out of his back pocket before tapping on the screen. "Okay... *Go!*"

My little brother takes off.

"Tell Mattie too!" I call after him.

"That'll mess up my time!" he shouts back, stomping up the stairs.

Neither one of us responds because for the first time since Monday, we're alone. Sadly, the length of the dining table separates us.

"You're so good with him." I've said this before, but he needs to know how much it means to me.

He shrugs. "It wasn't that long ago when Alex was his age. I remember some of the tricks."

I move around the head of the table, take two steps toward him, and stop. "I probably shouldn't tell you this, but you're making me nervous."

His expression clouds. "Nervous? Why?"

Heat rises to my face. "You said you wanted to talk."

The corners of his mouth turn up, but his dimples stay hidden. "And talking's bad?"

"Well, duh," I say, crossing my arms over my chest, my nerves escalating by the second. "Everyone knows talking's bad."

Luc's brows lower and he stalks toward me. When he's in my space, he grabs me by the belt loops of my jeans. "What about talking like this?" He pulls me to him until my nose brushes his collarbone and his lips meet my ear. "Is this bad?"

He smells amazing. Clean, like cut cedar. But warm and unmistakably male. I wrap my arms around him and inhale. His arms close around me too.

"Not bad, right?" he whispers.

I shake my head. "Not bad." I've kind of already forgotten how we got here, my nerves vegging out in the pheromonal glow of his body.

Rhythmic thumping overhead, the sound of Emmett on the stairs, kills the moment. I move to pull away, but Luc grabs me by the elbows and our eyes lock.

"I don't know what it was like for you before, Millie," he says, his gaze searching. "But talking with me won't ever be bad."

Wow. Okay. I feel a little better.

Enough to put away a Judice Inn burger, harass Emmett into taking a bath, and finally get the kids upstairs at eight-thirty. The twins won't be asleep for hours with all the homework they have, but Emmett should konk out by nine.

I find Luc on the sectional, but not sprawled out with one arm resting on the back like I'd prefer. He's sitting, but with his elbows on his knees, hands clasped.

Shit.

He looks up when I approach. "They're all good?"

"Yeah." I know I should join him, but my feet don't want to move.

Luc smacks the cushion next to him with two swats. "Come sit by me."

I make a hesitant noise. "Mmm. I have a bad feeling about this."

He cracks a smile. "What's it telling you?"

I don't mince words. "That you're about to say something I won't like."

Luc presses his lips together and tilts his head to the side, considering. "You probably won't like it, but we'll deal."

We'll deal?

It's the *we* part that frees my feet up to move toward him. "Is this about why you seemed angry earlier?"

I've taken him off guard. I can see it in his eyes. "Angry?"

"At the game."

A shadow passes over his face. "Oh. That... That was Papi." Luc shakes his head, his gaze dropping. "I don't want to talk about him."

I nod, but I don't like the look he's wearing. It's like a little of that anger from earlier has come back. Luc shakes his head again, almost like a dog shedding water.

"Come sit." He pats the couch again. I take two more steps.

"I'm just reminding you," I say softly, "that you said talking isn't bad, so I expect you to keep your word on that."

I say this—mostly—to make him laugh, and it works. If he's laughing, I can relax. At least a little.

He reaches a hand to me, and I take it, moving the rest of the way toward him before sitting.

"Even if we have to talk about something bad, like I said, us talking won't be bad." He cocks a brow at me. "This is ours, remember?"

At this, warmth pours through me. "I remember." And I squeeze his hand.

"Okay," he says, as if it's settled. Then his eyes narrow like he's wincing. "I gotta tell you something—"

"You're married," I blurt.

His brows shoot up. "What?! No! What the hell, Millie?"

I shake my head. "Sorry. Sorry. I just went with something really bad. Like ripping off a Band-Aid," I blather. "Now, anything you say will just pale by comparison."

Luc blinks at me, looking both confused and mildly concerned. I take a cleansing breath, rub my free hand up and down one thigh, and nod. "Okay, I think I got that out of my system. Go for it."

His brows downshift again. "Okay... So... On Monday?" He says it like a question, his voice dipping low, making it plenty clear he's talking about when we had sex. I bite my bottom lip because I just knew something was wrong.

Is it me?

Is there something wrong with my junk? Like a freak-of-nature thing? "Did you know that male cats have barbed penises?"

Okay, even I can't believe I just said that.

"Wh-ha-hat?!" If Luc looked confused and concerned before, he's downright horror-stricken now.

And, God help me, I can't shut up. "Yeah. They're covered with all these little spines that appear to make cat sex really painful for the female," I explain, my vet school training kicking in hard core. "But it's believed that the spines trigger feline ovulation."

"Millie—why?" Luc asks bug-eyed. "Why are you telling me this?"

I let go a breath. "Well... just that... maybe if something didn't feel quite right when we... you know—"

"Stop."

I stop.

Luc squeezes his eyes shut and runs a hand down his face. Then he blinks at me, looking like a man who has just been put through the wringer. He takes my hands with both of his, bouncing them on my knees with each word.

"Everything. Everything felt right, Millie. I swear to Christ."

"Then what—"

"Millie, the condom broke." He says this, and I realize that his face is going red, and it's getting redder. "That's all. I should have told you then, but I didn't want to freak you out."

I swallow. "Oh."

"Oh?" He blinks four or five times. "You mean, you're not freaked out?"

"Well…" All things considered, it's better than him telling me that sex with me felt like banging a cactus, but, honestly, it doesn't feel like news. "To tell you the truth, I'm not all that surprised."

This time when his brows fly up, I can see he's genuinely stunned. "What do you mean? Why?"

I lift and drop one shoulder. "Of course something like that would happen. To me, I mean."

"Why should that happen to you?" he asks, surprise morphing to curiosity.

"Because of The Cur—"

"Don't call it a curse," he interrupts, glaring a little.

"Okay, fine. Because of the supernatural-phenomenon-surrounding-my-fertility-and-that-of-every-woman-I'm-descended-from." I frown. "Doesn't really roll off the tongue, does it?"

Luc visibly fights a grin. "Millie, I'm being serious."

"Me too." I nod. "But, honestly, when you put it on—the condom, I mean—there was a part of me that literally thought *why bother?*"

"Seriously?" Astonishment rings from the question.

I shrug again. "Granted, I wasn't at my most rational at that juncture," I admit. "But, yeah, kind of. I mean, if my parents resorted to a vasectomy, and even that failed in the face of cosmic interference, what good is a little latex balloon?"

Luc narrows his eyes in a sinister expression. *"Little?"*

I smile huge. "Massive. Massive latex balloon."

Hello, dimples.

"Anyway, I figure we both know the score. You were warned at least."

Luc rolls his eyes. "I'm just glad you aren't upset. At first I wasn't going to say anything about it."

Something in his voice snags my attention. "What made you change your mind?"

"Because." Luc's face hardens in a way I've never seen before. "If you wanted to do something about it, there's still time."

Later, I'll look back on this moment and realize just how naive I am. But right now, I still have no clue.

"What do you mean?" Honest to God. No clue. "Time for what?"

His expression doesn't change. It's as hard as granite. "To get a prescription."

I stare at him, still completely *sans* clue.

"You know," he says with a shrug and a disconcerted frown. "Plan B."

When the penny drops, it's with a trumpet blare of adrenaline. I swear, I hear the blast as it enters my bloodstream. My vision tunnels, and my mouth turns to cotton.

"Plan B," I parrot. "Right." The words sound as dry as cornhusks.

I realize I've been standing in the center of hope, rocking in its orbit, like a girl with a hula-hoop. And it just clattered to the ground.

I'm not taking Plan B. I'd never take Plan B. That's not the problem. The problem is that I would have never expected Luc Valencia to suggest it. And because I never expected it, I feel like the dumbest person in the world.

Because *it's too much to ask*.

My life. Everything I am. What I'm destined to be. It's too much to ask.

And I knew that before I fell for him, and I still let myself fall.

Stupid.

Stupid.

Stupid.

"Millie? You okay?" he asks, eyes searching.

I paste on a smile. "Yeah. Fine."

He frowns. "Did I say something wr—"

"No. No." I shake my head. "I just… That's not for me. Plan B, I mean." I don't tell him how much I wanted the baby I lost. How if I things had been different, she—if she was a she —would be due in three weeks. If I had been able to keep him —if he was a him—I'd be complaining about my swollen feet and my sore back and needing to pee every ten minutes.

And loving every minute of it.

My dry mouth suddenly floods with saliva, and I swallow hard.

"I wasn't—" Luc stops, frowning. "I didn't mean to suggest—"

Reaching over the two inches that separate us—two inches that now seem like two miles—I pat him quickly on the knee. "No, no. Of course."

His frown etches deeper, and he sits up straight. "Because if you were preg—"

I shake my head hard. So hard, my brain might rattle. "I'm sure I'm not."

This is a lie. I'm sure of nothing. Not a damn thing.

"I'M PREGNANT."

It's the fourth time I've said it this morning, and for the fourth time, Kath gives me an exasperated stare. "Stop saying that. You know it's too soon to tell."

I make a noise of dispute in my throat while she unwraps her chopsticks. We're between appointments, and Kath grabbed Peking Gardens takeout for lunch. I poke at my Singapore Mai Fun, trying to decide if I'm nauseated or just too stressed to eat.

Reading my mind, Kath points her chopsticks at my to-go plate. "You're hungry. You told me yourself you skipped breakfast. Eat."

Repressing the urge to snarl, I hook a bite of noodles and shrimp and shovel it into my mouth. And it's good. Really good. When I eat another bite, Kath chimes in.

"See? You're getting yourself all worked up for no reason."

I shake my head, mouth still full. "Oh, there's reason. How could I have been so stupid?" I stab a fancy cut carrot with a chopstick. "I'd just had a shot of antibiotics. While on the Pill. I know that antibiotics mess with the Pill. Not that the Pill even works for me," I add with a shrug.

Kath winces. "I did read an article about that once. The pill doesn't work for a small percentage of women. Like not at all."

I snort. "Nothing—short of celibacy—works for me. And clearly not even that because…" I open my mouth to say Luc's name, but then shut it, afraid I'll start crying.

Why did I think this time would be any different? Why did I think *he* would be any different?

Because, a voice from deep within me whispers, *he's Luc.*

My throat wants to close on a sob. I shove another bite of noodles into my mouth and swallow them almost without chewing to force it open. The battle between constricting muscles and Chinese takeout is epic. Thank goodness the noodles win, or my life might hang in the balance.

As I recover, I admit to myself why I believed things would be different with Luc. Because he knew, even better than Carter did, what he might be getting into. He knows the Delacroix day-to-day—better than Carter ever did because Aunt Pru was still with us back then. Helping out. Keeping us afloat. And back then, we were still in a state of shock.

But Luc has seen us as a family redefined. He knows us from the inside.

And he was warned. Carter never took me seriously when I said my chances of getting pregnant were astronomical.

But Luc did.

At least, I believed he did.

How could he think for a minute I'd—

"Have you talked to him about it? Since Wednesday, I mean?" Kath asks.

I roll my eyes. "No." It's Friday, and although I'm spending time with Luc, I've made sure we're never alone when I do. Luckily, Emmett had to make a diorama Thursday night, and last night was another away game. "I know I need to talk to him. I just want to wait until I'm sure."

Kath raises a brow at me. "And what then?"

I swallow. "Tell him I'm pregnant—"

"You're not pregnant."

I sigh. Kath has no appreciation for the power of The... The... Whatever We're Calling It. Honestly, I can't even bring myself to think *Curse* anymore. Because if I am pregnant (who am I kidding? I'm so totally pregnant) it's Luc's.

And how could *that* be a curse? How could that be anything but wonderful?

I sigh again, but this one sounds completely different. Worshipful. Hopeful.

Yes. I hope I'm pregnant. (Again, who am I kidding?)

But I'm hoping for more than that. So much more. And this hope is almost too big to let myself feel.

"Fine," I concede just to move the discussion along. "*If* I'm pregnant, I'll tell Luc. I'll tell him everything's cool. That I don't expect anything from him. He doesn't even need to pay child support—"

"Millie!" Kath scolds with a scowl. "That's crazy!"

I shrug. "It's not like I—" the word halts in my throat, and I make myself say it hard, "*need* him for a roof over my head or —or to pay the bills."

This much is true. I don't need him for those things.

Not those.

I press my lips together and move my gaze to my lunch. The Singapore Mai Fun is suddenly no fun at all. The noodles now look like tapeworms, and I toss my chopsticks on the table between us, my appetite long gone. "Besides..." I say on a forced exhale. "I know better than to ask so much of someone."

"What do you mean, Millie?" Kath's frown deepens. "A father taking responsibility for his baby isn't too much to ask."

I shake my head. "Normally, I'd agree with you, but my situation isn't normal."

Kath just stares like she's waiting for me to elaborate, so I do.

"Luc has a pretty good idea of what it would be like if he stuck around," I explain. "If he really wanted that, why would he even bring up other options?" I try to make it sound like it's no big deal. Like I'm not involved.

Like my heart isn't either.

She so totally calls me on my bluff. "Do you care about him?"

I swallow. "Y-yeah."

Kath makes owl eyes at me. "I think telling a man you care

for that you don't need him is a bad idea." Seriously, I feel like a field mouse under that stare. Then she goes in for the kill. "And I know I never knew them, but I think your parents would have too."

I want to curl in on myself like I've been stabbed. Not really because Kath said it. But because she's right. I resist the urge. Keep myself open and hold her gaze.

"Yeah, that's true," I acknowledge. "But—like you said— what they would have wanted can't be applied to a world without them."

She blows a breath out of her nose, her bird of prey look turning wry. "I knew those words would come back to haunt me."

I'M SUPPOSED to be off on Saturday, but Dr. Loftin calls me in to help with an emergency surgery. Dachshund versus golf cart. Broken carpus and radius with tissue abrasions. Not a hopeless case, but one that requires time and skill. This is definitely one of those instances when two vets are better than one.

We finish up after closing time, and I transfer the little Dachshund to the emergency clinic where she can be kept under observation for the rest of the weekend. By the time I get home, it's after two p.m., and I need a shower.

And that's where it happens.

The prick.

No, not that kind of prick.

The one that feels like an acupuncture needle deep down inside me.

I felt it before. The last time. Except that was on the right side, and this one is definitely the left. I go completely still under the shower spray with the certain knowledge that within the confines of my body... it's not just me.

It's *us.* Me and baby.

And not just any baby. Not even just my baby. But ours. Mine and Luc's.

It's as though the water rushing over me is a benediction. A blessing the angels have poured over me.

And whether Luc wants me or not. Or whether he wants *us* or not, this baby—this blessing a thousand times over—is wanted and loved. Already.

And if we have to go it alone, so be it.

Chapter Thirty

LUC

Millie won't talk to me. Not really.

I know she's upset. She's been upset since I told her about the condom. She's keeping me at arm's length, and I'll be damned if she isn't finding ways to have the kids around when we're together.

But, as usual, she insists that she's *fine*.

Whoever thought that someone could grow to hate that four-letter word? I know she's not fine because I keep catching her watching me.

And it's not the way she used to watch me. Back before I kissed her. She watched me then like she couldn't help herself. The same way I couldn't help watching her.

Now, it's like she's on the lookout for sudden moves. And maybe I'm doing the same. Waiting to see if she'll bolt.

I dare her to try. I'm not letting her go anywhere.

It's Sunday night, and for once this week, there's not a game or a homework project or a recital. And I might just strangle my mother.

My plan was to pay the kids to babysit themselves again.

Millie and I haven't even been on a real date. She deserves one, and I want to give it to her.

But Mami called Millie an hour after she got home from work yesterday. She wants us to come over for Sunday Supper. Fried catfish tacos and churros with chocolate sauce. And Millie and her crew are suckers for anything homemade.

I can't really blame them. The Delacroixes have been eating takeout for weeks.

Maybe that's what I should do for a first date—if ever I get to take her on one—make her a home-cooked meal. At my apartment. I wonder how much I'd have to pay the kids to keep Millie overnight.

And if she'd ever agree to that.

Right now, I'd take having her spend just a few minutes alone with me. Even under the same roof with the kids. Just ten minutes so I could kiss her deep. Remind her what we have.

Okay, maybe twenty minutes.

Maybe I can steal her away from the crowd at my parents' house tonight. If Papi and Uncle Raul haven't commandeered the den for a game of pool, that would be a great spot. Just a few minutes to wrap her in my arms and chase her tongue with mine, show her that she is safe with me. Show her that I want her. Tell her again that I love her.

I pick up the Delacroixes at five-thirty. The twins vibrate with excitement. Emmett is practically levitating.

Millie seems *fine*.

At least, this is what I think until I hand her up into the Tundra, pressing my palm into the small of her back. She's wound tighter than a guitar string. The kids are climbing into the back, arguing with each other, so I steal an opportunity.

When her behind lands on the seat, I squeeze her thigh. Millie jumps, but at least she meets my eyes. And the expression in hers is guarded. Wary.

I hate it.

I squeeze her thigh again. "Before the end of the night," I tell her, my voice low, for her ears only, "we're talking. I don't care how late it is."

Millie triple blinks. Her mouth falls open. Then closes. If I had to guess, she's somewhere between startled and terrified. What the hell?

She opens her mouth again, but suddenly her blue eyes are awash in regret. "I don't know if I'm up for that tonight."

Not up for it? Talking to me?

A trap door opens in my stomach. My mind immediately swings toward the worst possible scenario. I told her about the condom. She's worried she's pregnant. And now, despite giving me her love, she's having doubts. About us.

About me.

"Why are you just standing there, Luc?" Emmett pipes up from the back seat, bouncing like he's spring-loaded. "Let's go!"

Part of me wants to drag Millie inside and have this out now. But I grit my teeth and close her door.

I drive, but the grip I have on the steering wheel is merciless. At first, my anger is a slow boil, just barely contained. She doesn't want to talk to me? Fine. She doesn't have the courage to tell me I'm not her first choice? That's fucking fine, too. It's not like I'm not used to that.

Ronni couldn't come out and say it. Left her phone with her messages open right where I'd see them. Right where I'd read her boss's dirty texts.

And Papi? Every time I talk to him, he comes as close as he can to saying he'd rather be pushing up daisies than watch me at the helm of the business.

The heat of my anger and the acid burn of bitterness are good at first. Distracting. Consoling. But by the time we get to my parents' house, I know they are just shields.

Because if Millie doesn't want me—if I'm not her first choice—it'll slay me. It'll hurt worse than anything.

She's mine. Mine in a way Ronni never was. Mine more than the business could ever be.

Mine because in the short time I've known her, somehow, my heart has moved out of my chest and now beats inside her hands.

We've said next to nothing on the drive over, relying on the kids' chatter to fill the cab of the truck. And I'm grateful for them because they rush inside, through the garage door, into the kitchen, and the voices of Mami, Abuela, and my cousins rise in greeting. Millie slips inside, and I bring up the rear, forcing a smile at the excited crowd.

The kitchen is so full, I have to squeeze in behind Millie to shut the door. Her hair smells like love. Selfishly, I lean in, pull her scent in deep. If I press her to talk tonight, this might be the last time I get close to her. I clasp a lock of her blazing hair between my fingers.

"*Dios ten piedad*," I whisper in prayer. "*Por favor, déjame conservarla.*"

Millie turns, looking back at me over her shoulder. Her gaze is so warm and curious, it gives me hope. "What did you say?" she whispers, her eyes searching.

I swear, I'm about to answer her truthfully, tell her that I'm begging God to let me keep her when Abuela, her face alight, pushes up from the kitchen table.

"*¡Dulce Cristo!*" she cries at Millie, clasping her hands over her heart. "*¡Estás embarazada!*"

"*¿Qué?*" Mami shouts, eyes wide.

"*¿Qué?*" My aunt and cousins ask each other.

"*What?!*" Mattie shrieks, turning to Millie, looking betrayed.

Millie throws her hands up. "What? What did she say?"

I drop a hand on Millie's shoulder, but before I can say

anything, Mattie blinks, her big eyes more worried than ever. "She said you're pregnant! Is it true?"

Both Emmett and Harry whirl to face Millie, bug-eyed. "Seriously?" Emmett squawks, his surprise quickly morphing to excitement.

I step beside Millie with one arm around her shoulder and one hand raised to calm everyone down.

"Guys, no," I say shaking my head. "I don't know what Abuela is talking about but—"

Abuela pokes a gnarled finger at us. *"Anoche soñé que ustedes cinco entraron así como acaban de hacerlo…"*

"Last night I dreamed," Mami translates for Millie and her family, *"that the five of you walked in like you just did…"*

"Y Millie llevaba una camisa morada como esa," Abuela says, pointing at Millie before pinching the fabric of her blouse between her fingers. The hair on the back of my neck stands at attention.

"And Millie was wearing a purple shirt just like that," Mami delivers, nodding to the purple top that Millie is wearing. At her words, Millie's spine straightens beneath my arm.

Abuela holds her hands out in front of her, making the universal shape of a pregnant belly. *"Pero su vientre estaba creciendo con un crío dentro."*

Aunt Luci clucks her tongue and gives Abuela an exasperated look. "That doesn't mean anything. *Eso fue solo un sueño."*

"¿Solo un sueño?" Abuela throws up her hands. *"¡Era una señal de los ángeles!"*

Aunt Luci rolls her eyes. "A sign from the angels? Really, Mami," she mutters, not bothering to reply in Spanish.

Abuela thrusts an emphatic hand toward Millie. *"¡Solo mírala! Ella está brillando!"*

The gaze of every woman in my family lands on Millie.

"She's right. Millie *is* glowing," Felicité murmurs.

I glance down at Millie. Sure, her face is flushed with the

embarrassment of all this attention, but beyond that, she is radiant. Her vanilla ice cream skin has never looked so brilliant. Her blue eyes shine with an almost angelic gleam.

How could I not have noticed it earlier? She's more beautiful than ever. By far, the most beautiful woman I've ever seen. Is the glow because—

"Millie?" My throat is so dry her name comes out a rasp. "Is there something I should know?"

She looks up at me dewy-eyed, her spice-colored lashes closing and opening like butterfly wings. "Well…" Uncertainty rings in the word. Something is on her mind, and she's unsure about telling me.

I take in the ten pairs of eyes watching us, her family and most of mine in that number, and I make a decision.

"We aren't doing this here," I mutter, grabbing her hand.

Millie still has her purse slung over her shoulder, and I don't care. Leaving the crowd of our families slack-jawed and lobbing questions after us in two languages, I drag her out of the kitchen, through the living room, and up the stairs. Two bedrooms flank the top of the stairs, Abuela's and Alex's. Passing both doors, I am for the third in the middle and throw the bathroom door open.

"Fucking God—Luc, what the hell?" Alex, shirtless and barefoot in jeans glares at me in outraged confusion.

I rear back and Millie gasps. "Sorry, I—"

But Alex's gaze falls on Millie and his eyes light up. "Mattie's here?"

"Jesus Christ," Millie mutters under her breath.

"Yes. Go say hi. And give us some space, yeah?" I urge.

My brother is moving past us before I even finish my suggestion.

"But put a shirt on first," Millie orders as he steps into the hall. She turns to me as he heads to his room. "One look at that, and she'd be—"

"Stop." I hold up a hand. "Wipe that thought out of your head."

Millie stares at me for a second. Then she gives me a sharp nod. "Right."

I hold out my hand, gesturing her toward the bathroom. She points. "Why—"

"Because it's the only place we're guaranteed privacy."

"I wasn't guaranteed privacy!" Alex calls from his room.

I glower at his closed door. "Use the damn lock."

"It's just me and Abuela up here," he hollers back. "And *she* knocks." His bedroom door opens, and Alex emerges, smoothing a T-shirt down over his chest. It's white except for the letters LSD written in what looks like pink, yellow, and blue cake frosting.

Millie narrows her eyes at the letters, and Alex looks down at his shirt. "Oh, don't freak out, Millie," he says, meeting her glare with a grin. "This LSD is the band. Not the drug."

"I know," she says through clenched teeth. "Mattie's been blasting 'Angel in Your Eyes' in her room the last three days."

Alex's teeth flash. "Must be our song."

I grab Millie by the wrist before she can push my brother down the stairs. "Go," I tell him.

Still grinning, my brother high tails it down the stairs. Millie pulls out of my hold, stalks into the bathroom and folds in half on the edge of the tub. Her purse falls to the floor and she drops her head in her hands.

"My God. She'll be pregnant by New Year's."

I step inside and close the door. I lock it for good measure and lean back against it.

"She won't get pregnant."

A curtain of red hair hides Millie's face. "She will," she moans. "We're doomed."

I push from the door, moving to her, but she whips her head up, eyeing me with alarm. "We have to break up."

I'm not gonna lie. Even though I know she's panicked and rattled and has her head in the wrong place, even though I know in my soul she is mine, her words land like a club to my gut.

I take a deep breath and absorb the blow. I empty my lungs slowly. "Millie, why are you saying that?"

Her bottom lip trembles, and I watch her swallow the emotion and steel her resolve. "Because. It's the right thing to do."

A bitter laugh cracks from me. "Right for who?" I'm standing over her, and the posture feels all wrong. Everything about this feels wrong. So instead of sitting beside her on the tub, I sink to my knees, lay my hands on her knees.

Her worried eyes are now level with mine. "Honestly?" she asks, her voice going squeaky. "All of us."

I shake my head. "Nope. Not good enough."

She clenches her jaw. "If I end this now, I can stop further damage."

"You end this now, there'll be nothing but damage." I speak the words like an oath. "It'll wreck me."

Millie closes her eyes and deflates. "But at least you'd be free."

My face becomes a scowl. "Free to do what?" When she doesn't answer me, doesn't open her eyes, I reach for her shoulders and give her a little shake. "Where is this coming from?"

So slowly, she lifts her eyelids and all I see is regret. "Nine months ago, I conceived a child with a man I thought I'd spend the rest of my life with," she says, and for the first time this Carter guy she's barely mentioned seems like a real threat. I want to brain him with a hammer.

"Even though it didn't feel like it at the time, losing him was not the worst thing to happen to me." Her eyes well, and she blinks and forces herself to smile. "It wasn't even in the top three."

The fight goes out of me, and I take one hand from her knee and grip her fingers in mine. She doesn't need to tell me her top three. Mother. Father. Child. In whatever order. Probably all tied for first.

"When he left, he said something to me I can't forget." Her voice is choked, stricken.

I squeeze her fingers, her knee. "What the hell did he say?" Yeah, I could still pick up that hammer.

Millie inhales through her nose and empties her lungs with resignation. "That this—us—me and the kids—this instant family was too much to ask." She shrugs. "And he was right."

"What?!"

Millie puts her free hand to her heart. "I know it is. I mean, I'm twenty-four, and I would have never signed up for this if we weren't talking about Harry, Mattie, and Emmett. I don't blame him."

"Millie, that—"

"No, just listen." She moves her hand from her heart to mine. "If we hadn't lost the baby..." Millie bites her bottom lip and frowns. "I think Carter would have stayed."

She lets the words hang there, and maybe it makes me a dick, maybe it makes me the most awful person in the world, but I'm so glad that fucker bolted. I'm sorry Millie lost her baby, but if things would have gone differently, he'd be here, and I'd be building a kitchen for an incredible woman I'd never have the chance to touch.

But I know, on my knees at her feet, I would have felt it. I'd have still gotten to watch her. Still gotten to know her. She'd be nine months pregnant, married to that asswipe, or home on maternity leave in my face every day, being her funny, fretful, fantastic self. And I would have felt the pull I felt that first night at the soccer game. Marveled over how strong she was. I'd have seen her patience and her passion, and I would have loved her anyway. Knowing I could never have her.

"So, you see, I have to break up with you," Millie says, jerking me from my fucked up day dream into an even more fucked up reality.

"*¿Qué carajo?* Millie, this makes no sense. I'm not—"

She grips the front of my shirt in her hand. "I'm all but positive I'm pregnant."

The air. The room. The whole world goes still. I've been ready for this. But even if you think you're ready to hear those words, they still hit like a shock wave.

I cover her hand at my heart. "Millie—"

"But it's fine," she says, her voice high-pitched and falsely bright. Her smile is false too. "I'm about as set for life as someone who's not a Kardashian could be. I can do whatever it takes. I can handle this by myself."

I shake my head. "No."

She rolls her eyes. "You don't have to prove to me you're a good man. I already know," she says, giving me a level look. "I'm not going to trap you and have you resenting me for the rest of our lives—"

"I wouldn't—"

"Because that's definitely what would have happened with Carter, and I won't have it happen—"

"*¡Maldición!*" The curse ricochets off the shower walls. "Millie, for God's sake, I'm. Not. Carter. And don't you ever lump me with that *cabrón*. He's too stupid to know what he lost."

She blinks, her lips parting. It's distracting. I'm so angry, I don't know whether to kiss her hard or throw something.

"You're right," she says, sounding startled. Millie shakes her head. "You're *nothing* like Carter. You are ten times the man he is. A hundred times. You are everything, *everything* I could want—"

Millie clamps her mouth shut, her eyes shining with unshed tears. In them I see all of her love. For me. Not anyone else. But right beside it is a sadness that scares the hell out of me.

"But—but Carter was right too." She looks so resigned. So defeated. "It is too much to ask."

Anger is the only protection I have.

"Are you asking? Are you even giving me a choice? Or are you just leaving me?" I don't think I've ever yelled in a bathroom before. It's fucking loud.

"I didn't want…" She leans down and reaches into her purse. "I was going to wait until tomorrow. Until I knew for sure." She pulls out a long, pink box. First Response Early Result Pregnancy Test. *"Can tell 6 days sooner,"* the label announces.

I stare at her, knowing with sudden clarity—and so much gratitude—that I am going to spend the rest of my life with a woman who has the power to drive me crazy.

"Marry me."

That mouth of hers falls open. Yep, damned distracting. *"What?!"*

I lick my lips. I've never done this before, but I know *What?!* Is not the answer I'm looking for. Correction. I'm going to spend the rest of my life with a woman who has the power to drive me crazy—if I can convince her to marry me. Now. Before she can take that stupid test.

At least I'm already on my knees.

I take a deep breath and clasp both her hands in mine.

"Millie…" I trail off because I realize I don't know it. How could I not know it? "Baby, what's your middle name?"

She grimaces. "Agnes."

My brows leap. "Agnes? *Really?*" What the hell were her parents thinking?

Millie wrinkles her nose. "It's bad. Awful, really."

I don't argue. "Millie Agnes Delacroix—"

"It's, um…" She bites her lip and wrinkles her nose again. "Actually, it's Mildred."

Dios misericordioso.

"Wow." I don't mean to say it out loud, but… "Wow."

She nods. "Tell me about it."

I blink. "Your initials spell *MAD,*" I blurt, then my voice drops with awe. "This explains so much."

Her brow executes a severe arch.

I look at her glowering at me, and I feel a smile that comes straight from my soul transform my face.

I'm going to spend the rest of my life driving her crazy.

"Mildred Agnes Delacroix." As the words leave my tongue, I realize it is the most beautiful name in the world. Because it's hers. "I fell for you at a soccer game when you wouldn't even look me in the eye, even though I knew you were checking me out—"

"I was no—"

I stop her mouth with my palm. "Let me finish. This is nerve wracking as shit." The glare she gives me is the most beautiful thing. Ever. "Then I found myself in the middle of your busy, full, crazy life, and I never want to leave."

The glare vanishes until there's nothing but her smooth, ivory brow and her soft blue eyes.

"I've watched you do the impossible—and do it with endless love and patience. And humor. I want a share of that. Of all of it. The responsibilities. The rewards. And most of all, the love." I squeeze her hands and uncover her mouth, but it's all I can do not to cover it again with mine. "I'll give you a ring tomorrow, but today I'm asking. Will you marry me?"

Her eyes are wide, hopeful, but still scared. She holds up the pregnancy test. "Don't you want to know first? Before you do this? I mean, maybe I'm wrong and—"

I snatch the box from her, turn and chuck it into Abuela's blue flowered wastebasket. I whirl back to meet her gaze.

"I don't care if you're pregnant or not. I want to marry you."

She glances at the trashcan with a frown. "That was thirteen dollars."

I shake my head. "Don't care about that either. I asked you a question, *linda.*"

Maybe I should be nervous that she hasn't answered, but I'm not. She can be nervous. I'm sure.

Millie bites her bottom lip. "You want to marry me?"

"Yes, *boba,* I want to marry you."

Blink. Blink. "Even if we have to spend the next ten years raising Harry, Mattie, and Emmett?"

"*¿Estás bromeando?* Especially if we get to spend the next ten years raising them," I promise. "And the next twenty or thirty raising our own."

"Twenty or th-thirty?" Those blue eyes go huge.

I shrug. "If everything you've told me about your family is true, you're going to be giving me babies for a while."

Her eyes soften again. "Giving you babies," she echoes, sounding kind of awed. I smile. It does sound pretty awesome. Her gaze shifts down, and I know she's looking at my dimples when she smiles, too.

"You mean it," Millie says, sounding surprised, but also, I note, sure.

I nod. "I mean it." But she'd better say yes. I'm ready to hear it. "So, what do you s—"

She grabs the front of my shirt with both hands and yanks me close. "Yes. Yes. Yes." The last *yes* lands on my lips right before hers do. She kisses me, and then I grab her behind her neck and at her hips, and I'm kissing her. Millie opens her knees, and I edge between them, tugging her closer, lungs pumping, pulse pounding, heart soaring.

When lips, tongues, and even teeth have had their fill and we are in danger of profaning my grandmother and brother's shared bathroom, I get us to our feet and smooth out Millie's clothes while she smooths out mine.

"Should we go down and tell them?" she asks, blushing.

"You mean if they're not all listening with their ears pressed to the door?"

She gasps.

"I'm kidding."

"Oh, thank God."

"But they're probably all at the foot of the stairs." This time I'm not teasing. We're talking about Mami and Aunt Lucinda. Not to mention Emmett, the little sneak.

I move toward the door, but Millie grabs my wrist. "I know what you said," she says before bending down to the waste basket. "But we're probably going to need this." She retrieves the pregnancy test.

I take the box from her, gently this time, and tuck it into her purse. "Keep it. But I don't want you taking it until after we're married."

Millie looks at me like I'm crazy. "Wait. *What?*"

"Let's get married first. Then take the pregnancy test."

"Um, Luc." She grabs my elbow, still wearing the *you're-crazy* look. "That would have to be *really* soon to—"

"Do you need a big, fancy wedding?" If she does, I'll give it to her. Whatever she wants.

Millie wrinkles her nose. "God, no. I don't have time for that."

I wrap my arm around her waist and cinch her close. "So we do it soon. The kids'll be off for Christmas break. We'll do it then."

"Where?" she asks, frowning.

I shrug again. "We could do it here. You know my family has the food covered." I smile at her, picturing it. "Mattie could play the piano. Harry could give you away. Emmett could be my best man."

Her mouth falls open. "You'd do that?"

I grin. What wouldn't I do for her? For them? "Sure."

She shakes her head. "What about Alex? Or your friend Cesar?"

Millie hasn't met Cesar, but I've told her about him. That'll be on my Daily Three tomorrow. Introduce Millie to Cesar.

"They'll both be cool about it," I reassure her.

"Mrs. Chen can play the piano," she says, her eyes shining. "I'll ask Mattie to be my maid of honor."

I nod. "That works." Another idea strikes. "And the kids can stay here while we go on a honeymoon."

Millie's eyes go wide. "That's a terrible idea. Mattie and Alex—"

"I meant what I said about sharing the responsibilities." I shake my head. "You don't need to worry about that anymore. I'll talk to Alex."

The tone of my voice seems to surprise her, but she doesn't look upset about it. "O-okay," Millie says with a grin.

Gripping the doorknob, I turn back to her. "Ready?"

"As I'll ever be," she says, color rising in her cheeks again.

I take her hand and then open the door. We're met with the sound of scurrying and urgent whispers coming from downstairs. When we step onto the landing, the bottom of the stairs is empty, but I know my family. They're just on the other side of the wall in the living room.

"Mami!" I call. Beside me, Millie's eyes bulge.

"What are you doing?" she hisses, squeezing my hand.

"Announcing it on our own terms," I whisper back.

My mother's voice, dripping with false innocence comes from the kitchen side of the living room. I know it's false innocence because she sounds a little out of breath. "What is it, *mi hijo?"*

"Trae a todos a las escaleras, por favor."

"What did you say?" Millie whispers.

"I asked her to bring everyone here."

Millie palms her face with her free hand. "Oh God," she moans.

From behind the living room wall, I hear Emmett. "Why are we going back?" Five or six mouths *shh* him. I chuckle.

"Oh, God," Millie pleads again.

But when the foot of the stairs quickly fills with every member of both our families, she drops her hands and stands up straight beside me. She's bright red, so I know what it's costing her, and I love her all the more.

I lead her down four or five steps with me so that we aren't quite so far from the gathered crowd, and as I do, it's my father's face that catches my eye. I expect to see a look of disapproval. And if it were there, I'd be beyond caring.

If having his blessing means not having Millie, I'd rather be cursed.

But he's not frowning or scowling. He looks... curious. Maybe even expectant.

I don't take time to puzzle it out. I glance over at Millie and find her looking down at the kids. Somehow they've made it to the front of the crowd with Alex right behind Mattie and the adults all fanned out behind them. Mattie, of course, looks worried. Harry's expression is watchful. But Emmett just looks ecstatic.

I know I have everyone's attention, so I give mine to Millie. Face flushed and lip trembling, she gazes up at me. In spite of the fact that I'm embarrassing her, she looks happy. Almost as happy as I feel.

"Abuela says we're expecting." The crowd of family seems to hold a collective breath. "Maybe we are. Maybe we aren't. We don't know." But our hands are linked between us, and I let the outside of my pinky brush her belly in silent greeting. Silent welcome. Silent promise.

From behind Emmett, Abuela mutters, *"Lo sé. Voy a ser una bisabuela."* Mattie and all of my cousins titter.

Judging by the smile on Millie's face, she understood Abuela perfectly, and I turn to give my grandmother a mock glare.

"All I know is I asked Millie to marry me, and she said yes."

Everyone cheers, including Abuela, who still insists on pretending she doesn't speak English. Mami breaks through the crowd to swarm the stairs, and before we know it, we are smothered in hugs. Valencia hugs. Delacroix hugs. For his size, Emmett threatens to squeeze the life out of me.

When Mami, Luci, and my cousins pull Millie toward the kitchen, peppering her with questions, I let her go. The kids and my Uncle Raul follow them, leaving just Papi and Abuela at the foot of the stairs with me.

She shoots my father a warning look that needs no translation before taking to her cane, and then it's just the two of us.

Papi clutches the banister with one hand and digs aimlessly in his pocket with the other. He's looking at the bottom stair as though trying to decide if it's level or not.

"You love her, *mijo?*"

"Yes, Papi. More than anything."

He doesn't look up from the step.

"That was fast," he mutters, glancing up to read my expression.

I shrug. "Feels like I've been trying to win her forever."

One bushy gray eyebrow bows like a caterpillar. He looks down again. "I thought she was toying with you." He toes the bullnosing of the bottom stair with the tip of his black shoe. *"Mami* and *Abuelita* told me I was wrong."

"You were."

His shoulders rise and fall. "Maybe I didn't want to watch someone else toy with you. Ronni did it for too long."

I jolt at his words. I never told my parents why Ronni and I broke up. Looks like I didn't need to.

"Millie is nothing like Ronni."

Papi nods. *"Sí."* I've never heard my father apologize for anything, so I get a second jolt when he says, "I was wrong about her."

I want to thank him, but sensing he has more to say, I stay quiet.

He raises his eyes to mine, and suddenly my father looks older than I've ever seen him. "A lot of things haven't gone the way I wanted them to go, Luca."

My heart squeezes painfully. "I know that, Papi."

He shakes his head. "You know it, but you don't know it. The whole time you were growing up, I couldn't be here. When I finally made it back into this country, you were nearly a man."

The squeezing moves to my throat.

"I started my own business—not only because I knew construction—but so I could have it for you." His hand grips the banister, and I know it's not just for balance. "To one day give it to you and Alejandro, sure. But first—and for years—to work beside you. To get back some of the time I lost."

Somehow, I always knew this. Sensed it in the way he talked about the business—even before I was old enough to work there. But he has never come out and said it like this. And it kills.

"Papi—"

"Ehhh," Papi grunts, waving off any sentiment. "We had a few years, right? Before all of this," he says, gesturing to his bad leg. The one he's still lucky to have. The one he may not be so lucky to have in a year or two.

He turns his hand up in a gesture of acceptance. Acceptance of a fate that could deal him such a shitty hand. "So maybe now you understand."

"I do." I understand why it's been so hard on him. Why he's been so hard on me. I think I always understood, but hearing it from him takes away the sting I've felt these last few months.

I reach over and grip him on the shoulder. Mami hugs everyone. Total strangers. She hugged Millie the moment she met her. For Papi, hugs between men are for when he hasn't seen someone in years. Like if they've been in Louisiana and you've been in Chihuahua.

But he didn't raise me. Mami did.

So I lean in and hug my father.

He lets me. I haven't been this close to him in years. He feels smaller than he did the last time. I try to remember when the last time was. Graduation? But before I do, he's slapping me on the back, a movement I match, to let him know I've gotten the signal that it's time for the hug to end.

Papi pulls back, looking embarrassed, teetering as he tries to pace on his bad leg. He clears his throat as though the raw sound of it could clear the air, bring us out of this awkward moment.

He frowns at me but does it while smiling. "So." He coughs and then blinks. "I might have a grandchild?"

My smile erupts. "We'll have to wait and see, Papi." Then I drop my voice. "But we might not have to wait long."

His expression doesn't change, but a light sparkles in his eyes.

"So maybe I didn't get to raise my oldest son," he says with a shrug. "And maybe I don't get to work with him either." He narrows his eyes, but the smile is still there. "But maybe he and his *blanca* wife would let his mami, and his abuela, and maybe his papi watch this grandchild instead of putting him in daycare?"

I'd like nothing better. "Maybe," I say, grinning.

Papi smiles. Really smiles. And then his brow screws up and

he looks at me with confused wonder. "What are the chances he'll have red hair?"

I split with laughter. "Probably as good as the chances as she'll have red hair."

Papi blinks, considering this. "I always wanted a daughter. But it wasn't meant to be for us." He smiles again. "A grand-daughter would be a great thing."

I nod, picturing that. The perfection of a red-headed daughter.

Papi shrugs. "But first, I think I'll get to know my daughter-in-law."

"Definitely a great thing. How about you start now?"

I lead Papi back through the living room and into the kitchen where Mami is handing out plates. Her kitchen island has become a toppings bar for the fried fish tacos, and the Delacroixes have been ushered to the front of the line. Harry, to be specific, leads the charge.

Papi limps right up to Millie and puts his calloused hands to her cheeks. *"Bienvenida hija,"* Papi tells her, smiling. "Welcome to our family, Millie."

Surprised, Millie glances to me just for an instant before thanking Papi and embracing him. But that one glance tells me everything. She knows things between me and Papi have been rocky these last few months. And in that one glance, she is asking if we have sorted things. She must see in my face that we did. Because I know Millie. She's loyal and protective of those she loves.

And she loves me.

The look lets me know if ever there are sides, she's taking mine.

And I love her all the more.

I step back and let Papi repeat his sentiments to Millie's brothers and sister, and I take the opportunity to grab my own brother by the shoulder. My grip is firm and he looks back at me, smiling.

I gesture toward the door that leads to the garage, and while the crowd's attention is still on my fiancée, I slip outside with him. Alex is all smiles as we stand between the door and Mami's Enclave.

I smile back. "I'm marrying Millie."

My brother's smile grows. "I know. It's really cool."

I nod, locking eyes with him. "Mattie is going to be my sister-in-law."

If it's possible, his smile grows even wider. "Yeah, I know. I'll get to see her, like, all the time."

I keep my grin but lift a brow. *"Hermano,* she's going to be family."

His brows move together just a fraction of an inch. He still looks happy. Just a little confused. "Right, but not really."

I shake my head. "No, really."

Now he frowns for real. "Nah. It's not like she's going to be my cousin like Rosa or Esme."

Rosa and Esme, Aunt Lucinda's two youngest daughters, are drop-dead gorgeous and just a few years older than Alex. He's probably had a crush on one or the other since he was old enough to notice girls.

"Maybe not," I say with a shrug. "But she's going to be *my* family. Under my protection."

His brown eyes narrow. "What do you mean? Are you trying to tell me I can't date her?"

I know better than that. The last thing I need is to give the two of them a forbidden-love complex.

"No, Alex." I drop my hand onto his shoulder again and grip it in a way that makes him squirm. "I'm telling you you can't touch her."

His eyes flare. "Not touch her?! But——"

"You know what I mean."

Alex's nostrils flare. "Let's pretend I don't," he says with swagger, wagging his head side to side the way only a Chicano teenage boy can.

I firm my grip until his breath hisses.

"No sex. And I mean. No. Sex. While she's living at home."

His eyes bug. "You expect us to wait until college?!"

I chuckle. *"Hermano,* I don't expect you'll be dating next summer."

He looks so hurt; I almost feel guilty. "Why not?"

I sigh. "Alex——" I start to tell him that it's just not realistic, but I stop. In a few months, he'll figure it out on his own. "Forget I said that. Just remember the part about no sex."

He scowls. "You're just saying that to me because I'm your brother, and you expect me to be just as perfect as you are."

This time, I laugh outright. "Alex, I'm going easy on you. Wait and see what I do to the other guys Mattie dates."

My little brother—who's not so little anymore—steps into my space. "There won't be other guys," he growls.

I almost—*almost*—step back. But I get into his space instead. "Good. Then I'll only have to say this once, little brother. You have sex with her while she's underage, and I. Will. Hurt. You."

Chapter Thirty-One

MILLIE

AFTER NEZZIE'S TACOS, CHURROS, AND LOTS OF WEDDING TALK, we head home. But the kids are still so wired from all the excitement that I cave when they ask to watch the copy of *Coco* Luc's cousin Felicité lent us. I make everyone—everyone except Luc—change into pajamas first so getting into bed after will be quick—or so I think.

When I come back downstairs in my Latuza pajama set and fuzzy socks, Luc's appreciative gaze makes me blush even though I'm covered from neck to toe. He starts the movie, wedged between Emmett and me, the two of us snuggled against him. But as soon as little Miguel finds himself among the dead, Emmett scrambles in between us so he can hug me.

I'm not at all prepared for the scene when Miguel plays the lullaby and Coco remembers her father. None of us are. And the living room echoes with the susurration of muffled sobs and sniffles.

"This is why I don't like school," Emmett whimpers into my shoulder.

I sit up straight, clutching him. "What do you mean, buddy?"

Emmett looks up at me, red eyed and nose streaming. Like the hero he is, Luc pauses the movie, reaches toward the coffee table, and plucks a tissue from the box in the middle of it.

Emmett takes it from him and wipes his nose. "This," he says, stamping his eyes with the tissue. "Crying like this. Even when I'm not watching a sad movie."

"Oh," I say, feeling helpless. "I know. It happens to me too."

"Grief attacks," Mattie says, shaking her head and reaching for her own tissue. "I hate them."

"Yeah," Harry says, his voice rough. "They suck."

Emmett blinks his watery eyes. "You have them *too?!*" Shock rings in his voice. All three of us nod, and I bite my lip, guilt swamping me.

"It does suck," I say, "but it's normal. Like I said from the beginning, it's normal to cry about it."

He looks at me, clearly stunned. "You didn't say it would happen *at school!*" His voice pitches with the injustice of it. "I thought it would only happen when I thought of Mom and Dad."

I smile, but gently, wistfully. "No, Em, it doesn't work like that. It can happen anywhere."

"Even at school," Mattie says.

"Or soccer practice," Harry adds grudgingly.

Emmett stares at the twins, disbelief written all over his face. "You cry at school and soccer practice?"

Mattie's smile must match mine, but Harry just shrugs his acknowledgement.

"Sometimes you can't help it," Mattie says.

"So, what do you do?" Emmett asks, his face screwing into a frown as he looks back and forth between the twins. "Nobody calls you a baby?"

"Who's calling you a baby?" I ask, but Emmett ignores me. Right now, it's Harry he needs.

"I keep a pair of sunglasses hooked to my shirt," my brother says, sounding supremely cool. "If one hits me in class, I put 'em on. Nobody but Mr. Craddock tells me to take them off, but by the time he does, I'm usually good."

Emmett whips his head around to me. "Can I get a pair of sunglasses?"

I fight to keep my smile in check. "We'll hit CVS on the way to school tomorrow."

His body practically wilts with relief. He turns to Mattie. "Do you have sunglasses?"

Grinning, she shakes her head. "Not for that. I usually just ask to go to the bathroom."

Emmett frowns. "But I don't need to go to the bathroom."

Behind Emmett, I catch Luc stifling his laughter.

"But you need privacy," Mattie explains.

Emmett aims his confused gaze at me. "Girls cry in the bathroom?"

"Sometimes," I say with a shrug.

Looking like the secrets of the universe have been revealed to him, his forehead clears. "No wonder they take so long in there."

Mattie rolls her eyes. "Can we finish the movie?"

Everyone agrees, so we do. It's a sweet movie, and the ending is both sad and happy.

As the credits roll, Mattie looks at Luc with wet lashes. "Do y'all do that?" she asks, her voice squeaking.

"Do what, Matt?" Luc asks gently.

My sister dabs her eyes with a tissue, her chin trembling. "Celebrate *Dia de los Muertos?*"

"We do," he says, nodding. "Mami spends days cleaning the house, and we make an *ofrenda* with *pan de muerto* and a lot of other foods and offerings to honor my grandparents and my Uncle Ernesto, Mami's older brother."

Emmett releases me and sits bolt upright. "Do they come

visit you?" he asks, looking equally spooked and hopeful.

Les Dimples stand out as Luc grins. "If you ask Abuela, she'll say they do." Then he shrugs. "Alex and I never knew them, but during the holiday... I don't know..."

Harry says nothing, but he leans in, resting his elbows on his knees. Mattie glances at her twin and then back to Luc.

"What do you mean?" she presses.

Luc shrugs again. "The house feels different on *Dia de los Muertos*. More... *open*. That's the best way to explain it. And even though I didn't know them, my grandparents and my uncle, I think about them. About the stories I've heard about them."

"Can we make one?" Emmett asks, looking at me with huge eyes. "An off-rend-oh?" he asks, butchering the word.

"*Ofrenda,*" Mattie corrects, her accent sounding pretty close to Luc's.

"*Ofrenda,*" he tries again, nailing it. "Can we make one for Mom and Dad?"

I glance at Luc, unsure what to say. I don't know the rules for this kind of thing. And I don't know if I can explain cultural appropriation in a way Emmett would understand.

But Luc doesn't hesitate. "Sure, *jefe*, we can do it together next year."

Emmett—no, all of my siblings—stare at Luc like he just invented flying cars and he's given them each a free one.

I freakin' love this man.

I cover his knee and give it a squeeze. When he aims those dimples my way, a little flutter dances in my middle.

My three siblings exchange glances. Knowing glances, I realize. Harry clears his throat. "So y'all are getting married in less than two weeks." It isn't a question. This is something we hammered out at Nezzie's. A small ceremony—Luc's family, my family, and a few friends—at his parents' house. December 21st. The Saturday before Christmas.

Last month I had no idea how we'd get through the holi-days. Well, this is how. With a wedding. New traditions. And The Valencias.

I've never felt so blessed.

"Yep," I say. "In less than two weeks."

Harry raises a brow at me. I can tell he's ready to ask for something. Argue for something if he has to.

"We've discussed it," he says nodding to Mattie and Emmett in turn, "and we think Luc should start living here now."

They've discussed it? *When?!*

Luc coughs next to me. A quick glance tells me he's equally surprised—and amused.

"Like tonight," Harry adds.

"Well, we haven't—" I start, but I don't get very far.

"We like it when Luc's here," Mattie says.

"Yeah," Emmett echoes.

"Hey guys, I like being here too," Luc says. "And I'm happy to hear you're ready for me to move in. But let me and your sister talk it out first, okay?"

"Sure," Harry concedes. Mattie and Emmett seem to follow his cue.

Once again, when they would argue with me, one word from Luc, and it's done. I could get used to this.

I can't help my smile. I *will* get used to this.

"Okay. Now that that's settled, you three get upstairs. It's late."

And to my surprise, they go. I give them a minute to get upstairs, fight over who gets the bathroom first, and then I go up to make sure everyone's good for the night. Emmett lets me hug and kiss him as usual. But tonight, the twins surprise me.

"I'm so excited for you," Mattie whispers, hugging me in her doorway. It's really sweet.

When I go to tell Harry goodnight, he gets up from his

unmade bed and comes to put his hands on my shoulders. God, he's getting so big. We're no longer eye-level. I have to look up at him, and when I do his face is so serious. So grown up.

"I'm really glad it's Luc."

I smile. "Yeah. Me too."

When he kisses my cheek, my throat goes tight. "Where are those sunglasses when you need them?" I say, and he laughs.

"'Night, Millie."

Clarence follows me downstairs where Luc waits on the sectional. He looks relaxed and perfect and beautiful. I'm a nervous wreck.

I move around until I'm facing him but then stop. "I feel like I have whiplash."

He smiles, and those dimples I love are there just for me. "Big day. I don't have any regrets. You?"

Some of my nerves quiet down. "No. None." It's true. Not one. Still, I bite my lip. "But I want to talk about something."

He pats the spot next to him. "I figured."

I sit, but apparently, it's not close enough. Because Luc hooks one arm around my back and swings my legs across his with the other. And some more of my nerves settle. He'll understand. He always does.

"What is it?" he asks. "You think we're moving too fast?"

I shake my head. "I mean, it's fast, but it feels right," I say. "Now that we're here, I can't imagine being anywhere else."

His smile grows, and he nods. "Me too. And I want to stay tonight." He searches my face for my reaction. "If you're okay with that."

Not smiling is impossible. So is not blushing. "I'm okay with that." I swallow. "And you can move in whenever you're ready."

His arm around me pulls me closer against him. "Tomorrow."

"Tomorrow," I say with a nod. "Perfect. I'm off tomorrow."

His eyes glint. "I know."

The promise in those two words makes a welcome heat prickle over my skin. What are the chances that any of the kids will come downstairs tonight? But I don't get the chance to calculate them.

"You wanted to talk about something?" Luc prompts.

My nerves rush back single file. "Um, yeah." I sit up a little straighter and clear my throat. No sense in dragging it out. If he's offended, he'll let me know. "I don't think I can take your name."

His puckered brow tells me this wasn't at all what he expected me to say. "Why not?"

I bite my lip. My heart thumps clumsily. *Millie Valencia?* I-It sounds like that poser band from the eighties."

His frown pinches tighter. Then his eyes fly open. *"Milli Vanilli?"* And just like that, he's laughing.

Really laughing.

I sigh. "When it comes to names, I'm kind of cursed."

His laughter quells as he nods. "Yeah, baby, that curse I won't argue with."

I get a tingle deep inside. In a place that could never be cursed. One that could only be blessed, and one I now desperately hope carries a blessing we've made.

Luc pulls me to him and plants a kiss on my lips. I think it'll be a quick one, but he slows it down, draws it out, and nibbles on my bottom lip before deepening the kiss again.

When I'm half breathless and hoping the kids are sound asleep, he pulls back.

"I don't need you to take my name, Mildred Agnes Delacroix," Luc says. "As long as you take me."

"Oh, trust me Luca—" I pause. Frown. "Wait. I don't know *your* middle name. How did that happen?"

I can't believe it. Luc blushes. He actually blushes and says nothing.

"Luc, what's your middle name?"

"It's Hugo."

I blink. *"Oogo?"* I repeat. Because it sounds like he just said *Oogo*.

"Yeah, spelled like *Hugo*, but the H is silent." He winces. "I've always hated it."

"Luca Hugo." But, of course, it sounds like Luca-Oogo. I press my lips together, fighting a smile.

He's still wincing.

"What?" I ask.

"Mami's maiden name is Lugo."

"Oh?" I shrug. "Okay."

Luc wrinkles his nose. "So, legally, my name is Luca Hugo Valencia Lugo."

I burst out laughing. "You're kidding, right?"

Luc's eyes narrow into a glare. "No."

And I laugh and laugh and laugh because I know without a shadow of a doubt that this is the man for me. While I laugh, he grips me tighter, glaring hard so he won't laugh too.

"Luca Hugo Valencia Lugo," I test it out, managing to keep almost a straight face. "Yeah, that's not much better than Mildred Agnes."

He arches that scarred brow.

"Okay, maybe it's a little better," I concede.

Luc nods.

"Let's just agree we'll be super careful with all of our kids' names, okay?"

He nods harder. "Yes. So careful."

I nod too and then put my hand on his chest. "But like I was saying…"

The dimples come back to me. "Yeah?"

"You, Luca Hugo Valencia Lugo, are definitely taken."

Epilogue

LUC

FOUR YEARS LATER

"WE'RE GOING TO HAVE A BABY."

My brother and Mattie sit across from us at the breakfast nook, their hands clutched together in front of them. Mattie's knuckles are white. So are Alex's lips.

But he looks defiant. Mattie just looks terrified. Under the table, Millie squeezes my wrist. This isn't something she needs to be dealing with right now. The twins—our twins—Marco and Mateo—turned three in August. They've been running circles around her these days.

And her morning sickness is so bad this time. She's exhausted. So much worse than when she carried the boys. That must mean it's a girl, right?

I glance at her and find her biting her lip. *Damn.* I don't want her to worry.

I fire a glare at my brother. "What did I tell you?"

Alex's brows shoot up. "You told me to wait. We waited until college."

"Alejandro!" Mattie jerks one hand free and covers her face

with it.

"*Mi melodia.*" Alex wraps an arm around Mattie's shoulders. "Don't be embarrassed." His eyes narrow on me. "We waited four years. No one could expect more than that."

Clearly mortified, Mattie moans behind her hand.

"I warned you this would happen," I hiss.

"Well, you would know," Alex snaps.

I sit up straighter, shoulders going back. Millie holds up a staying hand. "Hey-Hey," she says, eyeing me and Alex in turn. "We're all family, remember?"

Mattie risks a peek between her fingers. It's such a Millie thing to do, my tension and frustration eases. Just a little.

"Have you told Mami and Papi yet?" Millie asks. This is what she calls them. What all the Delacroixes call them. Since we got married.

Mattie shakes her head, dropping her hand. "Not yet. We thought we'd do it tomorrow—after Thanksgiving dinner," she adds, wincing. "What do you think?"

My wife snorts. "I think you need to be ready for Abuela to announce it to everyone as soon as you walk through the front door."

This is true. Millie and I found out about this baby before Halloween. When we brought Emmett, Marco, and Mateo over to my folks' for Dia de los Muertos and Abuela said nothing, we thought we were in the clear. We'd wait. Make sure everything looked good and then tell everyone.

And then Abuela had cataract surgery.

The day after the operation, she took one look at Millie and spilled.

My young sister-in-law looks at me with wide eyes. "How upset are they going to be?"

She looks so worried. I hate to see her worried. It's been my job for four years to make sure she was safe and secure. I shoot my brother another glare, but I gentle my voice for Mattie.

"I don't know. You two are a lot younger than we were." Then I focus on Alex. "What's your plan? I'm assuming you have one since you had plenty of warning."

His fist clenches on the table. I get the feeling he'd like to pound me with it. Well, the feeling is mutual.

"We have a plan. We're getting married." He squeezes Mattie's hand, looking at her with that all-in love he's had for her from the beginning. A shy—but utterly happy—smile shapes her lips. But then Alex faces me, and I watch him swallow. Did he just pale a little? "I'm going to quit school."

"You're *what?!*" I fire the question like a pistol. Alex and Mattie are three months into their freshman year at LSU. A long, long way from graduating.

"At the end of this year," he adds, as if that makes it any better.

Mattie sits up straighter. "And I'll transfer to UL. They have a piano pedagogy program too. I'll earn my degree here."

"And I'll come work with you," Alex says. And, yeah, his color is washed out. He's nervous about this. "Full-time. At least until Mattie finishes."

I frown. "You need to stay in school. If you quit now, you might never go back."

Alex shakes his head. "No. I need to take care of my family."

His family. I can't argue with that. And the hard look in his eye tells me it wouldn't do much good anyway.

"Besides," Alex says, likely sensing his advantage. "Do we both need a degree to—"

"Yes," I snap. This is non-negotiable. Mami and Papi worked and saved and sacrificed to give us more than they had. Neither one of them went to college. "We both need a degree."

Maybe I'm the one wearing a hard look now because he

changes tacks. "Fine. Then I'll go back after Mattie graduates," he says, then adds in a lower voice. "Part-time."

"Part-time?" I growl the question.

Alex leans forward, still clasping Mattie's hand. "Think about it, Luca. Mattie's going to be a teacher. Earning a teacher's salary. We're going to have a kid—" He flicks his gaze to Millie, the direction of it taking in her still-flat middle, a half-smile on his lips. "Probably more than one by that time. I'll get a degree if you insist, but, *hermano,* we're going to need my income."

For the second time in as many minutes, my little brother has shut me up. Eighteen, and he already has his life planned out.

Eighteen. It's so young.

"Are you sure, Alejandro?"

I watch his arm tighten around Mattie, his eyes moving to slits. "You really have to ask that?"

No. I don't. My brother has loved Mattie forever. I should know. I've been kicking him out of the house at eleven o'clock for four years. Until they went to LSU.

This was bound to happen.

My gaze moves to my little sister-in-law. As usual, she looks nervous—and embarrassed—but if I'm being honest, I've never seen her so happy. Her fair skin glows. Just like Millie's.

Abuela is so going to call it in two seconds.

"Have you told Harry?" Millie asks her sister.

Alex blows out a breath, and Mattie winces. "Not yet."

One look at my brother and I know telling me was the lesser of two evils. He and Harry have always been tight, but Harry has vowed repeatedly he'd beat Alex bloody if he knocked up his sister.

I don't think he was joking.

But Harry's not in from Centenary yet. His season just ended a couple of weeks ago. The Gents finished up 11-4-5 with four shutouts. Four shutouts that happened while Harry was tending goal. Yeah, he's had a good first semester. A great one, considering he is bringing a girl home for the holiday.

Maybe that will help Alex's cause. If Harry's in love, he might be able to forgive Alex. Or at least let him live. We'll find out in a couple of hours.

"So, can I come work with you?" Alex asks, his uncertain look returning. "In May?"

Like I'd say no. Like I even could. The name on the sign says *Valencia and Sons.* I glance at Millie, and just one glimpse lets me know what she's thinking.

He wants your support. Her eyes tell me. *He wants your blessing.*

I lock eyes with her, giving her the smile that she owns a controlling share of. She's right. Alex doesn't need me to bust his balls. Papi and Harry are going to take care of that.

"I can't wait," I tell my brother. A wave of relief passes over both him and Mattie, and I feel a prick of guilt for taking so long. I get to my feet and hold my hand out to Alex. His eyes widen in surprise, and he stands too. The handshake becomes a hug, and then I turn to Mattie, clasp her hand, and tug her out of the nook. She springs to her feet and into my arms, tears glinting in her eyes.

"I get to have you as my sister twice over."

The back door bangs open and the sound of males—human and canine—echo through the house. Clarence and his one-year-old sidekick Danté lead the charge, tearing into the kitchen and lapping simultaneously at the giant water bowl next to the fridge.

Danté is what Millie calls a foster failure. His first owner surrendered him at Millie's clinic when he couldn't pay to treat the pup's Parvo. Knowing the illness would be deadly if left untreated, Millie took him in and covered his bills. The plan was to get him well and then help him find his forever home.

Yeah, that plan lasted about a week. And then our boys all fell in love with the Labrador-Springer-mystery mix.

Okay, I did too.

And while Clarence merely tolerated him at first, within a few weeks, they were inseparable, wrestling or chasing after each other when awake and lying right beside each other while they slept.

Nothing has changed—except Danté has nearly quadrupled in size.

Emmett comes in on their heels, sees the four of us, and stops with a suspicious frown. "What's going on?"

Mattie turns away to dab her eyes, and Millie steps forward. "Not much. Where are the boys?"

At her question, the back-door slams shut. "Here, Mama!" Mateo shouts. He runs in, ahead of his brother. Mateo is the loudest. And he always has to be first. It's been that way since they were born. Marco is our observer. Our introvert. So much like his Aunt Mattie. But it's their twelve-year-old Uncle Emmett both our boys worship. If he is home, they're on him like a two-headed shadow.

Most of the time, Emmett's really good about it. Not always, but then again, he's just twelve. The kid hates it when Marco and Mateo wake him up on the rare Saturday or Sunday morning when he doesn't have a soccer game and he can sleep in. He also hates it when they go into his room when he's not home.

Emmett was nine by the time they were born, and out of the three of Millie's sibs, I think he was the happiest about their arrival. They wiped away his baby-of-the-family status. Doubly so. And I think he's always been grateful.

And maybe he also doesn't mind the hero worship.

"Can we have a snack?" Marco asks. He's our bottomless pit. Always wanting a snack. Just like his Uncle Harry. He swipes his hair out of his eyes. Both boys are dark like me, but they have their mother's blue eyes. *Dios mío,* they are the most beautiful babies I've ever seen.

If the next one is a baby girl with those eyes, I'll be doomed. She'll have me wrapped around her little finger.

"C'mon," Emmett says, waving the twins over to the island. "I'll make us peanut-butter-bananas."

See what I mean? He's really good with them.

"Thanks, Em," I say, meaning it.

Some of my buddies have asked what it's been like to start our marriage and raise our family in this full house. If we ever wished it was just us. Honestly? I can't imagine it any other way. Having newborn twins isn't for wimps. I never got to ask my in-laws about it, but I have a feeling Eloise and Hudson were probably super grateful Millie was ten years old when Harry and Mattie were born. I swear, there were times in the beginning when two felt like ten.

For weeks after we came home from the hospital, it was all hands on deck. In the beginning, when they were nursing Millie dry, they'd wake up crying at the same time like they'd planned it. No matter how many times Millie tried the football hold, she could never get them to latch on at the same time.

And it killed her to hear one of them crying while the other ate. She'd get so tense, her milk wouldn't let down. So my job was to rub her shoulders to help her relax while one of the kids tried to soothe the fussy newborn.

By accident, we discovered that Mateo would stop crying if Mattie played Chopin's *Fantasie-impromptu in C-Sharp Minor.* So Harry would hold him, Mateo's eyes wide open and blinking in wonder, as Harry paced around the living room while she played, stalling until Marco finished nursing. But Marco hated Chopin. Too busy. If it was Mateo's turn to eat first, Marco would only settle into a whimper instead of a wail if she played Satie's *Gymnopedie No. I.*

Emmett, at his age, was the only one I could enlist for

diaper duty. He wouldn't actually *change* any diapers, but he'd assist. Did you know infant boys will pee in their own faces if you don't take measures when you change their diapers? We learned that the hard way our first night home from the hospital. And it took more than one lesson to realize it wasn't a fluke.

I blame myself. *Señor ten piedad.*

Anyway, Emmett did a quick online search and learned that a dry washcloth draped over the quick draw was the answer. And so he became the Pee Goalie, a title that put him in danger of pissing his own pants every time he said it.

At two in the morning, when you've only slept a few hours to begin with, you have to laugh at shit like that.

So when friends have asked, I tell them truthfully I don't know how we'd have managed that first year without Harry, Mattie, and Emmett.

Emmett is taking down the peanut butter, addressing the twins like we can't hear him. "Maybe after our snack, we can figure out what the grown-ups are trying to hide."

Both twins, who are in the middle of making their climbs onto the barstools, whip their heads around to look at us.

"What'd you hide, Mama?" Mateo asks.

"Is it a puppy?" Marco adds.

Beside me, Millie stifles a snort of laughter. I cut my eyes to my brother, unable to resist. *"¿Es un cachorro, hermano?"*

Marco and Mateo's focus shoots to their uncle, who gives me a sour look. As planned, Mami, Papi, and Abuela keep our boys while Millie and I are at work. All Mami, Papi, and Abuela speak at home with them is Spanish. Neither one of the twins started talking before their second birthday, but when the words came, they came in both languages.

As it should be.

Millie's Spanish improved rapidly after that, learning whatever they learned. Teaching her words in bed might have been

a good start, but toddlers chatter about a lot more than *honey,*
delicious, heaven, and *love.*

Smiling at the thought of our Spanish lessons, I reach over
and grab my wife.

"*¿Es un cachorro, tío?*" Mateo asks Alex.

Alex shoots me another dirty look, but Mattie, now
composed, steps between us. "No, *niños,* it's not a puppy. It's a
surprise. We'll tell you after Uncle Harry gets home."

Mateo frowns, clearly disappointed. "When's that?"

"He'll be here by suppertime, baby."

My son looks offended. "*I'm* not a baby. Marco's the baby."

My second born might be the introvert, but he has a clear
sense of injustice. "I'm *not* a baby!"

Millie steps out of my touch to move between them. Twin
boys fight. A lot. Another reason why it's a good thing grown-
ups in the house—and I'm including Emmett here—
outnumber them.

"*Babies?!* I don't see any babies." Millie looks back at me
over their heads, wearing a mock confused expression. "Do you
see any babies, *mi amor?*"

Grinning, I shake my head. The boys have turned their
attention to her, all smiles. They know what's coming. "I don't
see any *babies,*" I say, emphasizing the word.

Millie takes a sniff. "I certainly don't *smell* any babies." She
sniffs Mateo's head before turning and doing the same to
Marco. They both giggle as her nose tickles through their hair.
"*Pew!* No, these smell nothing like babies. Babies smell like
clean laundry and cotton candy."

She sniffs again, as animated as a Sesame Street puppet.
Giggles bubble over. Millie shakes her head, looking
confounded.

"You smell them, honey. I can't figure it out."

I grab Marco by his tiny shoulders, he squeals and then

shrieks when I stick my nose into the hollow of his armpit, tickling him. Sweat. Dog. Dirt. This kid needs a bath.

"Ooph." I pull a face. "That's no baby, Mama." Wide-eyed with anticipation and a little wild terror, Mateo waits his turn. I grab one wrist and whip it into the air. He laughs so hard, he sags against the island. Alex, Mattie, and Emmett are laughing now too. I'm fighting to keep my own tremors in check, staying deadpan, but I've got nothing on Millie. That woman almost never breaks character.

"Put your nose way in there, Daddy. Tell me what that is," she says with clinical seriousness. It's the *way in there* that sets me off. I have to hide my face against Mateo's shirt so they can't see I'm laughing. But my babies are laughing so hard I'm afraid they'll fall off the stools.

Again, I smell sweat, dog, and dirt. "Ugh," I manage through my stifled laughter. "I'm... speechless."

Millie moves behind Marco, guarding him in case he lists any more to the right. "Honey," she says sounding solemn, and tucking her red hair behind her ears as if she's about to deliver bad news. "It's worse than I thought."

Dios mío, I love her so much. She makes every day so much fun. Just like this. I swallow, nodding. "Tell me. I can take it."

She faces me with a mad scientist gleam in her eye. "It's two... Stinky.... Sweaty... Dirty..." She jerks her gaze from me and gives her crazed look to each of our sons, and they dissolve in hysterics all over again. "Little boys!"

"No!" I gasp, pretending horror.

"YES!" Both boys shout.

Millie closes her eyes, nodding. "Yes," she whispers somberly. She opens her eyes, pressing her lips together with mock regret. "And there's just one thing you can do with their kind."

"What?" Mateo asks, breathless.

Millie reaches out and cups each boy's chin. "Give them a bath."

Matching blue eyes widen in dread. "No!" They bellow in twin cries. Emmett slides two plates across the island, a fruity, nutty stay of execution.

"Not yet, but after you've had your banana and peanut butter," Millie says, the ring of finality in her words.

The boys don't like it, and they'll fuss again in a few minutes, but now, their world is all banana and peanut butter goodness.

———

TEN MINUTES LATER, my little family is upstairs in the bathroom Emmett and Harry used to share, and Millie is drawing a bath for our boys. Emmett has claimed the guest suite, the one Millie slept in when I first met her. It gives him a little more space and privacy—when the twins aren't barging in on him.

When we got home from our honeymoon, a week-long trip to Costa Rica right after Christmas, the kids—no doubt with help from Mami, Aunt Lucinda, and my cousins—had moved Millie and me into the downstairs master suite. Her parent's old bedroom.

It was the best wedding present they could have given us. The thought had crossed my mind to move in there eventually, but I would have never asked, never wanting to suggest a move Millie and her siblings weren't ready for.

But after a week of living as husband and wife, nearly naked in a bungalow with an empty beach in front of us and the rain forest behind us, I had no idea how we'd go back upstairs with our room just a few doors down from Harry, Mattie, and Emmett.

It was Mattie's idea, Mami had told me, and her brothers needed no convincing. The memory of my sister-in-law's thoughtfulness brings me back to the present. I look at my wife, who is leaning over the tub, testing the water temperature against her palm. The boys are choosing bath toys from the bucket under the sink.

"Should we offer them a place to stay here?"

Millie's eyes widen. "Mattie and Alex?"

"It's her home too."

She straightens and dries her hand on one of the boys' bath towels, eyeing me doubtfully. "Where?"

I shrug. "Maybe we could talk Emmett into giving up the suite." Then inspiration strikes. "Or maybe we can knock out the wall between Harry and Mattie's old rooms and make that space into a second master suite and nursery. There's time."

Wearing an indulgent smile, Millie steps up to me and drapes her arms over my shoulders, raking her fingers gently down my scalp at the back of my head. Pleasure runs down my spine. Pleasure and a promise. In this full house of ours— getting fuller by the minute—we will find time and space for each other.

We always do.

"It's so sweet of you to offer that. To even consider it," Millie says, smiling up at me. Then she shakes her head. "But I don't think they'd want that."

I frown. "Why not?"

She quirks the sexiest of all brows. "Being right down the hall from our boys and Emmett? *Really?*"

I think about Marco and Mateo's tendency to burst into Emmett's room. And Emmett's recent discovery of eighties metal bands.

"You have a point." I narrow my eyes, but even I'm skeptical. "You think they'd move in with my family?"

Millie winces. "I don't think they'd have much more privacy there."

Alex shared an upstairs with Abuela his whole life. I doubt

he'd be eager to pick that up again. And then there's Mami. And Aunt Lucinda. And the cousins. They don't live there, but some days, they might as well.

"Honestly, I think they'd pick the twins if it came down to it."

Millie sniffs a laugh then releases me. She bends down and snags Mateo before whipping off his shirt and jeans. Socks and underpants go flying. I've got Marco stripped an instant later.

We get both boys in the tub and waste no time dropping to our knees. The first order of business at bath time is to wash the twins' hair—which they hate above all other things. All conversation ceases while we simultaneously rinse, lather, and rinse again. Well, all conversation except Marco and Mateo's shrieks of protest. It's fast—and it's furious.

When their heads are clean and dripping, Millie and I sit back on the floor, facing each other. The look of exhausted satisfaction on her face isn't the one I ache to give her, but "the shampoo shitstorm," as she calls it—or the "S.S." if the boys are around—is behind us once again.

We're leaning back on opposite walls while the boys forget their troubles with Boon jellies, and Millie taps her bare foot against my knee.

"I do have an idea, though."

I reach forward, grab her foot, and run my thumb along the bottom. Her breath hitches.

"What kind of idea?" My voice stalks like a predator.

She arches a brow. "Not *that* kind," she says, but she doesn't pull away, so I let my thumb retrace the move, and I'm rewarded with her sigh of pleasure. "I mean..." She blinks and regathers her focus. "About Mattie and Alex."

I sit forward, pull her foot into my lap, and get to it with both hands. Millie moans. It's one of my top three favorite sounds.

Her moans.

Her laughter.

Her calling my name.

Not just *then*. Anytime. Every time.

"You gonna share?" I tease. Because she's slipping down the wall, puddling just a little under my touch.

"Mmmm."

I grin, pleased with myself for being able to give her this right now. For seizing this moment to make her moan—even if it isn't strictly sexual—in the middle of this nightly chore. With a house bursting with family.

She narrows her eyes at me. "You and your dimples," she mutters, shaking her head. "What about that three bedroom that's for sale on St. Louis?"

My hands still. St. Louis is the street behind ours. The house she's describing is behind us, two doors down.

That would be great but… "They couldn't afford that. Not right now." Even getting an apartment would be tight. It's why I want to offer them a place here until they can get on their feet.

Millie shrugs, looking up at me with irresistible blue eyes. "They could if we bought her out."

I blink. "Of the house."

She nods.

The Delacroix's house—this house—belongs to all four of Eloise and Hudson's children. The plan has always been to keep it at least until Emmett leaves for school. Since that's still about six years away, we haven't really thought past that.

But as far as I'm concerned, this is home.

And if I had any doubts, the look in Millie's eyes would stop them cold. She wants this house. She wants to raise our babies here. All of them.

My smile grows, and I nod toward her belly. "We know it's big enough for us."

She gives me a wry look. "Well, for *now*, anyway."

"Three babies in four years," I say with a shrug. "If we run out of room before Emmett moves out, they can double up."

Millie tilts her head back and laughs. Then she meets my eyes again. "That's never scared you, has it?"

I lean forward. Come up on my hands and knees. And prowl up the length of her body. "You mean filling this house with our babies?" My knees are anchored on either side of her thighs. "Never."

She reaches for me again, her gaze soft with something like wonder. I go a little crazy when she looks at me like that. "I've always liked that about you."

I drop my mouth and brush my lips against hers. I trail them to her ear. "I want as many babies as you want to give me."

Her arms tighten around me. "Luc," she whispers my name against my ear, and it's just the way love is supposed to sound. She draws back and looks me in the eye, hers now hazy with desire. "So we can offer? To buy her out now?"

Millie is still part-time, but Valencia & Sons has grown in the last four years. And it doesn't hurt that we've never had a house note. "If that's what she wants, we'll make it happen." Then a thought occurs to me. "Do you think Harry and Emmett will mind? Us owning half the house and, let's face it, planning to buy them out later?"

She shakes her head. "We'll ask, but they're a long way from needing a five-bedroom house. And if we're here, at least their childhood home will stay in the family." Her gaze moves to my lips before she kisses them. Millie looks back up at me. "I think they'll be happy about it."

I grin. Her gaze lowers again, and I know she's looking at my dimples. "And you?"

She grins too. "Oh, I'm pretty happy." Her eyes flicker with a wicked gleam. "Almost as happy as I'll be later."

My brows lift. "Later?"

She bites her bottom lip and nods in a way that makes my spine tingle. "I think I'm gonna be pretty happy then too," I muse.

Her eyes heat. "I think so."

Turns out... she's right.

THE END

Acknowledgments

When writing a book, help and inspiration come from many quarters, some more obvious than others. My husband and I are in the habit of giving our dogs "old lady names." We think it's sort of funny, and Gladys and Mabel don't seem to mind. I've kept up the practice for some of my canine characters, like Clarence, and I even have a dog named Millie in *Leave a Mark.* When a childhood friend of mine named Millie read that novel, she laughed and told me that the only other Millies she knew were old ladies or dogs. Clearly, that stuck with me. I know only two Millies who are my age, and I had a great-aunt named Mildred who went by Mim. She never married and lived to the age of 97 in her childhood home along with three of her sisters. As a kid, this seemed like a horrific fate (no offense to my three sisters). Back then, I also thought Mildred was the *worst* possible name. I can't say I'm all that fond of it now, but I'm ever so grateful for the inspiration.

Although I wish I did, I don't speak Spanish, and I would not have been able to write the Valencias as well without the help of Heather Lamarche, Beth Acevedo, Juan Alvarez, Tatiana Milton, and Bria Lozada Wolf. Also, for the second book in a row, Bria has served as an invaluable alpha reader, and I am so grateful.

Millie Delacroix may be fictional, but Loftin Veterinary Clinic is not. In fact, Dr. William Loftin performed the very same cruciate repair surgery on my Gladys years ago as is described in Chapter Twelve (and the dog named Millie here is really Gladys in disguise!). And I owe Sarah Loftin a debt of gratitude for encouraging me to use the clinic as part of my setting. Thanks for that AND the chocolate dipped strawberries!

All of Millie's veterinary know-how came from my sister Emily Thomas, DVM. Not only is she always there for me and our many canine emergencies, she graciously answered all of my questions about sacculectomies, surgeries, feline abscesses, and the like. Thank you, Dee.

At the Valencia's Thanksgiving dinner, Luc's cousin Natalia teaches all the kids to balance spoons on their noses. For this delightful tradition, I must acknowledge my dear friend Michael Frederick and his lovely and talented wife Zabryna Guevara (seriously, look her up and watch her latest show *Emergence* on ABC). They have to be the world champions of nose-spoon-balancing.

Thanks to my friend and fellow author Kimberley O'Malley for all of the recommendations and the many shout-outs. The same goes for author Lexi C. Foss. Thanks to grammar goddesses Nicole Lobello and Karen Ladmirault. Once again, thanks to the amazing and intrepid Kathleen Payne. I treasure your talent, but I'm also so grateful for your cheerleading! Jena Brignola, thanks again for your time and expertise. To the incredible Cayla Zeek, thank you for giving Millie and Luc a cover that looks just like them! Thanks also to Marie Force's Formatting Fairies and InkSlinger PR for their services and support. You ladies are amazing!

On a much more serious note, I've dedicated this book to

my dear friends Tara and Shane Breaux and their angel baby Rebekah Grace. After losing Rebekah Grace midway through pregnancy, my friend Tara, who has a heart big enough to hold all the mommies, daddies, babies, big brothers, and big sisters who have traveled this devastating road, started a Forget Me Not Walk to Remember in Youngsville, Louisiana. She did this because she knew other mothers and families had to be carrying the same grief she and her family were, but searches online yielded almost nothing about support and community. The first time Tara held the walk ten years ago, she had eighty participants. This year, more than eight hundred took part. Her tireless dedication to this walk and her support of grieving families continue to inspire me. October is pregnancy, infant, and child loss awareness month. If you are living with this kind of grief, know you are not alone. If you can't find a community of supporters in your area, be the first to start one. You will be filling a great need.

As always, thanks to my daughter Hannah and my husband John. I can't even list the many ways you both help me to be a better writer and a more evolved human.

Finally, I'm so grateful to each and every one of my readers. I hope you enjoyed Luc and Millie's love story. It isn't really kind of cursed, but it is kind of magical. If you post a review, someone else will see it, pick up the book, and maybe fall in love with it. And that's kind of magical too.

About the Author

Stephanie Fournet, author of nine novels including *Leave a Mark, Shelter, Someone Like Me,* and *Kind of Cursed,* lives in Lafayette, Louisiana—not far from the Saint Streets where her novels are set. She shares her home with her husband John and their needy dogs Gladys and Mabel, and sometimes their daughter Hannah even comes home from college to visit them. When she isn't writing romance novels, Stephanie is usually helping students get into college or running. She loves hearing from fans, so look for her on Facebook, Instagram, Twitter, Goodreads, and stephaniefournet.com.

Other Books by Stephanie Fournet

Fall Semester

Legacy

Butterfly Ginger

Leave a Mark

You First

Drive

Shelter

Someone Like Me

Anthology:

Block & Tackle

Turn the page to read a sample from Stephanie Fournet's novel

Someone Like Me

Someone Like Me Chapter 1

DREW

I DON'T WANT TO GET OUT.

This place is surrounded on three sides by the Mississippi River. The fencing everywhere else is topped with razor wire. But in the last eight years, I've never needed those to keep me in.

This is where I belong. And everybody knows it. Ma. Annie. Grandma Quincy.

But out of the sixty-three hundred inmates here at Angola, I'm the one being released today.

It's morning, but it's not time for roll call yet. I know because, for Hickory, it's quiet. There's no such thing as silence in a dorm with eighty bunks to a hall. That's eighty men who talk, whisper, snore, fart, cough, jack off, and whatever the hell else they can get away with during lights out. But in the hour or so before dawn, like now, this place is as quiet as it ever gets, so I know I've got a little time left ahead of me.

Just not enough.

The thought of the outside world has my stomach clenching under the thin sheet. In a few hours, they'll process me out, and then I'll walk through the doors of Reception.

Annie will be there, and that'll be okay. That's not the part I'm dreading.

We'll get into her car — I have no idea what she's driving; we've never talked about that — and we'll make the two-hour trip down Highway 61 and along I-10. That's not the part I'm dreading either. Because that's just road and sky. There's plenty of sky here. I'm used to it. Nothing to be afraid of.

For the last five years, I've worked in the auto tech shop. Assistant to the foreman for the last two. I know I could swipe a six-inch screwdriver and sink it into a guard's thigh. Buy myself a whole lot more time.

I've thought about it. Really, I have.

But that would only be more blood on my hands, and I have enough already.

Enough already.

I've been able to picture the ride with Annie, I can get as far as crossing the Atchafalaya Basin Bridge, but as soon as I try to see us pulling off I-10 onto University Avenue, my mind shuts the fuck down.

I roll onto my back. The ceiling above me is a washed out gray in the pale, pre-dawn light. Top bunks are a trade off here. On the bottom bunk, you feel like the world is closing in on you. And with a two-hundred-pound man sleeping in the bed above you, on a noisy heap of springs and feathers, it's not hard to imagine all that shit coming down on you every time that bastard rolls over.

On top, there's nothing there to crush you, but it's hot as fuck up here. I may not be ready to get out and face everything and everyone waiting for me, but I'm not gonna lie. I've missed air conditioning. It's September, and September in Louisiana is like the inside of a baked potato. Steaming and still.

Today is September 18th. Eight years to the day the fool I was walked in here.

Walking out, I'll still be a fool, but I've learned some things inside. Back when I was eighteen, I had no idea that in the state of Louisiana an aggravated burglary conviction got you one to thirty. My lawyer made sure to tell me that ten years was a sign he'd done his job.

I'd said nothing to that. I would have taken the thirty if it hadn't been for Annie and Grandma Q. My sister said if I went away that long, I'd miss seeing her have kids, miss seeing them grow, and Grandma said I'd miss her altogether. Those are the little details I have to remember.

I shake my head at the ceiling. What's wrong with me? Those details aren't *little*.

But it's hard to remind myself that there are a few people I care about who don't want me to pay anymore for my crimes. And the fact that I disagree with them only makes them suffer more, and that's the last thing I want.

They are the reasons I "good-timed-out" when I had the chance. For them. Not for me.

The creak of springs and rustling of sheets snag my attention. I glance down to the bottom bunk on my right and find A.J. smiling up at me.

"It's here," he whispers, grinning. "Ya big day."

In spite of myself, I grin back. A.J. Lemoine is a goofy ass mother, and he makes me laugh at least six times a day.

"It's here," I whisper back, glad that seeing his smile makes my own show up. A.J. and I are tight, but I haven't told him how I feel about getting out. Like almost three-fourths of the inmates at Angola, A.J's here all day. A lifer. Second degree murder. No possibility of parole.

You can't tell a guy who'll never get out that you want to stay in. That's just cruel. In fact, half the guys I know have been smiling my way all week, happy for me. It gives them hope.

I feel sick just thinking about it, but I can't let on.

"Annie comin' for ya?" A.J. asks, his voice so low I almost can't make it out over the tide of snores that surrounds us.

I nod. A.J. first met my sister six years ago on a visiting day when his son was here at the same time. Since then, A.J. has asked about her almost as much as Annie's asked after him.

"She'll be happy," he says, nodding with approval. Then his eyes lock on mine like he's been seeing through my mask for weeks. "And everythin' else will work out alright."

I don't care what he did. A.J. doesn't belong here. A lot of guys don't. He's been inside since 1997. Last year he graduated from the Bible college old Warden Cain and the New Orleans Baptist Theological Seminary started decades ago, and now A.J. is an ordained minister. An ordained minister who will die in prison.

A.J. and I have talked about a lot — almost everything — but one of the things I've never come out and said is that it's crazy I'm getting out when he never will. If you ask me, it should be the other way around.

See, when A.J. was twenty-one years old, he got into a bar fight with this piece of shit. Piece of Shit started the fight, and A.J. finished it by breaking a bottle over his head. And that's how you can just be minding your own business one minute, nursing your Bacardi and Coke, and doing life without parole the next.

This is not the way A.J. tells the story. It's how I tell it. A.J. tells a story of a young man who took his gift of life for granted. Who needed to let God into his heart. Who needed to bow to love and forgiveness instead of hate and revenge.

But he didn't step into the bar that night intending to hurt anybody. He walked in there an innocent man. And he didn't ask Piece of Shit to hassle him, either. He was law abiding until that asshole touched him.

I cannot say the same for me.

Nothing that led me here was innocent. I'm guilty. One hundred percent. If I weren't guilty, I wouldn't be here. And Anthony would still be alive.

But I'm here. And he's not.

Someone Like Me Chapter 2

EVIE

"Evie!" Tori shouts from the bottom of the stairs. "Where's my Jazz Fest T-shirt?"

I press my pencil into the seam of my open book and push myself off the bed. *The Yamas & Niyamas* will just have to wait.

"It's not in your closet?" I ask, calling down from my bedroom door. I can't see my sister from here, but she can hear me better this way.

She makes a noise in her throat, like a little cough. "If it were in my closet, why would I be asking *you?*"

Any answer I give will only piss her off more, so I head downstairs. "I'll help you look for it."

She's standing there with her arms crossed over her pajamas, the beginnings of a sneer curling her lip. "Did you take it without asking me?"

"No," I say gently. "But maybe I washed it with my things." I move past her, heading toward the direction of the laundry room, and she whirls on her heel to follow me.

"Well, did you or didn't you?" Her voice drips acid.

Tori is in a bad mood. If I'm being honest, Tori has been

in a bad mood for about three years. Only it's gotten worse over the last month. For that, I blame Jason Watney.

"I washed and dried a load yesterday morning, but I haven't folded it yet."

She follows hard on my heels. "If you shrunk my shirt, I'm going to be so pissed," she seethes.

I seal my lips together, declining to point out that she's always pissed. Instead, I force the slightest constriction in my throat and inhale through my nose, taking a barely audible *ujjayi* breath. I feel the balancing and calming effects of the yogic breathing almost immediately. My shoulders drop away from my ears, and I challenge myself to feel the wood floor beneath my bare feet as I make my way to the laundry room.

Tori's glower seems to burn through the back of my slouchy tank as I dig in the basket, but I concentrate on my breath, the crisp smell of Meyer's geranium fabric softener, and the brush of fabrics against the skin of my hands. I spot the electric blue T-shirt and pluck it from the pile.

I attempt to shake it out to assess any damage, but Tori yanks it from my grip. "Give it here." Her jaw is clenched, and she doesn't even meet my gaze as she drapes the shirt over her front and smoothes it out.

It doesn't look like it shrunk at all, but I'm leaving nothing to chance. "I'll buy you a new one if—"

"That's not the point," she snaps, shooting me a scowl.

The look she gives me is so bitter and violent, I want to look away, back away, and leave her alone, but I don't. I have one guess as to why *this* electric blue Jazz Fest T-shirt is the only one she wants.

Jason Watney.

They went to Jazz Fest together to see The Revivalists and Cage the Elephant last May. Jason was over here almost all summer. But I haven't seen him since August. I've waited for

Tori to say something — anything — about what happened, but so far, zilch.

Mom keeps pumping me for information every time we Skype, so maybe it's a good thing I don't really know what happened. Mom's too good at getting information out of me.

Tori is still checking the shirt for shrinkage, smoothing it over her front a third time. Lo and behold, it still hasn't shrunk.

"I think it's fine," I dare to suggest.

She narrows her eyes at me. "No thanks to you."

Ujjayi breathing is miraculous. It's faster than a glass of wine and more mellow than a pot brownie. But I think I'm going to enjoy the hell out of my Ashtanga short form class this morning.

I like to leave more than an hour early for each class. This gives me time to get to the studio, settle energetically into the space, and center myself for a few minutes of meditation before my students show up. The more present I am, the better I see and feel what my students need from me.

And what they don't need is for me to be focused on a run-in with my sister.

I finish getting myself ready and tiptoe downstairs. Tori's bedroom door is closed, and I'm relieved I don't have to talk to her before I head out.

I'm also relieved when I step out into the garage and see that she didn't park her Fiat behind Mom's Volvo. I don't have my own car because I don't need one. Mom and Dad are only home twice a year for three weeks at a time so the XC40's almost always available.

My dad is a petroleum engineer for Chevron. Four years ago, he got transferred to the Abuja office in Nigeria. I was still in high school then, and Mom stayed home with Tori and me. But I'm pretty sure it was the worst year of her life. She missed Dad like crazy.

They've been married for twenty-seven years, but they still

act like newlyweds. They hold hands wherever they go. They smile and laugh at each other at the dinner table. And they slow dance in the kitchen.

When they sat us down three years ago and told us Mom would be moving to Nigeria with Dad now that I'd graduated, I can't say I was all that surprised. But it's one reason why Tori and I still live at home.

My house — my parent's house — is the most adorable two-story Tudor style home. It's where Tori and I have lived since I was five and Tori was nine, and it's where my parents plan to retire. Mom wouldn't dream of selling it, and I think the thought of renting it out while they're halfway across the world would actually give her hives.

So Tori and I get to enjoy a home right out of *Southern Living* in the heart of the Saint Streets while keeping the house lived in and looked after. And, really, I couldn't pay rent on my yoga instructor earnings. I only finished my 200-hour certification a year ago. I work part-time at the Yoga Garden, and I do about six private lessons a week, but that's not nearly enough to make up a living wage.

People — Tori, my parents, friends — have asked me when I'm going to get "a real job." I was studying kinesiology at UL, but I only finished three semesters because what I really want to do is teach yoga.

I know it's hard to make a living this way, but it's not impossible. The more students who show up to my classes at the studio means the more classes I'll get. And private lessons are hard to come by, but if I could even double what I'm doing now, I could swing a small efficiency, and I wouldn't really need more than that.

And, yeah, I'm twenty-one, but that's not too old to still be living at home. I don't make much, but I save what I can, and it's not impossible to think that one day I could own my own — perhaps very tiny — home.

My only expensive habit is that I like to travel. I want to go to India one day, of course, but I'd love to see other places too. Mom and Dad have taken us to England, France, and Spain, but I'd love to see Scotland… Greece… Italy… Ooh! And Iceland. And those are just the top spots on my list.

When my parents took us abroad to England and France, we stayed in luxury hotels, saw shows, and ate at fancy restaurants. It was great, but I don't need that either. A backpack, a solid pair of shoes, and a Eurail pass would be enough of a start.

Well, and a plane ticket.

But for right now, I'm happy just where I am. I have a great place to live, a car to drive, and the freedom to do what I love. But that doesn't make me I'm complacent. I mean, on Tuesdays, Wednesdays, and Thursdays, I offer free yoga classes at Parc Sans Souci. It's good practice for me, and it's a way to grow a client base. And sometimes my freebie students even tip.

I'm smiling about this when I pull into the gravel lot of the Yoga Garden. But as I step through the entrance and into the tea room, my smile slips.

Drake Jordan.

He's sitting at one of the tea room tables, stirring a cup of what smells like apple blossom tea. And he's leering at me. As usual.

"Hi, Evie." Drake Jordan could not look more wolfish if he had pointy ears and whiskers.

"Hi Drake," I say, and because I don't want to seem rude, I stupidly keep talking. "How are you?"

His grin slithers higher on his cheeks. "Better now."

I press my lips together and force a tight smile. Drake has asked me out twice, and both times, I've politely declined. You'd think he'd take the hint that I'm not interested, but he hasn't yet.

"I saw you were on the schedule today, and, lucky me, I have the day off." Drake is a server at Social. I know this because he's tells me almost every time he sees me. He has an employee discount. We can go to Social whenever I want.

I don't want, but I hate turning him down. I get this twisted up feeling inside like my guts are made of pipe cleaners and they're being wrapped around a toilet plunger.

"That's…nice." I step closer to Studio B where I'll be teaching. Jill, one of the teachers who has been here forever, has a beginner class going on right now in A, but B is just waiting for me.

Drake gestures at his tea. "Would you like to join me for a cup?" He lifts his wide brow. "My treat."

I swallow. "No thanks, Drake. I need to set up for short form."

He nods, grinning like he's in on a secret. "Looking forward to it." He leans back in his chair and crosses his arms over his chest. "What about having dinner with me tonight?"

Shit.

There goes that pipe cleaner feeling. The other two times he's asked me out, I've been able to tell him honestly that I was teaching that night. But tonight I'm free. Unfortunately.

"I…" I stretch out the word and then catch my lip between my teeth and gnaw it nervously. *Stall. Stall and think of an excuse,* I tell myself. "I need to check on something. I'll let you know after class."

Drake's face brightens. I've never seen a face look so happy and so wicked at the same time. "Great," he croons.

I suppress a groan. "I have to get set up," I say in a rush, crossing the tea room. "See you in class." I open the squeaky door and shut it firmly behind me. The rattle echoes across the wood floors. In another life, Studio B was someone's back porch. The house that is now The Yoga Garden is at least eighty years old. The doors rattle in their frames, the floor creaks, it's drafty year round, and I absolutely love it.

Studio B, now a sunroom, has picture windows on two sides. Flooded with natural light and facing the back yard, it's easy to forget that this place sits on one of the busiest streets in Lafayette.

I move across the room, drop my bag and mat on the floor, and breathe a sigh of relief. What the hell am I going to tell Drake?

Karma is absolutely real, and honesty is one of my values. Lying to him isn't an option for me. But I really don't want to hurt his feelings with the truth. I'm not attracted to Drake. Like at all. I feel like I need a shower after just talking to him. The way he looks at me… it's like his eyes have hands and they touch me without permission.

But he's a person. A being that carries the same divine spark we all possess. And he's a yogi, which means, in some way, he's trying to evolve. I have to respect that. And I have to honor it.

So I need to find another truth to tell him.

I unroll my mat and reach into my bag for my singing bowl, mallet, and bowl cushion. Making myself slow down and focus, I place these near my mat, arrange myself into a comfortable lotus sit, and on a deep inhale, strike the mallet against the bowl.

The soft chime washes through the room, and I close my eyes. I center my attention on my breath. I feel cool air on the edges of my nostrils and in the back of my throat. For a couple of breaths, I manage to stay with that sensation, but then my mind drifts back to Drake again, and I feel my stomach tense.

Okay, so don't fight it, I tell myself. *Focus on the feeling.*

I inhale again, but instead of sensing the rush of air into my lungs, my awareness moves to the tightness in my middle. There's a churning tension just below my diaphram, a nagging burn of unease. It's rare, but sometimes when I sit in meditation and allow myself to just listen to the sensations in my body, an insight will open itself up to me, and something I didn't understand before will become clear.

Watching the feeling, I note its size and shape, the way the muscles in the wall of my abdomen twitch and tense as if they have a mind of their own, as if they are trying to tell me *Pay attention to us. Don't ignore what we're trying to tell you.*

I begin to think about how the gut really is a second brain, full of neurons that are in constant communication with the brain that sits in my skull. And then I catch myself thinking instead of feeling. I take another mindful breath and try to settle in again.

Thirty minutes pass, minutes in which I am thoughts and feelings, breath and heartbeat, muscle, nerves and bone. And life. I open my eyes, at ease, centered, and with one goal in mind: to offer my students what they need from me. Moving slowly and with awareness, I rise to begin preparing the studio. I connect my phone to the bluetooth speakers and start my playlist. The soft notes of harp and flute fill the space, and I open the door to welcome my students.

Class won't begin for another ten minutes, but a handful of yogis have already arrived. We greet each other with smiles and quiet words, as is our routine, and they move through the room, unrolling their mats and setting out their towels. Ashtanga yoga is intense, and in short order, we'll all be sweating.

Drake is among them, and I am aware of his eyes on me, but I remind myself of my purpose, my intention for the day.

Of course, it doesn't help that he positions his mat at the front of the class as close to me as possible.

At noon, I stand at the front of my mat, and close my eyes, feel all four corners of my feet pressing into the mat. I bring my hands to prayer pose, open with chanting mantras, and begin the short form series.

I take the class through the sun salutations, leading from the front of the studio for the first round before moving through the room, subtly adjusting students as I pass. A palm on the back, a whispered suggestion, or an encouraging word. I do the same with the fundamental asanas, joining in only when I feel each yogi is safe on the mat.

It's during the finishing sequence when everything falls apart.

"Aah!" A sharp, masculine cry pierces the room. Everyone is in wheel pose, including me.

This is not good.

I quickly tuck out of the posture and rush to Drake. "My back!" he wheezes, his eyes screwed shut.

I stand with my feet by his hands, bend over him, and brace him behind his shoulder blades. "Tuck your tail."

He tilts his pelvis and hisses.

"Put your weight into your heels and lower your hips."

"Christ!"

I anchor my own weight so I don't collapse on top of him. I know if I did, my face would land in his crotch, and my crotch would probably end up on his mouth. Great. For the half-second it takes to lower him to the ground, I offer my soul to the devil to avoid this nightmare.

By some miracle or dark magic, I keep my balance and then shift to his side. "Your lower back's in spasm. Draw your knees to your chest."

Drake groans, and I sweep my eyes over the rest of my students. Some have come out of the posture and are watching us with concern. Some are still in wheel, plainly ignoring the sounds of a man in pain.

Honestly, I don't know which is worse. By the look on Drake's beet red face, he's mortified.

"If you're still in wheel, lower down carefully, rest your back onto the earth, and draw your knees up to your chest," I instruct.

Drake's breath is still jagged, letting me know that the muscles in his back are still protesting. I lower to my knees and lean down closer to him.

"Breathe," I remind him, my voice a whisper. "Then open your legs and clasp the arches of your feet in happy baby."

He opens his eyes and shoots me a glare. "I'm not doing that." He looks angry, but I know he's probably more embarrassed than anything else.

I raise my voice and address the class. "Let your knees fall open to your underarms and reach for your feet," I tell them. "Grab inside or outside. It doesn't matter, but try to let your knees sink down so you open up your lower back."

As the rest of the class follows my instructions, Drake narrows his eyes at me. I can see he's chafing under his humiliation, but there's a spark of something else in his look.

"You owe me a date now."

My heart sinks. As much as I don't want to go out with him, I can't turn him down now. Not after he's whimpered in pain in front of a class full of women.

I grasp at the only straw I have. "Not tonight. You need an epsom salt bath and heating pad."

He raises a wolfish brow. "Tomorrow night."

I chew the corner of my lip. "I teach the next three nights," I tell him, and I'm so glad it's the truth.

A smile breaks over his face. "Perfect. Friday night then."

Defeat washes over me. I swallow and nod. "Friday night."

Get *Someone Like Me*!